Dr Finlay's Casebook
Omnibus

Dr Finlay's Casebook Omnibus

A.J. CRONIN

BIRLINN

This edition first published in 2010 by
Birlinn Limited
West Newington House
10 Newington Road
Edinburgh
EH9 1QS

Reprinted 2014

www.birlinn.co.uk

ISBN: 978 1 84158 854 4

British Library Cataloguing-in-Publication Data
A catalogue record for this book is available from the British Library

Typeset by Hewertext UK Ltd, Edinburgh
Printed and bound by Grafica Veneta
www.graficaventa.com

Contents

Dr Finlay of Tannochbrae

A Delicate Matter

The building of the Caledonian, a great new international hotel, at Arrochar had caused only mild interest in Tannochbrae, where it was regarded with disdain as a further intrusion on the Highlands, but one unlikely to disturb the even tenor of life in this quiet Scottish village. Reading an account in the *Scotsman* of the luxurious furnishing and splendid appointments of the new hotel and the list of important people who had graced its opening, Dr Cameron looked quizzically at Dr Finlay over the edge of the paper.

'We'll be getting some grand new patients one o' these days, lad. The number o' lords and ladies mentioned here wad make ye blink. Ay, and there's important foreign personages as weel.'

'They'll not bother us, sir.'

'I wouldna be too sure o' that!' Dr Cameron teased. 'Ye're a verra weel kent man in this part o' Scotland. Your fame has gone before ye.'

Finlay laughed heartily at this joke against himself, then picked up his hat and his black bag and started on his daily round.

And indeed, as time went by, only fragments of news of the grand hotel filtered into Tannochbrae. It is true that Finlay, taking his usual weekly walk over the Hallerton Moors, would come across alarming scraps of evidence, such as would-be sportsmen astoundingly attired – some even in the kilt – shepherded with their guns by Tam Douglas, the keeper, and obviously looking for unsuspecting grouse, not yet in flight.

'Anybody got shot yet, Tam?' asked Finlay.

'That's what I'm trying to prevent. Although none o' them could hit a bird if it was sittin' looking at them, they're quite capable o' blowin' each other to bits. But they're quite content if I shoot a brace for them to take back to the hotel and brag about.' Suddenly he looked towards the western sky. 'Here, lad, take my gun, there's a flight coming over.'

'Thanks, Tam,' said Finlay. He took the gun and as the high, almost invisible, specks flew overhead he raised it to his shoulder.

Bang! Bang!

'He's missed,' shouted the bogus kiltie. But at that instant two birds dropped out of the sky and fell almost at his feet.

'Nice work, lad,' said Tam. 'I wanted them to see that I am not the only Scot who can bring down a brace.'

'Who is this good-shooting young gentleman?' inquired one of the group who had gathered around Finlay.

'He is Dr Finlay, the young doctor of Tannochbrae. One of the best doctors and best-loved men in the west of Scotland. Now see that your guns are unloaded, shoulder them and quick march back to the hotel.'

Finlay finished his walk and forgot about the incident, but in the hotel that night he was freely discussed. Men who shoot badly are as a rule excellent talkers and the story of Finlay's quick double-barrel action was further enhanced by the revelation of his medical skill. That all this talent should be buried in a little West Highland village was a tasty titbit for the gossips.

As for Finlay, he continued with his practice, totally unconscious of the stir he had created. It meant nothing to him that one wet morning more than a week later, while he was still at breakfast, a long, low Hispano-Suiza limousine drew silently to the front door. He called to Janet. 'They've lost the way. Tell them to drive straight ahead for the main road.' But when Janet went to the door she quickly returned.

'It's two very fine ladies, doctor, asking to see you. Shall I show them to the front parlour?'

'Na, na, Janet,' Dr Cameron intervened, 'let them go to the consulting room.' Then with a smile to Finlay, 'I'll bet you this is hotel stuff, we mustna turn them away.'

Finlay finished his breakfast, drank a last cup of coffee, then strode into the consulting room.

The two ladies were seated by the window and one glance assured him that they were of the highest class.

The younger of the two was extremely beautiful, with dark eyes and a pallor that indicated inner tension. The older woman was middle-aged and plainly English. She it was who spoke.

'Dr Finlay, we have heard so much of your skill as a doctor that my dear friend here wishes to consult you. As she is a Spanish lady with only slight English, she has asked me to speak for her.'

Finlay seated himself at his desk and the English woman drew her chair near to him.

'Doctor,' she began, 'we have heard so much of your skill, my friend would like you to treat her. The truth is, she is suffering from a suppression of the blood and for some weeks past has missed her period.'

'Continue,' said Finlay grimly.

'We thought, doctor – and I am an experienced woman – that a few strokes of the curette would soon cure this affliction and bring back a healthy flow of blood.'

'You are well informed, madam. How long have the periods been missed?'

She turned to her friend. 'Is it five or six weeks dear – or perhaps a little longer?'

Finlay immediately smelled a rat. But he could not jump to conclusions on insufficient evidence.

'Before taking any action in this matter, I must thoroughly examine the patient.'

'But is this necessary, doctor? A curettage is so simple.'

'You seem surprisingly knowledgeable, madam, but I can assure you I would never, but never, perform this operation, as minor as it may be, without a thorough examination of my patient.' He

5

paused. 'If you are looking for someone who will use such an instrument, and most probably a dirty one, on your friend, then *tout de suite* I bid you good morning. You will find what you are looking for in the shadier quarters of Glasgow or Edinburgh.'

There was silence in the little consulting room. Then with a sigh, came the words, 'I will not seek further, Edith, I trust this man. It must be he, or,' she gave a little sob, 'no one.'

'Come then, madam, I am a busy man. Remove your clothing and lie down on the couch. There is a soft Shetland shawl with which to cover yourself.'

When he saw that he was obeyed he went over to the wash basin, took off his jacket, and thoroughly washed his hands. When he turned back to the couch she had prepared herself and was lying on her back.

'Do not be afraid, madam, I shall not hurt you.' He removed the shawl. Yes, she was a superbly beautiful woman, quite young, and of course she was pregnant. The nipples were slightly pigmented, the breasts were veined and faintly full. He gently passed his hand over her abdomen, then, placing his stethoscope upon it, listened intently. Dear Lord, he thought, as he distinctly heard the foetal heartbeat.

'You can dress now, dear lady, and we will then talk together.'

'What!' cried the other woman. 'Aren't you going to do anything?'

'Madam,' said Finlay in a hard voice, 'you sound like a prostitute yelling after a client who has suddenly tired of her.' After seating himself at his desk he continued. 'This young lady, who you tried to trick me into curetting, is at least four, possibly five months pregnant. Her child is alive within her. Now, do you wish to take her to some filthy crook who will try to terminate her pregnancy and probably kill her and her baby too?'

'Oh, no, no, doctor,' wept the woman, 'I had no idea the case was so far advanced. I wished only to help Isabel, who has foolishly got herself into this condition without the knowledge of

6

her husband, a distinguished nobleman who is at present Spanish Consul in Rio de Janeiro.'

'She must make a pitiful confession and be forgiven.'

'Ah, doctor, you do not know her husband. He is an aristocrat of the old school, a true caballero. He would not forgive her. He would discover her lover and kill him.'

'Who is this lover?'

'A worthless Parisian boulevardier who found her alone at Maxims on her way to England. They danced and drank lots of champagne. Then, when she was powerless to resist, the worst took place.'

'She is a beautiful woman, she will have a beautiful child, wouldn't that cause her husband to relent?'

'No, no, the reverse, doctor. He would think, "This little bastard is not mine, it is the evidence and eternal reminder of my wife's sin. I don't want it. I hate the sight of it." '

'And he will blame his wife equally?'

'Oh, much more, doctor. In Spain, and especially to a man of his position, it is the unforgivable sin.'

Finlay was silent. He saw now that the Englishwoman's stupid attempt to deceive him was not a true presentation of the case. Finally he said, 'When does your Spanish friend return to her husband?'

'Oh! That is the real difficulty, doctor. For her husband is planning to visit her here in six weeks' time.'

Finlay reflected for a moment. This was a serious matter, possibly with fatal consequences. He turned to the Spanish lady who, in silence, was studying him with beautiful, tragic, imploring eyes.

'Your friend, dear lady, has almost prejudiced me by her stupid, misleading presentation of your case. But now I realise your true plight, I feel sorry for you in your trouble and want to help. First answer me these vital questions. On what date did you leave your husband?'

'On the morning of 1st of March.'

'On the eve of that day, possibly even in the morning, did your husband . . . make love to you?'

She flushed but answered bravely. 'Yes, doctor. On that very morning. And indeed on the evening before. He was so sad that I was leaving him.'

Finlay reflected. If conception dated from 1st March the child must now be almost seven months in utero.

'And your husband proposes to visit you?'

'In October. Just before the end of the shooting season.'

Again Finlay considered the dates. It would be a near thing but there was no alternative. After a moment, first glancing towards the English woman, he said, 'There is a possibility that the baby may be born before your husband arrives. You must write him a good, long letter with the news that you have just seen a doctor who tells you that you conceived on 1st March and that the baby will be born towards the end of November. You must then suggest that he delay his visit by a few weeks, since you will be in bed surrounded by doctors and nurses and you want everything to be over before he comes. Make it a very loving letter. Is all that clear?'

'Yes, doctor. Indeed it is.'

'One thing more,' Finlay looked at the Englishwoman. 'It would be thoroughly impracticable for the confinement to take place in the hotel where, at this season, there will be all sorts of festivities, bands, dances, all-night disturbances of every variety, and,' he paused significantly, 'reporters. It will be necessary for you to move to a house in the neighbourhood where I may attend you without publicity.'

'Oh, yes, doctor, I did think of that. But how can we rent such a house?'

'*I* will attend to that. Entirely without benefit or profit to myself. I hope to telephone you this evening and let you know what I have arranged.' He stood up. 'Now you must leave. My waiting room has been filling up while I have been occupied by you.'

They went quickly. In this way Finlay saved himself all manner of effusive thanks, and was able to call in the first of the twenty-odd legitimate patients awaiting him.

Finlay was, in fact, exceptionally busy all day, yet despite the pressure of work one thought persisted. What a fool he had been to entangle himself in a family mess, a dilemma that through his well-meaning interference might recoil upon himself and bring real disaster into his quiet, orderly and strictly God-fearing life. Nevertheless, he had given his word and he had a haunting premonition that, if he did not act wisely on behalf of his beautiful patient, she herself might come to grief.

So, that night after supper, when Janet was busy with the dishes and Dr Cameron had gone upstairs, Finlay telephoned his friend, Douglas Baird, who lived very comfortably with his wife in a country house halfway up the neighbouring glen.

'Doug, this is Finlay here. Tell me, are you proposing to go south this winter?'

'The wife is keen, Finlay, but I'm afraid this year the money won't run to it.'

'Here's something that might interest you. A patient of mine, a Spanish lady staying at the Caledonian, has booked me for her confinement – first baby, due towards the end of the year. Now the Caledonian, as ye weel ken, is very noisy and boisterous from now till New Year, so I have told my patient she must move to a decent quiet house, near enough for me to give her every attention. So, how about it, Doug? You and your wife could be off to the Riviera – isn't that where you usually go? – for six weeks or two months. You would leave your couple to keep house for my lady – I'll provide the nurse. How about it, Doug?'

'What's the figure, Finlay?'

'Your usual price is . . . how much?'

'Thirty pounds a month, and pay the servants.'

'I believe I could get you a hundred for the two months, Doug. And maybe a nice present if all goes well.'

'It's a deal, Finlay. But just a minute till I check with my Annie.'

A brief pause, then a woman's voice floated towards him.

'Is that Father Christmas?'

'His youngest son, Annie.'

'That's just what you are, Finlay. Here am I dying to get off to the French sunshine and sadly aware that the money won't run to it this year. Then up you come with your splendid offer. Of course we'll take it. And I promise you I'll leave everything in splendid order.'

'Good enough, Annie. Will you be moving out by the middle of the month?'

'Before that, Finlay. Tell me, I hear you're working for the Caledonian now.'

'Just this one patient. And as she's a Spanish lady she needs a little help.'

'If it's twins, Finlay, she must pay extra.'

'Sorry to disappoint you lass. I've already examined my patient and it's just one dear wee babby. But not to disappoint ye, I'll have your cheque for the two months delivered to you tomorrow.'

'Finlay, ye're aye such a darling, would a kiss reach ye over the wire?'

'One of yours would.'

Instantly a loud smacking noise came over the telephone.

'Thank you, Annie. That was just what I needed. Wait till I set out with you at the next Country Dance . . . Well, have a fine time in France.'

'We will, lad, thanks to you. And bless you for thinking of us.'

Five minutes later Finlay phoned the Caledonian and left a message for Madame Alvarez: EVERYTHING IS ARRANGED. PLEASE CALL ME FIRST THING TOMORROW.

Then, tired as if he had walked ten miles, he fell into bed and, almost at once, was fast asleep.

It is agreeable to relate that everything went according to Finlay's plan. The Bairds took off for the Riviera without delay and Señora Alvarez, accompanied by her English friend, moved into the comfortable villa on the Glen where precisely on the last day of November, Señora Alvarez was delivered of a baby girl. Finlay, who performed the ceremony and was the first to see the baby, noted with satisfaction that it took after its mother, with the same dark eyes and beautiful skin.

A few days later, when Madame Alvarez was able to sit up with the child in her arms, the señor arrived and Finlay, who witnessed the reunion of husband and wife, thanked heaven that he had preserved the love of this truly devoted couple.

When the day of departure arrived Señor Alvarez called on Finlay carrying an exceedingly handsome gun case.

'My dear doctor, nothing can adequately reward you for all that you have done for my wife, and all with the most perfect and scrupulous professional etiquette. But as we have been unable to shoot, I wish to give you in addition to your fee a present of my guns. They are by Da Costa, the best gunmaker in Spain, inlaid, as you will see, and the trigger has a pull as soft as silk.'

Finlay opened the case. What guns, compared with his own five quid lump of ironmongery! He picked one up. The barrel was finely inlaid with a thread of gold, the butt had a mounting of ivory.

'Oh, I say, sir.' He swung one to his shoulder. 'I never saw or used anything so splendid in all my life.'

'And the shot – dead true.'

'How can I thank you, sir?'

'How can I thank *you*, doctor?'

Finlay saw them off on the London train. The señora's eyes were moist as she pressed her doctor's hand.

'I am so happy, doctor. And it is all, all due to you.'

The train steamed out of the station and Finlay went home to admire his guns.

Professional Etiquette

In the passage of time, Finlay, from being the timid assistant nervously arriving at Tannochbrae, had come to shoulder most of the practice, which had indeed grown and extended well beyond the village. Dr Cameron was older now and less amenable to strangers, but he still had his patients, old friends who firmly believed in him and would never for a moment have passed him by in favour of his bumptious young assistant. What matter if Finlay were called personally to the posh new Caledonian Hotel ten miles north of the snug little village. Nobody in Tannochbrae gave a good Scottish damn for that swank establishment, stuffed with English snobs and stinking rich foreigners who 'didna ken one end of a gun frae the other but came back boasting frae the moors wi' grouse shot by the keeper'.

Such an opinion had indeed been voiced by Bob Mackie the grocer, one of Tannochbrae's leading citizens, and a lifelong friend of Dr Cameron.

'What did they ever do for me? Never ordered even a sausage, let alone a joint of my famous spiced bacon. All their stuff comes by special train from London.'

Dr Cameron had the habit of dropping in regularly at Bob's shop to pick up a piece of this famous spiced bacon to which, when freshly prepared, he was especially addicted and he was, consequently, regularly treated to Bob's opinion of the Caledonian. However, on this particular morning Bob was strangely silent on his favourite topic. He did, indeed, seem preoccupied and worried to such an extent that Cameron scoffed, 'Is it the hotel again, Bob?'

'No, man, it's not that at all. The fact is, I'm real worried over my young grandson, a boy I'm verra fond of. As ye weel ken, he's the son of my dochter Gracie, that married Will Macfarlane and moved to Beith. Weel, every summer young Bob – he's named after me – comes up to Tannochbrae for his holidays. Ye'll have seen him around.'

'I have indeed,' said Dr Cameron. 'A nice lad. I think Finlay takes him fishing in Gielstone Burn, odd times.'

'Aye, that's the boy, and he's clever at school too. But he's not looking near so weel this year. In fact I'm real worried about him. So if you wouldna' mind, while I'm wrapping the ham, I'd be much obliged if ye might take a step upstairs to look at him.'

'Certainly, Bob. Anything to oblige ye.'

Dr Cameron went upstairs and, most unusually, found young Bob, dressed, but stretched out on his bed.

As Dr Cameron appeared he sat up, looking ashamed of himself.

'Forgive me, sir, I was up and moving around but suddenly felt queer and had to lie down.'

'That's all right Bob. Your granddad just told me you hadn't been up to the mark lately. Have ye been studying hard at school?'

'Not more than usual. But the truth is, sir, all last term I felt as if I had no go in me whatsoever. Even here I'm just the same. First thing I did was to go up to the Gielstone Burn – it's my favourite walk – but if you can believe it, I could hardly get back.'

'I can see at once it's a tonic you're needing, Bob. But let's have a look at ye. Take off your shirt.'

The light in the room was not particularly bright but when Bob stripped off his shirt, Dr Cameron took out his stethoscope and went over the boy's heart and lungs thoroughly. The heart did seem a little tired but the lungs were sound. When he put his stethoscope away he smiled at Bob who had flushed nervously during the examination.

'Now, don't you worry, Bob. You're as sound as a bell. Just a

13

bit tired and run down. I'll give you a tonic that will soon put ye right.' As he wrote the prescription, he added, 'It's a well-proved medicine for hard-working students. I don't mind admitting to you that I took it myself when I was at college studying for my MD.'

'Oh, thank you sir, thank you ever so much. I'll get it from Mr Blair the chemists this morning.'

'Good lad! Mind you, it takes time to work so see that ye give it a fair trial.'

When Dr Cameron returned downstairs, the butcher looked at him anxiously.

'Nothing serious I trust, doctor?'

'He's a bit run-down, Bob. But I have given him something that will put him right. Mind you, it might take time to work but a couple of bottles should do the trick.'

'Thank you, doctor, most sincerely. I've wrapped up your ham and I picked one specially for ye.'

'Thanks, Bob. I'll look in and see the boy in say a week or ten days.'

With the big parcel under his arm, Dr Cameron strode proudly down the High Street. He was not ashamed to admit that he liked a good ham, and indeed the rich aroma of the bulky package would have revealed the fact even had he attempted to conceal it. At lunch that same day he said to Finlay:

'I was up to Bob McKie this morning to fetch your breakfast for the next month.'

'Oh, thank you, sir. Did you not bring something for yourself?'

'And when I was in the shop,' Dr Cameron continued, ignoring the interruption, 'Bob asked me to have a look at his grandson who's up as usual for his holidays.'

'Oh, good! I must get him out for some fishing. But tell me, is he not well?'

'A bit run-down from his studies, but I gave him something that will soon have him jumping over the burn with his rod.'

'What was your prescription, sir?'

'Did ye ever hear o' McKie's Tonic?'

'No . . . o . . . o, canna say I did, sir. What does it contain?'

'Weel, I'll enlighten you, m'lad. It's a standard tonic that we students used when we were run-down with examinations and hard work at the hospital wards. McKie's Tonic. Man, it's a famous remedy.'

'Can't say I ever heard of it, sir. But naturally I'll take your word for it.'

'Keep an eye on Bob Macfarlane and ye'll not need to take my word for it. Ye young doctors think ye know it all, but apparently ye never heard o' Dr McKie.'

After this discussion Finlay determined that he would keep an eye on his young friend. He was busy all next day but on the following morning, after his morning round, he walked up the Gielstone Burn and there, as anticipated, he found young Bob Macfarlane.

But Bob was not fishing. His rod was propped against a tree and he was sitting disconsolately on the bank.

'But you're not fishing, Bob!' cried Finlay, seating himself beside the boy and putting a friendly arm around his shoulders.

'Oh, I'm glad to see you, Dr Finlay. I hoped you might come up here. Yes, I did try a couple of casts then I had to sit down.'

'As bad as that! Are ye not takin' your tonic?'

'I have tried a few doses sir, but the truth of the matter is this. It makes me sick as a dog. In fact I brought up the last couple of doses. Vomiting something terrible, I was.'

'Then ye maun stop it Bob, on my authority. While ye sit there – don't get up – let me have a look at you.'

Bob submitted in silence while Finlay took his pulse, then peered into the boy's white, tense face. Finlay spent some time examining the boy's eyes in particular, everting the lower lids and studying the conjunctiva, which was not a healthy red but pallid and bloodless.

My dear old boss has missed this, Finlay thought, and it's the certain clue to the boy's condition.

'Tell me, Bob, did you have an accident of any kind before your holidays?'

'Yes, I did, sir. On the last day of term we were larking about in the carpentry room when another boy, quite by accident of course, stuck his cutting chisel into my bare arm. Well, I bled like a pig and before they could get the master with a proper tourniquet I had made a pool on the floor that was fearfully large. They wanted to fetch a doctor but I said no and they sent me home in a cab.'

'Good God, lad! And you came on here the very next day.'

'I didn't want to tell anyone sir. I felt such a fool. So I just came, but I admit, I felt awful in the train. And to tell the truth I still feel peculiar. Don't have a kick in me.'

And my dear old boss gave him a bottle of McKie's Tonic, thought Finlay, then aloud, 'Bob, you're coming with me to the hospital lab. Just wait here quietly till I return.'

Finlay took Bob's bicycle and rode down the glen to his car, which stood outside the surgery. Leaving the bike propped against the kerb he got into the car, returned and picked up Bob. In five minutes they were in the hospital laboratory.

'Take your jacket and shirt off and lie down on the couch, lad. And don't worry, I'm going to take just one tiny drop of your blood, for a test.'

The blood, pale and watery-looking, was drawn up into a hypodermic syringe then transferred to a test tube and within twenty minutes the tests were complete. Finlay gave an exclamation of satisfaction and turned to the boy.

'Now listen, lad, you have lost so much blood it would take you months of misery before you make it up. Fortunately you have the same blood group as myself, so I'm going to make you a present of some which I can very well spare. Lie still and I'll draw up my chair beside you.'

Within ten minutes this simple operation was completed. Finlay lay for a few moments beside his patient.

Then he said, 'How do you feel, lad?'

'Oh, sir, dear Dr Finlay. Instead of feeling like a wet empty sack, I want to run for miles, jump over walls. Oh, thank God, and thank *you* and bless you, doctor. I'm myself again, better than new.'

'Take it easy then. You must be quite still for half an hour. And I will rest too.'

'Of course. Oh, Dr Finlay, do you feel bad?'

'I'll soon be right as rain and all the better for the blood letting. Now listen carefully, Bob. No one must know of this, it's between you and me alone, for it would hurt Dr Cameron's pride really badly to think he had failed in diagnosing your trouble. And worse still that I, his assistant, had spotted your want of blood and cured it on the spot!'

'Oh, I won't tell anyone Dr Finlay. Although perhaps you would let me tell my mother when she comes up next week. But surely to goodness I don't need to go on with that beastly McKie's mixture.'

'You don't need it, lad, and never did. So quietly, quietly mind you, dispose of it down the sink or, safer still, the lavatory.'

'I will, doctor. I'll do everything you tell me because I trust you and love you.'

'Then get in the car with me and we'll drive to your bike, parked outside my surgery. Then you can take off for your gran-dad's. And remember, no gabbing, not a single word.' Back home Finlay felt the need of his tea and went to the kitchen to make it when Janet suddenly appeared, took off her coat and said reproachfully, 'Could you not wait five minutes till I got back from the town?'

'I was thirsty, Janet. I've been up the burn fishing with young Bob Macfarlane.'

'Ay, he just passed me on his bike goin' like steam. Dr Cameron will be pleased with him.'

'That's the truth, Janet. He's come on wonderfully since he took Dr Cameron's medicine.'

'I'm glad ye admit it,' Janet said kindly. 'Would you like a piece o' shortbread tae your tea? I made some afore I went out.'

'Thank you, Janet. I love your shortbread, it's the best in Tannochbrae.'

'Best in Scotland, ye mean, lad.' And Janet gave him one of her rare smiles. 'To find ye so polite and agreeable is just like the auld days when ye first came here. When the doctor was heid o' the family and me and you were his devoted children.'

'We're still devoted, Janet. You know I'd do anything in the world for the auld doctor.'

'I'm sure ye would, lad. It's just that sometimes ye seem to think that ye ken mair than him.'

'God forbid, Janet.'

'Well here's your shortbread, and it's a bigger bit that I meant to give you.'

Finlay departed with the shortbread and a respectful inclination of his head. Janet was sometimes difficult, but she could always be brought round by any appreciation of her worth, verbal or otherwise. He had barely nibbled the shortbread and sipped at his first cup of tea before a firm step was heard in the lobby and the door was flung open, revealing Dr Cameron still in full outdoor panoply – reefer coat slightly open, one of the many scarves knitted by Janet, and his hat cocked at a rakish angle.

'Well, indeed!' he exclaimed half jocularly. 'Tea without me! Is that the way to treat the head o' the house?'

Finlay stood up and said quietly, 'As you're very often not in for your tea, sir, preferring to take it at your club in the town, and as it had struck the half five without a sign of you, Janet very kindly gave me a cup.'

'Shortbread, too! Well I never. Ye fare well, my young sir, whenever my back is turned.'

Fortunately Janet scurried in with a tray, bearing more tea and an ample portion of shortbread, which she placed by the big armchair. Then receiving coat, scarf, gloves and hat from her master she scurried out to hang them in the hall.

'Well, lad! I ken ye were up the burn with my patient. What did you think o' him?'

'Wonderfully improved, sir, and a compliment to you!'

'Ay, thank ye, lad. As a matter of fact, Bob McKie hailed me in as I passed the shop to shake me by the hand. "Never," says he to me, "have I seen such a wonderful recovery. The dear boy was creeping about, white as a ghost. You prescribed for him, and after one bottle o' your medicine – for it's all gone – he is cured, looking better than I have ever seen him since he was a bairn." '

'Well, sir,' Finlay exclaimed, 'what a triumph for ye.'

Dr Cameron gave a self-conscious little laugh. 'Bob told me the whole town would be talking about it. Says he to me, "Doctors may come and doctors may go, but there's one doctor who will ever be with us, loved and respected for his kindness and brilliance." '

'He insisted in bringing down the boy, my patient. I'll confess to you, Finlay, that I was amazed by the improvement in him; his pulse, his colour, his briskness. I saw that I had just hit on the one correct medicine he needed. And it had done the trick for him, and, if I may say so, for me.'

'Well, sir, I am happy for you. And for young Bob. He's a thoroughly good, likeable lad. And as he was certainly seriously ill it's a God's blessing he is well again.'

'Thank you, Finlay. It's to your credit that never, ay never, have ye shown the least jealousy towards me.'

The old doctor then quaffed his tea and poured himself a second cup before filling and lighting his first pipe of the day.

The weather continued fine and young Bob Macfarlane was up every day fishing the full stretch of the Gielstone Burn where, as work was light in the practice, Dr Finlay regularly joined him. On several occasions they went further afield and Finlay took the boy over the high Darroch Moors where there was a chance of sea trout in the loch. Usually they came back with a few sizable fish and once they – or to be exact, Finlay – landed a seven-pound grilse. As they stepped off the Moors to the Tannochbrae road, young Bob carrying the fish, they observed a young woman stepping briskly towards them. And suddenly Bob let out a shout.

'Good heavens, it's my mother!'

Within five yards of them she stopped, looking them over, then in a tone of admiration and surprise she said 'Bob! I can't believe it's you! And Finlay! You don't look a day older than my big son. And both of you so brown and healthy, stepping off the Moor as though you'd walked ten miles to catch that lovely fish.'

She took her son in her arms and gave him a big kiss, then, unable to resist the impulse, she turned to Finlay and pressed her lips against his glowing cheek murmuring, 'Why didna ye, mon? Why didna ye?'

There was a long moment of stillness, then, recovering herself, she addressed her son.

'I came to Tannochbrae expecting to find you still pale as a sheet and here ye are, brown and healthy, better than I ever saw you.' She turned to Finlay, 'His grandad told me it is all due to some wonderful medicine Dr Cameron gave him, that worked like magic. It's the talk of the town.'

Bob, excited at seeing his mother, let out a wild exuberant laugh.

'Mother, dear Mother, I have to tell you.'

'Now, Bob, remember your promise.'

'I should be allowed to tell my mother, Finlay. It won't go further.'

Arm in arm the three had begun the long walk home. 'Listen, dear Mother . . .' Out came the whole story while his mother listened intently, half turning now and then to study Finlay's set face.

'So you see, Mother, here I am walking for miles with Finlay's good blood in me while that auld fraud gets all the credit for a bottle of medicine I never took but just poured down the lavatory.' He added, 'But for his transfusion, I'd still be crawling about like a broken-down ghost.'

Bob's mother did not reply but she looked at Finlay several times, then her grip on his arm tightened and in a quiet but determined voice, she said:

'I never in all my life have heard of such a cheap and beastly swindle. Here is my dear Finlay who diagnosed my son's condition and gave freely his own life's blood to save him, to put him back striding on the moors instead of crawling around like Hamlet's ghost while that puffed-up old Cameron, who doesna ken a transfusion from a bull's behind, has the whole town bowin' and scrapin' to him.'

'Hush, Gracie. Mind your language.'

'If you had lived with a man like my husband you would have picked up a few choice bits and pieces. Oh, Finlay, why didna ye follow on after that last dance at the Reunion? I was fair crazy for you and I could weel tell that you liked me.'

'Ah, Gracie, my love,' Finlay sighed, 'that's old history now. I was so young and inexperienced in my job, a miserable assistant. I spoke to Janet and she said there was no place for a wife in the house. I hadna the courage to tell ye I loved ye.'

'So you left me to Will Macfarlane, a worthy man according to his neighbours, but sae coarse and insensitive to a woman's feelings, I was shocked and disgusted with him before the honeymoon was over. Oh Finlay, how often have I missed you and longed to put the clock back. That night of the Reunion when you held me in your arms I could feel you loved me.'

'I'll tell ye one thing, Grace dear, I have never looked at or touched a woman since that wonderful night and that is many a year past.'

'That's proof ye loved me dearest Finlay. Surely I can see you mair often than I do now?'

'You'll be up occasionally visiting your big son.'

'My big son! He's as much yours now as mine. Well, darling, my train leaves in an hour's time. Would you walk up to the station with me?'

'I will, indeed, Gracie. Just bide here a few minutes, I have a patient waiting for me in the surgery.' When Finlay had gone Grace did not sit down but stood staring moodily out of the window.

Suddenly a voice made her turn round.

'So, you are off home tonight to your own dear husband. I thought I would look in to bid ye a pleasant goodbye.'

Grace swung round. She knew the voice. Her face hardened. 'Don't you wish me anything pleasant you two-faced, keyhole-listening, auld bitch. You're the one that botched up Finlay's chance to wed me. Ye thought it would be inconvenient for the lord and master that ye worship with all the dried-up blood in your veins. You were feared I might cook better, run up and down stairs quicker than you on your auld withered legs. So you frightened my lover awa' frae me. All for the great god o' the household. Well let me tell you this. It was *not him*, with his bottle of rotten physic, that cured my boy. It was Finlay, who diagnosed the case correctly, took him to the hospital and transfused his own blood into my poor bloodless boy. The change was instantan-eous. And now that Bob is totally cured, walking miles over the moors with Finlay's good blood inside him, who gets the credit? Your Lord and Master, whose medicine went down the mickey and who is now struttin' about the town as though he was God Almighty. And who keeps the secret? The Finlay ye took away frae me. He's warned my son and me not to say a word, to save your auld hero from being the laughing stock of Tannochbrae!'

As she spoke Janet's face altered dramatically. The prim self-satisfied expression simply fell apart. Speechless and aghast she gazed at Grace. And in that one dumb look, Grace felt that she had levelled the score with the selfish old woman who had destroyed for ever her one chance of happiness.

There was the sound of someone moving in the lobby, too slowly for Finlay. A few moments later Finlay stepped briskly into the room. Ignoring Janet he said, 'Have I kept you waiting too long, Gracie? I had two patients not one.'

Taking her arm he led her from the room. As they walked to

the station arm in arm, she said, 'Your extra patient gave me the chance to say a few words to Janet that I've been saving up for many a day. I think they'll do her good.'

Dinner that evening was a silent meal. Dr Cameron seemed preoccupied, Finlay was still mulling over Grace's visit, and Janet never let a word escape from her compressed lips. When the meal was over and they were drinking their coffee, Dr Cameron took a deep breath and turned to Finlay.

'My dear, most distinguished colleague, I have asked Janet to bring your morning tea to your bedroom, just as she does for me.'

'Oh really, sir, that is most kind of you. It's a bore having to get up, wash, shave, dress and come downstairs before that first delicious sip. I hope Janet won't mind?'

'Janet will do as she is told,' Cameron said concisely. Then, after a pause, he seemed to nerve himself to speak and in a loud voice he said, 'Coming in tonight, when I was in the lobby, I chanced to hear what I was not intended to hear, and what I most certainly did not wish to hear. And from Grace, who was angrily addressing Janet. I heard all, and I mean all, that you have done to completely cure Grace's boy. I heard also a very just criticism of my absurd assumption that I had cured the boy, when it was you by your correct diagnosis and splendid self-sacrificing transfusion who had immediately restored him to health.' He paused. 'I heard also of your most loyal silence, sparing me a most painful humiliation before the whole town. Dear Finlay, I have always respected you and loved you like a son, and now in gratitude and admiration I will henceforth regard you as a possible partner to myself. Look ahead to that day, my dear lad, when I will place my hand upon your shoulder and declare: "Finlay! You are no longer my assistant. Today, in the sight of heaven, I create you my partner." '

Suddenly, from the doorway, there came a wild skirl of laughter. And Janet, who had been listening, suddenly shouted: 'That will be a day I want to see. And never will. So long as ye dae a' the hard and difficult work, Finlay, he'll keep ye slavin' awa' under him. That's the way he's treated me. Years ago when I was young and bonny he made me hope for something better, but I'm still slavin' awa', workin' mysel' to daith just to fill his belly and mak' him comfortable.'

When she departed and the kitchen door closed with a deafening slam, Dr Cameron drew himself to his full height and looking benignly at Finlay delivered himself of this brief moral postulate:

'Even the worm will turn!'

The Shepherd of the Far Hills

Dr Finlay's love of hard exercise in the open air was well known in Tannochbrae and in the lands beyond. The Caledonia's game-keeper would always have him up for a couple of days' shooting at the end of the season. Often indeed, Finlay would go ranging far beyond the hotel's private land and come back with a brace of grouse, or maybe a salmon when the fish were running in the upper river. Even in the open season when no sport was possible and the practice was not unduly busy, Finlay would put an apple in his pocket and in thick-soled boots, corduroys and grey woollen jersey take off for a long day's tramp over the moors and into the wide blue yonder.

It was on one of these excursions that he first came across Willie Semple. Finlay was sitting by a stream eating his apple after a long hard grind that had taken him beyond the moors on to a high, rough stretch of coarse grass, and he was watching a little ripple by the far bank when a voice behind him said:

'Don't kill him. He's fu' of milt on his way to the lake.'

Finlay flicked a fragment of apple in the direction of the ripple and immediately there was a slow turn over in the water exposing the full side of a heavy fish. Finlay swung round. Close beside him was the oddly-clad figure of a young man, bearded and bare-headed, with long shaggy hair, who was holding a young lamb under one arm.

'Forgive me for butting in on ye, Dr Finlay.'

'So you know me?'

'You're weel kent, doctor. I've often seen ye lower down and hoped ye might come by. I'm Willie Semple.'

The name struck a chord in Finlay's mind.

'Are you the fellow they call the shepherd o' the far hills?'

'I don't know what they ca' me doctor, and I don't care. I live up here wi' my sheep.'

'All by yourself?'

'No, doctor. Wi' my mother. And that's why I took the liberty to speak to you, for it's far from my custom to talk to strangers.'

'Is your mother ill?'

'Very poorly, doctor. I wish you would take the trouble to look at her.'

Naturally Finlay could not refuse. And this strange young lad interested him. They set off up the hill together.

'You have a stray lamb with you?'

'Ay! My dear wee Jeannie is a wanderer. But she'll aye come to me when I blow my horn.'

Finlay now noticed a curved bull's horn slung from the boy's shoulders. 'Would you blow it now?'

'Ay, I'll gie it a toot to let my mother know I'm coming.'

Still supporting the lamb he put the horn to his lips and blew a long, deep, melodious note.

Soon they were at the summit of the hill, and there, in a wide circular hollow, was a low, poor farmhouse surrounded by sheep pens. Willie now released the lamb with a light tap on its rump and the injunction, 'Don't do it again, Jeannie!'

They entered the house and at once Finlay was struck by the poverty and disorder of the interior – simply a kitchen and a bedroom.

'I'm home, mother. And I've brought Dr Finlay to see ye.'

Finlay entered the bedroom, which contained a large bed and a narrow cot against the far wall. On the bed an old woman lay, half-dressed and, though struggling for breath, making an endeavour to get up.

'Lie still, dearie,' Finlay said. He saw at a glance that the old woman was seriously ill. When she lay back he felt for a pulse in the old withered wrist. Not a sign of one. Without a stethoscope he leaned over and placed his ear flat against the old woman's breast. Only the faintest flutter was discernible and the breathing was feeble and shallow.

'How do you feel, Mother?'

'I feel this, doctor. I've done my best for my boy, but I canna do no more.'

For a moment Finlay considered the possibility of moving her to hospital, then dismissed it. She was too far gone. She had given everything for her son. Nothing was left.

'I'll send a nurse to you. Just to look after you for a while.'

'There's nae nurse will ever put a finger on me, doctor. My son can do all that is required.'

'But you'll take the medicine I send you. And let me look in to see you when I'm on the hills next week.'

'Ye may come if ye wish, doctor. But I've never taken physic in my life and I never will.'

Finlay remained for some moments, stroking the poor old emaciated arm, then he stepped into the kitchen.

'Willie, your mother has put up a good fight but now the battle is over. In my opinion she cannot go on much longer. Any day now. Any minute. I could send a nurse, but she would only be able to help you with the funeral.'

Finlay felt his hand clasped in an iron grip. 'You're a good man, doctor. I read it in your eyes.'

'But what will you do, Willie? When you're all alone?'

'I can make shift masel', doctor.'

'Never, Willie. You're too young to be a hermit o' the hills. I'll see about that for you when the time comes.'

The time was not long in coming. Two weeks later the poor old woman went to her eternal rest and was buried in Tannochbrae churchyard. Willie was persuaded to sell his stock to an adjoining farmer who also bought the house and furnishings for his own occasional use. But Willie persistently refused to sell his favourite lamb, Jeannie, who had grown so attached to him that, suitably shorn, she followed him about like a little dog.

Finlay thought it wise to make some adjustment in Willie's appearance before exposing him to the public eye in Tannochbrae. He presented him with a safety razor and instructed him in its use. Although Willie refused to have his hair cut he allowed a slight trimming of the edges. And he accepted gratefully one of Finlay's suits, a soft brown over-check which Finlay had put aside as a mite too dashing for his own use.

Shaved, tidied up and wearing the suit, which fitted him perfectly, Willie Semple, with his dark eyes, flowing hair and fine aesthetic features, even without the lamb, was indeed a striking figure. Finlay felt proud of his creation and bravely chose the right moment to introduce him to the rest of the village. One Sunday, well after noon, when the churches were emptying and the streets were full of people in groups standing to talk, or promenading slowly in the middle of the road, Finlay and Willie appeared at the head of the town. Quietly followed by the lamb, they began to stroll slowly along the main street, across, into and around Victoria Square, then back and down to the far end of the town, where they vanished along the quiet, secluded residential part of Tannochbrae, known to the élite as Dunbarton Villas. Opposite one of these houses Finlay paused and, by a discreet movement of his left foot, directed Jeannie to the large grassy lawn where the intelligent animal, whose breakfast had been rather delayed, set to work. Finlay then mounted the three broad steps and discreetly pulled the bell.

A smiling maid, small and dressed for the street, answered the door and without interrogation admitted the two finely turned-out young men to the large drawing-room where a fire, by considerable skill, had been kept aglow.

'Mr Cairns will be down presently, sir. I am to tell you that he has thought over your telephone call and may be able to give you an answer.'

Looking about him Finlay decided that Cairns, corn-chandler for Tannochbrae and the surrounding countryside, had done well for himself and his grown-up daughter. At that moment the man of the house entered the room, shook hands with Finlay and, after close scrutiny, with Willie. As he seated himself, Finlay said quickly, 'I am sorry, sir, to be intruding on your privacy, especially on a Sunday, but when I phoned you last night you said I . . .'

'Don't apologise, Finlay,' he smiled. 'From what I see on my front lawn the case is remarkably urgent.' He reached for a pipe from an adjacent rack, filled it from his pouch, lit up and, after a few satisfactory puffs, saw that it was drawing well. 'Now,' he continued, 'from what you have told me it is quite evident that your young friend would never be content in a town job. I'm fully aware of the circumstances before his mother passed away when he worked hard and weel wi' his bit of a sheep farm. He's a countryman, born and bred.' Another pause while he puffed.

'I have gone through the list of a' my customers.' A pause. 'And there's just one likely farm that may fit the bill. The auld Macrae place, way out by Bridge. Ye'll maybe ken it.'

'Oh, I do sir, why it's past the . . .'

'Exactly,' Cairn cut in, unwilling to share his choice. Then, after a few puffs. 'Since auld Jock Macrae died, it's run down to the bone. The widow hasna bothered much for she's plenty o' money, but they still have sheep and raise a field of taters, but the rest o' the lands are completely run down. There's nae son, just a dochter awa' at some fancy school who'll hardly show her face there. But what am I thinkin' of? Let me offer ye some coffee. I'm wantin' some myself.' He gave the bell handle on the wall a violent pull that sent a tremendous jangling through the house.

Almost at once a pretty young woman came into the room. 'What do you think you're doing, Father? Deafening the ears off me. Didn't ye ken Cathleen has gone out to that church o' hers?'

'I'm sorry, dearie,' Cairns said humbly, 'I clean forgot. Like myself these two young men fancied a cup of coffee. Ye ken Finlay I believe.'

'I certainly should. He tried to kiss me often enough at the Reunion Dance. Is the other lad his brother?'

'No, Jessie. He's Willie Semple, a fine young man who's just lost his mother and is looking for a job. I thought he might work his way up on the Macrae farm.'

'That dump! Nae mair than a run-down potato patch, where the mother is aye at the bottle and the daughter a stuck-up bitch. This fine young man would be wasted out there.' She came into the room and seated herself beside Willie. 'Is that your wee lamb that just came in the kitchen? I gave him a big bowl of corn grits and milk. He's sleeping now before the kitchen fire.'

Willie flushed and smiled. 'Thank you most sincerely, Miss Cairns. You are as kind-hearted as you are beautiful.' He leaned forward, took her hand, and kissed it. The action was so simple and unpremeditated no one thought it peculiar. But Jess Cairns looked into Willie's eyes long and deep, and what she saw there caused a rich colour to mount in her tough little face, then fade, leaving her very pale. Then she in turn took Willie's hand and after a long moment she turned to her father.

'Dad! You're not sending this fine young man to waste and wither at that God-forsaken place. Ye can see at a glance he's worth more, much more than that. Now listen to me. Ye're aye complaining that ye need help in the yard and come home groaning about your back after lifting the heavy corn sacks. Why don't you take Willie as your assistant. I'll swear to you on my very life that he'll be worth it.'

Six months later Finlay received an invitation to the wedding of Jess Cairns and William Semple, Junior Partner in the firm of Cairns and Semple, Corn Chandlers and Stock Salesmen.

Perhaps Finlay was a trifle piqued to lose the beautiful Jess, but he consoled himself by sending the happy bride an expensive wedding present, a brooch consisting of a white-gold lamb with two little diamonds for the eyes.

The wedding of Willie and Jess was the great event of the season in Tannochbrae. The church was packed to the doors. Everyone who was anyone was there.

When Willie and Jess stood together before the minister, a sweet little creature with a curly fleece and bow of white ribbon round her neck and another on her tail slipped up and stood behind them.

A low murmur of appreciation and suppressed laughter rippled through the congregation. All eyes moved towards one figure, who stood reverential and absorbed in the first pew. In his buttonhole was a little white bow exactly the same as the one sported by the lamb.

As to the lamb herself, the origin and cause of this tale, she was induced to join a handsome young ram at one of the finest farms in the shire. Their first lamb was called Jess.

Janet is Not Herself

Readers of these chronicles must have observed, I trust with sadness, or at least mild regret, the slow deterioration, not in Janet's physical activities alone, but in that indefinable quality known in Scotland as 'her temper'. Now Dr Cameron was inclined to be indulgent to an old servant who had been with him for so many years but there came a day when even he had to admit that she had gone too far. This particular morning his breakfast egg was stone cold and in the good doctor's own words 'hard as a bluidy brick'.

Indeed, Dr Cameron took steps to settle the matter later that day.

'Don't ye think our Janet could do with a bit o' help?'

'Certainly, sir. If she can be persuaded to take it.'

'Aye, that's the rub, lad. But there comes a tide in the affairs of men. Ye ken what I mean?'

'Perfectly, sir. And without the aid of Shakespeare. I do agree that to have a fresh, cheery young face instead of Janet's "soor plooms" bringing in your breakfast wad not be a change for the worse.'

'Exactly, lad. I could not have put it better myself. Now tell me, you're always about the young folks – bein' young yourself – do you ken such a young lass as I'm speaking about?'

Finlay reflected. True enough, he was always about when the games, football or hockey, of the Academy boys and girls were being played. And there was one lass who had most favourably caught his eye.

'Bess Buchanan,' he said.

'Ay, Bob Buchanan the barber's dochter.'

'His only daughter, sir. And a splendid lass. Captain of the hockey team and the principal girl in the Kinderspiel last winter. She must be in her last term at school.'

'Ay, ay. She sounds as if she might stand up to Janet for a couple of weeks, maybe. I'll step in at Bob's this verra morning. I'm needin' a shave anyway.'

All day Finlay went about his round of visits, unconscious of time and the possible consequences of what he had started. Nor, at the midday meal, did Cameron say a word, though his silence was portentous. However, at four o'clock, the end of the scholastic day, a clear, strong young voice was heard in the house and presently a fine, smiling girl appeared before Finlay with the tea tray.

'Dr Cameron is out, sir, so I brought yours in first.'

'Oh, thank you, Bess. And please don't call me sir. To you, dear lass, I'm always Finlay.'

'Thank you, sir, I mean Finlay.'

'That's better! Now pour yourself a cup, take a big slice of cake and sit down. Dr Cameron is out visiting Miss Walker, she'll keep him a good hour.'

Finlay exerted himself to please and with another thick slice of cake (Janet's special) succeeded in correcting the icy reception Bess had received downstairs in the kitchen. Indeed Bess herself assured him, 'My father warned me she was an old harridan, and told me not to mind her!'

Dr Cameron was a long time coming for his tea, indeed, by wise foresight he missed it altogether. And his first words to Finlay were: 'Everything go all right with young Bess?'

So it appeared. Dead silence reigned below, and cheerfully and quietly, Bess served the dinner. But unfortunately the soup was cold, the potatoes hard as stones, and the milk pudding full of lumps.

'If only she had let me do it, sir,' Bess said to the defeated Dr Cameron. 'I often make the dinner at home. She just done it for spite.'

Cameron said not a word, but his brow was dark with sombre thought and suddenly he stood up and spoke.

'Get on your coats and hats both of the two o' ye. If she thinks I'm going to let you young people starve tae daith as weel as masel', she's sadly mistaken.'

Donning his own coat and hat, he led the way out of the house and into the High Street where an interested populace watched him barge into the fine new restaurant, known locally as the Swank. Undeterred by the interest he was creating the bold Cameron commandeered a table and, subtly guided by the head waiter, ordered a dinner such as he and his two guests had never tasted.

Oh, the deliciousness of it, after Janet's horrid offerings!

'Man, Finlay,' said Cameron when the caviar was served. 'This potted heid is the best I ever lipped.'

'Do you like it too, Bess dear?' asked Finlay, enjoying the company fully as much as the scrumptious repast.

'It's next to heaven.'

'I thought I occupied that privileged position,' Finlay murmured.

In reply to this, Bess blushed and looked down.

When the next course, *ris de veau à la crème*, had been served the manager sidled up followed by a young man whom Finlay immediately recognised as the reporter for the *Tynecastle Times*.

'Dr Cameron, sir, forgive my intrusion. We are a new enterprise anxious to promote ourselves by publicising the distinguished patrons who honour us with their custom. For instance, the Duke of Argyll was here last week and had some very flattering things to say of our cuisine. Now, doctor, you sir are just as well known as the duke, indeed locally, even better so. Do you feel disposed to say a good word for us, as he did?'

'I'll be outdone by nae duke,' said the worthy doctor, setting himself square in his chair. 'And I'll tell ye straight, sir, when a man is driven from his home by the worst cookin' in the world, a deliberate waste o' good honest food that's made to taste like pig's swill, fit to poison ye, then it's time for him to walk out to the best and nearest establishment where every bite ye eat is delicious, superlative, and at the same time fully nutritious.'

The usually imperturbable face of the tough, experienced manager, actually flushed with pleasure. 'Did ye get a' that, Willie?' he whispered.

'Every word o' it, sir. And it will be a banner headline in the *Times* the morn's morn, "RENOWNED LOCAL PHYSICIAN SCORNS HOME COOKING, PRAISES 'SWANK' CUISINE SKY HIGH!" '

'That's it, Willie! That will bring them in.' Then he turned to Cameron, 'Dr Cameron I feel favoured by your generous unsolicited compliment and in return, permit me to extend to you, freely and without charge, the courtesy of dinner here, for yourself and your companions, for the further period.'

'Including tonight,' prompted the wily Cameron.

'Most assuredly, sir.'

When the good doctor and his adherents reached home their usual snack of porridge and buttermilk awaited them, but none of the party seemed to fancy it.

'We'll just leave it,' said the bold Cameron. 'It will teach *her* a lesson.'

Next morning, the breakfast appeared as usual: porridge and sweet milk, boiled eggs and good Scottish rolls.

'We'll no' stuff ourselves,' said Cameron. 'Save up for our dinner tonight.'

At lunch, which consisted of fresh Dover soles, nicely fried, with a full complement of crisp fried potatoes, there was no question of stinting themselves.

'We've taught her a lesson. This is just as good as the Swank.'

'Better,' said Finlay mildly. 'Do we want to go out again tonight?'

'Tuts, lad. We're invited, we canna refuse.' Then, when night fell, without a word to Janet, the bold doctor led his party to the Swank where their table of the night before had been reserved for them. In the manager's absence – he was obliged to officiate at a private dinner party – they were courteously received by the head waiter who, by his accent, revealed his Scottish origin.

'Well, doctor, sir, what shall we begin with tonight?'

'For me, I'd like nothing better than that special potted heid.'

'The caviar, sir?'

'Is that what ye call it?'

'It has to have a fancy name, sir. Ye see, it's nothing but the rotted guts o' a Russian fish.'

Cameron sat, stunned, while Finlay and Bess ordered tomato juice.

Presently the waiter returned.

'Seeing you fancy it, doctor, I've brought you an extra large portion, and mind you sir, this stuff costs a fortune.'

Silently, Cameron studied the black mass on the lovely white plate.

Costs a fortune! he thought. Well, I like it, so I'll no' waste it. Bravely he began on the caviar, but the words 'rotten Russian fish guts' kept ringing in his mind. And strangely, perhaps because it lacked the accompanying brandy, it tasted different, in fact just like rotten guts. But the waiter was watching with great interest, so too were Finlay and Bess. He must clear the plate, somehow get it down. But no, at last nature protested, he faltered, then suddenly dropped the fork and rushed through the swing doors into the cool, dark night. Alas, the horrid sounds of retching rent the air and came back to the listening pair as a man-size Russian vomit.

'We should go to him,' whispered Bess.

'Ach! He'll find his way home. Janet will see to him. Let's enjoy our dinner together.'

And so they did. Going straight on to lovely pink roast beef with mashed potatoes and sprouts.

'Isn't this lovely, dear Dr Finlay,' murmured Bess.

'Nothing could be nicer, darling,' Finlay agreed, looking into her eyes. The waiter, watching them, was quite paternal.

'Another fine slice o' the beef for both of you?'

'It's delicious, Willie.'

'Ay! Ye'll get nae Russian fish guts frae me.'

Bess sighed softly. 'This would be perfect, Finlay, if it wasna for my best boy.'

'I'm your best boy, Bess.'

'What I mean is that I'm supposed to be engaged to Alex Douglas. In fact I can see him looking through the window at us now.'

'I'll settle him when we get outside.'

'No, no, no, Finlay! I'm not wanting a common fight over me in the public street. My parents would hear of it and it would disgrace me for ever.'

'Then who do ye want?'

Dead silence. Then in a little whisper:

'I'm afraid I've gone sae far wi' Alex.'

'Ye mean he's . . .'

More feebly still she replied, 'Yes . . . several times.'

My God, thought Finlay, rotten fish guts and now this, all in one night. And for me, what a close shave. After a moment he said firmly. 'Well Bess, away out to Alex now. He'll see ye home. Goodnight, dear.'

When she had gone Finlay ordered himself a brandy. When he had downed it he said goodnight to Willie, then set off through the empty streets alone.

There was a light in the dining-room. And there, sitting together over a wee drop of goodness, were Dr Cameron and a penitent Janet. Finlay thought he'd leave them to it.

The next morning, at seven o'clock prompt, porridge and sweet milk, soft boiled eggs, new-baked scones and strong coffee appeared on the table.

As Finlay watched the good doctor humbly eating this magnificent repast he could not, as he sat down, resist a final word.

'Better than that Russian stuff, eh sir?'

A Moral Dilemma

All was now sweetness and light in the home of the good Dr Cameron. Never was the worthy doctor so forbearing to his patients, so pleasant to Dr Finlay, so courteous to his faithful housekeeper. Now that the no-longer-needed Bess had departed, presumably of her own free will, all was peace in the kitchen. And, as any good Scotsman will testify, when all is well below stairs, then you have a happy home.

Only one member of the household seemed not quite at ease. A worried frown disfigured the noble brow of Dr Finlay; his eye was clouded and remote. On several occasions when Dr Cameron addressed him, he was obliged to stir himself and murmur, in apology, 'What was that you said, sir?'

Experience had shown that to disturb Finlay in these moods of introspection was to court disaster. If for instance some well meaning acquaintance, meeting him in the street, were to say, smilingly, 'What's on your mind, Finlay, old boy?' he might receive the sombre and totally unexpected answer, 'Mind your own damn business, and let me mind mine.' With these offensive words, Finlay reserved the right to solve his own problems, and when the opportunity presented itself, to act upon them as he thought wise and proper.

Some ten days later Finlay entered the establishment of Robert Buchanan, Barber and Hairdresser, and seated himself quietly to await his turn. This was not long in coming since Finlay was now an acknowledged and esteemed personality in Tannochbrae. And soon Bob Buchanan himself came bustling out of his office to seat Finlay in the special chair by the window.

'Is it the usual, Finlay? Cut and trim?'

'Please, Bob. But first I would like to apologise for the treatment your splendid daughter received from our jealous auld bag o' a housekeeper, who couldna bear to see your sweet lass do everything so easily, ay, everything she groaned and complained about hersel'.'

'Ay, Bess is a good lass, though lately she hasna been quite hersel. Mind you, Finlay, she liked working for ye, and had hoped ye would teach her to dispense the medicines.'

'And so I would have, Bob. I think the world of your lass and certainly would have helped her to take her dispenser's certificate. In fact, it's because I esteem her so highly I would like your permission to speak of her today. Bob, as a father, what is your view on children – boys and girls – having full, complete, and unrestricted knowledge of each other without the consent of their parents?'

Bob was so surprised, he actually stopped snipping.

'Why, Finlay, I . . . I think it would be abominable, disgusting and sinful in fact.'

'These are exactly my views. For the fellow it's little enough, he may or may not decide to marry the girl. But for the girl it is the ruination of everything that's sacred and can very easily end in disaster. What would Tannochbrae think of a dear wee lass who faces the village with a little bastard in her pram?'

Bob stopped clipping altogether. 'Finlay! I fear ye have something on your mind. Come into the office with me now.'

Quickly, he brushed Finlay's hair, whipped off the sheet, and led the way into his office. There, facing each other, the two men sat knee to knee in silence.

At last Finlay felt obliged to speak:

'Bob, my dear friend, whom I have known all my days, even when I was a bairn and my mother took me to you to have my curls cut. Bob, it breaks my heart to tell you, for I dearly love your Bess . . . but it is my duty and I must do it. Bob, your daughter has been raped, used like a common whore and still is twice a week, behind a dyke, in the woods, anywhere at a' and is abused by a man we both know.'

A deathly stillness settled over the little office, and Finlay prayed that he had made the right decision. He waited a few moments then said, as calmly as possible, 'Now, dear Bob, this painful information came to me as an admission from your daughter. I have struggled day and night with the problem of whether or not to tell you, but in the end I saw that it was my duty, to you – and to Bess whom I love with all my heart.'

Again silence filled the little office. Then Finlay felt his right hand grasped as in a vice and slowly he was drawn towards Bob until his cheek rested against the other's tear-drenched face. At last the words came as though wrenched from clenched teeth: 'I'll kill the scoundrel.'

With an effort Finlay broke free.

'Be calm, Bob. Calm and strong. For the sake of Bess, whom we both love, don't act on impulse.' He paused for a few seconds then continued, 'It's quite clear that these two are infatuated, not so much with each other as with the pleasure, illicit thought it is, they derive from each other. In other words that attraction for each other is purely physical, and only physical force will stop it.'

'If you mean to thrash that young blackguard I've already tried it, Finlay. I gave him a damn good hiding, and it only made her go to him all the more out of pity.'

After another, more lengthy, silence Finlay spoke again. 'Bob, I have given a good deal of thought to your problem, and there is only one way to deal with it. As I said just now the attraction between these two is physical, easy and accessible contact. They must therefore be separated.'

He paused to let this sink in, then he resumed. 'Now, at my university in Glasgow, they have instituted a scheme to deal with the Spanish War orphans. Boatloads of them have just arrived at the Broomielaw. My old teacher, Professor Sinclair, is now calling for young people to help in the reception and care of these poor little waifs. Now listen Bob, I have kept in touch with

Professor Sinclair and if I let him know the circumstances, he will give Bess work that will fit her case, work in a country settlement that will certainly touch her heart and absorb her interest and attention. She will go to her cot – in a dormitory of girls – too tired even to think.'

In the silence that followed Finlay felt his hand gripped again.

'So you agree Bob. I thought you would!'

The answer came instantly. 'Of course I agree, dear Finlay, with all my heart, and I beg you to ring your professor, right away, soon, soon!'

Finlay replied quickly and firmly, 'I have already telephoned him, Bob! It's all arranged. Ye may send Bess off first thing tomorrow. Tell her to go straight from the station to Professor Sinclair at the university. I've got him really interested in her case and he will take care of everything.'

Six months later on a fine autumn afternoon Finlay had just come in from a brief foray on the moors when Janet called to him, 'There's a lady and gentleman to see you. It's such a fine afternoon they're waiting outside in the porch.'

Finlay put down his gun and a brace of partridges then walked round to the porch. Immediately a young man stood up and held out his hand.

'Forgive us for disturbing you at this hour, Dr Finlay. My wife was so anxious for us to visit you that we came directly to you from the station, before going on to my dear wife's home. The name's Sinclair, by the way.'

Shading his eyes against the sun Finlay saw the young man to be well set up, handsome, quietly dressed in tweeds and wearing a university 'blues' tie. Sinclair? thought Finlay. Suddenly the light struck.

'You are Professor Sinclair's son?'

'Yes, indeed, sir. He sends his very best regards and remembrances to you. And this lady here, my dear wife, surely you know her?'

'Bess! Bess Buchanan!'

'Now Bess Sinclair, darling.' And rising Bess planted a soft, warm kiss on Finlay's cheek, whispering, 'How much I owe you dear doctor. You must realise that when you look at me. I am happy, so happy, and am at last truly and serenely in love!'

For a moment Finlay was too overcome to speak.

'It's the orphans who did it,' he muttered, at last.

'And weren't you responsible for the orphans?' countered Bess warmly.

This was too much for everyone. Even Janet, who had been listening at the door, went away cackling to the kitchen. At last Finlay said, 'How good of you to come first to me, Bess. Will you take tea here? Or would you like me to drive you home?'

'Home, darling,' said Bess.

Janet, watching from the window as they piled into the car, threw up her hands and wailed:

'That's Finlay for ye! After I've made him a lovely tea, wi' the treacle scones he's sae fond o', he's off like a flash and I'll no' see him till his evening surgery. Ah weel! I canna waste such a lovely tea, I'll just sit down in the kitchen, stir up the fire and eat it a' masel'.'

Dr Cameron's Appendix

Lovely autumnal weather was blessing Tannochbrae with blue skies and bright sunshine that warmed the crisp, cool air. Of course, the practice was always busy at this time of year but, as he sat down to a good breakfast of porridge and sweet milk followed by grilled kippers and toast, Finlay felt that he might manage to get off to the moors with his new gun for an hour in the early afternoon. As Janet brought in his second kipper he remarked pleasantly, 'I'm surprised that Dr Cameron has not appeared for breakfast – he loves a morning like this.'

'No, Dr Finlay,' Janet formally replied. 'Our chief is not down yet. In plain truth I question if he will come down at all. When I took in his morning coffee and his shaving water he was still in his bed, without a word, layin' there prostitate.'

'Prostrate, surely, dear Janet,' Finlay corrected with a laugh.

'It may amuse you, Dr Finlay. But if you had seen him, ye might have thought it was no laughing matter.'

Finlay was certainly not laughing at his chief's indisposition, slight though it may be. He knew very well that Dr Cameron was essential to their joint practice; not only to take over a fair portion of the work, but to lend his authority and support in all important and difficult decisions.

With this in mind, Finlay, having downed his second kipper, and third cup of coffee, hurried upstairs to his chief's room, expecting to find him shaving, a lengthy and serious task with, of course, the open blade.

Dr Cameron had risen from his bed, and though unwashed and unshaven, was trying to dress himself in his full professional attire. The will was obviously there, but when he saw Finlay, the worthy old doctor staggered slightly, just saving himself from falling by a dramatic clutch at the big wooden end of his bed.

'No, sir, you must not get up. Not under any circumstances.' And supporting him with both arms Finlay laid him back again on the bed, studying him with an anxious eye.

'I'm heart-sorry to bother you, dear Finlay, but I don't feel quite up to the mark this morning.'

'Do you have any pain, sir?'

'Some twinges in the left lower abdomen.'

'Let me have a look, sir.' As Finlay gently passed his hand over the affected area his chief winced perceptibly. 'Is there any stiffness there, lad?'

As Finlay gently touched it with the flat of his hand, the muscle stiffened and became tense.

'It seems to me, sir, that your appendix is involved.'

The sufferer emitted a sigh that was half a groan.

'That damned appendix of mine has been troubling me off and on for years.'

'Surely you think it time for you to have it out, sir?'

'What! At a time like this, the turn of the seasons, one of our busiest o' the entire year?'

'But sir, when your health is concerned . . .'

'Do you think I would lie down now, give up at our busiest time o' the year?'

'But, sir . . .'

'Leave you to carry the whole weight o' the practice on your own back, with anything up to thirty cases to visit every day; and the surgery chock-full every morning and night, and odd times o' the day as weel! Never, Finlay. I'd see myself in my grave first.'

Ignoring this panegyric Finlay produced his thermometer and placed it between the good Dr Cameron's lips. A minute later the patient himself withdrew it, gave a loud sigh of annoyance and shook it down.

'I'm not showing you this, lad, or you'll have me laid up for a week.'

Finlay did not reply. He picked up his thermometer, wiped it with his handkerchief and replaced it in its case.

'You are to stay in bed, sir, whether you wish it or not.' He then withdrew the key from the inside of the door, passed through, and locked the door from the outside.

To Janet, who, of course, had been listening in the passage, he handed the key. 'Janet dear, don't let the good doctor up till I come in from my round. Give him only liquid and light food. I'll see him when I get back. Tell me, are there many in the surgery?'

'It's chock-full to the door, doctor. And there's three mair calls has just come in from the Anderston Building. But listen to me, sir, ye're not getting out of my sight till ye've had a big strong cup o' hot coffee and a piece o' hot buttered toast. I've kept it warm . . .'

A faint tinkle from the sick room interrupted her. Her lips compressed slightly. 'Ay, I thocht so! It will be runnin' up and down for me a' day. But he'll have to wait till I see you off first, warm and weel fed.'

Indeed, thus fortified, Finlay went into the teeming surgery and almost two hours later braved the chill, wet streets to begin his visits. At noon these were still uncompleted, but by putting his back into the task, he was home by half past two. His first words to Janet were 'How is our invalid?'

'I'm going to see you eat your dinner first, sir. I've kept it a' nice and hot for you.'

Chilled, tired and hungry, Finlay did not resist. Janet watched him with concern as he hungrily swallowed everything she put before him.

'Feel better now, sir?'

'Thanks to you, my own dear wee Janet, I feel more like myself.'

'I was feared to tell you sir, until you had ate, sir, that three mair calls came in from that same Anderston Building.'

'Damn! They've got a regular 'flu epidemic there! Well, never mind. How is our own patient?'

Janet's lips drew tight together. 'As snug and comfortable as my carrying out his orders can make him. He has a lovely fire in his room, fruit juice and fresh pears by him on his bedside table, and he's lyin' back against his pillows readin' this morning's *Chronicle* where I noticed there's a bit on the front page about hissel'! "Our patrons will read with regret of the illness of our most worthy and beloved Dr Cameron. During his enforced absence his practice will be sustained by his young, active assistant *Dr Findlater*." '

Grimly, between set teeth, Janet ground out the words, 'How dae ye like *that*, Dr Finlay, sir? I'd swear by my own Bible I never in a' my life kent such bluidy insolence!'

'It could just be a printer's error, Janet.'

'Printer's error be damned. He wrote it out hissel', put it in an envelope and last night, bid me take it tae the office o' the *Chronicle*. If I had kenned whit it was I'd have put it down the closet. For it's a' part o' his plan to blow himself up and keep you down.'

Finlay managed a smile, but his jaw was set firm. After half the day in the pouring rain, in and out of the sick rooms of Anderston Buildings, this was the last straw.

'Has the poor invalid asked for anything special?'

'He wanted a hot clout, wrung out, just before ye came back and had me lay it on his belly. But when I went upstairs a minute later, it was flung on the floor.'

Finlay reflected deeper. 'Janet! D'ye think all this is put on for our benefit?'

'For his *ain* benefit, ye mean, sir. This is the second time in succession that he has brocht out his cursed appendix just at the busiest time o' the year. Aye, and let you slave your guts out while he lies cosy in bed wi' all sorts of delicacies to his hand.

Believe it or no, he wants me to run out for a jar o' the best calf-foot's jeely.'

As they left the dining-room together Finlay spoke firmly. 'Dear Janet! If this is real appendix trouble he must have it out *immediately*. If it's no', I want to find out exactly *what is the matter wi' him!*'

'He has it fixed in his heid, sir, that his appendix is the trouble. You'll never shift him.'

'Then we'll shift his appendix!'

And Finlay went straight to the phone. Then, having closed the door of the cabinet, he rang an old professor, Mr Nicol, MS, FRCS, one of his teachers at the Royal Infirmary of Glasgow. Not to anyone did Finlay divulge the nature of his conversation. Even Janet who listened hard outside, heard not a word of it.

But early that afternoon a beautiful shining ambulance, complete with uniformed driver, attendant and white-clad nurse seated beside a soft-blanketed couch, drew up at Arden House. Immediately the attendant descended, bearing a portable stretcher, and accompanied by Finlay, entered the sick-room, guided perhaps by the invalid's sonorous snores.

Three minutes later, borne on the litter by Finlay and the attendant, that same invalid was in the ambulance, tended by the nurse, with Finlay and the uniformed attendant on the outside seat beside the driver. Then with a low Rolls-Roycean purr the ambulance sped off en route to Glasgow.

What the good doctor's thoughts might be as he lay in comfort being driven he knew not where, only Dr Cameron could tell. Finally he murmured a single interrogation to the nurse. Whereat she replied, 'To the finest hospital in Scotland, sir. Where the best surgeon in Great Britain will examine and treat you.'

'No operation I hope, dear nurse, I'm no' *that* bad.'

'Do you feel able to undertake all your professional duties?'

'Who kens, nurse. It a' depends on how I feel the morns morn.' There was a pause. 'Ye ken, dear nurse. I've aye had a tendency to this appendix trouble in the winter. Not a great deal o' pain in the stomach, mind ye, I can aye eat well, but nae strength at all, ye ken, nae incentive to work at a'.'

'Weel, try and get a wee sleep now. I'll wake ye when we're at the Royal.'

Although he did not sleep, the good doctor was silent until they drew up at the huge hospital.

'Tell Finlay to bide with me,' he exclaimed as he was borne into the intimidating recesses of the giant infirmary. Once he was safely in a side room on the surgery floor Finlay left him and sought out Professor Nicol, who welcomed him warmly, then listened intently as Finlay described Dr Cameron's symptoms.

'And all this comes on exactly when the work in your practice is at its heaviest and hardest?'

'Aye. I've scarce had a moment to myself all day.'

'Ye've not examined him?'

'No, sir! He'll submit only to an expert.'

'Well!' said Professor Nicol grimly. 'Bring him in right away.'

In a few moments the patient was wheeled in, completely stripped and covered with a sheet.

'Greetings, fraternal greetings, Dr Cameron. How are you feeling now?'

'Verra weel indeed, professor. In fact absolutely perfect.'

'Ready to start work in your practice this very minute?'

'That, professor, with a' the good will in the world, I could scarcely guarantee it. Ye see, it's this business of my appendix.'

'Ah, what a pity, dear doctor. It pains you?'

'It's not exactly a pain, professor, sir, it's a kind of a sort of *weakness*!'

'I understand perfectly, dear doctor. Now perhaps you will permit me to examine you.'

'That's exactly why I am here, sir.'

Quickly, Professor Nicol removed part of the sheet and studied the left region. Then, gently, he placed his hand on the affected part. Immediately the patient stiffened his muscles till his lower abdomen was hard as a brick.

'Exactly as I feared,' said the professor. Then turning to his smile. 'A clear, cut-and-dried case of psychotic phobia centred immediately.'

'Dear heaven, professor! Ye're not going to cut me open sae soon!'

Without deigning to reply, Professor Nicol watched the patient being trundled out, then turning to Finlay with a grim smile. 'A clear, cut and dried, case of psychotic phobia centred on the appendix. Didn't you realise that yourself Finlay?'

'I did suspect it, sir. But what on earth can one do about it?'

'Operate immediately! Remove the affected part and the fixation disappears. At least he'll have no appendix to blame for lying in his bed and stopping off work!'

In the operating theatre Dr Cameron was already prepared and under the anaesthetic. Quickly Professor Nicol washed and prepared his hands, then took up his scalpel. After a few swift and expert strokes the incision was made; and a small, exceedingly healthy-looking appendix was exposed and skilfully removed. The small incision was then re-stitched.

'What a wonderful operation, sir. So neat and swift,' Finlay exclaimed. 'But what a pity the appendix is so small. It's just a wee healthy thing. He'll never believe getting that thing out had cured him.'

'I have precisely the same thought, dear Finlay. Come with me. I think a trip to my Pathology Department would be in order.'

Leading the way into an annexe at the end of the corridor, Nicol selected a jar from the end of the shelf. 'This came out of a sick, really sick, old woman this morning. Isn't it a beauty – for our purpose?'

Dangling in the spirit that almost filled the jar was the longest, most hideously inflamed and peptic appendix imaginable, complete with a bag of pus at the end. It was the worst Finlay had ever seen, and yet, for his purpose, the best appendix ever.

'This should convince Cameron, the lazy old dog,' Nicol laughed. 'He can display it with pride, as evidence that he is cured. Now come lad, and have a coffee and a bun with me. I can see that ye've been sadly overworked lately. But now we'll be having no more of that nonsense.'

Half an hour later, when the patient was again in the ambulance, smiling happily and lovingly clutching his specimen, Nicol repeated his injunction, 'You may start work in the surgery without fail next Monday.'

'Thank you professor, sir, with a' ma heart. I've the evidence that I'm cured right before me.'

Indeed, when they reached home Cameron stepped nimbly out of the car and into the house.

'Janet, Janet, woman! My appendix is out. See for yourself.'

When Janet had looked and shuddered, Cameron moved off to his consulting room and placed the specimen on the mantelpiece.

'That will show my patients that I'm cured!'

'Would you like to spend the night here looking at it?' Finlay asked testily.

'Not on your life. Now it's here and no' inside me I feel I'm better. But consider for a moment, dear colleague, and perhaps I may say, friend. Consider what it was like to have that beastly, horrid *beeling* growth inside my fine body. Do you wonder I had to lie up and refrain from work. Had I forced myself to, I should have burst it and expired in the street, among the slush and rubble of Anderston Buildings.'

'Ay, ye were wise to let me run a' the risks, sir.'

'Do not be unfeeling, Finlay, I beg of you. I am still suffering from the effects of the operation.'

'Tut, tut, man. Professor Nicol definitely ordered you to take *both* the surgeries. Indeed, he told me, on the way to the ambulance, that if you did not begin to exercise yourself by getting up and moving around, adhesions might set in and damage your kidneys!'

'He did! Bless my soul. Ah well, I maun buckle to it and keep my kidneys clear.'

'Now it's time for some o' that nice hot, strong chicken soup Janet has ready for me. It'll strengthen me for a hard day's work tomorrow.'

As he walked to the dining-room he took Finlay's arm and murmured tenderly in his ear.

'Dearest Finlay, best assistant in a' the world, I was sair afraid our wonderful partnership was broken, and all our adventures tegether over and done with. But now, please the good Lord, now we're all set to carry on our good work and to establish new records of our achievements in the annals of Scottish medicine which may honour us, not only before our colleagues but, please God, in the eyes of our compatriots.'

Sad News and an Old Flame

One fine evening that autumn, when Finlay had a free half-hour after his surgery, he strolled, bareheaded, down the Gielston Road to enjoy the cool air and catch a glimpse of the setting sun as it vanished in a blaze of glory behind the Lammermuir Hills. Alone at this hour and in such a place his mood was meditative and, as had been his habit during the past few months, inclined to sadness and regret. Possibly, in his profession, he had been a success of sorts. But in his personal life? Ah! That brought neither pride nor consolation to his thoughts.

So many of his contemporaries were married, each with a wife and children to bless and harass them. But he had failed to achieve this natural consummation of a man's life. His one chance to achieve love and happiness he had been too timid to accept and treasure when it was offered. And in the swift passage of time it was gone, lost forever. Destined when he retired to become that pitiful object, a lonely bachelor; condemned to nights of solitude, without even a dog to lie beside him while he read, or dreamed, the evening away.

Abruptly he turned – the sky had lost its radiance – and at a brisk pace he started off for the house of Dr Cameron which he must perforce call home.

He had not gone far before his name was called and the quick patter of running footsteps caused him to turn round.

A boy, with a strapped bundle of books under one arm, was smiling, and calling to him by name.

'Dr Finlay, sir! I've finally caught you. Every night this week I've been taking my evening run out here in the hope of meeting you.'

'Bob Macfarlane! Dear Bob!' Finlay embraced the lad. 'What in the world are ye doing back in Tannochbrae?'

'It's rather a long story, doctor, and a tragic one. Did you not read all about it in all the newspapers?'

'I rarely have time for the papers, Bob.'

'Well, it's just this, Finlay. You know that my father was constantly engaged in steel construction work. The last one was a huge new block of flats in Anderston. Dad was always in demand, for he could climb and balance on the big metal girders like a monkey. Dangerous work but wi' big, big wages. It was a treat to look up from far below and see him leap across a huge gap, from one narrow girder on to another still floating on the cranes.' Bob paused, then said steadily: 'One morning Dad tried too wide a jump, missed the other girder,' a pause, 'and fell three hundred feet to the concrete pavement. Thank God he suffered no horrible injuries. He was killed instantly.'

Shocked by this terrible news Finlay was silent. Then he said, 'Surely your mother got some compensation!'

'The big London company offered her £500. She would have accepted it but fortunately Charles Dean, a young lawyer my mother knows, stepped in and said "No!" He told mother he would not stand by and see her swindled. He returned the cheque and started a suit against the company for culpable negligence, responsibility for the death of one of their employees and damages thereon. Apparently my father should have been provided with a belted sling support from the overhead crane. The company tried to buy him off, but they didn't know Charlie Dean. He wouldn't have it. He fought tooth and nail for my dear mother and, in the very end, when the London newspapers got word of the case and were preparing to make a big story out of it, the company finally gave in. Mr Dean was able to present my dear mother with a cheque for £20,000. And what's more, he wisely invested it in gilt-edged stocks so that we have a sure and steady tax-free income of over £500 a year.'

For a moment Finlay was silent. Then, in an odd voice, and pointing to a wayside bench, he said. 'Let's sit here, Bob.' Presently, having apparently collected himself, Finlay said:

'What a blessing for your dear mother that this brave young lawyer was there to help her.'

'Oh yes, Finlay, he really stood up for her. We had known Mr Dean even before the accident to my dear dad. In fact, he and my mother were intimate friends, very intimate. To be quite honest Finlay, he was deeply and truly in love with her, well before the accident.'

'And she was with him, of course.' Finlay managed to bring out the words.

'Dear Finlay, with Mother it is hard to tell. There's no doubt but that, for a long, long time she was terribly in love with you. But, as you never said the word, it's possible she felt free to look elsewhere.'

'And if she did, Bob, who is to blame her. I have loved your mother ever since I first saw her. My love has so grown that I have never looked at, never laid a finger on another woman. But circumstances prevented me from speaking. So now, who would blame that dear, lovely lass, if she were to take to her bosom this young lawyer who has fought and won a fortune for her, and who would expect her to remember the man who has loved her, will love her a' his life, in steeled, suffering silence? Let her forget him, as if he, too, were dead. Let her wed, and be happy with this lawyer who has really proved how much he loves her.'

Here Finlay broke off with heaving breast and Bob saw that this fine man whom he loved and admired was weeping, anguished tears falling in scalding drops on the wooden bench.

A long silence prevailed. Then Finlay, again master of himself, said quietly: 'So here you are, Bob, at the Academy to brush up your Latin, before ye go to the university.'

'Yes, Finlay, and also to see you, my blood father!'

'Then let's meet often, Bob, and go fishing for burn trout in the high moorland streams.' He paused. 'Your mother will be holidaying with her lawyer friend?'

'No, Finlay. She has gone alone to the Baths at Harrogate Spa. She says she wants to wash herself clean of her past life before she comes back to Tannochbrae to meet you.'

A long silence. Then, as they paused before approaching Tannochbrae Finlay said firmly: 'Not a word of my weakness to your mother!'

'I reserve the right to open my heart to my dear mother whenever I wish, and I am writing her a long letter this very night!'

The Flame is Extinguished

One fine morning, almost a month later, Finlay finished his leisurely breakfast and, assuring himself that Dr Cameron was dealing with the surgery, went out to stroll up and down in front of the house, enjoying the cool morning air. Long days of striding across the moors with Bob had left their rugged mark on him. He was at his best, tanned, erect, his shoulders square, his movements supple and easy. Momentarily his attention was caught by signs of activity in the house next door, a fine old Georgian building that had long been empty. Often Finlay had gone through it, admiring the lovely rooms, beautiful antique furniture, the rich carving of the woodwork, and from the upper floor the magnificent view of the surrounding countryside and the distant Lammermuir Hills.

Now the signs of activity increased and indeed the big old FOR SALE sign was being taken down and removed.

Finlay, who knew everyone in Tannochbrae and was well liked by all, shouted across the big garden.

'What's up, Davie? Don't tell me the house is sellt.'

'Ay, deed an' it is, Dr Finlay, sir.'

'Who's bocht it, Davie?'

'Dinna ken, sir. It's our ain lawyers in the town that have managed the sale. And forbye, they're managing a' the cleaning, painting, doing over and everything else. I believe the garden is a' to be done over as weel, a' the lawns reseeded, and the broken stonework built up.'

'Good enough. Maybe we'll have the duke back as our neighbour.'

'Seriously, sir, that's the talk in the town. For him or the duchess for, as ye ken weel, at one time it was their hoose.'

As Finlay moved away, Janet, who had been listening to the conversation called out: 'Sir! Did he say when the duchess would move in?'

'Not until you've had news of it, Janet.'

Having delivered this long-delayed compliment, Finlay looked in at the surgery to assure himself that Dr Cameron was dealing with a manageable number of patients and then walked casually along the Gielston Road to see if the burn was running full enough to be fishable. Never had he felt so well, so much master of himself and, in plain truth, the practice, as if he had become the head doctor and not Dr Cameron, with his bogus appendix stuck on the mantelpiece.

As the days passed, the old house next door, so long neglected, began to re-emerge, recreated as the beautiful residence it once had been. Not pretentiously large but perfect in structure and design. So, too, with the garden which began to bloom in company with the house with green lawns, replanted flower beds and a paved walk down the side of the house, which would give access to both the side door and the sunken garage, also with a paved courtyard.

Steadily the house advanced towards completion and still Janet had failed to pierce the mystery of the new owner. The lawn was now a mass of primroses, daffodils and crocuses.

'Dr Finlay, sir,' said Janet one morning. 'I've had the great privilege of seeing inside *the hoose*. Early this morning one of the workmen, Jock Blair, let me in to look round, and I can tell you, from what I have seen with my own eyes, that it's absolutely lovely. All the fine antique furniture has been polished, and the wonderful carpets spread out – Jock tellt me they was frae Persia and Turkey, and worth a pretty price. Mind ye, sir, when ye're inside it dinna seem big, it's as snug as can be. I'm sure it's the duchess who has bought it. I'll keep my eye skinned to see when she arrives.'

Spring had now come and with the onset of the warm weather the restored house and resplendent garden did indeed become a delight to the eye. All the workmen had left, and it stood alone in its beauty. As the practice was light Finlay would stroll up and down after breakfast enjoying the perfect scene, often joined by Janet who, with a lively interest, awaited the arrival of the duchess.

One morning a car appeared quite suddenly, rounding the far corner. It was a big, shining, continental car, and one of the highest quality. The lady at the wheel drew up at the kerb and stepped nimbly out, enabling the onlookers to observe that she was quite lovely and fashionably attired in a smart grey dress, scarlet silk scarf and a fetching black toque. After having scanned the house intently, she turned, ran up to Finlay and flung herself into his arms. Showering him with passionate kisses, she murmured, 'My dearest darling! At last, at last! And forever!'

Janet, shocked out of her wits, uttered a mild shriek. 'Oh God! The duchess is kissing our Finlay! Kissing and kissing him.' And with a final strangled cry she ran like mad into her kitchen.

Meanwhile the lovers continued to cling to each other in a close embrace.

'Oh, Grace, my darling. I felt this would never come true. For years I have wept for you, longed for you . . .'

'And now I am yours, my dearest, most faithful love. Our son has told me how you wept for me.'

'Ever since our first tender kisses, I have loved, loved only you, and no other woman.'

'Well, now, my darling Finlay, your fidelity will be rewarded. Come and look through the lovely home I have bought for us.'

Encircling his waist with her arm she led him to the house, took the key from her pocket and snapped open the door. Then, still leading her beloved, she took him round the house and showed him all its treasures.

'Is this all yours, my angel?' he faltered.

'Ours, dearest one.'

'But the cost, beloved! How on earth could you?'

'Finlay!' She looked him straight in the eyes. 'The place has been mouldering away for years. You'd be surprised how eager the Town Council were to find someone who would do it all over, from top to bottom. And do you know what the clincher was, lad?' She paused. 'The fact that you would be the owner! I got it practically for the price of the renovation!'

'But Grace, dear, I am not the owner and never will be the possessor of this lovely house. In effect you lied to the Town Council.'

This demanded another long embrace. But Finlay ventured a sly remark, 'How did ye ken, for sure, that I would have ye, lass?'

'Because I know you, dear love. Even without Bob's letters I knew that you were true to me. And before the God o' Heaven, so also was I to you. That good wee lawyer that fought and won my case . . . he was dying to have me. Not a chance! I was yours and here I am with a lovely home, ready to wed you.'

'You've been mine, my sweet, ever since we kissed after the Reunion Dance. But tell me, how in all the world do you still expect me to carry on my medical practice?'

'Darling, your days as an ordinary country GP are over. You are far, far too good for that. You may tell Doctor Cameron that you wish to continue the private practice, here in the special apartments, with a side entrance which I have already shown you. And I assure you that *more* private patients will come to you here. And I am convinced that you will soon have an appointment, with your own wards, at the new Tannochbrae Hospital. Now isn't that better than having Janet waken you at two in the morning with "There's a call from the Anderston Buildings", with your beloved Cameron too lazy to get up? Your talents and your fine personality deserve much, much better. We'll go over together to Cameron and make an amicable arrangement. Then, my love, we'll have a quiet wedding at the altar of St Thomas's, with all of Tannochbrae present, open carriages to bring us home and a champagne party that will go on forever and ever.'

During this recital and the remarks that preceded it Finlay's expression had gradually changed and he said firmly: 'Grace dear, I'm sorry to put an end to your rosy dream but there are several points I wish to take up with you.' Finlay took a long breath. 'First, it was downright dishonest to say I would be the owner of the house, and it could get us both in jail. Second, how the devil do you expect me to practise medicine in that wee bit of a cupboard you call my consulting room, where there's barely enough space for a couch to lie on?'

'Not all your patients need to lie down,' Grace said pertly.

'So that's it! A young woman comes in and she's hardly past the door before I say, "Do you want it standing up or lying down?"'

'How vulgar you can be, Finlay. You've changed frightfully.'

'It's no' me that's changed. It's you wi' your face a' powdered and your lips made up, and you stinking with perfume. Now I see ye in a good light the first thing I'd want tae do is wash your pretty wee face. When you was takin' the waters why didna ye plunge your heid in?'

'How dare you, Finlay!'

'You don't even kiss the way you used to. Instead o' a good face to face cuddle ye put your jaw to my lips.'

'Since you do not relish my kisses, I shall in future refrain from embracing you.'

'And the worst thing of a' – never mind your faked up kisses and the smell o' perfume that would make all the cats in the town follow ye in a line – the worst thing of a' is this. Ye expect me to ditch my dear auld Cameron, who has worked side by side wi' me summer and winter for many and many a year. Now, especially when he's bye his best and needs me mair, I'm to stroll over and say casual like, "By the by, auld fellow, I'm leavin' you! A young wumman has bocht me a cupboard in her big new house where I'm to work up a high-class practice, nae trash, just high-class gentry that can be gi'en a private prescription without even takin' their shirts off." As for auld Janet, how in the world will she ever get up in time to gie the boss his breakfast, if I'm no' there

60

to pull the quilt off her bed at 7 a.m.? Aye, and gie her a clout on the backside if she'll no' move quick enough?

'It's true enough that I loved a Gracie years ago and the memory o' her has lingered. But you're a different woman now, hard as nails, and your heid swollen wi' the fortune you got when your old man jumped off the girder to his death. The young jerk o' a lawyer who got you the cash can come up to you here in your house. Since you've missed out on me, take *him* to your bosom. But you can let me tell you this. If he says one word to me that's in any way objectionable I'll smash his face with a single punch.'

With that final word Finlay turned and walked out of the house, almost colliding with Dr Cameron, who in a thick over-coat and muffled to the eyes was starting out on the morning round.

'Sir! Where are ye bound for? What's that paper in your hand?'

'Dear Finlay, it's my calls in the Anderston Buildings.'

'Hand it to me, sir! Don't you know I always do the Anderston district?'

'But, dear Finlay. I, we, all of us thought you were detained by the lady next door.'

'Not on your life sir. Not now, not ever. In fact *never*.' He snatched the paper from Cameron's gloved hand.

This was too much for the old doctor. He put an arm round Finlay's shoulders and drew him close.

'Dear lad, when I thought I had lost you, my heart was like to break. But now it's alive again and overflowing with joy. God bless you, lad. I look upon you as my own dear son.'

He stood watching Finlay step briskly along to the lower road, then he turned back into the house, where Janet at the window had seen all.

'Janet,' he said, 'rejoice with me. Finlay is back to us. And see ye keep the porridge hot on the stove.'

'I've kept it on, sir. I felt sure our Finlay wouldna have lipped my breakfast. That woman we a' thocht was the duchess wad never have thocht o' such a thing, for she's nae mair nor poor Will MacFarlane's widow who they say treated puir Will sae bad, he jumped off that building wi' a broken heart.'

'Oh, come now, Janet. It wasna like that!'

'Weel, whether or no, sir, she'll never get a civil word out o' me. The very idea that she wad have the impudence to try and take our Finlay awa' frae us is enough to finish her, even without the stink o' that fancy scent o' hers. Mark ma words, sir, she'll no be long our neebour, ye may trust me to see to that, if it's the last thing I was to dae for ye.'

Finlay was late in coming back for his long-delayed breakfast but he seemed well satisfied with his morning's work.

'What kept you, Finlay?' Dr Cameron inquired.

'As I had some time to spare, chief, I took a walk up to the Town Clerk's office. You see, I wanted to correct the impression that I had any interest at all in the house next door. Somehow they were misled into believing that I would be the responsible proprietor of the restored mansion. It was because of this assumption, entirely false, that the house had been so perfectly restored and furnished at an exceptionally reasonable price.'

'So you withdrew yourself completely from the transaction?' said Dr Cameron.

'No sir, not completely. I reserved the right to purchase the house within a period of three years, in the meantime allowing public admission for a restricted period twice a month.'

Dr Cameron thought for a moment, digesting this information, then he gave out a cry that held both triumph and exultation.

'She named ye the owner of the house to get better terms for herself, and now, having paid for it in your name, she has publicly deeded it to you . . . at least she has given ye the whip hand in any transactions she may wish to make.'

At this point Janet brought a steaming bowl of porridge and another of fresh sweet milk. Poising himself with an outsize spoon Finlay delivered the final dictum.

'She named me the proprietor because she was so sure she had me completely under her thumb. Weel, now that I'm free of her, we'll just sit back quietly and wait and see what she'll be up to next.'

Suffer the Little Children

Now that Finlay was definitely back in harness all went smoothly and easily in the practice. The onset of good weather lightened the burden of the Anderston Buildings, where the blessing of warm sunshine cleared up a variety of coughs and colds that had kept Finlay busy during the winter months. Now he was able to cast an eye on the uplands where the sodden moors were losing their sheen of mist and gradually drying out under the persistent sun.

The neighbouring house was silent in all its beauty, its only habitant the housekeeper who could occasionally be seen by Janet as a shadow moving silently behind the curtained windows. The smart black car was not on view, from which Janet deduced that its owner had departed for some destination, as yet unrevealed. Grace was not mentioned in conversation between Dr Finlay and Dr Cameron, the subject was apparently dropped. And while Finlay kept an alert eye out for Bob on the Gielston Road, the boy had long since disappeared, probably to sit his first examination for Glasgow University.

Following his interview with the Town Clerk, Finlay had made an appearance before the entire council and had honestly and frankly defined his position, from the very first meeting with Grace at the Reunion Dance. He stated, under oath, that he had not had the slightest pre-knowledge of the lawyer's desire to put the purchase of the house in his name. His quiet manner and the unquestionable veracity of his answers to all the searching questions put by the committee were so convincing that its decision was emphatic and unanimous. After consultation with the committee, the Town Clerk addressed Finlay in these words:

'Dr Finlay, I am empowered to advise you that the decision of the Committee is immediate, emphatic and unanimous. They have no doubt whatsoever that the house was deeded to you without your knowledge or consent. Although such deeding was solely intended as a legal device to trick the council into selling the house at a figure commensurate with the esteem in which all members of the committee – and indeed everyone in Tannochbrae – hold you, it is nevertheless valid and binding. You have not only the opportunity to buy the house for your own occupation at a favourable figure, but also – note this – the positive legal right to deter any other person from so purchasing the property.'

Finlay's face was such a study of astounded innocence that the members of the council rewarded him with a sustained round of applause. As the meeting finally broke up, the Town Clerk put his arm round Finlay's shoulders and drew him into a little side room.

'My dear Finlay, you are so universally beloved in our community that I would wish you to know that all of us are delighted that this positively criminal use of your name without your knowledge or consent should not only rebound against the perpetrators, but result legally and positively, in your favour. The historic house adjacent to where you reside at present may be purchased by you complete with all repairs, alterations and improvements for a sum which takes into account the sympathy extended to you by the Town Council for the manner in which you have been abused. This privilege will be extended to you for a period of three years, and the price at which you may purchase the entirely renovated house is that price fixed for the old, unrenovated property.'

Before Finlay could speak or recover from the shock of this magnificent, unexpected and unsolicited gift, the Secretary continued, concluding, 'The committee make this gesture with all their good will and gratitude for the splendid service you have

rendered to the community from your earliest days as a quali-
fied medical practitioner.' Then in a quiet voice, intimate and
friendly, 'Come away down to my office lad, and we'll celebrate
your good future wi' a wee dram o' Glenloch.'

Naturally, Finlay was delighted with his acquisition and often,
when unobserved, would slip down quietly to enter the house
and examine all the fine furnishings which also had so unexpectedly become his own. And slowly the question formed in
his mind: what should he do with this treasure? If only he were
married, his dilemma would be solved. And what a marvellous
and appropriate gift for the woman he loved. Alas, there was no
such woman. Unkind fate had so arranged his life that he seemed
fated to be, and to remain, a bachelor.

What then must he do with his house? The good Dr
Cameron, somewhat slighted by the preferential treatment
shown to his assistant, did not fail to drop a little acidity into
the situation.

'And when will ye be moving into your grand new house,
Finlay?' or, 'Don't ye think ye should advertise in the local
Tribune: "Gentleman, handsome and distinguished, with large
furnished house, desires wife. Apply with photograph and testimonials".' While Finlay took this in good part it crystallised his
purpose to stop treating his house as a beautiful toy, but instead to
put it to good and useful purpose. He sat down and wrote a long
letter to his friend, the matron of a children's hospital, explaining
his purpose and asking her to call and see him – and his house.

The matron came immediately and, to Finlay's surprise and
discomfiture, was not at all the motherly figure he knew so well.
No, she was not grey-haired, stiff in the knee joints and visibly
corseted. As she advanced unsmiling, with hand outstretched in
greeting, he saw that she was young, tall and supple, with neat
feet and lovely legs. As if that were not enough to disarm him
she was, absolutely and without question, a very beautiful young
woman.

'Although we have never met, I assume that you are Dr Finlay. I am Miss Lane, the new matron at the children's hospital and I gratefully accept the offer of your house and garden as a convalescent home for our children, subject of course, to the completion of certain necessary arrangements.'

'Such as?' inquired Finlay.

She smiled, a calm superior smile. 'You cannot convert a beautiful private house to a home for young children without certain adjustments. May I therefore have the privilege of inspecting your house now?'

Finlay immediately got up and, without a word, led the way through the lovely garden to his house, and flung open the door.

She entered gracefully, as one accustomed to luxurious surroundings and, followed by the silent Finlay, closely examined the house and its furnishings. Examining minutely the carpets of the large dining-room she said mildly, 'You know of course what you have here, doctor?'

'Of course,' Finlay said shortly, 'Orientals.'

She shuddered visibly. 'For God's sake, don't use that atrocious word which encompasses all the rubbish sold at Shepherd Market. This, for example,' (she indicated an elegant rug with a beautiful floral design), 'is a perfectly lovely Kirman Lavar, a Persian Flower Carpet of the ninth century with thousands of stitches in a single six-inch square. Why, a peasant woman may have given her entire lifetime to the creation of this noble work of art. Now this rug, and your others, which are equally fine, must be removed and in their place the floor must be covered with a coconut fibre carpet.'

'Is this really necessary, matron?'

'It is in your best interests, Dr Finlay, otherwise heaven knows what will happen to your priceless carpets with messy and often incontinent young children in the house!'

Finlay was silent. This was an aspect of his philanthropy he had failed completely to discern. Meanwhile the matron continued. 'I also strongly advise you to remove all breakable objects. These fine K'ang Hsi plates on the sideboard must be stored, so also that beautiful Ch'ien Lung vase and the Ming bowl. These enticingly coloured objects would immediately attract the children, who would either climb up to pull them down or throw stones at them.'

Finlay was silent; then, sarcastically, he said, 'Ye ken a lot about antiques, madam. Ye must have served your time in one o'them second-hand junk shops.'

'Unfortunately no, Dr Finlay. The little knowledge I possess was acquired from my dear father, Regius Professor of Oriental Studies at Oxford University, whom I frequently accompanied on his visits to the East.'

'He should have left you there, madam. One of them sheiks would have given you what you rightly deserve – a damn good shaking and whatever would follow it.'

'No man yet born will ever shake me.'

'Indeed, madam?' said Finlay putting his hands on her shoulder and giving her a gentle shake.

Immediately he found himself sprawling on the floor.

'I should have told you, doctor, that when I was at Girton I took a special course in self-defence which gives me the ability to deal with any attacker as I have dealt with you.'

While still in his ignominious position, Finlay laughed heartily as though at an excellent joke until, without warning, a sudden spring put him back on his feet with his hands firmly gripping her waist. Then she was lifted from her feet and laid tenderly on her back on the Kirman rug, with her skirt over her head and her white knickers exposed, paying tribute to the skill of her laundress and the slender beauty of her legs. To ensure her immobility Finlay seated himself upon her stomach, murmuring, 'No man, madam? What about Girton now?'

At that precise moment there came a knock on the door and Janet entered with a tray.

'I thought ye'd be wantin' coffee, sir, for yourself and your lady guest.'

'Thank you Janet. Serve it now.'

'No sugar for me please, Janet.' The request came from some-where about Finlay's nether regions. And at this evidence of hardihood Finlay stood up and taking hold of both hands of his victim, lifted her to her feet and placed her tenderly in a Louis XVI armchair.

'Don't talk about this, Janet,' said Finlay as he received his cup. 'Miss Lane was just showing me some exercises she learned at her college.'

'It seems to me, sir,' said Janet as she departed, 'that the lady was showing ye more than her exercises.'

'Well, now that we are seated and in our right minds, dear matron, may I enquire if the coffee is to your taste?'

'Delicious, you great brute. I'll take another cup if you have it.'

'Certainly, Miss Lane,' Finlay responded. approaching with the coffee pot. 'I believe you are *Alice* Lane, if I am ever permitted to address you by your first name?'

'You may do so now, Dr Finlay. To be absolutely truthful I came here so fed up by all the praiseworthy things said of you in the paper and elsewhere that I thought I would teach you a lesson. Instead it is you who have so taught me.'

'Oh, nonsense, Alice! I would not dream of behaving rudely to a lady so charming as you and one in so useful and important a position as that to which you have been appointed. I can now tell you, emphatically, that you may do as you think fit here for your little ones. Your arrangements are accepted before they are made. For why in the name of heaven should I act as the proud proprie-tor of a house that only fell into my hands by a series of accidents, sanctioned by the kindness and goodwill of the Town Council?'

She seemed about to speak but instead smiled and pressed his hand.

'So now,' Finlay went on, 'may I regard you as a dear friend?'

Her smile deepened and, as she had not relinquished his hand she pressed it again.

'How can I say "no" to a gentleman who has seen me in my drawers?'

The alliance between Finlay and the new matron prospered rapidly. All the rugs and precious china were stored and locked in the little side room once intended for Finlay's consultations. Coconut matting was laid on the beautiful polished-oak floors and half a dozen hospital beds were set up in the big drawing-room for those children not yet able to walk.

'Does that suit you, matron?' asked Finlay as they finished a tour of inspection together. To which she replied, 'Could not be better, doctor.'

Then on a lovely sunny day the ambulance started to run between Barton Hills and the new convalescent home. At the same time a flood of photographers descended upon the house and would not be denied. Shots were taken of everything and everyone, inside and outside the converted house. Finlay was photographed in his shirt-sleeves carrying the children from the ambulance. One absolutely marvellous shot portrayed him with a little crippled girl of five in his arms while the child, leg irons dangling, raised her head to kiss him on the cheek.

This photograph was a 'natural' for the Press. It appeared in all the Scottish papers, then in the London dailies and finally found its way into the pictorial magazines – the *Sphere* and the *Sketch*. Accompanying the photograph was a heart-warming account of the young Scottish doctor who had sacrificed his fine house for that most worthy of all charities, the treatment and care of crippled children. Finally the climax was reached when a well-known journalist, noted for his acid ability to denigrate the rich and the famous, strolled unannounced into the home where Finlay, stripped to the waist, was giving the children, two by two, their weekly bath in an atmosphere of steam, splashing, soap suds and general merriment. What he saw caused him to stay, not only for all of that day, but for the entire week. He then returned to London and wrote, from the heart, an article entitled 'My Selection for the Man of the Year'.

Although this remained unread by Finlay and his matron, its general effect was profound. The Caledonian Hotel began to fill up with visitors whose main purpose was to see or at least catch a glimpse of this young Highland doctor, a Scottish paragon who had given up his fine house to the treatment and care of crippled and disabled children whom he personally fed, bathed, carried about, massaged and exercised, with the help of a young and supremely beautiful matron.

Taking advantage of this influx, Finlay fixed a big collection box on the gate with three simple words emblazoned on it: FOR THE CHILDREN.

'What a good turn that journalist chap has done us,' Finlay remarked to his matron as they took tea in the kitchen, one of the few moments of the day they were alone together. 'You know I was beginning to run out of money.'

'Your own money?'

'Certainly, and why not? This is my show! Sorry, Alice dear, *our* show.'

She thought for a moment. 'I wonder how much we've been given by those kind people. Twenty pounds perhaps?'

'You're joking, child! These most generous visitors gave, all in all, over five hundred pounds!'

'Now *you* are joking, surely?'

'Come on down with me to the bank and see for yourself then.'

Together, arm in arm, they set off for the town, leaving Janet to keep an eye on the children. Firmly clasped in his right hand Finlay carried his historic black bag, now emptied of instruments but even heavier than before. As they walked down Church Street every eye was directed towards them – the good burghers of Tannochbrae simply stopped and stared.

'I say, Finlay, isn't this a bit too much! Let's go a quieter road.'

'Most certainly not. Next time I'll bring our collection box with us.'

At the bank Finlay asked politely if they might see the manager and almost immediately they were shown to his sanctum, being greeted with the utmost cordiality by Mr Ferguson himself.

'Come in, come in, the pair o' ye, and sit down. I ken the both
o' ye, but if I didna I'd have only to look at the *Herald*. It's full o'
ye both, with photographs and all.'

'Thank you, sir, for your kind reception. And possibly you
may know the reason of our visit. Collections have been coming
in so fast for our Children's Home I would like to bank what
we have in hand, and place it in a new account specially for our
Home and of course the children.'

'Well, then, let's see first what ye have.' Accepting the bag
from Finlay, he emptied the contents on to his desk.

Rapidly he counted the notes and the silver. Then, with a
smile, he looked at Finlay. 'Young man, ye are a lot richer nor
I thought. What do ye want done with this considerable sum?'

'Banked in the name of the Home, sir, for the sole benefit of
the children therein.'

'What, lad! You have over £500 here. And not a penny for
yourself who does all the work, or your lady here who assists
you?'

Finlay exchanged a glance with Alice. 'We wish it all to go for
the benefit, care and comfort of the children.'

'And for all the good food they eat,' added Alice.

Mr Ferguson leant back in his chair and studied them both.
'Surely in reason, in common fairness, you are entitled, each
of you, to a reasonable salary? And you, Finlay, a rent for the
premises?'

'Miss Lane and I have decided to give our services free for this
most worthy cause. For the same reason I want not a penny of
rental for my house.'

Again the manager was silent. Finally he said: 'If we, the bank,
were to give a special donation of £100 how would you use it?'

Without hesitation Finlay said: 'Sir, I would buy a special apparatus to cure a little girl who cannot walk, who is now wearing leg
irons that she will never be free of. Just think of it sir, paralysed
for life. I am now giving her special massage and electrical treatment. If I had this apparatus definitely available I believe it might

encourage her to do what she has never done – to try, herself, to walk.'

There was a brief silence, then the manager said, 'Finlay, I will see that £100 is paid into your *own* account today. And perhaps, later on, you will permit me to visit you to see this apparatus in action.'

'Come, sir, by all means,' replied Finlay at once. 'Just give me a few weeks to get the treatment started.'

Wisely, the manager waited three months before making this promised visit, and what he saw gladdened his heart. While the other children were playing noisily in another part of the garden, a little girl was trying to walk. Supporting herself by leaning on the aluminium handle-bars of a contrivance with little rubber-tyred wheels, she was slowly pushing forward her little machine, encouraged by Finlay.

'Good, good, lass! Bend the right knee, again, again! Well done, lass. Now take a rest on the saddle.'

The child slid herself back on the seat of the machine and turned towards Finlay with a little smile that was good to see.

'Now dearie,' said Finlay, 'you'll be pleased to know that you went twenty yards under your own power. And now you are coming for your wee walk with me. And after that, you'll have your lovely hot bath and fifteen minutes of massage for your good new muscles.'

Standing back unnoticed in the shadows, the manager saw Finlay lift the little girl from her saddle and set her down carefully on her feet. Then, holding her hand and arm tightly, he walked with her for another twenty yards, momentarily releasing his grasp of her hand so that she actually, for a brief moment, walked alone. Then with a triumphant cheer Finlay carried her indoors.

The manager did not reveal himself. What he had seen had touched him, and his tears were flowing freely, almost blinding him, as he turned and made his way back to the world of commerce and the bank.

Teresa

Summer had passed, autumn had come, and the fall of leaves had kept the children busy, sweeping and brushing the drive and the woodland paths. In the early dusk there would be bonfires to delight and enliven childish hearts. Some of the children were now so greatly improved they would soon return to the parent institution at Muirhead, possibly for return to their own homes, if these were judged to be suitable. In any case, Dr Finlay's house was only for the warm weather. In winter, without adequate heating, it must close until spring came again. And now Finlay, with time on his hands, was free to give more help to his long-suffering partner in the practice. Aided by the comforting sight of the horrendous appendix on the mantelpiece of the consulting room, Dr Cameron, rejuvenated, had come through the slack season without apparent difficulty. But now, with winter looming ahead, Finlay saw that he must be back to resume his normal occupation, and to shoulder, once again, the heavier portion of the work of the practice.

On such an evening, when the mist had begun to fall, and Finlay was pacing meditatively down the avenue of leafless trees, he heard a light step behind him and, before he could turn, a warm familiar hand was placed in his, and a comforting voice said, 'You looked so sad, sir, I felt I must join you.'

'Don't call me sir, or I shall lapse into deep and uncontrolled melancholy.'

'It *is* a sad season. I suppose we'll be closing soon for the winter?' She had fallen into step beside him. 'And you'll be losing all your darling children.'

'And their mother! I'm going to miss you sadly, Alice.'

'Yes, dear Dr Finlay, it is a bore, this enforced separation. I have so loved being with you, for your cheerful companionship and,' she hesitated, 'yourself.'

'Enigmatic as ever.'

'Oh, you do know what I mean. Your ability to behave cheerfully and happily with a woman without wanting . . . to put her on her back.'

'Didn't I do that the day you arrived?'

'Oh, that was lovely, adorable fun, and I wouldn't have missed it for the world.'

'Yes, it was fun, in the beginning.' He paused. 'May I have the privilege of visiting you when you are back at your house in Sussex?'

There was a silence, somewhat prolonged. Then she said quietly, 'Finlay, I am obliged to tell you the sad truth. I am spending the winter with my father and . . . a young fellow from the Brigade of Guards, who has a house, inherited from his mother, in Amalfi.' Casually she murmured: 'As a matter of fact, he is my fiancé.'

A silence, prolonged and vibrant, then Finlay said quietly:

'I'm pleased for you. After all your hard and marvellous work here, it's just what you need: rest, sunshine and companionship with people of your own class.'

They continued to walk up and down under the trees, but in silence. At last she dared to look at him. His jaw was set, his lips formed a smile, but his cheek was wet with tears.

Finally he said, 'Your kind of people don't send picture postcards but I shall think of you, sunning yourself by the blue sea, and dashing into it, through the surf, with your friend.'

'Thank you for your sincere good wishes. I shall not forget them, or you. Now you are aware that I am off today. My taxi is ordered for tomorrow morning. Shall we say goodbye now?'

Facing him, she held out her arms. With his heart pounding painfully he took her in a close embrace, not touching her lips, simply holding her to him, in silence, as if they were already one.

At last he let her go, saying, 'I thank you with all my heart for your help and sweet companionship. Don't let us write to each other. Let our parting now be a clean break, sharp and final. I know you are too good for me, a common fellow with common manners and no aristocratic background, while you are born and bred a gentlewoman, and from your earliest days accustomed to fine society and destined to marry one of your own class. So, goodbye, dear heart!'

Before she could speak he turned and went into the house where, in his own room, he flung himself into a chair and closed his eyes. One thought alone consoled him, that she too had wept when he said goodbye. Only hours after Alice had turned from him and finally gone did he stir from his chair and go to bed.

The next morning he sought the company of the little girl who was now so proficient with her apparatus that with its support she could easily manage a tour of the grounds, alone.

Indeed, as he went into the garden there she was, leaning on 'bicycle', as she had named it, waiting for him.

'I hear good news of you darling. Once round, on your own.'

'Twice, doctor. And all without stopping.'

'Spendid! You *have* worked hard. Now come and give your old doctor a kiss.' As he spoke he lifted her from her machine and sat down with her on his knee. When he had exacted the kiss he continued: 'By the bye, what is your proper name, darling? I can't go on calling you "lass", you must have an identity of your own.'

'I don't think I have a right name, sir. I've just been called "kid". You know, "Get the hell out of the way, kid." '

Finlay thought for a moment, massaging the child's legs, then he said, 'I'm going to give you a name.'

'Oh, that's a treat, sir. I never thought I'd be that lucky.'

'Well, from now on you are going to be Teresa,' Finlay said, choosing the name of his favourite saint.

'Teresa,' the little one exclaimed. 'That's a lovely, classy name.'

'Very classy.'

'Oh, sir, let me go out to the far end of the garden, and call me.'

She took one step to her machine and fell on to the handle-bars. In another minute she was behind the trees, invisible, at the end of the garden. Finlay then got to his feet and at the pitch of his lungs shouted, 'Teresa! Teresa!'

Immediately there came a joyful answering call and very quickly the child was back, hugging Finlay's knees.

'Oh, it's lovely, sir. Having a name! Could we do it just once again?'

The game was repeated, successfully, again to the child's delight.

'Now,' she exclaimed, 'I'll be able to tell the other kids who I am.'

'Listen then, Teresa,' Finlay said seriously. 'Your little handle-bar machine has done its job, and a very good one too, but now we are going on to the next step. This morning you are going to learn a little dance called the Sailor's Hornpipe. It's very easy to learn and will help to strengthen your legs. Let me show you.'

Singing the refrain Finlay executed a few simple steps, greatly to the delight of his little companion. 'Now you try it, Teresa.' Holding her hands he succeeded in teaching her the steps which, indeed, she picked up quickly. Finally, halfway through the dance, he released his hold of her tiny hands, so that she was doing it without support.

'You have picked that up quickly, Teresa!' He took her on his knee. 'And I'm pleased, because I want to be proud of you when we go to Mr Ferguson's house for tea on Saturday afternoon.'

'Good gracious, sir. Am I really invited?'

'Really and truly, lassie. You remember that Mr Ferguson gave you your bicycle. That's why I want you to do a little dance for him.'

'Oh, I will, sir, I'll practise very hard.'

Saturday afternoon was so fine that Finlay regretted that his little lass was not more appropriately dressed for the tea party. But though her old grey frock was drab enough, nothing could dim the brightness of her small face, shining with expectation. Since parking was always difficult in Tannochbrae on Saturdays, Finlay had ordered a taxi. As he helped her into the rear seat beside him her expression was one of sheer delight.

'Just think of it, Dr Finlay. Teresa in a taxi for the first time in her life. Going to her first tea party.'

Since the bank was closed on Saturday afternoon both Mr Ferguson and his wife, a fine, full-bodied woman, were waiting for them, upstairs, in the big roomy house. And how warmly welcomed were Finlay and his little companion. In the front room the table was laid for a magnificent tea, with a beautiful iced cake, crystallised fruits, and crackers to be pulled.

It pleased Finlay to see how well Teresa behaved and how quickly Ferguson and his wife took her to their hearts.

'I do wish, Mrs Ferguson, that I had found a proper party dress for the little one, but you see, I'm not good at these things.'

'Don't worry, doctor,' said Mrs Ferguson, 'I think I have just the thing for the lass.' Holding out her hand she said: 'Come with me, Teresa, and we'll look for a pretty dress for you.'

With a glance at Finlay, who replied with a reassuring smile, Teresa went out of the room with Mrs Ferguson.

A silence followed; then Ferguson said: 'Some years ago my wife and I had the dreadful misfortune to lose our own little girl, killed by a drunken driver who, without warning, and travelling at high speed, ran off the road and on to the pavement where she was standing . . . Anyway, my wife insisted on keeping everything that had belonged to her, all her clothes, books, toys – everything.'

Finlay was silent. What could one say? And already, with dreadful premonition, he was beginning to fear the possibility that lay awaiting him. And, indeed, at that moment the inner door opened and Teresa made her entrance, dressed in a beautiful full-skirted white-silk frock, with silk stockings and fine patent-leather shoes. Her hair had been brushed back and clasped by a silver fillet. A necklace of silver and amethyst adorned her slender neck. She looked at Finlay, shyly conscious of her altered appearance, then flung her arms around him and kissed him fervently.

'Oh, Dr Finlay, don't you like to see me nice? And underneath I am even nicer, with what Mrs Ferguson calls my "undies". Would you like a look?'

'If Mrs Ferguson is satisfied, dear, then I am too.'

'I don't call her Mrs Ferguson now. She likes me to call her "Mama". Now I am to go down and show my new self to Nora, the cook.'

When she had gone, Ferguson looked at Finlay in silence. Then he said: 'My dear, my very dear Finlay, the little lass has explained the situation better than I could ever have done. It will be hard on you, I well know. You have saved her from a crippling infirmity. You love her as your own. And yet, Finlay, is she not better off in a comfortable home with a mother, a loving mother who will care for her, and bring her up as though she were her own daughter? Only a woman can properly care for a young growing girl, maturing to womanhood. Don't you feel within yourself that whatever your sacrifice it would be wise to let Teresa come to us, as our own child?'

Finlay bent forward and raised his hand to his brow. Yes, he thought, for the sake of my little one I must let her go.

'Yes,' he said finally. 'I see the reason of what you say. And I consent. I must consent.' He paused. 'Don't ask me to stay for the feast. Teresa will not miss me. And it is better so. I am happy at her good fortune for I know that you, sir, and your wife will do everything you can to make her life a happy one.'

Finlay had risen and was prepared to go, when Ferguson rose and shook him by the hand.

'What we will never, never forget dear Finlay is that but for you, our beautiful little daughter would be a helpless, hopeless cripple.'

Finlay walked home slowly, in a mood that verged on despair. What is wrong with me, he thought bitterly, why am I destined for such misfortunes? I lose the only woman I have ever loved, and now, for every good reason, I must relinquish my own, my dearest child.

Janet's Bairn

Several days later, Finlay received a call from the Caledonian Hotel. His mood was still heavy and unpropitious. From past experience, he was always wary of commands from the luxury hotel, which might prove rewarding or completely the reverse. Seeking information from his friend Bill Scott, the telephone operator, he received this reply: 'They're a foreign couple, Finlay. Spanish, from Bolivia in South America. Great style and a' that, but if I were you I'd get my fee in my hand before leaving. It's the woman, Señora da Costa, who is wantin' you. She asked me for the best doctor in Scotland, so I had to say you. But look out Finlay, she's a regular bitch.'

'Thanks, Bob. I'll watch my step.'

With this friendly warning Finlay drove slowly to the big hotel across the valley and high on the ridge above. At the hotel, since most of the ground staff were local lads, Finlay was greeted with smiles and shown to the lift which bore him to the seventh floor and to the luxury apartment of Señor and Señora da Costa.

The Señora was sitting up in bed, supported by two voluminous pillows and wearing a bed jacket that could only have come from Paris.

'Ah, doctor, you are here at last.' As she looked Finlay over she added as if to herself, 'And young, handsome, intelligent . . . when I had feared the worst. Sit down, doctor.' She drew a long hoarse breath.

'Madam,' said Finlay mildly, 'the atmosphere of this room is stifling. I must open a window.'

81

'No, doctor, I beg of you. Look first at my throat.'

Finlay opened his bag and took out his spatula, drew the bedside light nearer and said briefly, 'Remove your false teeth, madam.'

'But doctor, I have no artificial . . .'

'Kindly remove your plate, unless you wish to swallow it.'

As she still seemed reluctant Finlay pushed his forefingers between her jaws and pulled out a king-size dental plate bordered by a number of perfect white teeth.

'Now, madam, open your mouth wide, very wide.'

Visibly discomposed, she reluctantly obeyed, causing her cheeks to sag dramatically.

'Wide, madam. Wider, please.'

Finally, after much manoeuvering, Finlay got a really good look at her throat. He then withdrew his instrument and, handing back her dentures, turned his back while she replaced them. As she struggled with this somewhat delicate manoeuvre, Finlay picked up a narrow box from her bedside table and extracted one of the short, dark cigars it contained. Rolling this article between his fingers, he studied it, then bit it hard. Already he was convinced, but to be certain he tasted the dark oily liquid that oozed from the cut and bruised tobacco with the tip of his tongue.

She watched him carefully during this operation, and when he placed the cigar in his pocket she said acidly, 'You make free with my possessions, doctor.'

'This is merely for a final confirmation of my diagnosis, madam.' He paused while a nerve in her cheek began to twitch.

'I must first relieve your mind, madam. You do not suffer, as I had feared, from a cancer or some such other fatal growth. Your throat is merely inflamed, but savagely so. If you obey my instructions your throat will be normal within four weeks. You will be cured.'

'Oh thank you and bless you, doctor. They told me you were the best doctor in Scotland and it is the truth.' She closed her eyes, made the sign of the cross and, beginning 'Madre de Dios', made a short little prayer of thanksgiving.

'Here is my prescription, Madam,' said Finlay without handing the sheet of paper to her. 'This medicine must be taken at 10 p.m., when you have retired. You will find that it gives you a much better sleep than these poisonous cigars. You must never ever smoke these cigars again. The fumes that you inhale are loaded with a dangerous drug. If you disobey my instructions you will assuredly end with a cancer of your throat. Have I made myself clear?'

'Oh yes. Oh yes, dear doctor. I will obey, obey your commands. Please give me the paper.'

'First, madam, you must give me my fee of three guineas.'

Her face assumed a shocked expression. 'Dear, clever doctor, you are most ungallant to speak of money to your patient, a lady of distinction, while she is still in her bed. Surely you understand that your fee will be remitted to you the moment we receive your account.'

'Madam, I am no Shylock to tear my beard and cry "Give me my ducats". No, madam, I am a simple country doctor who has several times been swindled by residents of this hotel who depart without settling their just debts. I therefore have a fixed principle: "No pay, no prescription".'

She studied him again, seeking a sign of weakness in his stern young face, then in a loud voice she called out: '*José, venga aquí.*'

Now for the first time, Finlay saw a little boy with dark eyes in a very pale face lying on his stomach on the floorboards in a corner by the window. Now, very stiffly, he got up, stumbled to the wardrobe, and after opening the door produced a woollen work-bag which he handed to his mistress. As he returned to his corner Finlay noticed, with horror, that under the thin singlet the little boy's back was scarred with ugly red weals.

Meanwhile the Señora was fumbling in her bag with an air of distress. Finally she exclaimed: 'What a pity! Such a nuisance! Dear doctor, is it not embarrassing for me? I find I have not enough of small "*vueta*" to discharge your account.'

83

'Then I will hold your prescription, dear madam, until you actually have the amount you require.'

Again she studied him. Then, without further delay, she handed Finlay three rather dirty pound notes and three separate shillings.

When he had pocketed the cash, Finlay stood up and, with a bow, handed her the prescription.

She accepted it with a shriek. 'What! No liquid! No medicamenta!'

'The excellent chemist in the town, madam, will supply your medicine according to my prescription.'

'Ha! So I must again pay. The English are all cheats!'

'Scottish, madam,' Finlay corrected mildly, turning towards the door which the small boy had already opened for him.

As he entered the passage and the door closed behind him he felt that he had a shadow behind him. Turning, he saw that the boy had followed him out of the room.

'Señor doctor, I implore you, please heal my wounds.'

Finlay could not resist this pitiful appeal. He removed the boy's shirt, then gazed in horror at the deep, raw weals that had broken the skin and cut almost to the bone.

'Who did this?'

'The master, doctor sir. When I do not please the mistress she reports to her husband.'

Finlay studied the boy in silence. The child was undernourished to the point of emaciation. And pitifully beaten.

Finlay did not reflect even for a moment. Wrapping his coat round the boy's shoulders, he led him into the lift, then quickly through the swing doors and out into his car. As they drove off, the boy crouched beside Finlay shaking with tears of joy.

'How come you understand English?'

'I study greatly at school, señor, hoping to run away to an English family.'

'To escape the flogging?'

'It is not always flogging. I leave to get food.'

'Don't they feed you at the hotel?'

84

'I am not registered at the hotel, señor. I eat only what madame leave on her plate. If nothing, I lick plate.'

Dear God, thought Finlay. Could anything be worse? He was silent until he reached home, then lifting the child gently from the car he carried him into the kitchen. 'Janet, dear, this poor little boy has been maltreated and starved. I see you have porridge on the hob, please give him a big plateful with lots of creamy milk. I'll be back in a few moments.'

In the surgery, Finlay collected together everything he required, wrapped them in a big towel and left them by the couch, so as to have them close at hand. He then returned to the kitchen. There he sat with Janet who, entranced, was watching the little boy eat.

'Oh, Dr Finlay,' she whispered. 'The boy is starved to death.'

'Very near to it, Janet. Give him a second helping if he asks you.'

'He has already,' she answered, rising to replenish the empty plate, already licked clean.

'Lovely, lovely porridge, sir. After more I am again strong.'

'Are you going to keep him, sir?'

'Nothing else for it, Janet. He hasn't a friend in the world. And of course I'll never, *never* send him back to those South American bastards at the hotel.'

When the second plateful of porridge had disappeared Finlay lifted the boy and carried him to the surgery, where he laid him face down on the couch. It was absolutely essential to clean the sores, some of which had become infected.

'I must hurt you a little, José. It is necessary.'

'I will not cry, sir.'

Using pure ether, Finlay thoroughly cleaned the sores, then covered the child's entire back with damp boric lint and carried him back to the kitchen.

'Janet! This is your boy as well as mine. Could you spare him a wee corner o' your bed? And if you have an old chemise, that could serve him as a night-shirt till I get him some proper clothes.'

Janet flushed with pleasure. 'I can certainly see to him, sir. He'll be real cosy wi' me forbye.'

Receiving the child from Finlay she disappeared through the doorway that led to her room, just behind the kitchen.

Finlay could now hear Dr Cameron moving about the surgery and it became necessary to consider the main business of the day. His list of visits, already made out, was on the hall table.

'Good morning, sir,' he called loudly. 'Have you any more calls for me? I am just starting out.'

'No, I have no calls, so I'll do the surgery. But Finlay, have ye had your breakfast?'

'I was out early, sir, and forgot about it. I'll have my coffee now.'

Back in the kitchen, his coffee and fresh roll awaited him. Janet, with a portentous air put a finger to her lips as she whispered, 'Our wee laddie is fast asleep, sir. But I'm sorry there's nae parritch left, he's ate it a'.'

Finlay had no serious cases on his list and he finished his round before midday. He then drove into the centre of the town and drew up before the double-fronted shop which bore the sign: GENERAL AND CHILDREN'S OUTFITTERS.

For about half an hour Finlay remained in the shop, emerging with the manager, who deposited a bundle of parcels in the back of the car, then remarked, with a significant smile, 'Your other order for the buttons uniform will be ready for the try-on by the end of next week.'

With a glance at his watch Finlay saw that he still had enough time to make his final visit. Leaving the car he walked across the street to the Central Police Station.

Here Finlay remained for another thirty minutes or so and when he emerged he was accompanied down the steps by the Chief Constable.

'I'll have a word with the Registrar, Finlay. It will be perfectly simple: father – unknown; adoptive mother – Janet MacKay.'

The two men then shook hands and Finlay got into his car and drove home.

'Janet,' he called, 'here's lots of good things for your wee laddie.' Aided by a very bright-eyed little boy, Janet and Finlay unloaded the goods and carried them to the kitchen where a fire burned cheerfully. As the parcels were unwrapped one by one it was a joy to watch the child's face, alight with joy and wonder. Everything he needed was there: little white and blue shirts; underwear; socks; two pairs of shoes, one for the house, the other for out of doors; a little soft hat; two ties; two pairs of trousers, one grey flannel, one blue; two sweaters; and a lovely blue reefer coat.

As Finlay turned to observe the effect of his purchases, Janet was actually weeping. 'Oh Dr Finlay, dear Dr Finlay, to think that ye bought a' these lovely things for my wee laddie!'

'And he really is yours now, Janet. I fixed it all with the Chief of Police – and the Registrar.'

'There's just one thing that I must humbly thank ye for, doctor: your skill and gentleness that made the birth o' my bairn absolutely painless. Ye must a gi'en me a great big dose o' the chloroform, for it's the God's truth I never felt a thing till I woke up wi' the dear bairn in ma airms.'

Finlay studied her, kindly. Better, yes, better by far to let her cherish this fulfilment of her dream.

Now, indeed, Janet yielded to all her years of frustrated motherhood. A woman too plain to attract a man, yet longing in her heart to have a child. She sat down, holding her little boy tight, and let the warm tears flow.

Dr Finlay's Hopes are Dashed

In Tannochbrae winter was at last over, a warm sun had dispersed the lingering mists, and the budding trees proclaimed the advent of spring. This was the season especially beloved by Finlay – it seemed to herald the joys of the outdoor life, the very soul and substance of his being. Yet there was no joy in Finlay's heart. He looked sadly at his beloved guns, and his fishing rods stood unused in their corner of the garage.

As if in contrast, activity in the house, such as the annual spring-cleaning, had never proceeded with greater gusto and good-humoured thoroughness. Janet, the leader of the assault, had never been in better form. Aided by Joseph (no longer José), she scrubbed, scoured, swept and polished as though she were twenty years younger. Complimented by Finlay in these terms she nodded in agreement and said, 'It's a true word ye've spoken, Finlay, sir, I'm a new woman since I had ma braw son.'

'And he's a great help to you, Janet.'

'A help and a comfort, sir, you should see how he snuggles in to me in bed. I sleep far better nor I ever did.' She smiled tenderly. 'And then in the morning, he's up to bring me my cup o' tea the minute I'm awake!'

'He's growing up a fine boy, Janet. And since he's got his smart new buttoned uniform it's a treat to see him answering the front door bell and showing the patients to the waiting room.'

'Och, sir! He's a help everywhere. You should see how he tidies our bedroom. Even empties my chanty for me.' She paused and suddenly began to shake with laughter. 'Sir, this will kill ye.

At first when my wee laddie didna ken ony better he lifted the chanty, fu' to the brim, and shooshed it out through the open window just as Dr Cameron was passing! Och, sir, it was a near shave. As I served lunch the boss says to me: "Janet, the roof gutter is leaking. Have it seen to at once. I nearly had a bath this morning." '

Finlay rejoiced in the old servant's happiness. Yet, in his own heart, there was no such joy. Now was the time to reopen his house as a holiday home for the children. But though this had been such a wonderful success last summer, he could not bring himself to take the decisive step. Where would he find a matron? No, he could not face the prospect of the old dame from the hospital, hobbling round with the help of her stick. Perhaps she would send one of the senior nurses, all starch and spectacles? Finlay shuddered at the thought. Nothing would match that wonderful summer of a year ago, when every day was a joy – or a joyous battle.

On the first day of April, when Finlay had finished the morning surgery, Janet directed his attention to a group of workmen standing by a pantechnicon outside his house.

'They've been shouting across the gairden for ye, sir.'

Finlay strode towards the half dozen workmen but before he reached the group the foreman touched his hat and said, 'It's just the key, sir, that we're wanting, to get into your house.'

Finlay recognised the man. 'Andy, who sent ye?'

'Hoo should I ken, Finlay? The word musta came tae the office. The manager just stepped oot tae the yaird and says: "Finlay's hoose, lads, exactly the same as last year." '

'But, Andy, I never said a word.'

'Then it musta came frae the weans' hospital, sir.'

A dull feeling of acceptance came over Finlay. He had set the pattern, yes, he must accept it. He followed the men as they entered the house and watched as they expertly set about their work, removing and storing his lovely rugs and fine china, then rolling out the drugget over the polished floors. Suddenly he heard the tapping of a stick and a high-pitched voice pierced his eardrums, 'I wish to assure myself that all is perfect . . .' That was enough for Finlay. He shut himself in one of the lavatories, shot the bolt and sat down on the seat to brood. Yes, it was the old matron. He had let himself in for it. Well, it was too late now. He must stand aside and let her go ahead.

A copy of the children's paper *Comic Cuts* was on the floor, left by one of last year's cheerful horde. On the upturned page was a drawing of a sad little fat man left with his baggage on a pier, while a liner was steaming away into the distance under clouds of smoke. The caption read, 'The man who missed the last boat for Kingdom Come.'

I am that fellow, thought Finlay. I had the chance of sublime happiness and let it sail away from me.

At last he picked himself up from his ignoble throne and, from force of habit, flushed it.

Back home he took the evening surgery, a very light task as the good weather had largely reduced the number of his patients. Upstairs, he found little Joseph awaiting him with a smile. 'Nice postcard for you, sir. Of course I do not read it, but the picture is most funny.'

While the boy watched him with a smile, Finlay took the postcard and studied it with a diagnostic eye. The postmark was San Remo and the picture, in the crudest of colours, depicted a pretty young woman in negligible bathing attire fleeing along a beach, hotly pursued by an elderly man in a top hat and frock coat. With the card there was a letter written in a very small, neat hand, immediately recognisable, which made his heart beat frighteningly fast.

Dear Maestro,

Aware of your fondness for comic coloured postcards I could not resist intruding on your majestic, stoical silence. I would have written you sooner but being anxious not to disturb your winter hibernation, I awaited first a brief word from you. Alas! No word came and our good Italian postman looks pathetically sad when he shakes his head and murmurs a soft Italian negative. I would then retreat to the sad sea shores, with a picnic lunch – anything to get away from that infernal little Army bore, a snob who talks endlessly of the 'Brigade', and his association with the highest level of British aristocracy. Even my dear father is sick of the man and has developed a pain in his side which worries him, and me. Well, as the result of all this we have decided to leave for England by sea and will be arriving in London on 25th April at 11.30 a.m. I realise sadly that you are much too busy to greet us, but what a relief it would be, might I say a joy, to see your dear, noble face at Southampton when we arrive.

Yours,
Alice

To Joseph's surprise and delight, Finlay began to sing, and execute a few dance steps of the Highland Fling.

'Oh, sir,' the little boy exclaimed. 'You are pleased and happy!'

'Both,' said Finlay, picking up the child and continuing the dance. 'But tell me, Joseph, have I got a noble face?'

'You got the best, ugliest face in all the world, ever!'

Finlay's happiness reached its climax when, very early on the morning of 25th April, he stepped into his car and drove, as fast as he dared, to Southampton. Here, pacing up and down, he anxiously awaited the arrival of the 11.30 boat. When it arrived he posted himself at the end of the gangway where its passengers would soon be appearing, his heart pounding. First came Italians, then an elderly English couple, some women without escorts, another elderly couple, more Italians – probably workmen – and finally a small, immaculately attired Englishman.

With a crushing, overpowering sadness Finlay realised that his beloved was not on board. He was about to turn away when the elegant Englishman addressed him in accents of the parade ground: 'I'm Pimmy. You, I believe, are Dr Finlay.' He paused. 'If so, I have a letter for you.'

Finlay was too stunned to answer. Blindly he accepted the letter.

'Aha! Aha! Bit of a shock for you, old man. She likes dealing them out! Huh! As we are presumably in the same boat, why not a quick one before taking off?' Clutching Finlay's arm, as though he had known him for years, he gently steered him to the refreshment room.

In a welcoming dark corner Finlay was relieved to sit down, while his obliging companion brought two stiff whiskies from the bar.

'I say, old boy, you looked completely knocked out. Want to hear the worst?' As Finlay nodded silently, he went on: 'You know, I believe, that the worthy professor was ill, kidney or liver, I can't say which, but he was sufficiently poorly to want to get home. But yesterday afternoon, with everyone set to go, there came an intervention.'

'Yes, yes,' said Finlay. 'Please go on.'

'An Italian fellow had heard of the old man's illness. He had apparently been a student at Oxford, taught by Professor Lane. He immediately called for a specialist who refused to let the old man travel. Whereupon our Italian benefactor invited us all to his lovely big villa at Grasse. Naturally I jibbed. I have to get back to my regiment, y'know. But, with almost sacramental devotion, father and daughter were whisked off to the villa, a stunning great place – six gardeners someone informed me. I also gathered that Don Alphonso, the Italian, is by way of being a count with an absolutely historic château out in the wilds.' He broke off. 'I say old man, you look absolutely ghastly. Do let me get you another reviver.'

He did, and Finlay, who felt like death, swallowed it in one gulp.

'Well, I think you have the picture,' said his companion. 'Do you want to look at the letter and see what the lady says?'

Finlay found the letter, ripped open the envelope and withdrew the small single sheet.

Dear Finlay,

Father is too ill to travel – a specialist has so decreed. And a dear friend, ex-pupil of Father at Oxford, has moved us to his lovely villa where Father will have every comfort and attention from trained nurses, while the specialist will call every day. Of course I cannot leave him. Naturally I am sorry not to be joining you at the children's summer home.

With regrets,

Alice Lane.

Father will have every attention from the nurses, noted Finlay, and I will have every attention from Señor Alphonso.

There was a long, vibrant silence. Then Pimmy got up.

'I say, old man, don't get into your car for at least half an hour. When you start cursing, it's safe to drive.'

He held out his hand and gave Finlay's limp fingers a firm grip.

As directed, Finlay sat in sad, stony silence for the specified time, then he got up, found his car, and slowly drove back to Tannochbrae where his summer home, swarming with kids, was held in thrall by the old matron with her shrill voice, unpredictable knees and ever-present stick.

Alice Regrets

Finlay had suffered a severe blow from his obvious rejection by the girl on whom he had built his romantic hopes for so long. But when he suffered a hard blow he had the capacity to pick himself up again, square his shoulders and his chin, then get on with the business in hand. Although he occasionally muttered, bitterly, sarcastically, the words 'With regrets, Alice Lane', he threw himself into the task of making the children happy and, not least, of winning the approval and regard of the old lady with the shrill voice, piercing gaze and the stick which tapped relentlessly into the most unsuspected quarters.

The children, many of whom had been there before, were soon Finlay's boon companions. He would often play their games with them: rounders, hide and seek, French cricket; races of all descriptions, from sack to egg-and-spoon while, with every consideration of safety, and on the low branches, he taught them the noble art of tree climbing.

His efforts did not pass unnoticed by the old matron, who gradually began to like this enthusiastic and generous young man and when he arranged that she should have the 'elevenses' of coffee and hot buttered toast to which she was long accustomed, she finally took him to her heart. To Janet, who now brought in the 'elevenses' she would remark 'What a fine young man you have here!'

'Have ye only discovered it now, matron. If ye kenned how he manages almost all the practice, now that the auld doctor is a'most by wi' it ye might think even mair o' him.'

'Is he a Christian, Janet?'

'He's no' a kirk Christian, matron, if that's what ye mean, turnin' up his eyes at what he doesna like. But he's got a'maist a' the Christian virtues. If he sees a hard-workin' woman in distress, he'll step in and take some of the burden off her back.'

'I can see that he has helped you, Janet, as he has helped me.'

'Ye have spoken a true word, matron. And a' the time, if I'm ony judge, he is suffering himsel'.' And as Janet moved away she placed her hand, significantly, on her heart.

Some weeks passed in this fashion, all well with the children and the practice. The fine sunny weather had cut down the number of patients while, revived by the glorious weather, Dr Cameron had been stirred to some activity and would even answer calls to the dreaded Anderston Buildings.

One fine morning in July, Janet burst in upon Finlay with the local newspaper, the *Tannochbrae Herald*. 'Dr Finlay, sir, here's a piece of news that might interest you.' She handed him the paper where, already marked by a cross under the heading 'Social Events' he read the following:

Tannochbrae welcomes the arrival of Count Alphonso and his Countess who are staying at the Caledonian Hotel. The Countess is, of course, the lovely Alice Lane, who won all our hearts by her splendid work for the children at the Summer Home inaugurated by our own Dr Finlay. While rumour had it that the attachment of these two was more than professional, the noble Count and the blue Italian skies deprived our well-loved local hero of his merited reward.

When he had read the paragraph Finlay returned the paper to Janet without a word – with an expression that deterred all questions. After a long pause he said, simply and firmly: 'We will not see them down here!'

For almost a week Finlay's observation remained true. But on the following Monday a taxi drew up at the front door and a woman, quietly dressed, stepped out and rang the bell.

Janet, who answered the summons, admitted the woman, who asked to see Dr Finlay as a patient.

'And the name, madam?' asked Janet.

'Don't you know me, dear, kind Janet? Have I changed so much?'

Janet looked again then cried: 'You're our own Miss Lane! But Lord, how you have changed.'

'Yes, dear Janet, I am greatly changed. And for the worse.'

This, Janet could not deny. In silence she showed her into the consulting room.

And it was here, some minutes later, that Finlay found her weeping with her back to the window. Before he could speak she turned and said: 'This is not a sentimental visit, doctor. It is purely professional, since I have great need of your aid.'

Finlay, who had set his mind firmly against tears and kisses, was deeply moved.

'You are in some physical difficulty, madam?'

'In such atrocious difficulty I would expose it, and myself, to no other doctor but you. Because,' she added, 'I know that as well as being skilled, you are *good*.'

At this, Finlay sat down beside her, and took her hand.

'Tell me everything. You have my complete confidence.'

There was a silence; then, haltingly, she began: 'You are aware of my unexpected marriage, when carried away by the title, the luxury and sense of position, I gave my consent to a man I knew absolutely nothing about, except superficially, for I was blinded by his good looks and Latin charm. Now,' her voice expressed bitterness and disillusion, 'now, I know, to my cost, that man to be the destruction of my life.'

A silence followed. Finlay could not speak. She quietly resumed:

'After my marriage, with all the ceremony the Italians excel at, it was not long before I discovered that my husband was . . . not a normal man . . . but in matters of sex an unkind, unspeakable maniac. My wedding night was a nightmare, but I bore it, thinking it would soon be over, that he would change, but no, again and again, every night . . .' She paused and then forced herself to continue her harrowing story. 'My husband,' she laughed bitterly, 'the man I married, is given to uncontrollable rages, and as soon as we are alone in the evening he beats me unmercifully.' She saw Finlay's expression of shocked incredulity. 'You don't believe me? He is careful to aim his blows where his friends cannot see them and realise what kind of man he is . . .'

'Stop, you mustn't go on torturing yourself like this . . .'

'No, let me finish what I have to say. You have no idea what a blessing it is to have a friend to confide in after all this time. At first it was hard to believe that he could do such a thing, but now I realise that he actually found some kind of perverse pleasure in it . . . God! This last week has been the worst . . .'

Finlay was again silent, overcome by inexpressable compassion and disgust.

'You poor wounded creature, I'm afraid that it is essential for your own safety that I examine you without delay.'

Without a word, she removed her clothes and lay down on the surgical table. As she did so, he was painfully reminded of that wonderful morning of their first meeting not so long ago, when she lay flat on the living-room floor, with her skirt over her head.

My God! thought Finlay, torn between shock and disgust. The area from her creamy neck to her delicate knees was a mass of cuts and purple bruises. Something must be done at once.

He reflected for only a moment then left the room, took up the telephone and dialled.

At once a female voice answered: 'The Convent of Bon Secours, Maberley. Who is calling please?'

'Dr Finlay. May I speak to the Mother Superior?'

'Oh, certainly Dr Finlay. Just one moment please.'

There was a brief interval, then another voice came on to the phone, gentle yet commanding. 'My dear Finlay, at last you condescend to telephone me. I hope this is the preface to one of your rare visits.'

'Yes, dear Mother Superior, I am coming to see you at once. And I am bringing with me a lady, one of my patients, who urgently requires your care. Have you a vacant room?'

'For you, dear doctor, we can always find a place. Who is your patient?'

'She is a Scots girl who chose to reject me and marry an Italian count.'

'And now she is ill and regretting her mistake.'

'It is nothing so trivial, Reverend Mother. The man she married has turned out to be a brute. She has now the most horrible injuries inflicted on her by her husband. As I feel that no ordinary hospital would be suitable, so I thought immediately of you and your infinite mercy and compassion. You alone can tend her horrible wounds, and heal the terrible damage to her soul. Do this, I beg of you, my best and holiest friend.'

'Dearest Finlay, you sound exactly and precisely as did your uncle the archbishop when he wished a favour of me.'

'And I am sure, Reverend Mother, that you granted it.'

'Ah! He was a most endearing man, as well as a holy one. We nuns would have done anything for him. Now tell me at once what you want of me.'

'The best room in your house, not in the wards though, Reverend Mother. And expert medical attention.'

'When will you be coming?'

'We shall be with you in an hour.'

'All will be ready for your patient, dear Finlay, do come. And the Lord be with you.'

Exactly one hour later Finlay passed through the well-kept grounds and gardens and drew up before the Convent of Bon Secours.

Turning in his seat he took the hand of his patient, who lay on the back seat of the car.

'This is the end of our journey. No one shall know that you are here, where you will find undisturbed, peaceful rest, and skilled treatment of your wounds. I will personally ensure that no one disturbs you in this lovely spot.' As two nurses appeared bearing a stretcher, he added: 'May the good Lord heal and bless you.'

Skilfully she was borne away and into the hospice. Finlay then parked the car at the main entrance, jumped out and made his way to the Mother Superior's office.

'Dear Finlay!'

'Dearest Reverend Mother.' He picked her up and kissed her on the brow, before returning her to her official seat at the desk.

'All this show of affection won't give you absolution in advance dear Finlay. Now tell me, what is this load of trouble you have just brought me?'

Finlay did not hesitate. He began with his friendship and affection for the lovely girl who had come to help him in the garden with his crippled children. Then on to Italy, the sudden death of her father and her intimacy with Count Alphonso which quite soon led to their marriage. And now this. 'She is broken in heart and spirit. And . . .' he added in a lower voice, 'her body has been brutally beaten and abused. Now she needs such care, treatment and reconstruction of her life as you alone can give her in the peace of your convent, Reverend Mother.'

A silence fell in the little office, then the Reverend Mother said quietly, 'Dearest Finlay, looking at you now I recognise you as a splendid product of Stonyhurst where, amongst other distinctions, you were captain of the School Football XI. You were also Head Boy in Classics, much to the satisfaction of your reverend uncle, then Bishop, now Archbishop Finlay.' She paused, then went on, 'With all this in mind I find it hard to understand why you are never present at our Holy Mass, ten o'clock, every Sunday and Holy Day in the year.'

There was a silence, then Finlay said, humbly and contritely, 'You have a strong case against me, dear Mother. The truth is simply this, I am often as busy on Sundays as I am on weekdays and if I am not working I am tired and need rest. If there were a Catholic Church in Tannochbrae I would certainly drop in at ten or eleven o'clock, but as this is the nearest place of worship, the thought of the long drive here and back tends to rather get the better of me.'

'If other matters "got the better of you" so easily you would not be so highly regarded as you are now.'

'One other little difficulty, Reverend Mother. If in Tannochbrae I were to acknowledge myself as a Catholic I would be *shunned*, an outcast.'

She laughed sarcastically. 'My poor little Finlay – no longer regarded as a hero.' Her tone changed, hardened. 'In the name of God, wasn't our dear Lord Jesus shunned and despised, mocked, flogged, and crucified between two thieves? Did he say he was too tired when he took the long, hard, uphill walk to Calvary?'

There was a pause then Finlay said:

'You bring tears of shame to my eyes.'

'You know that I love you as a mother, dear Finlay. But your success, your easy friendly manner, your physical attributes, your skills on the moors in shooting and fishing, yes, even your success in your practice, all these have made you too secure, too proud. If a man insulted you, without hesitation you would knock him down. Finlay, can't you see that your public image has become your god and you would defend it with your life?'

'Dear Reverend Mother, your estimation of my character is only too true. Even at school I wanted to score the winning try. Is that a fault?'

'Would it not have been a nobler action if at the last moment you had passed the ball to the weakest member of the team, a boy unsure of his place, and allowed him to score?'

'If I had passed to him he would almost certainly have dropped the ball in sheer surprise.'

Irresistibly she laughed, and Finlay joined her.

Silence followed this almost profane merriment.

'Finlay,' said the Reverend Mother, taking his hand, 'just promise me this: if your patient should decide to join us here when she is well again, would you come to our celebration when she is accepted as a postulant in our Order?'

'That I definitely promise you. And I have one good quality amongst my many sins, I never, but never, break my word.'

When Finlay reached home that afternoon and had garaged the car he went immediately to the telephone. He had one more duty to perform, to thrash the villain responsible for this unspeakable crime. He rang the Caledonian Hotel.

'I wish to speak immediately to the Italian Count Alphonso.'

'But, Dr Finlay, he is no longer here!'

'What!'

'Yesterday, suddenly and in great haste, he left the hotel. We understand he had a reservation on the evening train.'

Finlay replaced the receiver. Such a man could only be a coward at heart.

So Finlay's life continued, undisturbed by external events. He carried on, in his usual thorough manner, with the practice, yet in his spare time his thoughts reverted to his patient at Bon Secours. All seemed well with her, and it was apparent that the rest and the complete security there had healed her both in body and in spirit. Although she was often on his mind, Finlay thought it better not to visit her. Moreover, he occasionally had word from the Mother Superior which confirmed the wisdom of his decision.

After a short and verdant spring, summer came in a blaze of sunshine that lit up the colours in Finlay's garden, where the children that occupied all his free time laughed and played to their hearts' content. This was enough to engage Finlay, and to distract his thoughts from more serious affairs.

Yet serious affairs were impending and would not be denied. On the morning of 7th July he was called to the telephone.

'Finlay, dear boy, I have some wonderful news for you.'

'Yes, Reverend Mother?' He had recognised the voice at once.

'First of all, dear Finlay, you will be pleased to know that your patient here is now fully and completely recovered. Yesterday she played the entire game of hockey between the Juniors and the

Seniors. And what's more she scored a winning goal that decided the game in favour of the Juniors.'

'Dear Reverend Mother, I am overjoyed! Such wonderful news. Soon, she will be back in circulation.'

There was a pause then, 'Not exactly! Within the next few days you will receive a splendid gold-edged invitation card.'

'Don't tell me you're arranging a dance, Reverend Mother.'

'Not exactly,' she replied, laughing. 'I am so happy. I rejoice to tell you that your Alice has decided to become a postulant in our Order. The ceremony of her acceptance will take place at eleven on the morning of Saturday 14th July and will be a truly joyful occasion.'

Finlay took a long breath to steady himself, then, repressing all personal feelings and with all the fervour of a noble heart he said, 'That is the best decision she could make. I rejoice with you, dear Reverend Mother, and you may be sure that I shall most certainly be there.'

This news was too much for Finlay to take sitting down. Replacing the receiver, he got up, went into the garden and with a deep frown began to walk up and down the gravel path, taking vicious kicks at various perfectly innocent pebbles. Suddenly little Jeannie, his special favourite amongst the children, came skipping up to him gaily.

'Weel, what do ye want of me now, ye wee pest?'

Her face fell instantly and she seemed ready to cry. 'Oh, what have I done wrong? You look so angry.'

'Nothing, my wee darlingest.' Relaxing, he picked her up and cuddled her. 'If a' the lasses in the world, big and wee, were as sweet as you, there wad be a lot less bother. Come on, now, and I'll gie you a big high swing.'

When this was accomplished, with mutual screams of delight, Finlay carried her into his office.

'Which is the right and proper place to find something for my own wee Jeannie?' She pointed to the lower right-hand drawer which, when opened, revealed a delicious-looking fruit sweet, gaily wrapped in coloured paper depicting some lovely strawberries.

'Oh, my favourite kind!'

'Don't eat it till after your lunch.'

'No, I won't.'

With the sweet tucked safely in the pocket of her pinafore, she kissed Finlay and ran off to the garden to join the others.

With a strange expression on his handsome face, something between a smile and a frown, Finlay moved towards his office, muttering.

'The poor wee Mother Superior is just kidding hersel'. That lass in there fully recovered and sae fu' o' beans she scores goals at hockey, would nae mair be a Postulant in her Order than I wad' be the Pope in Rome. It's no my place to tell her so, but before long she'll find out to her cost.'

The Escapee

In the children's garden several days passed in complete tranquillity and, as the practice was very light due to the holiday season. Dr Finlay spent much of his time there. When Dr Cameron had seen the few patients in the surgery he would watch benignly as Finlay played with the laughing children, filled with consciousness that all this childish gaiety was by his special permission and consent. Janet, too, when she had cleared and washed the breakfast dishes, would often step out for a few minutes to stand respectfully behind the doctor, making such comments as might propitiate and please.

"'Tis a cheery scene, sir, and yin that is maistly due to your good self, allowing Finlay the time off.'

'I am lenient, Janet, in a good cause. Even if it puts a greater burden on my shoulders. Finlay, you know, is still a boy, and it benefits him to run and tumble with the bairns.'

'While you do the hale o' the surgery, sir.'

'Tut, tut! My dear Janet! In all our many years together you must have perceived that I have a most generous, yes, even a sacrificial nature.'

'Ay, sir, ye are good tae us all. Just for example, this verra morning, there was a hale fried kipper left over at breakfast, since Finlay hadna ate his. Weel, I knew I could have it. So I took it to the kitchen, boned it and made a real tasty kedgeree for ma lunch. Now in maist big houses that kipper wad have to have come up again next morning. But not in yours, sir.'

'Ha, ha, hum,' said the doctor testily. 'I'm gey fond o' kipper kedgeree, masel'. Maybe you . . .'

'I couldna for one moment think of offering ye Finlay's leavins',' said Janet quickly. 'Now, I'll away and see if the post is in.' And briskly she set off to the front door where, although the postman had not come, the daily paper, the *Tannochbrae Herald*, was stuffed through the slit in the letterbox.

Janet picked it up, straightened it, then cast an experienced eye over the front page. Suddenly she started, her entire frame vibrating from the impact of a piece of news. 'Weel, weel!' she muttered audibly. 'Did ye ever in your life hear o' such a thing. *She's flown the coop!*'

Excitedly she moved into the adjoining waiting-room, sat down and read the item again and again, as if attempting to memorise it. Then, sitting back, she said aloud, 'Cameron mustna' see this. I'll pass it to Finlay in the gairden.'

Quickly she opened the front door, closed it quickly behind her, then stealthily made her way round the front of the house into the garden. Here, she buttonholed Finlay and led him into the summer-house.

'Finlay,' she whispered impressively, 'I've a rare bit o' news for ye. It fair puts my back up. After all ye have done for her, she's gone, escaped!'

With this she handed the paper to Finlay, pointing to the article:

ESCAPEE FROM BON SECOURS

Friends and admirers of The Good Mother Superior at the convent of Bon Secours will learn with regret of an unfortunate event, the first in the annals of this most worthy institution, which took place yesterday near midnight. One of the inmates, a postulant sister, made her escape by climbing down a long rope from a top-floor bathroom window. The rope had been previously secured from the garden and secreted under the escapee's bed. Once she was at ground level this dauntless young woman divested herself of her robe, which she hung at full stretch on the hedge bordering the lawn, thus revealing herself to the moon in the smart tweed suit which she had worn when entering the convent.

For so young and dauntless an adventuress it was an easy matter to climb the high-barred entrance gate and land on the open highway. Once here, did our nimble young Diana start out on the long hard walk to civilisation and security? Not so! Not, as she herself might say, on your ruddy life, pal! With noteworthy and, in other circumstances, commendable prudence, she had timed the passage of the last bus from the hamlet of Whinberry to Tannochbrae. Lest her signals might not be observed, she stopped the lumbering vehicle by the single expedience of standing in the middle of the narrow road. Once the bus was stationary she climbed up cosily beside the driver, who will verify her remark: 'Sorry to stop you, but I just had word my poor old mother is dying. If you drop me off at the Tannochbrae post office there's a ten bob note in your pocket.'

Spurred by the double incentive of a human action and this tangible reward, driver Boscop did not hesitate. In his own words, 'I stood on the gas. And let me tell you mo' she didna say a word. She was the cosiest bit o' goods that ever squeezed up there beside me on the dickey!'

Dropped off at the post office our young lady paid the offered fare and set off in search of a hotel. This morning a discreet survey of the various hotels reveals the fact that our charming and courageous escapee is bedded down and sleeping peacefully in the Princess Suite of the Royal Hotel. What can one say of this midnight adventure? While the few Holy Romans in our little town might look down their noses and shake their heads in sorrow, we others, while sympathising with the Good Mother Superior, would regard her brave and daring midnight adventure with admiration and respect.

While Finlay was reading the account of her adventures, Alice Lane awakened from a delicious sleep to find herself the heroine of Tannochbrae. Idly she rang for breakfast, which appeared immediately, a very different meal from the plain fare she had unwillingly endured in the Convent of Bon Secours. To say that she enjoyed it, while at the same time reading that portion of the *Herald* dedicated to herself, would be an absurd understatement. She revelled in it, stretching her beautiful long legs against the fine linen sheets as she drank the finest mocha and crunched on the excellent toast with her strong white teeth.

When the breakfast tray was removed by none other than the head waiter himself, she turned to the telephone and rang the local Scottish Provincial Bank, where she was immediately assured that her balance of £2000 remained intact. She replaced the receiver with a self-satisfied smile. How wise she had been to secure this from her beastly husband in the early days at the Caledonian Hotel. Indeed, her next call was to that same hotel, where the manager not only promised to send on her brass-bound trunk from storage, immediately, but suggested a change of air to his own Guest Suite.

If these attentions had not sufficiently convinced our little escapee of her news value she was certainly assured and reassured by the proliferation of attentions and invitations now showered upon her over the telephone and by the masses of letters brought into her on a tray by the first postal delivery. With these her natural discretion and *savoir faire* came into play. Requests that she should address the Philatelic Society, the Young Women's Club, the Anti-Popery League and the Boys' Brigade went instantly into the waste-paper basket. There were others, however, demanding further attention. And on reflection she committed herself to a Press Luncheon and, above all, to a dinner party, given for her at his private house by Mr Albert Caddens, a gentleman of high standing and considerable substance (in more ways than one).

This invitation she accepted immediately in a witty little personal note, not exactly provocative but as near to that as an escaped nun might go. But, alas, there was no letter, no phone call, not one word from the person with whom she longed whole-heartedly to re-establish the tender relations that had once, to the delight of her heart and soul, existed between them.

But then, she reflected consolingly, dear Finlay was always a shy boy, although she had created many opportunities for him to fall into her arms he had always retreated from the edge of rapture. Yet, now, surely, in the light of her brilliant return to him, he must yield. Already she felt him in her arms. This induced her to dress in the light summer frock she had worn at their first meeting.

Precisely when she was ready and a satisfying flush had been coaxed, with some assistance to nature, into her perfect complexion, the telephone rang. It was the hotel desk.

'The car is waiting for you, madam. Compliments of Mr Albert Caddens.'

'I shall be down presently.' As Alice gave this reply she smiled to herself in the mirror. No need to jump at the cherry. Dear old Albert seemed hers for the picking.

After a cigarette, puffed languidly, she appeared downstairs, where a succession of bows ushered her to the waiting car. Not a Rolls, as she had hoped, but a big, roomy, shining Daimler. However, the chauffeur was quite perfect, young, slender, dark-eyed, handsome, smartly uniformed. His hand lightly touched hers as he showed her to her seat.

'I first wish to go to the house of Dr Finlay.'

'Of course, madam.'

Her voice had quivered slightly as she breathed out that magic name. Yes, she was returning to him. And in style. A woman famous for her exploits, her courage, resolution and unyielding loyalty to the man she loved. As she approached his home her heart beat faster. Yes, he was there, in the garden, suntanned, splendidly muscled in shorts and white singlet, surrounded by the children. All were watching the big shining car as the chauffeur flung open the door, permitting her to descend in state.

Fortunately she had brought her parasol and, flicking it open, she strolled across the lawn under its shade. What a picture of charm, and easy, smiling nonchalance.

'It's our lady, Finlay!' cried the children as she advanced towards the group.

'Yes, darlings, of course it is. Back to play with you as she did last year.'

'Aren't you a nun, madam?' asked one little boy, as another said 'Is your Italian gentleman gone?'

Ignoring these rather personal questions she held out her hand to Finlay. 'I am back, darling Finlay, free of all my encumbrances, drawn to you as a needle to the Pole.'

'I don't feel at all magnetic this morning, madam.'

Finlay did not accept the proffered hand but, looking her in the eye, he said firmly, 'I cannot possibly receive you now. Your conduct and recent statements thereon have done a great injury to a lady I revere and love, and also to her splendid institution, which has done great service to me and to other doctors. Why, you yourself must realise what Bon Secours has done for you. You went there desperately ill, your body a wreck. How do you repay her? Although you could have walked out of the front door unhindered at any moment of the day, you chose to stage an absurd midnight escapade which made you appear a heroine, daring and astutely avoiding the crushing, unwanted oppression of a Catholic nunnery. And this, madam, to a respected institution and a woman, my dear Mother Superior, who with her own hands tended and healed your wounds. She made you once again a healthy, desirable woman. How do you reward her? By holding her up to the public gaze as the wardress of a prison in which, but for your own courage and adroitness, you would have been condemned to serve a life sentence!'

Alice had turned pale. As she did not speak he continued, 'All this, naturally, is like manna to our little Scottish town where we poor Catholics are held in contempt, disliked, despised, even hated.' Again a silence till he concluded, 'Naturally, madam, you are the heroine of the hour. You will be congratulated, admired, fêted.' He paused. 'I advise you to take full advantage of your triumph in this town. You will not find it here.'

With that final word, Finlay rose and walked back towards the children. Alone she sat, perfectly still and pale as death. But gradually the colour returned to her cheeks. She compressed her lips, rose, and seething with rage and disappointment walked directly to the car. Once in the safety of the big saloon she said, 'Home, to your master. Drive slowly.'

During the leisurely progress through the town with the near window open Alice was agreeably conscious of being looked at. Then the car drew up before the substantial villa of Mr Albert Caddens, in the secluded quiet of College Road.

'Shall I wait for you here, madam, or garage the car?'

'Garage it, please. And see you get a good lunch for yourself.'

'Thank you, madam, for your kind thought.'

As Miss Lane went up the stone steps and into the house she did not fail to observe, as she entered the big dining-room, that the table was sumptuously set for two with superb china plates and sparkling silver cutlery, while at the big sideboard her host, immaculate in fine white shirt and a blue suit, was expertly sharpening the carver on a steel.

He turned for an instant to bow and smile, saying, 'Oh, my dear Miss Lane, I am so glad to find you so punctual. I have a superb piece of beef here, cooked to perfection and I find it positively heartbreaking if it is not served and eaten *au point*. Do, please, be seated.'

A manservant, in a yellow striped waistcoat and green tails, seated her with extreme courtesy, and a moment later placed before her a delicious plateful of pink, wafer-thin roast beef, two floury potatoes simply bursting their sides and a crusty wedge of the best-looking Yorkshire pudding she had ever set eyes upon.

'Dear Mr Caddens,' she exclaimed, 'what a delicious sight for a very hungry young woman.'

He chuckled, watching approvingly as she set to voraciously. 'That's the spirit I like to see. I have nae time at all for women who shrink frae the finest roast beef and cry out for pastry and tea.'

'That's not my style, dear Mr Caddens. But do tell me where to get this superb beef, for it's surely the best I ever tasted.'

'It's frae my own stock farm, lass,' he gloated. 'I kill my ain beasts. Nae butcher's trash for me, I like the finest.' And with a side glance at her he added, slyly, 'That's why I like you!'

As the butler was now pouring beer into his master's tankard she thought it wise, at this early stage, to ignore the remark. With the same tact, when the butler approached her with the beer, although she hated the stuff, she permitted him to half fill her glass.

'And did you have a nice drive this morning, in my Daimler?'

'I just took a quiet little turn round the town, Mr Caddens, but enough to appreciate the magnificence of your wonderful car. But I'm surprised, sir, that a man of your position and, forgive me, wealth, should not have his own, more personal car, such as a sports model, preferably a Bentley, a Jaguar, or a Ferrari.'

He laughed heartily, slapping his thigh with one hand. 'That would be more to your taste, eh, ma dearie?'

'Well, I tell you truthfully, Albert, oh, forgive me Mr Caddens . . .!'

'Naething to forgive lass. I like ye to be on first-name terms wi' me, and in return I'll ca' you Alice!'

She smiled, bewitchingly. 'Thank you, dear Albert. Well, reverting to cars, my dear father promised me just such a car. But, alas, he was taken from me, almost a year ago.'

'So, beside the loss o' your dear father, ye lost your lovely sports car.'

She inclined her head silently and for a moment touched her handkerchief against the corner of one eye.

'Oh, my poor dear lass,' and he pressed her little soft hand, which lay conveniently near.

'How would it do, ma dearie, if on your next birthday, you looked out of the window and there, drawn up outside, a' shinin' and sparklin', was the car o' your heart's desire?'

Now, indeed, real tears flowed as she exclaimed, 'Oh, Albert darling, you couldn't be so wonderful. And my birthday is so soon, next month in fact.'

Now she had surrendered her hand completely and he was caressing it as he said, 'Let's have the date o' your birthday, dearie, and the name o' the car ye fancy.'

'It's the 25th July, and I would adore a twin-exhaust two-seater Ferrari. But I'll write it down for you later. Oh what wonderfully soft hands you have, Albert. From a great strong man like yourself a woman would naturally expect roughness and heaviness.'

'No, lass, no' frae me. When my wife was alive she wad often say to me: "Albert, big and heavy as ye are, ye are the gentlest creature in all the world." Ye see, lass, even in the pleasures of the bed everything was accomplished in the tenderest way.' Quickly he added: 'I tell ye this, lass, no frae indecency, but so ye may ken the true me. Strong in will and body, gentle in touch and caress.'

A short silence followed in which she was permitted to comprehend and digest this most relevant information. Then, as her hand continued to be stroked, she murmured, 'It was noble of you, Albert, to tell me this – since, if I may be as frank as your dear self, it was the one thing that held me back.'

'Then, ye'll no' be all by yoursel' much longer darlin'.'

Thus begun, the subjugation of the good Mr Caddens proceeded apace during the ensuing weeks. The worthy stock farmer, who could face an angry bull without turning a hair, was soft as butter in the hands of this experienced enchantress, upon whom he showered gifts of astounding munificence to the eyes of Tannochbrae. On a quick visit to Edinburgh the shops in Princes Street were raided and, on the following Sunday, Mr Caddens was accompanied to the kirk by a beautiful young lady so smart in a cashmere blue suit, snappy mink coat and capôte of the same fur that every eye in that hallowed edifice was fixed, fascinated, upon her. The gentleman himself was equally smart, indeed rejuvenated, in a frock-coat of Bond Street cut and the very latest trim white spats on his new patent leather shoes. As they emerged after the service into the gathering outside, a voice was heard, 'When is the announcement, Mr Caddens?'

'If you are interested,' came the reply, 'I advise ye to look in tomorrow's local paper!'

Then the handsome couple stepped into the Daimler and were borne out of sight.

'Oh, Albert, darling, wasn't it simply wonderful?'

'Aye, lass,' agreed the bold Albert. 'Naebody ever looked at the meenester. Every eye was on us.'

'And yon were lookin' so smart, my dearest. Were you not pleased I had togged ye up so well?'

'Aye, lass, I felt I was gettin' my share o' attention, thanks to you.'

This exchange of compliments continued until the Daimler reached the house in College Road, where Albert immediately composed the announcement of their engagement, which he himself posted in an adjoining pillar-box. Then followed the stupendous Sunday lunch, whereat their success at the kirk was dwelt upon and more thoroughly enjoyed.

'With all this going on, dearest Albert, I hope ye havena forgot about my wee car.'

'Not on your life, dearie. Last Thursday I was up to Hughie Ferguson at his big garage and showroom. He's right against the Ferrari, he says it's all noise and glitter. But he's all for the new Jaguar. Fast, yet fit for a lady to handle and silent as a cloud. In his showroom he has one just arrived frae the works, Oxford blue, just your colour. It's a real beauty.'

'Oh, dearest Albert, my sweetest, kindest darling . . . May I go up to town to look at it?'

'No need, my wee pettie. It'll be at your front door at ten o'clock tomorrow morning.'

'Oh, you darlingest Albert in all the world.' In her excitement the future Mrs Caddens could barely keep still, bouncing up and down in her chair.

'Another interesting thing for tomorrow, dear, is that the star reporter of the local paper wants to interview you tomorrow, to get your story. Since it would mean a tidy fee for you I said he could come. Eleven o'clock tomorrow.'

'Oh, good! How much do you think that would be, Albert?'

'I've fixed it for you, darling. If you can deliver the goods – five hundred pounds down, into your own dear wee hand.'

'Oh, Albert! Between love of you, the new Jaguar, and five hundred in cash, I'll be the happiest young woman in all the world.'

Next morning, everything fell out according to plan. The Jaguar was inspected, delightfully approved, and a trial run arranged for the following Saturday. Then, at eleven o'clock, Alice was ready in her new blue dress to receive Mr Donald Douglass, the star reporter from the *Herald*.

After coffee had been served the reporter laid a cheque on the table before the interview began.

'I imagine, Miss Lane, that you were not very happy in the convent?'

'Happy, sir! For a good Protestant lass like masel', it was hell.'

'You found your incarceration unbearable?'

'It was like being shut up in a cupboard.'

'Or perhaps a cell?' kindly suggested Mr Douglass.

'You've hit the word sir.' She had spotted the figure '500' on the cheque. 'And a' the time they were ding-dangin' away at me wi' those hymns and prayers and masses, far into the night.'

'Didn't they give you anything to help your insomnia?'

'You may be sure, sir, I was well drugged a' the time I was there.'

'Sleeping draughts?'

'Would you understand what I mean, sir, when I say it was the needle?'

'Ah! Hypodermics! Much more potent I assume.'

'Ay, they knocked me out as if I had been pole-axed, and next morning when I came to, I felt like hell.'

'Ah! What a splendid phrase! Might one say, you *felt* you were in hell!'

'That was my exact meaning, sir.'

'Did you have interviews with the Mother Superior?'

'Several, sir.'

'Of what nature?'

'As sweet as sugar. She was full o' pretended pity, telling me to forget the past and begin a new life.'

'With her in the convent?'

'Aye, she would love to have nabbed me. I would have been what they call a reclaimed sinner!'

'I believe that you have spoken elsewhere of cells. Did you see them? Were you ever actually shut up in one?'

'I saw them all right. I was looking around the premises one wet day, and there they were, two together, right at the back.'

'Made you shiver, I suppose, you poor girl?'

'Oh, sir, I could tell you . . .'

The interview continued on these lines for a further half-hour then, with a smile, Mr Douglass pushed his notepad towards her, 'Just sign here, my dear young lady, and the cheque is yours.'

She signed with alacrity, and the cheque was immediately in her hand. With the most cordial good wishes Mr Douglass then departed.

Giving him a bare ten minutes to get clear, the bold Alice took the cheque to the bank, cashed it, and received the entire amount in brand new crisp bank notes: three hundreds, two fifties, and the remaining hundred pounds in tens and twenties.

After locking the larger notes safely in her suitcase, Alice set off into the town on a wild spending spree, lashing out on a snappy yellow hat she had already seen and fancied in the local milliner's, pairs of sheer stockings from the same shop, a large box of Fuller's best chocolates, new light doeskin gloves, a sweet little bunch of dainty fresh violets for her lapel, a pair of patent leather shoes and a tiny bottle of Mille Fleurs, her favourite perfume. Finally she popped into the local Woolworth's and picked up a cheap tie for Albert in a very serviceable grey that would go with anything.

What fun she had! What a splendid time! She gave a little boy a penny to carry home her booty.

As Albert had not returned, she tucked away her treasures safely in her bedroom, bringing down only the presentation tie, from which she had carefully removed the Woolworth's label and price tag.

All that afternoon and evening she enchanted Albert with her gaiety, and when evening came and he tucked her into her little bed he said, lovingly, 'Not long now darling, till we are cosy together in the big bed.' He added, 'It was sweet o' you to buy me that fine tie, out of your own wee purse. I can tell it's an expensive yin, for there's nae label or price on it.'

'Darling Albert! Nothing but the best for you!'

Libel!

Next morning dawned fine and warm. Finlay awoke early, sensing that his favourite season of the year, glorious summer, was on hand. He leaped out of bed, put on shorts, sweater and canvas shoes, then set out on his usual three mile run round Gielston Old Toll, up Garston Hill and back home by Church Street.

Although he concentrated on his running, it became apparent that many more people than usual were on the streets. And all, without exception, were reading the *Herald*. When he reached home he called to Janet, who was busy preparing his coffee, 'The paper in yet?'

She came to the kitchen door to look at him. 'Ay, it's in, Finlay, sir. And there's something in it that will interest you.'

'Just hold it a minute, Janet, until I have my shower.'

He ran upstairs, showered in cold water, rubbed down with a rough towel, put on his underwear and, in five minutes, was down by the kitchen fire in his dressing-gown.

'Here's your coffee, sir,' said Janet, 'and I beg o' ye to drink it before you touch this dirty rag!'

'Something really bad, Janet?'

'Ay, sir, it doesna concern us, thank God, but it's enough to make ye spew.'

Thus warned, Finlay dispensed with his coffee and a slice of toast before glancing at the paper. Then, as he saw the headlines, he turned pale and a look of sick anger dimmed the brightness of his eyes:

BON SECOURS AT LAST EXPOSED: THE HORRORS AND MISERIES OF A PAPAL PRISON FINALLY REVEALED BY ESCAPED NUN

Only the courage and daring of a brave young Scottish lass, one of the finest in Tannochbrae, has enabled us to publish this true story of her life in, and escape from, this Popish hell. Yes, dear readers, our own Alice Lane, risking horrible punishments, even incarceration in the dreaded dungeon cell has risked her life to give our star reporter, Donald Douglass, the true story, signed on oath, of her life in and her escape from this damnable sealed enclosure, where under the threat of fearful ghastly punishments – so called penances – young girls are moulded to the iron will of that relentless, inscrutable woman, the Reverend Mother.

Alice Lane first came to this woman, brought by her doctor, another unspeakable character in this fiasco, for a slight ailment that quickly cured itself. Induced by false promises and other blandishments our young innocent was induced to become a Postulant to the Order.

Alas! Once she had donned the black robe of service and muttered the Latin balderdash of initiation, she was anointed with the Seven Oils and accepted into the Secret Sisterhood.

For weeks, bound by fear and dread of punishment in the underground cell, this poor young woman submitted to the iron discipline of the convent. But at last her brave Scottish spirit revolted. She attempted to escape, was caught and punished so severely that her health was almost undermined. Nevertheless, though her body was almost broken by punishments for supposed faults, her spirit was undaunted, her brave heart still beat steady, and true within her noble breast. 'Twas this courageous spirit that said, one unmentionable day, 'thus far and no further'.

Calmly, bravely, staunchly and steadily she made her plans and, in full knowledge of her fate were she caught, set herself courageously to carry them to a life-saving conclusion. A coil of thin rope, left by one of the nun gardeners for future use in the orchard, was secreted under her robe and smuggled up to her room where it was pushed far back under her bed. The window of her little bedroom was barred, making her tiny private cubicle a prison cell. However, next door was another, smaller room the window as yet unbarred, since it was destined to be a guest room. But as our little heroine inspected the long fall to the ground her heart almost failed her. Yet, one starless night, after a day of terror and oppression, she realised with all her being that it was now or never. Better a clean death from this precipitous fall than months, perhaps years of incarceration in a dungeon cell. Bravely she made her preparations. She carried the rope to the unbarred cubicle, fastened one end to the iron stanchion of the bed, opened the window, dropped out the free end of the rope until, far down it dangled, almost to the ground.

It was now or never. Offering herself to the God of all good Protestants she climbed out through the window and clung to the rope. Oh, dear heaven, what terror struck into her young heart as she dangled, a hundred feet above terra firma. Why not let go and finish it, now, once and for all? No! She had borne the terrors of the nunnery, now she would not yield. Dangling, swinging wildly on the rope, she slid down, tearing the skin and flesh from her hands. At last she was at the end of the rope but, dear heavens! Her feet did not reach the ground, With a stifled cry she released the rope and fell, with the help of the Lord, only one or two feet.

So far so good. Bravely, she picked herself up, but there was another difficulty ahead. The huge iron-spiked gate of the convent was locked and bolted, as immovable as that guarded by Cerberus, the keeper of the Gates of Hell!

Again, there was no recourse. She must climb. And climb our little heroine did. Struggling, straining, clutching the iron spikes with her torn and bleeding hands, breathless, agonised, she finally surmounted the top spikes and slid down, half dead, on the far side of hell.

Yes, she was free, but not yet safe. Five miles lay ahead to Tannochbrae. Perhaps a country bus would pass, or a car with a friendly driver. Alas, no such good fortune for our brave Alice. She must foot it all the way, arriving spent and breathless at the Royal Hotel, where she begged a room for the night. On the morrow she was received into the fine home of our worthy citizen and church member, Mr Albert Caddens where, thank God and Mr Caddens, she lies slowly recovering from her wounds.

Citizens of Tannochbrae, the *Herald* calls upon you to arise and strike this plague spot from our neighbourhood. Let the fateful story of Alice Lane be your weapon and your cause!

Janet had remained with Finlay watching his face all through his long perusal of the paper. And now timidly she asked, 'Is it bad, Finlay dear?'

'Stinking, filthy bad, Janet. It is bigoted lying evil, every ridiculous word of it.' He paused. 'I'm going out now Janet and may not be back for a few hours. Tell any important cases I'll be here this afternoon. Dr Cameron will look after the others.'

To implement this remark Finlay went along the passage, knocked at Dr Cameron's door and went in. The good doctor, lying back on a nest of pillows, was enjoying a hearty breakfast from a well-stocked bedside table.

'Sorry to disturb you, sir. I have some urgent business in town. When you've done the surgery, which should be light this morning, would you mind seeing to anything urgent coming in for me?'

'Certainly, certainly, my boy. Take all the time you need. I'll hold the fort.'

'Thank you, sir. I'll be back after lunch.'

Finlay then went into the garage, opened the doors and stepped into his car. It was not a long walk to the top of the town but the matter on his mind was urgent. In four minutes he drew up before a beautiful, large old house which bore discreetly on the door a small burnished plate inscribed with the words: 'Alexander Cochrane & Co., Solicitors and Officers of Law', the name of the oldest, and best and most widely known firm in the west of Scotland.

Finlay walked in directly to the room at the back where a large man in a tweed jacket and another of subordinate appearance were bending over the morning's *Herald*, laid flat on the table before them.

'Hello, Finlay!' said the big man, looking up. 'Gold again this morning?'

'Another day, Alex,' said Finlay, drawing a chair up to the table. 'This morning I want to hit something bigger than a little white ball.'

'I understand, Finlay. Scott and I have just been through this rot for the third time. It would be funny if it were not so damnably serious. It is of course actionable on every damn paragraph. That afternoon after our golf when you took me in to the Mother Superior for tea, I thought I had never met such a sweet, gentle person. And now this . . . with her dungeon cells . . . Didn't old Colonel keep his dogs there before the house was sold to the convent?'

Finlay nodded. 'The two Great Danes. Rather too much for the Sisters to handle. The two kennels were used for storage – old boxes, garden tools, anything bulky and unwanted.'

'The escape is the best bit. As I understand it, the big wooden gate is never locked.'

'Never, it stands wide open day and night. Many a stranded wayfarer, an old tinker or a gypsy has walked through to find a night's refuge, free of charge.'

'I loved the bit about the long walk to Tannochbrae,' Alex laughed. 'Davie here rang Jock Boscop, who makes that night run. He picked her up at the open convent gate and delivered her to Tannochbrae near the Royal Hotel.'

'Where she walked in and ordered the Princess Suite, the best in the house,' said Davie.

'Then she picked up Fatty Caddens, and now I believe she has the best of everything in *his* house.'

'Well, Finlay, it's up to you now, the big Number One question: how much should we sue for? The *Herald* is stinking rich and they should damn well be punished for this double page o' lies.'

'You name it Alex! You are the expert.'

'I'm going to stagger you, Finlay. For that dear Mother Superior held to shame and ridicule, I am going to get five thousand pounds.'

'What a heavenly godsend that would be for her, Alex. The old Colonel let his house run down a lot and if she had the cash Reverend Mother could bring it into shape again, and add to it, too.'

'Splendid,' said Alex. Then, after a pause he asked seriously, 'Finlay, old boy, when I was at Rossall and you were at Stonyhurst, and we met on several occasions in fierce conflict on the football field, did I ever regard you as unspeakable?'

Finlay laughed, 'No, Alex, I should think not. We were too busy killing each other.'

'My dear, very dear old friend, I raise this matter since in this totally filthy article you have actually been referred to as "an unspeakable character". Now that is a slur that in itself is actionable.'

'Well, Alex, we'll not get in the way of the big action or the big money, but you can refer to it when you have me in the box and I'll not fail to speak the truth.'

'Good lad, Finlay. Now, how about lunch?'

'Another time, Alex. I've left Cameron on his own, and I must first run out to console Reverend Mother. They take the *Herald* there. So I'll brief her on what we're going to do.'

'Right, Finlay. Bye.'

'Bye Alex! And bless you!'

Dr Cameron Triumphant

When, with the rapidity common to all Scottish towns, the news percolated in Tannochbrae that their beloved *Herald* was being sued for damages by the Reverend Mother Superior of Bon Secours, a shock-wave of disbelief passed through this snug little community. Any temptation to laugh the matter off was checked not only by the enormity of the sum but by the astounding fact that the sponsors of the action were none other than Finlay, their well beloved doctor, and Alexander Cochrane, the best and most highly regarded lawyer in the county.

'It's just a try-on!' This first impression was immediately countered by, 'What! Wi' Finlay and Cochrane baith ahint it?'

In the great *Herald* building which housed the offices of the paper there was something like panic.

'It's that damn stupid adjective we pinned on Finlay, "unspeakable" that has put his back up. Could we offer him a hunner to withdraw?'

'He'd spit on your hundred and throw it back at you!'

'Should we offer to compound the damages, say about five hundred?'

'Dinna be a bloody fool, man! That wad undermine our whole position.'

A quiet voice, that of the Chairman of the Board, quickly stilled the meeting. 'Gentlemen, we have made a crassly stupid and damaging blunder. Now there is nothing for us but to face the music and make the best o' a bad job.'

When it became known that the *Herald* would fight the case, the date being set for the fifth of next month, excitement in the town ran high and intensified in a rush to secure places in the gallery of the court, admission being only by stamped ticket. These precious squares of cardboard were bartered in the local pubs and as the date drew near changed hands for unbelievable amounts of cash.

During this preliminary turmoil both Finlay and Alex Cochrane remained perfectly quiet and in good spirits. In fact, they played several games of golf together, returning to take tea at the convent. On one of these visits Finlay left behind a large oblong box which carried the label of a first-class women's shop in London.

At last, in a final surge of excitement the fateful day arrived. From an early hour crowds gathered outside the Assize Court, so impatient for news that it took a solid barrage of police sergeants to keep the more boisterous from rushing the gates. When the *Herald* management arrived, accompanied by their legal advisers, they received a greeting of mingled cheers, boos and hisses. Nothing was seen of Finlay and his lawyer, who had reached the court by the upper entrance accompanied by a lady who, naturally, was veiled. Below, as the lucky holders of tickets poured in, they were greeted jealously by shouts, groans and every conceivable variety of filthy abuse, together with abortive attempts at ticket snatching.

At last the town clock struck ten sonorous strokes and, with the court filled to capacity, the proceedings began.

When the jury had been sworn in, the Clerk of the Court read out the charge against the owners and management of the *Herald*: that the article printed in the issue of 26th July was false, bigoted and seriously damaging to the persons specified therein.

The order was then given that the specified article be read aloud. In an even, unemotional voice, the Clerk of the Court slowly read the article in question, a performance greeted in the gallery by cheers and laughter, immediately suppressed.

Mr Alexander Cochrane then rose. His first question was to the lawyer for the defence, a Mr J. M. Taylor, from the City of

Edinburgh. 'Do your clients stand by every word of the article in question?'

'They do, sir, every word is the living truth.'

This brought more cheers from the gallery.

Mr Cochrane then proceeded to call to the witness box the various individuals mentioned in the specific article.

The first to be called was Mr Jock Boscop. When Jock was in the box, freshly shaved and sharp as a whip, Alex Cochrane said, 'Jock, is it correct to say that you make the night run from Whinberry for your employers, past the convent to Tannochbrae, returning by the same way?'

'It is correct and a fact, sir!'

'On the night of the supposed escape did you pick up a young lady who hailed you outside the convent gate?'

'I did indeed sir. I see her there now, sitting very lovely with the *Herald* gentlemen.'

'You picked her up, Jock, and gave her a lift to Tannochbrae?'

'I did indeed, sir. And a verra cheery companion she was, sir. We chatted and laughed all the way to town.'

'Did she appear distressed in any way?'

'Not in the slightest, Mr Cochrane, sir. I coulda' gaen a lot furder wi' her than just to Tannochbrae.'

Mild laughter from the gallery.

'So the young lady did not walk one foot of the road to the town?'

'Not a foot, sir.'

Mild sensation in court.

'Jock,' continued Mr Cochrane, 'did you happen to notice the condition of the convent gate, that great big steel gate with sharp steel points on the top bar?'

'Are ye coddin' me, sir – that convent gate is a wooden three-bar field gate and forbye it's never shut. It's aye open and that's how it was on the night ye mention.'

'Thank ye, Jock. Just one more question: Did the lass seem depressed, worn out, beaten up?'

Jock laughed heartily. 'You're certainly kiddin' me, sir. The lass was in high spirits, laughin', talkin' and singin' all the way home. "I'm for fun, now, Jock," she says, "and I'll make some money, the easy way." '

'Did she give you anything for all your trouble?'

'Certainly she did, sir. Out came a ten bob note frae her purse. I didna want to take it, for I thocht it might be mair fun tae tak' her out another nicht.'

'Jock, you're a man of your word. Did she seem like she might gie ye some fun?'

'That's a true word, sir.'

'So she wasn't all beaten up, worn out, with her hands cut and bleeding?'

'Sir! Now ye are coddin' me again. There wasna a mark on her. She was fresh as a daisy.'

'Thank you, Jock. Every word you have spoken has the ring of absolute truth.'

The opposition lawyer got to his feet.

'Boscop!' Jock remained on the stand. 'Are you not generally regarded as a drunkard, who would do, or say, anything for a good stiff whisky?'

'Produce the man what says that and I'll mak' him eat his words.'

There was dead silence in the gallery, then a man stood up and shouted at the pitch of his lungs:

'I have kenned Jock Boscop all his days and never once have I seen him drunk or tell anything that wasna true!'

'Enough, Boscop,' said the lawyer for the defence. As Jock retired Mr Cochrane got to his feet.

'May I ask Miss Lane to take the stand.'

After she had done so, to great cheers from the crowd, Cochrane addressed her as follows:

'Miss Lane, here we have a report which gives the lie to your written statement. Firstly, the convent gate. You describe it as a high steel structure, firmly closed, with steel spikes that ripped and tore your hands. Do you admit that this description is a complete and deliberate lie?'

'I wanted to make my report as bad as I could.'

'So you lied! Was it for this reason that you slid down a rope from your window instead of quite simply walking out of the front door?'

'The same.'

'And when you arrived at the Royal Hotel did you beg humbly for a little room, or proudly demand the best suite in the house, the Princess?'

'I demanded the Princess Suite.'

'And asked for all your beautiful clothes to be sent to you from storage?'

'Why torment me, sir? I dressed up in my very best then went out to visit Mr Albert Caddens.'

'You captivated him?'

'That was unnecessary. When he saw me he went down like a felled bull!'

A laugh, quickly suppressed followed this.

'You were in great form when he took you to view the beautiful Jaguar sports model that he wanted to give you.'

'I love beautiful cars.'

'That afternoon, being sure of the Jaguar, and with the *Herald*'s £500 cheque in your pocket you went happily out on the town, cashed the cheque at the bank and with all this money in your pocket, you bought yourself a hat, sheer silk stockings, a pair of fine yellow doeskin gloves, a large box of Fuller's chocolates, and a pair of the finest patent leather shoes. And, in this orgy of luxurious spending on yourself, you bought, for Mr Caddens, your aged lover, a very cheap Woolworth tie! Upon arriving home, you locked the balance of the *Herald* money safely away in your trunk, a good sum of more than £400.'

'Yes I locked it away and much good it will ever do me now. I have lied myself into such a mess I will never get out of it. If only I could be back again in the convent, to find peace again. I realise now that I was really happy there. We had the prayers, but we had lots of games and fun, and walks out into the country. And to speak humbly and truly, I had begun to like the prayers. They made me realise that the Lord God was with us and that we were his children.'

As she broke down, pandemonium broke out, shouts of abuse but also of sympathy and pity. In the midst of it all, from her seat in the front row of the auditorium, a figure in a neat, light grey dress stepped out to the centre of the court and, with arms outstretched, embraced the weeping girl and held her closely, saying, 'Of course you may come back to me my poor child, whenever you are free and permitted to do so. You will find there are no dungeon punishment cells, no steel barrage gates with nails fixed all over the bars. You will come back to a large and lovely garden, a little chapel in which you may pray at will and, above all, to forgiveness and forgetfulness that will in time heal your wounds. Love will conquer all.'

Now, indeed, as the Mother Superior ceased to speak, a great roar of mixed emotions soared to the roof of the court. Cries of sympathy and pity, yells of derision centred mainly on the *Herald*, and cheers and more cheers for one man who, in the face of the entire town had dared to bring the case to court and, against public opinion and so powerful an antagonist as the local paper, had brought light out of darkness, justice against bigotry and perjury.

At this point, an interruption occurred. Alex Cochrane was on his feet, demanding silence. Then, in the stillness of that great mass of humanity he spoke, loud and clear.

'My lord, I pray you! Before you close this case and give judgement may I bring to your notice a horrible unjustified calumny in the *Herald*. My best friend, whom I have known since boyhood, a man who spends his life helping the sick, who has been praised and honoured by the Town Council, is referred to in the *Herald*

report as being *unspeakable*. This word is a disgusting, deroga-
tory term. One might say unspeakable filth, a low unspeakable
brute, an unspeakable rascal, cheat, thief, or even an unspeakable
cad. To apply such a word to the young doctor who, from the
moment of his arrival, has served this town faithfully, brilliantly,
with all his energy and skill, who has won both local and national
esteem by the splendid manner in which he has given his house,
a gift of the town, to the treatment and care of sick and handi-
capped children, is in itself unspeakable. May I inquire if this slur
has been slung at my dear friend because he has had the courage
to stand up to defend and protect an aged Catholic woman, head
of an establishment where many of Finlay's patients have been
tended and cured, yes to stand up against the rage and hatred of
religious bigotry.'

A short, electrifying pause, then Alex Cochrane continued, 'It
has been my great good fortune to know and become friendly
with Finlay when we were boys at school – I at Rossall and Finlay
at Stonyhurst, an equally famous school that has been called the
Catholic Eton. Finlay's father died when his son was only seven
years of age. However, Finlay's uncle was not a man to shrink
from his responsibility. He sent the boy to Stonyhurst where,
as he grew up, Finlay not only became captain of the football
team, but captain of the school as well. Ah! What battles he and
I fought on the football field. These were surely the beginning of
the affection and admiration I have for him. Meanwhile Finlay's
uncle and benefactor had moved ahead in his spiritual profession,
first Bishop, and now Archbishop of the See of Dee and Don in
Aberdeenshire.'

A pause followed, so tense that Alex delayed for a full minute
before delivering his final punch.

'With such a history, do you wonder that Finlay's response to
the poor maligned Mother Superior was immediate and impera-
tive. Of course he is a Catholic, for so he was brought up. Does
that make him unspeakable? Now that you know his history do
you want to put him in the pillory with the Mother Superior?

Mind you, I am not saying that our Dr Finlay is scrupulously faithful to the rules of his religion,' a slight pause while a wave of suppressed amusement passed over the listeners, 'but he is, yes Finlay is, a Catholic. Now, I ask you, does this make him unspeakable?'

A great roar of negation came from the mass that crowded the gallery and was followed by such cheering as had never before been heard in that old and dreaded building.

Now, indeed, the *Herald* and its supporters were silenced, defeated and routed. When at last order was restored the judgement was firm and immediate.

'The voice of the public has spoken. And not for the first time, has expressed correctly, completely, convincingly, the judgement of the law, which awards damages in the amount of £5,000 to the Mother Superior of Bon Secours and five hundred to the most worthy, most esteemed, most beloved member of our town, Dr Finlay.'

A great burst of cheering greeted this verdict and was continued and maintained until the court was cleared, and Finlay had wisely made his escape by the lower inner door. Quickly he reached his car, parked in the private garage, and quickly he was home where, with open arms, Janet awaited him.

'Oh, Finlay dearest lad! I could jump for joy. Now quick! Here's some special beef broth I have ready for ye! Drink it smartly! They'll be down after ye!'

As Finlay drank the delicious soup he said inquiringly, 'And Dr Cameron?'

'He's done no' bad, sir, when he thocht ye were gonna be bate he was quite chirpy, and went about the hoose whistlin'. But the verdict cam' out that ye'd won yer case and a' the money, he just took to his bed. He's there the now.'

Now came the sounds of a great crowd approaching and surrounding the house, shouting for Finlay.

'I'll have to go on to the balcony, Janet. Get Dr Cameron up there, even in his dressin'-gown.'

With that Finlay stepped out through the open windows of the front bedroom and was immediately greeted by a great surge of cheering from the enormous crowd.

'Finlay! Finlay for ever! Finlay belongs to us!' The shouts continued until Finlay raised both arms.

'Thank you! Thank you, dear friends of Tannochbrae! Just when I needed you, when I had been libelled in our good paper, you gave me your support. Now that I am free of worry, you see me here, back on the job, ready to serve you in sickness and in health with my two wonderful colleagues.' At that precise moment Janet pushed out Dr Cameron in his dressing-gown and, as Finlay caught her by the arm and pulled her out, she stood between the two, blushing all over her face.

The tableau was perfect, as Finlay shouted at the pitch of his lungs. 'Here we are, dear friends, the little team of three who have served you in the past and, I now assure you, will continue to do so, with all the skill, energy and enterprise we possess. So now, on behalf of all three of us, I thank you for your continued loyalty and support. We have weathered the storm and are now looking forward to the good days that lie ahead.'

The cheers were renewed. Someone started to sing 'Happy days are here again!' and soon the crowd picked up the refrain which swelled and echoed in the twilight of this memorable day. Finlay then flung open the swing window behind and ushered his companions from the balcony, remaining only to open both arms wide in a gesture of embracing the cheering multitude.

Once inside the room Janet pressed her hands together in ecstasy. 'Never in all my born days, I'll never forget it, my dearest Finlay. Now come away, both of you, and get your dinner. Some more of that lovely soup and a nice grilled steak wi' roast taters and grilled ingins.'

When she had gone, Dr Cameron turned to Finlay: 'You did well, lad, to show me to my fellow townsmen. My appearance stirred them to the depths o' their hearts. I knew they would give me their best and loudest cheer, and they did. Come lad, give me your arm. We might have just a wee nip o' the "cratur" *to celebrate my greatest triumph*!'

Adventures of
a Black Bag

Finlay's Drastic Cure

Often, when Finlay felt himself in need of exercise after a long day's driving in the gig, he would walk in the evening to the Lea Brae.

At this period, before successful burghers started dotting its summit with their bandbox villas, it was a favourite walk, approached from Levenford by a gentle incline and sweeping steeply westwards to the Firth.

From the top the view was superb. On a still summer evening with the sun sinking behind Ardfillan hills, the wide water of the estuary below, and the faint haze of a steamer's smoke mellowing the far horizon, it was a place to stir the soul.

Yet for Finlay it was ruined by Sam Forrest and his wheeled chair.

Up Sam would come, red-faced, bulging with fat, lying back on the cushions like a lord, with poor Peter Lennie panting and pushing at the chair behind him.

Then at the top, while Peter gasped and wiped the sweat from his brow, Sam would majestically relinquish the little metal steering rod, pull a plug from his pocket, bite enormously, and, mouthing his quid like a great big ox, would gaze solemnly, not at the view, but at the steep hill beneath, as though to say: 'Here, my friends! Here was the place where the awful thing happened!'

It all went back a matter of five long years.

Then Peter Lennie was a spry young fellow of twenty-seven, very modest and obliging, proprietor of the small general stores in

College Street which – not without a certain daring timidity – he had named Lennie's Emporium.

In fiction the convention exists that meek little men have large, domineering wives, but in reality it is seldom so. And Retta Lennie was as small, slight, and unassertive as her husband.

In consequence, in business they were often 'put upon'. But for all that, things went pretty well, the future was opening out nicely, and they lived comfortably with their two children in a semi-detached house out Barloan way, which is a genteel quarter to which tradesmen in Levensford aspire.

Now, in Peter Lennie, the humble little counter-jumping tradesman, there lurked unsuspected longings for adventure. There were moments when, lying reflectively in bed with Retta of a Sunday morning, he would stare frowningly at the ceiling and suddenly declare – while Retta looked at him admiringly:

'India!' (or it might be China). 'There's a place we ought to see some day!'

Perhaps it was this romantic boldness which led to the purchase of the tandem bicycle, for though at that moment the craze for 'a bicycle built for two' was at its height, in the ordinary way Peter would never have done anything so rash.

But buy the tandem he did, a shining instrument of motion, a wicked pneumatic-tyred machine, which cost a mint of good money, and which, being uncrated, caused Retta to gasp incredulously:

'Oh, Peter!'

'Get about on it,' he remarked, trying to speak nonchalantly. 'See places. Easy!'

It was, however, not quite so easy. There was, for instance, the difficulty of Retta's bloomers. She was a modest little woman was Retta, and it cost Peter a week of solid argument and persuasion before he could coax his wife into the light of day in these fashionable but apparently improper garments.

Peter himself wore a Norfolk jacket, the belt rather gallantly unbuckled so that, even merely wheeling the tandem, it gave him a terribly professional air. Then, being competently clothed, Peter and Retta set out to master the machine.

They practised shyly, towards dusk, in the quiet lanes around Barloan, and they fell off in an amusing way quite a lot.

Oh! It was great fun. Retta, in her bloomers, was extremely fetching; Peter liked to lift her up as, red-cheeked and giggling, she sprawled gracefully in the dust.

They had their courtship all over again. And when finally, defying all laws of gravitation, they spun round Barloan Toll without a single wobble, they agreed that never before had life been so thrilling for them both.

Peter, significantly producing a newly-purchased road map, decided that on Sunday they would have their first real run.

It dawned fine that Sunday; the sky was open and the roads were dry. They set off, Peter bowed dauntlessly over the front handlebars, Retta manfully pedalling her weight behind. They bowled down the High Street, conscious of admiring, yes, even of envious stares.

Ting-a-ling, ting-ting, went their little bell. A great moment. Ting-a-ling, ting-ting! They swung left – steady, Retta, steady – over the bridge; put their backs into the Knoxhill ascent, then dipped over the crest of the Lea Brae.

Down the Brae they went, faster, faster. The wind whistled past them. Never had flight been swifter than this.

It was great, it was glorious, but, heavens! It was awful quick! Far, far quicker than either had bargained for.

From a momentary exaltation, Retta turned pale.

'Brake, Peter, brake!' she shrieked.

Nervously he jammed on the brakes, the tandem shuddered, and Retta nearly went over his head. At that he lost his wits completely, loosed the brake altogether, and tried to get his feet out of the pedal clips.

The machine, from skidding broadside on, took the bit between its teeth and shot down the hill like a rocket gone mad.

At the foot of the brae was Sam Forrest.

Sam had been down looking for drift on the Lea Shore; that, indeed, was one of Sam's two occupations, his other being to support with great industry the corner of the Fitter's Arms.

Actually, Sam was so seldom away from the Fitter's Arms that it never was in any real danger of falling down.

The plain fact is that Sam was a loafer, a big, fat, boozy ne'er-do-well, with a wife who did washing and a houseful of clamorous children who did not.

Sam, with an air at once fascinated and bemused, observed the bicycle approach. It came so quick he wondered for a second if he were seeing right. Saturday, the night before, had been a heavy night for Sam, and his brain was still slightly fuddled.

Down-down-down whizzed the tandem.

Peter, with a face frozen to horror, made a last effort to control the machine, collided with the kerb, shot across the road and crashed straight into Sam.

In point of fact, it hit him fair in the backside as he turned to run. There was a desperate roar from Sam, a loud clatter as the pieces of the machine dispersed themselves, followed by a long silence.

Then Retta and Peter picked themselves out of the ditch. They looked at each other incredulously as if to say – It's impossible; we're not really alive.

Stupefied, Peter grinned feebly at Retta, and Retta, who felt like fainting, smiled weakly in return. But suddenly they recollected!

What about Sam? Ah, poor Sam lay groaning in the dust. They rushed over to him.

'Are you hurt?' cried Peter.

'I'm dead,' he moaned. 'Ye've killed me, ye bloody murderers.'

Terrible silence, punctuated by Sam's groans. Nervously Peter tried to raise the fallen man, who was quite double his weight.

'Let me be! Let me be!' Sam roared. 'You're tearin' me to bits.'

Retta went whiter than ever.

'Get up, Sam, do.' she implored. She knew him well, having refused him credit the week before.

But Sam wouldn't get up. The slightest attempt to raise him sent him into the most terrible convulsions, and his big beefy legs seemed now no more able to support him than watery blancmange.

By this time Retta and Peter were at their wits' end; they saw Sam a mutilated corpse and themselves standing palely in the dock while the Judge sternly assumed the black cap.

However, at this moment help arrived in the shape of Rafferty's light lorry.

Rafferty, the butter and egg man, to whom Sunday – with early Mass over – was as good as any other day, had been down at Ardfillan collecting eggs. And with his help, Sam was hoisted up amongst the eggs and driven to his house in the Vennel.

A few eggs were smashed in the process, but Peter and Retta didn't mind; they would pay, they protested passionately. Oh, yes, they would pay; nothing mattered so long as Sam got safely back.

At last Sam was home and in his bed surrounded by his curious progeny, sustained by the shrill lamentations of his wife.

'The doctor,' she whined, 'we'll need the doctor!'

'Yes, yes,' stammered Peter. 'I'll fetch the doctor!'

What had he been thinking of? Of course they must have the doctor! He tore down the dirty steps and ran for the nearest doctor like the wind.

At that time Dr Snoddy had not married the wealthy Mrs Innes, nor removed to the salubrious Knoxhill. His premises still stood, quite undistinguished, in the High Street adjacent to the Vennel. And it was Snoddy who came to Sam.

Sam lay on his back with his mouth open and his eyes closed. No martyr suffered more than did Sam during the doctor's examination.

Indeed, his groans drew a crowd round the house, in the belief that he was once again leathering his wife, though when the truth emerged the sympathy for Sam was enormous.

The doctor, while puzzled, was impressed by Sam's condition – no bones broken, no internal injuries that he could find, but something seemingly wrong for all that, the patient's agony was so manifest.

Snoddy was a small, prosy, pompous man with a tremendous sense of his own dignity, and finally, with a great show of knowledge, he made the ominous pronouncement:

'It's the spine!'

Sam echoed the words with a hollow groan. And horror thrilled through to Peter's marrow.

'Ye understand,' he whispered, 'it was us to blame; we take full responsibility. He's to have everything that's needed. Nothing's too good for him! Nothing!'

That was the beginning. Nourishment was necessary for the invalid, good strong nourishment. Nourishment was provided. Stimulant – Peter saw that the brandy was the very best. A proper bed – Retta sent round the bed herself. Towels, linen, saucepans, jellies, tea, nightshirts, sugar, they all flowed gently to the sick man's home. Later – some tobacco – to soothe the anguished nerves. And a little money too, since Mrs Forrest, tied to Sam's bedside, could not do her washing as before.

'Run round with this to Sam's,' became the order of the day.

Snoddy of course was calling regular as the clock.

And finally there came the day when, taking Peter aside, he articulated the fatal word 'paralysis'. Sam's life was saved, but Sam would never use his legs again.

'Never!' Peter faltered. 'I don't understand!'

Snoddy laughed his pompous little laugh.

'Just watch the poor fellow try to walk – then ye'll understand.'

It was a staggering blow for Peter and Retta. They talked it over late into the night – over and over and over. But there was no way out.

Retta wept a little, and Peter was not far off tears himself, but they had to make up their minds to it; they had done it, they alone must foot the bill, and Sam, of course, Sam, poor soul, his lot was far far worse than theirs.

A bath-chair was bought – Peter sweated when he saw the price – and Sam and his chair assumed their place in Levenford society.

On the level his eldest son, aged fourteen, could wheel him easily enough and 'down to the emporium' became a favourite excursion of Sam's. He would sit outside the shop, basking in the sun, sending in for tobacco, or a pie, or dried prunes, of which he was particularly fond. Now, indeed, there was no talk of refusing him credit. Sam's credit was unlimited, and he had his weekly dole from Peter as well.

When the nine days' wonder of the wheeled chair subsided, Levenford forgot. Hardly anyone noticed it when Peter and Retta relinquished the cosy little Barloan house, and moved into the rooms above the shop, when the little girl gave up her music lessons, and the boy suddenly left the academy to earn a wage in Gillespie's office.

The grey creeping into Peter's hair and the worried frown deepening on Retta's brow, evoked little interest and less sympathy.

As Sam himself put it with a pathetic shake of his head: 'They have their legs, at any rate!'

This was indeed the very phrase which Sam employed to Finlay on that fateful evening on the first July.

It was a fine, bright evening, with the view looking its very best. Finlay stood on the brae, trying to find tranquillity in the sight.

Tonight his surgery had worried him, the day had been troublesome, and his mood, taken altogether, was cantankerous.

At length the soothing quiet of the scene sank into him; he lit his pipe, beginning to feel himself at peace. And then, over the crest of the brae, came Sam in the wheeled chair.

Finlay swore. The history of Sam and Peter had long been known to him, and the sight of the big, bloated fellow, fastened like a parasite on the lean and hungry Lennie, goaded him immeasurably.

He watched them draw near, irritably observing Peter's physical distress, and, as they reached the summit, he made a caustic comment on the difficulties of propelling inert matter uphill.

'He canna complain,' sighed Sam. 'He has his legs, at any rate.'

And then, instinctively, Finlay looked at Sam's legs as they lay snugly in the long, wheeled chair. They were, strangely, a remarkably stout pair of legs. Fat, like the rest of Sam, bulging Sam's blue serge trousers.

Peculiar, thought Finlay, that there should be no atrophy, no wasting of these ineffectual limbs. Most peculiar! He stared and stared at Sam's legs with a growing penetration, and then, with a terrible intentness, he stared at the unconscious man. My God! he thought all at once. Supposing – supposing all these years—

And suddenly, as he stood beside the wheeled chair on the edge of the brae – suddenly with a devilish impulse, he took the flat of his boot and gave the chair a frightful push.

Without a word of warning the chair shot off downhill.

Peter stood gaping at the bolting chair like a man petrified by the repetition of dreadful history; then he let out a nervous scream.

Sam, roaring like a bull, was trying to control the chair. But the chair had no brakes. It careered all over the road, dashed at frantic speed into the hedge, overturned, and shot Sam bang into a bed of nettles. For two seconds Sam was lost to view in the green sea of the stinging nettles; then, miraculously, he arose.

Cursing with rage, he scrambled to his feet and ran up to Finlay.

'What the hell!' he shouted, brandishing his fists, 'what the hell did ye do that for?'

'To see if ye could walk!' Finlay shouted back, and hit Sam first.

Peter and Retta have returned to the Barloan house. The wheeled chair is sold, and Sam is back at his old job – supporting the corner of the Fitter's Arms. But every time Finlay drives past he curses and spits upon the ground.

Pantomime

As a rule, Levenford saw little of the theatre.

At the annual Fair, the Bostons and Roundabouts were usually accompanied by a canvas 'geggie', where, in an atmosphere of naphtha smoke and orange peel, you could, for twopence, see 'The Girl Who Took the Wrong Turning', or 'The Murder in the Red Barn'.

At the other pole, of course, stood the Mechanics' Concerts. There, on Thursday nights during the winter season, a bevy of refined ladies and gentlemen entertained an equally refined audience to songs and readings.

'Mr Archibald Small will now give—'

Whereupon Mr Archibald Small would advance, blushing, in squeaky boots and a hired evening dress, and sing – 'Thora! Speak ag-hain tu mee!'

Between these extremes Levenford went dry of drama, and the stern spirit of the Covenanters was appeased.

Imagine then, the commotion when it became known early in December that a pantomime was coming to the Burgh Hall for the week beginning Hogmanay.

Pantomime! For the children of course! Yet it woke a thrill of interest in the austerest heart, and caused a perfect flutter amongst the burgh's amorous youth.

Even 'Doggy' Lindsay, the Provost's son, allowed his interest in the pantomime to be known – a superior interest, naturally; a rather sophisticated interest – for Doggy was a 'blood', the centre of a little coterie of 'bloods' who set a dashing fashion in dress and manners in the town.

He was a pasty-faced youngster, was Doggy, with a tendency to pimples, a loud empty laugh, and a tremendous heartiness of style – instanced by a maddening tendency to slap his intimates upon the back and address each boisterously as 'Old Man!'

'Brandy and splash, old man?' That, indeed, was Doggy's usual greeting, as he stood knowingly within the parlour of the Elephant and Castle. He wore bright shirts, effulgent cuff-links, and, in season, a racy topcoat with huge pockets and a collar that invariably rose up to Doggy's protruding ears.

He affected manly pipes with terrific curvatures, and rattled a heavy stick as he strode along. His knowledge of women was reputed to be encyclopaedic. And once he had kept a bulldog.

Actually, there was not an ounce of vice in Doggy. He suffered from a rich father, a doting, indulgent mother, and a weak constitution. Add the fatuous desire of the small town masher to be thought the most devilish of rake-hells, and you have Doggy at his worst.

The pantomime arrived, a number five company from Manchester, which had wandered to these northern wilds in the hope of putting Cinderella over on the natives. But the natives had been less amenable than expected.

In Paisley, not bouquets but tomatoes had rained on Samuels' Touring No. 5, and in Greenock there had been a deluge of ripe eggs. So, by the time Levenford was reached, the morale of the mummers was wilting.

The comedian wore a slightly tarnished look; the chorus had 'the jumps'; and Mr Samuels was secretly considering urgent business which might call him suddenly back to Manchester.

Two days after the opening night in the Burgh Hall, Finlay met Doggy Lindsay in the High Street.

''Lo, old man!' cried Doggy.

He rather cultivated Finlay as one versed in the occult mysteries of the body. Doggy's was a simple mind whose libido expressed itself in yearnings for an illustrated anatomy book.

''Lo, old man! Seen the panto?'

144

'No!' said Finlay. 'Is it good?'

'Good!' Doggy threw back his head and roared with laughter. 'My God, it's awful! It's rotten, it's terrible, it's tripe! But for all that, Finlay, old man, it's a scream!'

He roared again with laughter, and taking Finlay's arm, demanded:

'Have ye seen Dandini?'

'No, no! I tell you I haven't been near the hall.'

'Ye must see Dandini, Finlay,' protested Doggy, with streaming eyes. 'Before God, ye must see Dandini! She's it, Finlay. The last word in principal boys. An old cab horse in tights. Ye ken what I mean. Saved from the knacker, and never called me mother. Fifty if she's a day, dances like a ton of bricks, and a voice ye couldn't hear below a bowl – oh, heaven save me, but the very thought of her puts me in hysterics.'

He broke off, quite convulsed by merriment; but, mastering himself, he dried his eyes and declared:

'Ye must see her, old man. 'Pon my soul, you must. It's a treat not to be missed. I've front row seats for every night of the show. Come along with me tonight. Peter Weir is coming too, and Jackson of the Advertiser!'

Finlay looked at Doggy with mixed feelings; sometimes he liked Doggy quite a lot, sometimes he almost loathed him.

On the tip of his tongue lay a refusal of Doggy's invitation, but somehow a vague interest, call it curiosity if you wish, got the better of him. He said rather curtly:

'I might drop in if I have time. Keep a seat for me in any case.' Then, refusing Doggy's effusive offer of a 'brandy and splash', he strode off to continue his calls.

That night Finlay did 'drop in', having first sounded Cameron on the propriety of the act. Cameron, regarding him quizzically, had assented.

'Away if ye like, and I'll finish the surgery. Ye'll be doing no harm if ye keep young Lindsay out of mischief. He's a brainless loon – but I'll swear there's good in him.'

The pantomime had scarcely begun when Finlay slipped into his seat, yet already the audience, composed chiefly of young apprentices from the yard, was giving it 'the bird'.

It was actually a poorish show, but acute nervousness on the part of the performers made it quite atrocious. And there was, of course, Dandini–Dandini, principal boy the second – Dandini, mirror of fashion, echo of the court, dashing satellite of the Prince!

Finlay looked at his programme; Letty le Brun, she called herself. What a name! And what a woman. She was a big, raddled creature with a wasted figure – a hollow bosomed, gaunt-faced spectre, with splashes of rouge on her cheek-bones and palpable stuffing in her tights.

She walked without spirit, danced in a sort of lethargy. She was not called upon to sing one song. Indeed, when the chorus took up the refrain, she barely moved her lips. Finlay could have sworn she did not sing at all. But her eyes fascinated him – big blue eyes that must once have been beautiful, filled now with a mingled misery and contempt.

Every time she got the laugh, and it was often, those tragic eyes winced in that set and stoic face. It got worse as the show went on; whistling, catcalls, and finally jeers. Doggy was in ecstasy, squeezing Finlay's arm, rolling about helplessly in his seat.

'Isn't she a scream? Isn't she a turn? Isn't she the funniest thing since grandma?' as though she were some new star, and he the impresario who had discovered her.

But Finlay did not smile. Deep down in his being, something sickened as at the sight of a soul's abasement.

At last, amidst a hurricane of derisive applause, the final curtain fell. And Finlay could have cried out with relief. But Doggy was not finished – not, he assured them, by a long, long chop.

'We'll go round,' he informed them with a wink, 'behind the scenes.'

Something more subtle, some richer satire was in store for them than the crude spectacle of a fusilade of eggs.

Finlay made to protest, but they were already on their way –
Doggy, Jackson and young Weir. So he followed them along the
draughty stone corridors of the Burgh Hall, up a creaky flight of
steps, into the dressing-room of Letty le Brun.

It was a communal undressing-room of course, vaguely parti-
tioned, with torn wallpaper and walls that sweated, but most of
the company had already departed – glad enough, no doubt, to
scramble to their lodgings while they could.

But Letty was there, sitting at a littered table, slowly fastening
up her dress.

Closer inspection revealed how ravaged was her figure. She
had washed the greasepaint from her face, but two bright spots
still stood on her cheek-bones, and there were dark shadows
under those big blue eyes.

She inspected them dumbly.

'Well, boys,' she said at length, not without a certain dignity,
'what do you want?'

Doggy stepped forward, with a notable pretence of gallantry –
oh, he was a card right enough, was Doggy Lindsay!

'Miss le Brun,' said he, almost simpering, 'we've come round
to compliment you and to ask if you would honour us by coming
out to supper?'

Silence, while behind, young Weir struggled with a guffaw.

'I can't come out tonight boys. I'm too tired.'

'Oh, but Miss le Brun—' insisted Doggy, 'a little supper! Surely
an actress of your experience wouldn't be too fatigued.'

She took them all in with that sad and almost tranquil gaze.
She knows he's guying her, thought Finlay with a pang, and she's
taking it like a queen.

'I might come tomorrow night, if you cared to ask me.'

Doggy beamed.

'Capital! Capital!' he gushed, and he named the time and place.
Then, covering the ensuing pause in his customary brilliant style,
he flashed his gold cigarette-case at her.

But she shook her head.

'Not now, thanks.' Her lips made a little smile. 'I've got a smoker's cough.'

Another rather awkward pause. It was not turning out to be so funny as they expected. But Doggy rallied.

'Well, Miss le Brun, perhaps we'd better say au revoir. We'll expect you tomorrow night. And again congratulations on your marvellous performance.

She smiled again quietly as they went out.

On the following morning, across the breakfast table, Cameron tossed a note that had just come in, to Finlay. 'Ay!' he announced dryly. 'You'd better take this call, seeing you're so interested in the theatre.'

It was a note asking the doctor to call on Letty le Brun at her lodgings.

So it came about that Finlay went in the forenoon to No. 7 Church Street. He went early, impelled by a strange curiosity and a strange shame.

Something of this emotion must have shown in his face as he entered the room, for Letty smiled at him – almost reassuringly.

'Don't look so worried,' she said with less than her usual impassiveness. 'I wanted you to come. I found out about you when you'd gone. You were the only one who wasn't trying to make game of me.'

She was in bed, surrounded by a few things obviously her own – a photograph in an embossed silver frame, a crystal bottle of Florida water, a little travelling French clock that was now sadly battered but had once been good.

There was, indeed, a queer fastidiousness about the common room which she alone could have imparted to it. Finlay felt this deeply, and in his voice was a singular constraint as he asked her what he could do for her.

She motioned him to sit down, and for a moment lay back upon the pillow before she answered:

'I want you to tell me how long I've got to live.'

His face was a study. It might even have amused her. For she smiled faintly before going on.

'I've got consumption – sorry, I suppose you'd prefer me to say tuberculosis. I'd like you to listen to my lungs and tell me just how long I've got to put up with it.'

He could have cursed himself for his stupidity. He had been blind not to see it. Everything was there – the hectic flush, emaciation, the quickened breathing – everything.

Now there was no mystery in that strange pathetic lassitude of her performance on the night before. He rose hurriedly, and without a word took his stethoscope. He spent a long time examining her chest, though there was little need for lengthy auscultation, the lesions were so gross.

Her right lung was completely gone, the left riddled by active foci of the disease. When he had done he was silent.

'Go on,' she encouraged him. 'Don't be afraid to tell me.'

At last, with great confusion, he said:

'You've got perhaps six months.'

'You're being kind,' she said studying his face. 'You really mean six weeks.'

He did not answer. A great wave of pity swept over him. He gazed at her, trying to reconstruct that haggard face. She was not really old; illness, not years, had aged her. Her eyes were really extremely beautiful; she must once have been a lovely woman – manifestly a woman of taste. And now, mincing grotesquely in the tenth-rate pantomime, the butt of every provincial boor!

Despite himself, his thoughts came clumsily into words.

'You'll not bother about that supper tonight. Clearly you're not fit to go.'

'Oh, but I'm going! It's a long time since I've had a supper invitation. It's likely to be longer before I have another.'

'But don't you see—' he broke in.

'I see,' she answered. 'But if they like, let them have their little joke. That's what life is – just a little joke.'

She lay staring away through the window.

Then, as if recollecting herself, she took her purse from under the pillow and asked to know his fee.

Finlay coloured violently; her circumstances were so obvious. But there was tact in him, for all his rawness. He had the breeding to name the fee – it was not large – and he took it from her silently.

As he went out, she said: 'I shall see you tonight, I hope.'

All that day he couldn't get her out of his mind.

He found himself longing for the evening to come. He wanted to see her again, to help her if he could, to solve the baffling enigma she presented. Yet, in a sense, he dreaded the evening too. He feared to see her hurt by Doggy's insufferable ridicule.

Eleven o'clock came at last, the hour fixed for the supper party. The place was a little restaurant which had recently been opened in Church Street by a man named William Scott, a decent enough spot, frequented chiefly by commercial travellers, and known to Levenford inhabitants – perhaps because of a certain refinement in napery and glass – as the Swank.

Of course, the Swank was closed long before eleven, but Doggy, who knew everybody and everything, had induced Scott to set out a real good supper before a blazing fire in the smaller room.

It was, in fact, a very pleasant room with a good carpet and a piano – that was wheeled to a larger hall for dances – standing in the corner by the red plush curtains.

Finlay was early, but it wasn't very long before the others arrived, Doggy bursting in first with an air of great consequence, as if to announce that he escorted Royalty.

'Dandini,' he cried with a flourish. 'Here comes Dandini!'

Jackson and young Weir had evidently been primed to take their cue from Doggy, for with exaggerated deference they made way for Letty as she came up to the fire.

She was dressed very plainly in a dark blue dress, and, perhaps because she had rested all the afternoon, she looked better, certainly less haggard about the face.

They sat in to supper straight away; some excellent tomato soup, followed by a cold chicken and a fine jellied tongue.

Then Doggy, with a knowing air, popped the cork from a bottle of champagne and creamed Letty's glass magnificently.

'You drink champagne, of course?' he queried, with a wink at Weir.

She must have seen the wink but she ignored it. She replied simply:

'I used to like Veuve Cliquot. But I haven't tasted it for a very long time.'

'Come, come, Miss le Brun,' remarked Doggy. 'You can't mean that. You pantomime stars do yourselves pretty well, I imagine.'

With complete equanimity, she answered:

'No! We have perfectly atrocious food on tour. I haven't had a decent meal for weeks. That's why it's such a treat for me to have this.' She drank a little champagne.

'It's very good.'

'Aha, Miss le Brun,' mocked Doggy. 'It's well seen you're a connoisseur. You've been to many a supper party in your day. Come on, now! Tell us about all these midnight suppers you've been treated to.'

She looked dreamily into the fire, stretched out her hand as though to capture something of its warmth.

'Yes, I've been taken out to supper. To Romano's many times, and Gatti's, too, and the Café Royal.'

Doggy grinned. It was getting good at last; she was rising to the bait. In a minute he'd have her making speeches on the table.

With a leer he filled up her glass.

'That was when you performed in London?'

'Yes – in London.'

'Naturally you've played in – well – bigger pantomimes than this, Miss le Brun. An artiste of your genius—'

Finlay gritted his teeth at Doggy's rudeness, but before he could interfere she shook her head.

'No! This is my first attempt at pantomime,' – she shot a glance at Finlay – 'and my last.'

'Grand opera was perhaps your speciality?' suggested Doggy insiduously.

This time she nodded her head quietly.

'Yes. Grand opera.'

It was too much, oh, too much. Grand opera! They collapsed. Young Weir let out a guffaw, even the stolid Jackson sniggered. But Doggy choked back his laughter, for fear it should spoil the fun.

'Excuse them, Miss le Brun; a little champagne has gone the wrong way, I imagine. You were talking about opera, Miss le Brun – grand opera, Miss le Brun.'

She looked at him with those sad and tranquil eyes.

'You ought to stop calling me that silly name. It's only part of the pantomime. My real name is Grey – Letty Grey – a common name in Australia, where I come from, but it's the name I sang under.'

A curious little silence followed.

Then Jackson, who prided himself on his press memory, and carried the histories of celebrities in his head, let out a long, derisive whistle.

'Letty Grey! You're not trying to make out that you're *the* Letty Grey!'

'Don't believe me if you don't wish to.'

'But Letty Grey was famous. She came over from Australia to sing at Covent Garden. She sang "Isolde", "Aïda", "La Bohème". She had a triumph in "Madame Butterfly". Ten years ago Letty Grey was the toast of London.'

'And now she's here.'

Jackson stared at her incredulously.

'I don't believe you,' he declared bluntly. 'Letty Grey could sing. But you cannot sing for toffee.'

She emptied her glass. The champagne whizzing through her head had set an unaccustomed sparkle in her eyes, and her cheeks were deeply flushed.

'You've never heard me sing,' and there was a strange scorn in her tone. 'I haven't sung for years.'

She looked again at Finlay.

'He could tell you why. But I've a mind to sing now. Yes, I believe I will sing now. I'll sing to the gentlemen to pay for my supper.'

Now she was like a queen talking to a group of country bumpkins.

Doggy and Weir watched her with their mouths agape as she rose and walked over to the piano.

She opened the piano and let her fingers fall upon the keys. She paused – a long, dramatic pause. Then, throwing back her head, she filled her chest deeply and began to sing. She sang in German – one of Schubert's lieder. Her voice, uncertain for a moment, like an instrument long unused, swelled up in the little room with a purity that was divine.

Up, up, up went the voice, lifting them with it, thrilling the very air with its celestial harmony.

There fell a deathly silence when the song concluded.

Jackson stared like a man who has seen a ghost, and in young Weir's eyes was something cowed and bitterly ashamed. But she had forgotten them. Breathing quickly, bent a little forward, she sat at the piano with that dreamy distant look upon her face.

Then, as for herself alone, she sang again – the Love Song from 'Isolde'.

When she had finished, they still sat petrified. But at last Doggy stirred.

'My God!' he whispered humbly. 'That was marvellous.'

She turned to them, and with that half-smile upon her lips, said:

'Let me sing "Allan Water".'

Finlay, watching her face, the panting of her breath, jumped up from the table.

'No, no!' he cried. 'For God's sake, don't – don't sing any more.'

But she had begun. The moving words of the old Scots song flowed out with a pathos unbelievable:

> 'On the banks of Allan water,
> When the sweet spring time had fled.'

There were tears in Finlay's eyes; Doggy bowed his head upon his hands. But as they listened, spellbound, her voice, rising at the second verse to one last supreme note, broke suddenly and failed.

She swayed upon the seat; a tiny foam of scarlet came upon her lips. She looked at them rather stupidly; then, helplessly, she toppled sideways.

Finlay caught her before she fell. As the others rose clattering from the table, Jackson gasped:

'What's wrong?'

'Haemorrhage,' snapped Finlay. 'Bring some cold water, quick!'

He carried her to the sofa in the far corner of the room.

Doggy stood blubbering: 'It's all my fault! It's all my fault! Oh, God! What can I do for her?'

'Get a cab, you fool,' said Finlay. 'We must get her to the hospital.'

When they got her to the Cottage Hospital, she had recovered consciousness. Indeed, she rallied a little for the next few days, then slowly she began to sink. She lived altogether for three weeks more.

She was completely tranquil. She had no pain; she had everything she desired. Doggy saw to that. He paid for everything. He took her flowers every day – great masses of flowers which brought to her sunken features that faint, elusive smile.

He was with her when she died, and when he left the hospital that cold January afternoon, there was written on his face a strange new firmness.

★   ★   ★

Letty Grey lies buried in Levenford Cemetery.

Every week Doggy walks up there with his big stick and his pipe. He has lost his gush, his empty laugh, and something of his taste for brandy-splashes. But there is something more about him of the man.

The Sisters Scobie

That sharp September morning, while Finlay stood warming his boots at the fire before stepping into them, Janet entered the room with a slip of paper in her hand.

'There's a call,' she remarked, 'for Anabel Scobie.' And she held out the paper with a singular expression on her face.

He took the paper, a curious, narrow strip which somehow impressed him as having been cut carefully to pattern, and let his eye fall upon the angular, old-fashioned script—

Miss Beth Scobie requests the doctor kindly to call upon her sister Anabel, who is unwell.

'All right, Janet,' he nodded. 'I'll make a note of it.'

She stood for a moment, watching him make the entry in his book, burning, simply, to tell him something of the Scobies. The conflict between her imposed dignity and a frightful inclination to gossip made the corners of her down-drawn lips twitch – like a cat within sight of forbidden cream. Glancing up suddenly, he caught that thirsting look fixed on him. He laughed outright.

'Don't worry, Janet,' he said amiably. 'I've heard about the Scobies.'

She bridled.

'It's just as well. For not one thing would ye have heard about them from me.'

With her head in the air she turned on her heel, and in high indignation swept from the room.

The fact is that most folks in Levenford knew about the Scobies. They were sisters. Two maiden ladies, well past fifty, who occupied the little grey stone house at the end of Levenford Crescent.

It was an old-fashioned house situated beyond the Green, right on the edge of the Estuary, a wind-blown little house, with a wonderful view of ships and open water and a taste of salt, so to speak, washed into its very mortar.

It looked the house of a seafaring man, and so, indeed, it was.

Captain Scobie had built the house when – a widower with two grown daughters – he retired at long last from fighting the Atlantic gales. And he had built it snug and proper within sight and sound and smell of the sea he loved so well.

He was a short, trim, genial man, Abernethy Scobie, who had served his time in sail, stood his watch on the old paddle-pushers that made their clanking passage to Calcutta in the eighties, and come finally to command the *Magnetic*, the finest twin screw ship that ever left the Latta Yards for the southern trans-Atlantic route. That, in a sense, is ancient history, for Captain Scobie was dead these eighteen years past. But his daughters, Beth and Anabel, still lived on in the solid, spray-stung house which their father had built upon the Estuary shore.

Beth was the elder, a small, dark, dried-up woman with black, forbidding eyebrows and hair drawn tight as wire.

Anabel was two years younger, very like her sister, except that she was taller and more angular. She, had, however, a shade of colour in her cheeks, and sometimes, alas, when the wind blew sharp, in her nose as well.

They dressed alike – two regular old maids – the same style in shoes, gloves, hats, stockings of the same ply wool, and gowns always of black, with a thin white edging at the neck and cuff.

And they had the same expression – that bleak and vaguely hostile look which seems somehow to become ingrained in the faces of elderly spinsters compelled by usage to live too much together. For they were always together.

In fifteen years they had not once been apart. *But for fifteen years they had not spoken a single word to one another.*

This stupendous fact seemed incredible. But it was true. And like most incredibly stupendous facts it had arisen in the simplest, the silliest manner possible. It had arisen over Rufus.

Rufus was a cat, a large ginger cat belonging equally to the sisters, and equally esteemed by them. Every evening they took in turn the duty of calling Rufus from the back garden, where, like a sensible cat, he habitually promenaded before stretching himself luxuriously upon the kitchen hearth to sleep.

'Rufus! Rufus! Here, here!' Anabel would call one night. And on the next Beth, not to be thought copying her sister, would exclaim—

'Pussy, pussy! Here, Rufie, here!'

It went like clockwork until that fatal night of fifteen years ago. Then Beth, glancing up from her knitting, or it might have been her crochet, towards the clock inquired—

'Why haven't you called Rufus, Anabel?'

To which Anabel replied, without rancour—

'Because it isn't my turn. I called him last night.'

'But no!' Beth countered. 'I called him last night.'

'You did not, Beth Scobie.'

'I did!'

'You did not!'

'Allow me, but I did! I remember because he would keep hiding in the currant bushes.'

'That was the night before! I remember fine you telling me when you came in. It wasn't last night.'

'I beg your pardon, but it was last night.'

Then they both lost their tempers and went at it hammer and tongs. Finally Beth determinedly demanded:

'For the last time, Anabel, I ask you. *Will* you go and call the cat?'

And Anabel, with equal determination, hissed:

'It is *not* my turn to call the cat.'

Whereupon they both rose and went to bed. Neither of them called the cat.

All might have been well, but for the fact that Rufus, finding himself so unexpectedly at large, took it into his stupid feline head to wander.

Next morning Rufus was lost – not only lost, but lost beyond recall. And when it was known that Rufus was irreparably gone, Beth turned to her sister like a viper that has been trampled on.

'I will never,' she declared with concentrated venom, 'speak to you again as long as I live until you go down upon your bended knees and beg my pardon for what you have done.'

'And I,' Anabel retorted passionately, 'will never speak to *you* again as long as I have breath in my body, until *you* go down on *your* bended knees and beg pardon of me.'

Such vows have been taken before in the course of family squabbles! But the strange thing about this vow was that the Scobie sisters kept it; and even stranger perhaps the manner in which they kept it.

It fell out, then, at half-past eleven on this particular day when he got word to call on Miss Anabel, that Finlay walked up the white pebbled path of the Scobie house and knocked discreetly at the Scobie door, Beth Scobie opened the door herself.

Though the sisters were comfortably off, with an income derived from a joint annuity, they prided themselves in keeping no maid.

'Please to step this way, doctor,' Beth observed, showing him into the front parlour, a freezingly clean apartment with horsehair furniture, marine paintings on the walls, some excellent Satsuma china in a case, and a heavy marble presentation clock ticking solemnly upon the mantelpiece.

In the same colourless voice she added: 'I'll see if my sister is ready for you yet.'

Then she left the room.

When she had gone Finlay turned instinctively to warm himself at the fireplace. It was blank, however, of any cheerful blaze – the grate hidden behind an incised lacquer screen. But on the mantelpiece beside the clock his eye was arrested by a neat pile of paper slips, each exactly like the slip upon which had been written the message asking him to call. Beside the little pile of papers lay a pencil.

Finlay stared at the papers and the pencil, while a dim understanding worked to the surface of his mind.

Suddenly he observed two crumpled slips lying in the grate behind the screen, and, impelled by an odd curiosity, he stooped and picked them up.

On the first, written in pencil, were the words—

I don't feel well, please send for the doctor, and on the second: *A pack of nonsense fancying you're ill.*

Finlay dropped the papers in amazement. So that, he thought, that's the way they've worked it all the time.

Just then a noise made him swing round. Beth stood before him at the door.

'My sister will see you,' she declared evenly. And he could have sworn she was crushing a slip of paper in her palm.

He went upstairs, at her direction, for she did not follow, and entered one of the two front bedrooms.

Anabel lay in the big brass bed covered by a beautifully worked bedspread. The linen of the sheets and pillows was very fine. And Anabel herself was far from being fine.

It took Finlay just five minutes to discover that she had influenza – the early symptoms – and that she was going to have it pretty bad.

Her skin was dry, her temperature on the rise, her pulse bounding; and already there was a suspicious roughness creeping round the bases of her lungs.

She submitted grimly to his examination. She had none of that skittish modesty which so often besets the elderly unmarried female. And at the end she went straight to the point.

'I'm going to be ill, then, by the look of ye?'

'You've got influenza,' he admitted. 'There's a regular epidemic of it about. It's sharp while it lasts, but not serious.'

At his evasion she laughed shortly, which brought on her cough.

'I mean,' he amended, colouring, 'you'll be over it in a week or ten days.'

'Of course I will!'

'In the meantime, I'd better get you a nurse.'

'You'll do no such thing, doctor.'

The dour look settled back in her deep-set eyes.

'My sister will look after me. She'll make a handless nurse, no doubt, poor creature, but I maun just put up with that.' Pause. 'She's stubborn, ye know, doctor. Stubborn to a fault and quarrelsome, forbye. But I've tholed it in health. And I can thole it in sickness.'

There was nothing more to be said to Anabel. He folded his stethoscope, snapped his bag shut, and went downstairs.

In the parlour, amongst the horsehair furniture, the marine paintings, the Satsuma china, and the little pile of papers by the monumental clock, he addressed himself to Beth.

'Your sister has influenza.'

'Influenza! Is that all? Well, well! Anabel was aye one to be sorry for herself.'

'Don't you understand?' he exclaimed curtly. 'Your sister is definitely ill. She'll be worse before she's better. Much worse. This influenza is no joke. It's the real pulmonary type she's got. She'll want a lot of looking after.'

Beth made a slight ironic gesture.

'I can look after her. And look after her well. Though I've little doubt she'll make a poor, poor, patient. She's stubborn, ye know, doctor. Stubborn to a fault and quarrelsome, forbye. What I've had to endure ye wouldn't credit. But sin I've endured it from her when she was well, faith, I can endure it now she's ill.'

He stared at her astounded. At length he said:

'There's just one difficulty.' He paused to clear his throat awkwardly. 'You and your sister don't appear to be on speaking terms. You can't possibly nurse her under these conditions.'

She smiled her gaunt, humourless smile.

'We'll manage! We've managed well enough these fifteen years!'

There was a silence. With a shrug of his shoulders Finlay accepted the situation.

He began to explain at some length what had to be done. Having made his instructions clear he took his hat and left the house.

So Beth began to nurse her sister in that same stubborn silence which had lasted fifteen years. At the beginning it was easy enough.

As yet Anabel was not acutely ill, and notes flew between the sisters like swallows on the wing. Propped up on her pillows, the invalid would scrawl:

'Give me beef-tea instead of gruel tonight.'

And the nurse with a frigid face would countersign: 'Very well. But you must take your medicine first.'

Ludicrous, of course! But ludicrous or no, the habits of fifteen years are hard to break.

Late on the second afternoon, however, something went wrong with the well-tried system.

Anabel was worse; much worse; for several hours she had been lying still, looking very queer. Now darkness was falling, and sunk back on the bed with flushed cheeks and unseeing eyes, she lapsed into a light delirium.

Nonsense it was she talked, like scraps of words and phrases, but suddenly, in the midst of that rambling incoherence, she spoke – spoke to her sister. Out came the words—

'I'm that thirsty, Beth. Please give me a drink.'

Beth started as though a lance had pierced her.

Anabel had spoken to her – after all these years – Anabel had spoken first. Her face, her whole body quivered. She pressed her hand against her side. Then she gave a cry.

'Yes, Anabel, I'll give you a drink. Look! Here it is—' And she rushed forward to the bed, supported her sister's head with her arm, offered her the cup.

The sound of Beth's voice seemed to stir Anabel from her unconsciousness. She looked at her and smiled.

At that Beth began to sob, harsh dry sobs that tore and racked her narrow bosom.

'I'm sorry, Anabel,' she wept. 'I'm dreadfully sorry. It's been all my fault. And all about nothing.'

'Maybe it was my fault,' Anabel whispered. 'Maybe it was my turn to call him.'

'No, no,' Beth sobbed. 'I'm thinkin' it was mine.'

That night when Finlay called he found Beth waiting for him in the parlour. All her grimness had gone, and in its place there stood a real anxiety.

'Doctor,' she asked straight away. 'My sister's worse. You don't think – you don't think she's not going to get better?'

He studied the marine painting on the opposite wall – the *Magnetic* passing the Tail o' the Bank.

'I think she'll get over it,' he said eventually. 'With a bit of luck, you know.'

'She's got to get over it,' Beth cried hysterically. 'Don't you understand, doctor – we've made it up. This afternoon she spoke to me.'

And without warning she burst into tears.

In spite of himself Finlay was moved, moved by those tears – so foreign to this hard nature, they were like waters struck miraculously from barren rock.

He saw as something strangely beautiful the reconciliation of the two sisters, two crabbed and arid beings who had turned a trifling quarrel into such savage animosity, and linked their lives by speechless hatred.

With sudden poetic vision he reflected – if only he could save Miss Anabel, how marvellous to see the unfolding of these warped, malignant cords, the rebirth of affection, the progression of these twin natures into a rich and generous old age.

And such was the intensity of the thought that he declared aloud:

'We've got to save her!'

But it was not easy.

The days slipped in, and Anabel hovered between delirium and reason, her fever rising and falling, her pulse flickering feebly at the wrist, her strength gradually failing.

The infection ravaged her. She seemed to verge upon a secondary pneumonia which could have ended everything. That, at least, was Finlay's fear.

At times he almost despaired of her, her crisis was so long delayed. But she was tough, her fibre fashioned of a stern material. She lasted bravely. And she lacked for nothing.

Beth nursed her devotedly, wheedling her, coaxing her, humouring her with the utmost tenderness.

'Come away, my dear, and take your physic. Try some more of this nice chicken tea. This blackcurrant jelly should ease your cough.'

At last the reward came; reward for Finlay's vigilance and Beth's self-sacrificing care. A full fourteen days after the first day of her illness Finlay was able to pronounce that Anabel would recover.

At the news Beth sank down beside the bed and buried her head in the pillow beside her sister.

'Thank God!' she sobbed. She was overwrought from anxiety and loss of sleep. 'Thank God, you're to be spared to me. I don't know what I'd have done without you.'

From that moment Anabel progressed rapidly towards recovery. Perhaps because the acute period of her illness had been prolonged, her convalescence was extraordinarily swift.

In ten days she was able to be up in her room, to sit by the window and watch the fascinating procession of ships as they stole up or down the Firth.

In a fortnight she was downstairs, in another week she was able to go out. And at the end of the month Finlay proclaimed her as good as new.

'Indeed, ye're right, doctor,' she affirmed with a self-satisfied smile. 'To tell you the truth I feel better than I did before I was taken ill.'

He smiled back at her as he took his departure.

'I'll look in just once again before I finish with you. Say in a week or ten days. Will that suit you?'

'It'll suit me fine, doctor,' she returned primly.

When he had gone she continued swaying herself gently backwards and forwards in the rocking-chair.

'He's a nice young fellow that,' she ruminated amiably. 'A nice young lad he is. Mind you, though, when all's said and done, I wouldna go so far as to say 'twas him that saved me.'

She paused significantly.

'No, no! What really gave me the turn was you speakin' to me like ye did.'

Another pause, vaguely triumphant.

'Ye see – the very idea that you had given in, Beth – speakin' first like that – bad as I was – fair uplifted me.'

Beth sat up on the sofa, a little flush colouring her cheek. 'What are ye talkin' about, my dear? It was you, Anabel, who spoke to me. "Give me a drink" says you as plain as I'm speakin' to ye now.'

'No, no,' Anabel gently shook her head. 'I mind fine how it was. Over ye came to my bedside and knelt down. Then, with tears in your eyes, ye said – " 'Twas all my fault, Anabel, dear. I've been to blame for everything." '

'What!' threw out Beth, stiffening in every limb, glowering at her sister from beneath those black brows of hers.

'Ay,' tittered Anabel. 'And you even said ye'd been wrong all along. "'Twas my turn," says you. "It really was my turn to call the cat." '

'It's not true!' shouted Beth.

'Eh? What's that?' exclaimed Anabel, stopping her rocking and slowly reddening.

'It's not true,' Beth repeated, viciously. 'It was you yourself said you were mistaken. You admitted it was your turn to call the cat.'

'I did nothing of the kind.'

'You did so.'

'I did not. It was *not* my turn to call the cat.'

'It *was* your turn.'

'It was *not*.'

On they went. On, on – right to the bitter, inevitable end.

And so, when Finlay called at the end of the week, silence reigned once more between the Scobie sisters. Beth and Anabel were passing notes exactly as they had done for fifteen years.

He went out of the house, stupefied, pressing his head between his hands. Then – after the manner of Cameron – he invoked the high heavens above.

'My God! If one of these auld deevils takes ill again I'll see she doesn't recover – if I've got to poison her myself.'

Wife of a Hero

For days Levenford had talked of nothing but the match. Of course they were always 'daft on football' in these parts. They had the tradition, you see. In the good old days, when centre-forwards wore side whiskers and the goalie's knickers buttoned below the knee, Levenford had been a team of champions.

That they had languished since those Homeric triumphs – languished to a low place in the Second League – was as nothing. Levenford was still Levenford. And now, in the first round of the Scottish Cup, they had drawn the Glasgow Rovers at home.

The Glasgow Rovers – top of the First Division – crack team of the country – and at home!

In the shipyards, the streets, the shops; in every howff from the Philosophical right down to the Fitter's Bar, the thrill of it worked like madness.

Total strangers stopped each other at the Cross.

'Can we do it?' the one would gasp. And the other, with real emotion, would reply: 'Well! Anyhow we've got Ned!'

Ned Sutherland was the man they meant – Sutherland, the idol, the prodigy, the paragon! Sutherland, subject of Bailie Paxton's solemn aphorism – 'He has mair fitba' in his pinkie than the hale team has in their heids.'

Good old Sutherland! Hurray for Ned!

Ned was not young; his age, guarded like a woman's, was uncertain. But those in the know put Ned down at forty, for Ned, they wisely argued, had been playing professional football for no less than twenty years. Not in Levenford, dear, dear, no!

Ned's dazzling career had carried him far from his native town – to Glasgow first, where his debut had sent sixty thousand delirious with delight, and then to Newcastle, from there to Leeds, then down to Birmingham – oh, Ned had been everywhere, never staying long, mark you, but always the centre of attraction, always the idol of the crowd.

And then, the year before, after a short interval when all the big clubs – with unbelievable stupidity – ignored his 'free transfer', he had returned magnificently to Levenford while still, as he said, in his prime, to put the club back upon the map.

It cannot be denied that there were rumours about Ned, base rumours that are the penalty of greatness.

It was whispered, for instance, that Ned loved the drink, that Newcastle had been glad to see the last of him, and Leeds not sorry to watch him go.

It was a shame, a scandal, an iniquity – the lies that followed him about.

What matter if Ned liked his glass? He could play the better for it, and very often did.

What matter if an occasional drink gaily marked the progress of his greatness? If his wanderings had been prodigal, was he not Levenford's famous son?

Away with the slanderers! So said Levenford, for when Ned returned she took him to her heart.

He was a biggish man, was Ned, rather bald on the top, with a smooth pale face, and a moist convivial eye.

He had the look, not of a footballer, but rather of a toastmaster at a city banquet.

In his appearance he was something of the dandy; his suit was invariably of blue serge – neat, well brushed; on his little finger he wore a heavy ring with a coloured stone; his watch chain, stretched between the top pockets of his waistcoat, carried a row of medals he had won; and his shoes – his shoes in particular were polished till they shone.

Naturally Ned did not brush his shoes himself. Though most

of the Levenford team held jobs in the shipyard and the foundry, Ned, as befitting his superior art, did not work at all. The shoes were brushed by Ned's wife.

And here, with the mention of Mrs Sutherland, is reached the point on which everyone agreed.

It was a pity, an awful pity, that Ned's wife should be such a drag, such a burden on him – not only the wife but those five children of his as well. God! It was sickening that Ned should have tied himself up so young – that he had been forced to cart round the wife, and this increasing regiment of children upon his famous travels.

There, if you like, was the reason of his decline, and it all came back to the woman who was his wife.

As Bailie Paxton put it knowingly – with a significant gesture of distaste – 'Could she not have watched herself better?'

The plain fact is that Levenford held a pretty poor opinion of Mrs Sutherland, a poor dowdy creature with downcast eyes. If she had been bonny once, and some would have it so, Lord! she wasn't bonny now.

Little wonder if Ned was ashamed of her, and most of all on Saturday afternoons, when, emerging from obscurity, she actually appeared outside the football ground to wait for Ned.

Mind you, she never came to see the match, but simply to wait outside till Ned got his pay. To wait on the man for the wages in his pocket. Lord, wasn't it deplorable?

It must be admitted that some stood up for her. Once in the Philosophical, when this matter was discussed, Dr Cameron, who, strangely enough, seemed to like the woman, had sourly said:

'With five bairns to feed, she's got to steer him past the pubs – at least as many as she can!'

But then Cameron always was a heretic who held the queerest notions of things and folk. And Ned's popularity, as has been said, was far beyond the cranky notions of the few.

Indeed, as the day of the match gradually drew near, that popularity drew pretty near to glory.

Ned became a sort of god. When he walked down the High Street of Levenford, thumbs in his armholes, medals dancing, his smooth, genial smile acknowledging here, there, everywhere, they almost cheered him. At the Cross, he had a crowd about him – a crowd that hung on every word that passed those smooth convivial lips.

It was at the Cross too, that the memorable meeting took place with Provost Weir.

'Well, Ned, boy,' said the Provost, advancing his hand, affable as you like. 'Can we do it, think ye?'

Ned's eyes glistened. In no way discomposed, he shook the Provost's hand and solemnly delivered himself of that:

'If the Rovers win, Provost, it'll be over my dead body.'

One night, a week before the match, Mrs Sutherland came to the doctor's home.

It was late. The evening surgery was over. And, very humbly, Mrs Sutherland came into Finlay, whose duty it was to see cases after hours.

'I'm terribly sorry to trouble you, doctor,' she began, and stood still, a neat, poorly-dressed figure, holding her mended gloves in her work-worn hands.

She was a pretty woman, or rather once she had been a pretty girl. For now there was about her a faded air; a queer transparency in her cheek and in her look, something so strained and shrinking, it cut Finlay to the quick.

'It's foolish of me to have come,' she said again, then stopped.

Finlay, placing a chair beside his desk, asked her to sit down.

She thanked him with a faint smile.

'It's not like me to be stupid about myself, doctor. I really should never have come. In fact, I've been that bothered making up my mind I nearly didn't come at all.'

A hesitating smile; he had never seen anything so self-effacing as that smile.

'But the plain truth is I don't seem to be seeing out of one of my eyes.'

Finlay laid down his pen.

'You mean you're blind in one eye?'

She nodded, then added: 'My left eye.'

A short silence fell.

'Any headache?' he asked.

'Well – whiles they come pretty bad,' she admitted.

He continued to question her, as kindly and informally as he could. Then, rising, he took his opthalmoscope, and darkened the surgery to examine her eyes.

He had some difficulty in getting the retina. But at last he had a perfect view. And, in spite of himself, he stiffened.

He was horrified. He had expected trouble – certainly he had expected trouble – but not this.

The left retina was loaded with pigment which could only be melanin. He went over it again, slowly, carefully – there was no doubt about it.

He turned up the light again, trying to mask his face.

'Did you have a blow in the eye lately?' he inquired, not look-ing at her, but watching her reflection in the overmantel.

He saw her colour painfully, violently.

And she said too quickly: 'I might have knocked it on the dresser – I slipped, last month, I think it was.'

He said nothing, but he tried to compose his features into something reassuring.

'I'd like Dr Cameron to see you,' he declared at length. 'You don't mind?'

She fixed her quiet gaze on him.

'It's something bad, then,' she said.

'Well,' he broke off helplessly – 'we'll see what Dr Cameron says.' Wishing to add something but unable to find the words, very lamely he left the room.

Cameron was in his study, smoothing the back of a fiddle with fine sandpaper, humming his internal little tune.

'Mrs Sutherland is in the surgery,' Finlay said.

'Ay,' Cameron answered, without looking up. 'She's a

nice body. I knew her when she was a lass, before she threw herself away on that boozy footballer. What's brought her in?'

'I think she's got a melanotic sarcoma,' Finlay said slowly.

Cameron stopped humming, then very exactly he laid down his fiddle. His gaze fastened upon Finlay's face, and stayed there for a long time.

'I'll come ben,' he said, rising.

They went into the surgery together.

'Weel, Jenny, lass, what's all this we hear about you?' Cameron's voice was gentle as though she were a child.

His examination was longer, even more searching than Finlay's. At the end of it a swift look passed between the two doctors, a look confirming the diagnosis, a look that meant the death of Jenny Sutherland.

When she had finished dressing, Cameron took her arm.

'Well, now, Jenny, would that husband of yours look in and see Finlay and me the morn?'

She faced him squarely, with the singular precognition of women who have known a life of trouble.

'There's something serious the matter with me, doctor.'

Silence.

All the fineness of humanity was in Cameron's face and in his voice as he answered:

'Something gey serious, Jenny.'

Now, strangely, she was more composed than he.

'What does it mean, then, doctor?'

But Cameron, for all his courage, could not speak the full, brutal truth.

How could he tell her that she stood there with her doom upon her, stricken by the most dreadful disease of any known to man, an unbelievably malignant growth which, striking into the eye, spreads through the body like flame – destroying, corrupting, choking! No hope, no treatment, nothing to do but face certain and immediate death!

Six days the least, six weeks the utmost, that now was the span of Jenny Sutherland's life.

'Ye'll have to go into hospital, lass,' he temporised.

But she answered quickly:

'I couldn't leave the bairns. And Ned – with the big match coming off – it would upset him too, oh, it would upset him frightful – it would never do at all, at all.' She broke off, paused.

'Could I wait, maybe, till after the match?'

'Well, yes, Jenny – I suppose if you wanted you could wait.'

Searching his compassionate face, something of the full significance of his meaning broke upon her. She bit her lip hard. She was silent. Then, very slowly, she said:

'I see, doctor, I see now. Ye mean it doesna make much difference either way?'

His eyes fell, and at that she knew.

The morning of the great match dawned misty, but before the forenoon had advanced the sun broke through magnificently. The town was quiet, tense with a terrific excitement.

As early as eleven o'clock, in the fear that they might not be able to secure a place, folks actually started to make their way to the ground. Not Ned, of course! Ned was in bed, resting, as he always did before each match. He had a most particular routine, had Ned, and this day more particular than any.

At ten Jenny brought him breakfast, a big tray loaded with porridge, two boiled eggs, a fine oatcake specially baked by herself. Then she went into the kitchen to prepare the special hough tea which, with two slices of toast, made up his light luncheon on playing days.

As she stood at the stove, Ned's voice came through complainingly:

'Fetch me another egg when ye bring in my soup. I'm thinkin' I'll need it before I'm finished.'

She heard, and made a little movement of distress; then she went into him apologetically.

'I'm sorry, Ned! I gave ye the last egg in the house this morning.'

He glared at her.

'Then send out for one.'

'If ye would give me the money, Ned.'

'Money! God! It's always money! Can't ye get credit?'

She shook her head slowly.

'Ye know that's finished long enough ago.'

'My God!' he exploded. 'But ye're a bonny manager. It's a fine state of affairs when I'm sent on to the field starvin'.'

'Bring in my soup quick then, and plenty of toast. Hurry up now or ye'll not have time to rub me. And for Heaven's sake keep those brats of yours quiet. They've near rung the lugs off me this morning.'

She went silently back to the kitchen and, with a warning gesture, stilled the two young children there – the others had been dressed quite early and sent, out of their father's way, to play on the green.

Then she brought him his soup, and stood by the bed while he supped it noisily. Between the mouthfuls he looked up at her and surlily demanded:

'What are ye glowerin' at – with a face that would frighten the French? God knows, I havena had a smile out of ye for the last four days.'

She found a smile – the vague, uncertain travesty of a smile.

'Lately I haven't been feeling too well, Ned, to tell you the truth.'

'That's right! Start your complaining and me on the edge of a cup-tie. Damnation, it's enough to drive a man stupid the way ye keep moanin' and groanin'.'

'I'm not complaining, Ned,' she said hurriedly.

'Then away and get the embrocation, and give us a rub.'

She brought the embrocation, and while he lay back, thrusting out a muscular leg, she began the customary rubbing.

'Harder! Harder!' he urged. 'Use yourself a bit. Get it below the skin.'

It cost her a frightful effort to complete the massage. Long before she had finished a sweat of weakness broke over her whole body. But at last he grunted:

'That'll do, that'll do. Though little good it's done me. Now bring in my shaving water, and see that it's boiling.'

He got up, shaved, dressed carefully. A ring came to the door bell.

'It's Bailie Paxton,' she announced. 'Come with his gig to drive you to the match.'

A slow smile of appreciation stole over Ned's face.

'All right,' he said. 'Tell him I'll be down.'

As he took his cap from the peg she watched him, supporting herself against the mantelpiece of the room. Sadness was in her face, and a queer wistfulness.

'I hope ye play well, Ned,' she murmured. How many times had she said these words, and in how many places? But never, never as she said them now!

He nodded briefly and went out.

The match began at half-past two, and long before the hour the park was packed to suffocation. Hundreds were refused admission, and hundreds more broke through the barrier and sat upon the touch-line.

The town band blared in the centre of the pitch, the flag snapped merrily in the breeze, the crowd was seething with suppressed excitement.

Then the Rovers took the field, very natty in their bright blue jerseys.

A roar went up, for two train loads of supporters had followed them from Glasgow. But nothing to the roar that split the air when Ned led his men from the pavilion. It was heard, they said, at Overton, a good two miles away.

The coin was spun; Ned won the toss.

Another roar; then dead silence as the Rovers kicked off. It was on at last – the great, the glorious game.

Right from the start the Rovers attacked.

They were clever, clever, playing a class of football which chilled the home supporters' hearts. They were fast, they worked the ball, they swung it with deadly accuracy from wing to wing.

And, as if that were not enough, Levenford were nervous and scrappy, playing far below their best, shoving the ball anywhere in a flurry. All but Ned!

Oh, Ned was superb! His position was centre-half, but today he was everywhere, the mainstay, the very backbone of the team.

Ned was not fast, he never had been fast, but his anticipation quite made up for that – and more.

Time after time he saved the situation, relieving the pressure on the Levenford goal by some astute movement, a side step, a short pass, or a hefty kick over the halfway line.

Ned was the best man on the field, a grand, a born footballer. He towered – this bald-headed gladiator in shorts – over the other twenty-one.

It had to come, of course – one man alone could not stem that devilish attack.

Before the half-time whistle blew, the Rovers scored. Not Ned's fault. A slip by the Levenford right-back, and quick as thought the Rovers' outside-left pounced on the spinning ball and steered it into the net.

Gloom fell upon the Levenford supporters. Had the score-sheet remained blank their team might have entered on the second half with some much-needed confidence. But now, alas, a goal down, and the wind against them – even the optimists admitted the outlook to be poor.

There was only one chance, one hope – Ned – and the memory of his emphatic words: 'If the Rovers win it'll be over my dead body.'

The second half began; and with it the precious moments started to run out. Levenford were more together, they gained two corners in quick succession; when attacked they rallied, and rushed the ball forward in the teeth of the wind. But the Rovers held them tight.

True, they lost a little of their aggression. Playing on a small pitch away from home, they faded somewhat as the game went on, and it almost seemed as if they were content to hold their one-goal lead.

Quick to sense this attitude of defence, the crowd roared encouragement to their favourites.

A fine frenzy filled the air, and spread from the spectators to the Levenford players. They hurled themselves into the game. They pressed furiously, swarming round the Rovers' goal. But still they could not score.

Another corner, and Ned, taking the ball beautifully, headed against the crossbar. A groan went up of mingled ecstasy and despair.

The light was fading now, the time going fast, twenty, ten, only five minutes to go.

Upon the yelling crowd a bitter misery was hovering, settling slowly. Defeat was in the air, the hopeless wretchedness of defeat.

And then, on the halfway line, Ned Sutherland got the ball. He held it, made ground, weaving his way with indescribable dexterity through a mass of players.

'Pass, Ned, pass!' shouted the crowd, hoping to see him make an opening for the wings.

But Ned did not pass. With the ball at his feet and his head down, he bored on, like a charging bull.

Then the crowd really roared – they saw that Ned was going in on his own.

The Rovers' left-back saw it too. With Ned inside the penalty area and ready to shoot, he flung himself at Ned in a flying tackle. Down went Ned with a sickening thud, and from ten thousand throats rose the frantic yell:

'Penalty! Penalty! Penalty!'

Without hesitation the referee pointed to the spot.

Despite the protestations of the Rovers' player, he was giving it – he was giving Levenford a penalty!

Ned got up. He was not hurt. That perfect simulation of frightful injury was part and parcel of his art. And now he was going to take the penalty himself.

A deathly stillness fell upon the multitude as Ned placed the ball upon the spot. He did it coolly, impersonally, as though he knew nothing of the agony of suspense around him. Not a person breathed as he tapped the toe of his boot against the ground, took a long look at the goal, and ran three quick steps forward.

Then bang! The ball was in the net.

'Goal!' shouted the crowd in ecstasy, and at the same instant the whistle blew for time.

Levenford had drawn. Ned had saved the match.

Pandemonium broke loose. Hats, sticks, umbrellas were tossed wildly into the air. Yelling, roaring, shrieking deliriously, the crowd rushed upon the field.

Ned was swept from his feet, lifted shoulder high and borne in triumph to the pavilion.

At that moment Mrs Sutherland was sitting in the kitchen of the silent house. She had wanted badly to go to the park for Ned; but the mere effort of putting on her coat had shown how useless it was for her to try.

With her cheek on her hand, she stared away into the distance. Surely Ned would come straight home today, surely he must have seen something of the mortal sadness in her face.

She longed desperately to ease the burden in her breast by telling him. She had sworn to herself not to tell him until after the match. But she must tell him now.

It was a thing too terrible to bear alone!

She knew she was dying; even the few days that had passed since her visit to Finlay had produced a rapid failure in her strength – her side hurt her, and her sight was worse.

An hour passed, and there was no sign of Ned. She stirred herself, got up, and put the two youngest children to bed. She sat down again. Still he did not come. The other children came in from playing, and from them she learned the result of the match.

Eight o'clock came and nine. Now even the eldest boy was in bed. She felt terribly ill; she thought, in fact, that she was dying.

The supper which she had prepared for him was wasted, the fire was out for lack of coal. In desperation she got up and dragged herself to bed.

It was nearly twelve when he came in.

She was not asleep – the pain in her side was too bad for that – and she heard the slow, erratic steps, followed by the loud bang of the door.

He was drunk, as usual; no, it was worse than usual, for tonight, treated to the limit, he had reached a point far beyond his usual intoxication.

He came into the bedroom and turned up the gas.

Flushed with whisky, praise, triumph, and the sense of his own ineffable skill, he gazed at her as she lay upon the bed; then, still watching her, he leant against the wall, took off his boots, and flung them upon the floor.

He wanted to tell her how wonderful he was, how marvellous was the goal he had scored.

He wanted to repeat the noble, the historic phrase he had coined – that the Rovers would only win over his dead body.

He tried sottishly to articulate the words. But, of course, he got it mixed. What he said was:

'I'm going – I'm going – to win – over your dead body.'

Then he laughed hilariously.

The Resolution that
Went Wrong

Though poets have assured us that man is the master of his fate, and novelists presented us with heroes who, having once set their teeth, grimly pursue their purpose to the bitter end – in reality things don't happen that way.

Life makes sport even of those gentlemen who so splendidly clench their molars; and, in spite of the poet's assertion to the contrary, the bloody head is almost always bowed.

It would be pleasant to exhibit Finlay in the best Victorian tradition – a strong and silent youth whose glittering pledges were never unfulfilled. But Finlay was human. Finlay had as much to put up with as you or I. And, often as not, circumstances played spillikins with his most fervent resolutions.

One afternoon, some months after he had come to Levenford, he was sitting in the surgery doing nothing. He was, in fact, quite glad to be doing nothing, for his morning round had been arduous, his lunch heavy and late.

With his hands in his pockets and his legs stretched out, he reclined in his chair feeling the soporific quality of Janet's suet dumplings steal pleasantly upon his senses.

His eyes had just closed, his head nodded twice, when the surgery bell jangled violently and Charlie Bell barged into the room. Standing on no ceremony, Charlie exclaimed:

'I'm wanting my mother's bottle!'

Charlie didn't say it like that; what he did say was, in the roughest dialect of Levenford, was— 'Am wan'in ma mither's bo-all.'

But Charlie's phonetics defy polite comprehension and must, with infinite regret, be sacrificed to more normal speech.

Finlay started in annoyance, partly at being disturbed, partly because he felt sure he had bolted the side door of the surgery, but most of all because of the rudeness of Charlie Bell.

He answered curtly:

'The surgery's shut at this hour.'

'Then, what way do you leave the door open?' Charlie retorted irritatingly.

'Never mind about the door. I'm telling you the surgery's closed. Call back again this evening.'

'Call back! Me!' Charlie jibed contemptuously. 'I'll call back twice for nobody.'

Finlay glared at Charlie – a thickset, burly youth of about twenty-five, with terrific shoulders, a pale, hard face, small, derisive eyes, and a close-cropped, brick-red head.

Well back on this bullet sailed a cap – known locally as a hooker – which he had not troubled to remove, and round his short neck a flamboyant red muffler was knotted carelessly.

Charlie's air was altogether careless; from his earliest days he had never given a damn – not for anyone, had Charlie. As a boy he had played truant, been flogged, and played truant cheerfully once again.

He had rung bells, broken windows, and led a juvenile gang, had frequently been drowned – almost – by bathing out of his depth in the River Leven.

If ever a stranger appeared in the High Street of Levenford, you may be sure Charlie's voice was the first to raise the ribald yell – 'Haw! Luk at his hat!' – or his boots, or his face – as the case might be.

He excelled at every game from football, played with a tin can in the gutter, to fighting – oh! fighting best of all.

Expulsion from school, when it inevitably arrived, was sheer delight. Then Charlie became a rivet-boy in the yard, where he heated rivets and tossed them to the holders-on aloft, not forgetting occasionally to drop one into the jacket of a colleague – a blazing pocket made glorious sport!

That was years ago, of course. Now Charlie was a riveter himself, acknowledged leader of the crowd who hung about Quay Corner, the owner of a whippet bitch called Nellie, a regular lad, known to his intimates as Cha, tougher, harder than the rivets that he battered into the iron hulls of ships.

And now, warming under Finlay's stare, Cha thrust his head forward pugnaciously.

'Luk at me! Go on and luk at me! But do ye hear what I'm saying? I'm askin' ye to make up my mother's bottle.'

'It's made up,' said Finlay in a hard voice, and made a movement over his shoulder towards the shelf. 'But you can't have it now. It's against our rules. You must call at the proper time.'

'Is that a fact?' declared Cha, breathing hard.

'Yes,' said Finlay heatedly. 'It's a fact. And when you do come again, perhaps you'd mend your manners just a trifle. You might remove your cap, for example—'

'Holy gee!' Cha laughed insolently. 'An' supposin' I don't?'

Finlay got up slowly. He was flaming.

Taking his time, he approached Cha.

'In that case we might teach you to do it,' he answered in a voice that trembled with anger.

'Aw. Shut yer face,' Cha answered flatly.

He stopped laughing to arrange his blunt features in a belligerent sneer.

'Do ye think *you* could teach me anything?'

'Yes,' shouted Finlay.

Clenching his fists he rushed in at Cha.

By all the ethics of fiction there should have been a great fight – a magnificent combat in which Finlay, the hero, finally knocked Cha, the villain, for a boundary and six runs.

What actually happened was quite different. One blow was struck – one sad, solitary punch.

Then, two minutes later, Finlay woke up in a sitting position with his back against the wall, dazed and slightly sick, with blood trickling stupidly from the corner of his mouth.

By this time Cha, with his mother's medicine in his pocket, and his cap more insolently atilt on his ginger head, was striding down the middle of Church Street, whistling a lively air.

Finlay sat where he was for a long time; then, with his head ringing dizzily, he picked himself up. Inside him everything was black and bitter as gall.

He burned at the memory of Cha's insolence, raged at his own hopeless inadequacy. He was young, strong, thirsting to batter Cha's ugly face, and yet – he groaned in a perfect agony of humiliation.

As he went to the sink and bathed his face, he set himself doggedly to puzzle the matter out. Cha could box, so much was obvious, while he couldn't box at all. He had never thought about it even, never come up against a situation like this. And then, like a lamb, he had walked straight into that devilish punch of Cha's.

Cha! How he hated him – the insolent swine! Something had to be done about it – something must be done about it. He couldn't lie down under an insult like that.

To this effect he swore a tremendous oath – after which he felt better.

Then he finished drying his face and, knitting his brows, he sat down at the desk to think.

The result of that profound self-communion was to bring together Finlay and Sergeant A. P. Galt.

Archie Galt was 'at the barracks'. Indeed, the worthy sergeant had been at the barracks, without appearing to grow one hour older, as long as most folks could remember.

A tall ramrod of man with a dried–up face, waxed moustache, tight trousers, and the chest of a prize pigeon, Archie Galt combined the duties of recruiting sergeant and Drill Instructor to the Volunteers.

Fitness was his fetish; he had muscles all over his body, muscles which stood out like billiard balls in the most unexpected places at the word of command.

And he had medals – medals for wrestling, for fencing, for boxing; indeed, rumour had it that in his day Archie had been runner-up in the army heavies.

Whether or not rumour lied is no matter; the fact remained that Archie certainly could box.

That first afternoon in the big, draughty drill hall he hit Finlay hard and plenty – not, mind you, as Cha had hit him, but calm, judicial blows which jolted and rattled and shook and searched everywhere, beautifully tempered blows, any one of which – had the worthy sergeant chosen to let go – would have stretched out Finlay in undignified oblivion.

And at the end of it, Galt pulled off his enormous gloves sadly.

'It's nae guid, sir,' he observed broadly – for Africa, India, and the whole Sudan had not conquered Archie's Doric. 'Ye'd better stick to your doctoring. Ye havena the first idea about handlin' yerself.'

'I can learn,' panted Finlay. The sweat streamed down his face; the last punch but one had taken him in the bread-basket and left him gasping. 'I must learn. I've got a reason—'

'Umph!' returned Archie, doubtfully twirling the waxed moustache.

'It's my first lesson,' Finlay doggedly persisted, gulping in the air. 'I'll stick in. I'll try hard. I'll come every day.'

The shadow of a grin broke over Archie's impassive face, and vanished instantly.

'Ye're no' feared,' he said noncommittally. 'And that's aye something.'

So the campaign began.

Finlay stopped the stroll he usually took of an evening to the Lea Brae. Instead, he came to the Drill Hall, entering quietly by the back way after dark and slipping quickly into a sweater and shorts.

Then he set to with the sergeant, learning the mysteries of the straight left, the cross, the counter, the hook, learning to feint, to use his feet, his head – learning everything the sergeant could teach him.

He took some awful hammerings. The more he learned the harder Archie hit him. He found how soft he was – he – Finlay – who had always prided himself upon his rude health.

He went into terrific training. He rose early, took a run and a cold bath before breakfast. Without a pang he cut out Janet's delicious pastry from his diet.

Deliberately, wickedly, he set out to make himself hard as nails.

Cameron, of course, sniffed something in the air. His eye, penetrating and caustic, often lingered upon Finlay when he passed a dish at table or came down in the morning with a slight thickening of his ear. But, though once or twice he nearly smiled, he said nothing. Cameron had the gift of silence.

By the end of one month Finlay was boxing well; by the end of three his improvement was really extraordinary. At the end of May he came on with a rush and, one night, having gone six fast three-minute rounds with Archie, he finished up with a terrific wallop to the jaw which rocked the sergeant to his heels.

'That's enough to be going on wi',' said Archie decisively, as he peeled off his gloves. 'I'm not taking no hammerin' from a laddie half my age.'

'What are you blethering about?' Finlay demanded, in wonder, with his gloves on his hips.

Archie took a slug at the water bottle, and professionally squirted it from the corner of his mouth. Then he allowed himself the pleasure of a smile.

'I mean just this, sir. I've taught ye all I can.' He grinned broadly. 'It's high time ye found somebody your own age to hit.'

'Am I any good, then?'

'Good! Man, ye're damned good! This last couple of weeks ye've come on like a house on fire. But I aye said ye had the makings of a bonny fechter.'

He paused, then, with a sudden curiosity, went on—

'Now that we're as guid as I can make ye, maybe ye'd be telling me something. What was that reason ye spoke about, if it's not too big a question?'

Finlay stood silent for a minute, then he told Archie about Cha. And again that slow grin broke over the sergeant's rugged face.

'Bell,' he declared. 'I ken him well – the bull-necked rowdy. He's a slugger if ever there was one. But you've got the measure of him now. Ye'll teach him a lesson he's long been needin'.'

'D'you honestly think so, Archie?'

'Man, I'm sure on it. I'm not sayin' but what it'll be a bonny fecht. But as I'm a sodjer I wouldna like to be in Cha Bell's shoes by the time ye've done wi' him.'

Finlay went home that night with determination in his eye. During those weeks of preparation he had somehow managed to keep the matter out of his mind, but now he knew himself to be fit and ready for the fray, all his black rage against Cha boiled up afresh.

The memory of the scene of the surgery stung him more bitterly. The recollection of the rare occasions when he had subsequently encountered Cha, of Cha's impudent stare crossing his own studiously detached gaze, of the shout of derisive laughter following him down the street, these burst on him with new violence and goaded him beyond the limit of his endurance.

As he strode up the drive of Arden House he thought wickedly: 'I'll make him pay. I'll take it out of him. Not another day will I wait. I've suffered long enough. Now I'm going to get my own back.'

In this mood he entered the hall, and there, oddly enough, on the slate which was hung specifically for this purpose, he found a call written up for Mrs Bell at the little house in Quay Side.

Odd, in a way, but not unusual, for Mrs Bell was something of a hypochondriac, and once a month or thereabouts Finlay was obliged to call and reassure her on the origin of some vague pain or indeterminate symptom.

It suited him down to the ground. He would visit the old woman tomorrow – which was Saturday – prescribe for her, and blandly leave word that Cha was to fetch the medicine from the surgery in the afternoon.

The same circumstances, the same time, the same place – but oh, how different the result! Finlay set his jaw hard. 'I'll give him medicine,' he thought viciously, 'I'll give him a dose he won't forget.'

The next day came, and Finlay made straight for No. 3 Quay Side the moment he was through his morning consultations. It was a lopsided, single-gabled, old-fashioned bit of a house perched right on the river front behind the Elephant and Castle, and it protruded slightly in the rambling row as if the pressure of its neighbours had squeezed it out of shape.

Mrs Bell met him at the door, her fat, round face pulled into an anxious frown.

'Oh, doctor, doctor,' she protested. 'It was last night I wanted ye to come and not this mornin'. What way did ye not come when I sent down word? I've been worried fair sick the livelong night.'

'Don't you worry now, Mrs Bell,' he reassured her. 'We'll soon put you to rights.'

'But it's no' me,' she wailed. 'It's no' me at all. It's Cha!'

Cha. Finlay stared at her with an altered face; then, very thoughtfully, he followed her up the narrow wooden stairs into a little uncarpeted attic room.

There, propped up in a chipped truckle bed, garbed in a not very clean day shirt and the famous muffler, with a sporting newspaper on one side and a packet of Woodbines on the other, was Cha.

He greeted Finlay derisively.

'What do you want? The rag and bottle man doesn't call till Tuesday.'

'Be quiet Cha, now do!' pleaded Mrs Bell. 'And show the doctor your arm.' Turning to Finlay – 'It was a scratch he got at his work, doctor, the back end of last week. But it started to heal, and, oh, dearlie me, it's come up something fearful.'

'My arm's fine,' Cha declared rudely. 'I'm not wantin' ony make-down doctor to look at it.'

'Oh, Cha! Oh, Cha!' groaned Mrs Bell. 'Will ye not mind that terrible tongue of yours!'

Finlay stood with a stiff face trying to control his temper. At last, in a difficult voice, he said:

'Suppose you show me the arm.'

'Aw, what the hell!' protested Cha. But from beneath the patchwork counterpane he produced the arm, heavily, as though it were made of lead.

Finlay took one look at it, then his eyes widened in surprise. An enormous swelling stretched from wrist to elbow, an angry boggy tumefaction – of the diagnosis there was not the slightest doubt. Cha had acute sellulitis of the arm.

Making his attitude detached, completely professional, Finlay set about his examination. He took Cha's temperature – Cha's remark as he stuck the thermometer rakishly in his mouth being:

'Whit do you take me for – an ostrich?'

But for all Cha's pretence of coolness his temperature registered 103.5 degrees Fahrenheit.

'Have you any headache?'

'Naw,' Cha lied. 'And don't think you'll present me with one.'

There was a pause; then Finlay looked at Mrs. Bell.

'I shall have to give him a whiff of chloroform and open up the arm,' he declared impassively.

'Not on your life,' said Cha. 'There's no chloroform for me. If you're going to butcher me at a', ye can butcher me without it.'

'But the pain—'

'Aw! What the hell!' Cha interposed scornfully. 'Ye know fine ye're wantin' to hurt me. Go ahead and see if you can make me squeal. Now's the chance to get a little of your own back.'

The blood rushed to Finlay's face.

'That's a lie and you know it. But just you wait. I'll get you better. Then I'll teach you a lesson that you won't forget.'

He swung round abruptly, and, opening his bag, began to prepare his instruments. Cha's answer was to whistle: 'The Bluebells of Scotland' with satiric variations.

Cha didn't go on whistling, of course – though, no doubt, he would have liked to.

It was a nasty business opening the mass of inflammation without an anaesthetic.

His stocky figure went quite rigid, and his face a dirty grey, as Finlay made two swift, deep incisions, then started to probe for pus.

There was very little pus, a bad sign – merely some dark serous fluid which oozed from the drainage cuts, though Finlay looked at it with almost painful care before he packed the wound with iodoform gauze.

When it was finished, Cha drew a stump of cigarette from behind his ear, lit up, and hardily regarded his bandaged arm. 'You've made a bonny hash of it, right enough!' he exclaimed critically. 'But what else could we expect?'

Then, with the cigarette in his hand, he promptly fainted.

He came to, of course, but he was far from being right. That afternoon when Finlay called again he found him in the grip of a raging septicaemia. The infection had spread into the blood stream. Cha was delirious; his temperature 105, his pulse 140; he was dangerously ill. Mrs. Bell resolutely opposed his removal to hospital.

'Cha wouldn't have it! Cha wouldn't have it!' she kept on repeating, wringing her hands. 'He's a guid son to me for all his wildness. I winna go against him now he's badly.'

So the whole responsibility of the case fell on Finlay.

For a whole week he battled for Cha's life. He loathed Cha – yet he felt that he must save him. He came three times a day to the house in Quay Side, religiously dressing the arm himself; he sent specially to Stirrock's in Glasgow for some new anti-toxin;

he even went into Paxton's in the High Street, and ordered the nourishment which kept Cha alive.

Not a labour of love, you may be sure; for lack of a better phrase you might call it a labour of hate.

At last, after a horrible week, Cha had his crisis on the eighth day. As he sat late into the night beside Cha's bed, Finlay saw positively that Cha would recover. Indeed, towards midnight Cha stirred and opened his sunken eyes, which, out of his gaunt, unshaven face, fastened themselves on Finlay. He looked and looked, then, moving his pale lips, he sneered:

'Ye see – I'm getting better in spite of ye.'

Then he went off to sleep. During his convalescence Cha was even worse. The stronger he got the more outrageous he became.

'Thought ye'd take my arm off so ye'd have the beating of me!' or 'Ye'd have finished me, I suppose, if ye'd had the guts to do it!'

Not that Finlay stood it stoically. Oh dear no! With Cha out of danger, he dropped his professional dignity and thoroughly let himself go, Hammer and tongs they went at it, slanging each other unmercifully, the young riveter and the young doctor, until Mrs Bell would thrust her hands upon her ears and run in terror from the room.

Finally, when Cha was up and ready to depart for a month at the Ardbeg Home, Finlay took him pointedly aside:

'Your treatment's finished now. You're better. You're going down to get braced up at the seaside. Well, when you're back again and thoroughly fit, come and see me at the surgery. I'm going to give you the hiding of your life.'

'Right!' Cha nodded defiantly. 'That suits me down to the ground.'

The four weeks passed slowly. Indeed, they passed extremely slowly.

One by one Finlay counted the days. He hated Cha so much he missed him. Yes, he actually missed him.

Life was rather flat without Cha's scornful grin and bold, satiric tongue. But eventually, on the last Saturday of the month, Cha returned and came bustling into the surgery, bronzed and fit, as strong, stocky and sardonic as he had ever been before.

Up he came to Finlay. They faced each other. There was a pause. But what happened next was terrible – so terrible it can hardly be set down.

Finlay looked at Cha. And Cha looked at Finlay.

They grinned at each other sheepishly. Then, with one accord, they delightedly shook hands.

Wee Robison's Lost Memory

If that Friday evening had not been so fine and inviting for a walk, Finlay might easily have postponed his call on the Robertsons, of Barloan Toll, until the morning.

He suspected something trivial, for Sarah Robertson was such a fusser. A large, full-bosomed, heavy-footed woman with a plain, flat face and a heart of gold, she fussed over her big daughter, Margaret, and her small husband, Robert, until Robert at last could hardly call his soul his own.

She aired his flannels, knitted his socks, escorted him to church, selected his neckties at the sale, religiously superintended his diet – ('No, no, Robert, you may like these curds, but you know they always bind you, dear. Tit, tit, take the dish away from your father, Margaret!')

Among her bosom friends of the Toll she was rightly known as a paragon.

'Ours is the happiest marriage that ever was!' she would frequently exclaim with an indrawing of her lips and ecstatic upcasting of the whites of her eyes.

She was the best kind of devoted wife. Or the worst.

But, however much her proprietory fondness redounded to Sarah's credit, the unkind of tongue in Levenford – and they were perhaps a few – found mild amusement in Robert's submission to the wifely yoke.

'He's a hen-pecked little deevil,' Gordon had once declared in the club, and Paxton had acquiesced with a snigger – 'Ay, it's her that wears the breeks all right.'

Although a master at the Academy, Robert did not belong to the club – it had been laid down kindly that smoking and drinking were 'not the thing' for him, at all, at all.

It was extraordinary, in fact, the number of things that were not the thing for Robert. He seemed to go to so few places; never to the football matches, or to the bowling green, or to Glasgow with the other masters to visit the theatre.

He was a small, mild, unassuming man of about forty-four, rather round-shouldered, with a habit of saying very little out of school. He had dog-like, rather harassed brown eyes, a fine tenor voice, and was known affectionately to his class as 'wee Robison'.

His voice apparently was useful, for Sarah, the lady wife, always pressed him to sing when they had company, and through Sarah's more influential pressing he secured year after year the single honour – for it could be nothing else – of preparing the children of the parish church for the cantatas, sacred or otherwise, which they regularly gave about Christmas.

Such was 'wee Robison', and all this passed through Finlay's mind as he strolled towards the Toll through the balmy evening air, already sweet with the breath of early summer.

He rang the bell of Robertson's house and he was not kept waiting long, for Mrs Robertson, in a flurry, pranced to the door and showed him in.

'I do declare, doctor, I'm awful glad you've come,' she cried in the parlour, where, supported by the big, gawky Margaret – nineteen years old and almost the image of her mother – she stood in devoted concern over Robertson.

He was wearing a discomfited look, and moved restlessly in his chair under the chandelier and the inquisition of their united stares.

'Nothing serious, I hope, Mrs Robertson?' said Finlay cheerily.

'It's nothing at all,' protested Robertson uncomfortably. 'Nothing, nothing! I don't know what in all the world they fetched you out for.'

'Now, you be quiet, Father,' said Margaret warningly, 'and let Mother speak.'

Robertson subsided, and Finley looked interrogatively at Mrs Robertson, who drew a long sibilant breath of wifely concern.

'Well, it's like this, Dr Finlay. I don't say it's serious, mind you, far from it, but still I'm worried about my Robert. He's been fair overdoing it lately! Mr Douglas, the master of the class above his, has been away for some reason or another, and Robert's been taking the two classes together. It's an absolute put upon, if you ask me; he's been working himself to death.

'And, forbye, there's the cantata. They're going to give a special performance of "The Lady of the Lake" come Saturday week on account of the church jubilee. It's just one thing after another that's come on the poor man, and you know I'm the most devoted wife in the whole world, and—'

'Yes, yes, but what's all this got to do with fetching me out here?' interposed Finlay, smiling.

'Why, everything, doctor!' expostulated Mrs Robertson with an air of supreme concern. 'It's got Robert into such a state of nerves that the man doesn't know what he's doing. I'll swear he's losing his memory.'

'For God's sake, woman,' muttered Robertson, 'it's nothing at all. You know I was aye absent-minded—'

'Now, Father,' cut in Margaret again, reprovingly.

'It's not just as if it was the once,' went on Mrs Robertson, bending forward towards Finlay in another spasm of wifely anxiety.

'He never knows where he puts a thing now. He forgot my wool I asked him to buy this afternoon. He forgot Margaret's music yesterday. It's one thing after another, forgetting this and forgetting that. He's in such a state he'll be forgetting where he lives next.

'And so, doctor,' continued Mrs Robertson, 'will you take the poor man in hand, for goodness sake, and tell him not to work so hard and what to do and everything, for I am fair worried. I wouldn't have him miss the cantata for worlds.'

Finlay could have laughed out loud at the terrible solicitude of Mrs Robertson. He felt it was wholly unjustified, and yet he did not know either.

Perhaps Robertson had been overworking. He was such a downtrodden little man he was likely to have everything shoved upon him, and besides, he did look oddly nervous, fidgeting with his hands, letting his eye roam about the room with a queer and rather restless look.

Finlay sat down and, in his own particular way, making himself at home, he talked to them. He reasoned with Robertson upon the dangers to the mind of overworking. He talked pleasantly and reassuringly on the subject, and then, before he rose to go, he warned him, referring to a case which had actually come within the bounds of his own experience.

'You know,' he said, 'real overstrain does throw the memory out – aphasia we call it. And it happens quite suddenly. I remember when I was at the Royal I saw a case. It was a businessman. He had forgotten who he was, or rather, he thought himself somebody else. He had come all the way from Birmingham, and he had been living for a fortnight in Glasgow before his people got in touch with him.'

'My goodness!' exclaimed Robertson with an almost startled look in his eyes. He sat up in his chair. 'Is that a fact, doctor?'

'It's a fact,' Finlay reaffirmed.

'So you see now,' put in Margaret, 'you'd better be careful, Father, and do as Mother says.'

'I wouldn't have believed it,' gasped Robertson in that same queer tone, staring in front of him like a man distracted.

'Well, maybe you will now,' said Mrs Robertson in a pleased, justified voice.

As she showed Finlay to the door, she thanked him for having spoken so plainly.

★   ★   ★

Next morning Robert awoke early after a night which had been singularly troubled.

It was Saturday, a beautiful day. Through the open window the air blew sweetly down from the Winton Hills. He lay quietly in bed with his eyes fixed on the ceiling.

He was faced with the rehearsal of the cantata at the Rechabites' Hall, where the fifty-odd children – big and small, wet- and dry-nosed, of all sexes, the same whom he taught wearily every day of the week – would be waiting for him to appear with his tuning fork and little pointer.

He rose, dressed, and had his breakfast. Sarah accompanied him to the door to give her parting instructions.

'Now be careful, dear. You'll come straight back, and you'll sit in the garden with me this afternoon. Then we'll both maybe take a bit walk together. There's a hat in the window we might look at for Margaret.'

Robertson nodded in meek acquiescence, then turned and went down the road, across the Common and towards the Rechabites' Hall.

But at the end of the Common a strange thing happened. All at once a change came over his face. He lifted his gaze from the ground where it habitually rested, and fixed it upon infinity, as if hypnotised. Instinctively his pace quickened, and, swinging round from the direction of the Rechabites' Hall, he started off towards Church Street.

In Church Street, with the same queer hypnotic absorption, he entered the bank. Here he drew out the sum of thirty pounds.

When he came out of the bank he turned and walked straight off towards the station. Two people standing about, Dougal Todd, the sign painter, and old Lennox, the butcher, called out to him in greeting, but no recognition came upon his face.

He marched stiffly up the station steps on to the platform and without a trace of hesitation he entered a train which had just drawn up.

In an empty first-class compartment, surrounded by unusual luxury, he sat with impassive face. Presently he took off his hat, the dingy bowler hat which he had worn for some ten years, and laid it on the seat beside him.

He stared out of the window at the flashing panorama of green fields and woods and the opening estuary of the lovely Firth.

Half an hour later the train drew to a stop. It was Craigendoran Pier. He got out of the train and walked straight onto the pier as if he meant to walk right off the end of it. Fortunately, however, a steamer lay at the end of the pier. It was the Lord of the Glens, and with complete composure he walked aboard.

A moment later the ropes were cast off, the paddles flashed, and the boat put off. A band broke gaily into music. The breeze blew soft and fresh, the sun shone, and the prow of the steamer was set towards the Kyles of Bute.

Bare-headed, for he had left his hat in the train, the little man paced the deck with his hair blowing in the wind, and some time later he went downstairs and ate a large meal – soup, cold salmon and cucumber, roast beef, pudding, biscuits and cheese. Then he came up, faintly flushed, but still queerly automatic, and began to pace the deck again.

'Tickets, please; tickets, please.' The young purser appeared, and the little man put his hand to his head as though bewildered. He had no ticket.

'Kirn, Dunoon, or Rothesay?' asked the purser, pulling out a book of counterfoils.

'Rothesay.' Mechanically – like that!

The purser wrote out a slip. He looked up casually, then his expression changed—

'Why, it's Mr Robertson, isn't it? I was in your class ten years ago—'

'What,' asked the bare-headed passenger, 'in all the world are ye talkin' about?'

The purser flushed in confusion.

'Sorry,' he said awkwardly. 'My mistake.'

At Rothesay the little man stepped ashore briskly, mechanically, and opposite the pier his eyes took in a large boarding-house decorated with a gilded sign – Cowal Cliff. He went straight in.

'I'd like a nice room,' he said.

The manageress looked up cheerfully from behind the little window.

'Yes,' she said. 'Have you booked?'

'No, I've just come off the boat.'

'Oh, I see. Your luggage will be along later?'

'Yes.'

'I can give you a nice front room. What name, sir?' She offered him the pen.

He hesitated. Since he was not Robertson he must be somebody else. His face clouded, then cleared, as if remembering something.

'Walter Scott,' he said, almost to himself. And he wrote it down.

When he had been shown to his bedroom and had washed his face and hands, he went out and strolled along the front.

He went into a draper's shop, where he bought himself a small portmanteau, nightshirt, various odds and ends, and finally a yachting cap.

Perching the yachting cap jauntily on his head, he ordered the other purchases to be sent up to the Cowal Cliff, and went into an adjoining tobacconist's.

In the tobacconist's, with a strange intentness in his eyes, he bought himself some cigars – large cigars, cigars each circled by a beautiful band.

With one of these smoking in the corner of his mouth, the yachting cap set rakishly on his head, and an expression at once blank and complacent, he strolled along the promenade, as though enjoying the sunshine and fresh air.

Although he seemed so curiously detached and hypnotised, it seemed that everything was an entertainment to him.

Towards the end of the promenade he passed a young lady

with dark eyes and wind-blown hair tucked under a red tam-o'-shanter. She walked with her hands in the pockets of her short jacket, and there was something soft and roguish and solitary about her.

In the same absent-minded fashion, he swung round and began to stroll behind her. When she stopped to look at a sailing boat which lay close inshore in the bay, he stopped to look at it, too. In the same absent fashion he remarked—

'A bonny boat, isn't it?'

She agreed.

'And it's a bonny day,' he said, his voice expressionless and innocent.

Again she agreed, smiling.

'Where are you staying?' he asked.

'At the Cowal Cliff,' she replied.

'Fine!' he said. 'I'm there, too. Isn't it time we were back for tea?'

She burst out laughing.

'Don't think I didn't see you at the end of the promenade. You're a wicked one, picking up decent girls. I saw there was a wicked look about you.'

'Oh, no,' he said, 'not at all.'

'Come on,' she teased him, 'I'm waiting for you to say we've met before.'

'Maybe we have,' he replied strangely. 'I don't remember.'

As they walked along towards the boarding-house, she told him about herself.

Her name was Nancy Begg, and she worked in a big store in Sauchiehall Street. She had drawn her holidays a little earlier than usual in the ballot, and she admitted that she had been very lonely since her arrival at the Cowal Cliff. She liked Rothesay better in August.

She seemed to him to be about twenty-seven, and was lively and self-possessed.

'But you haven't told me anything about yourself,' she said,

'What do you do?' Envisaging the yachting cap, she remarked archly, 'Something to do with the sea, I should think.'

'That's right,' he said. 'A purser on a ship.'

'You can always tell,' she agreed smiling again. 'There's something – I don't know what. Something dashing, I think.'

At the high tea they sat next to each other, and he helped her to everything. After tea he said—

'What are you doing this evening?'

'Well, what do you suggest? There's the entertainers – they're awful good.'

They went to the entertainers. He took the best front seats, and bought her a box of chocolates. By the time they came out a soft darkness had come down upon the bay. The end of his cigar glowed brightly, and on the way home, in that absentminded fashion, he slipped his arm round her waist.

'You're a nice chap, Walter,' she whispered.

The next few days were fine and sunny. The time passed quickly, while Walter and Nancy enjoyed each other's company. They walked together, took drives together, and a cruise round the Kyles. They even danced together, for, on the eve of her return to Glasgow, as they passed beside the Cowal Hall they saw a placard displayed—

GALA ASSEMBLY TONIGHT. ALL WELCOME
GLOVES OPTIONAL: SLIPPERS ESSENTIAL

Nancy sighed wistfully, hanging on his arm, and asked—

'Do you dance, Walter?'

'I think I might dance,' he said with the odd, noncommittal caution with which Nancy was now familiar.

He had changed visibly; his shoulders were more erect; he was slightly sunburned; his eye, though still, alas, extremely distant, was bright and daring.

She was to leave by the five o'clock boat, and that afternoon they took a final walk up past the golf course beyond the Skeoch Wood.

Nancy was very silent. Presently she complained that she was tired, and they sat down. They were enclosed by a sea of young bracken, above which the tree trunks and feathery bushes framed a strip of blue sky.

Far away they heard the throb of a streamer going down the Kyles, and then a deep stillness fell.

'You won't forget me, will you, Walter?' Nancy whispered, afraid to break this quietness.

'I don't know,' he said queerly. 'I'm not very good at remembering.'

At that she gave a little sigh and her arms went round him. Absentmindedly his went round her.

Then it was time to return for Nancy's boat. She took Walter's arm, and in silence walked very close to him.

They had reached the promenade leading to the pier, when suddenly a large and portly figure blocked the way.

'Hello, hello!' he exclaimed in a tone of wonder. 'It's you, Robertson! Well, I'll be damned!'

'I beg your pardon,' said Walter in a stiff voice, 'You're making a mistake.'

'What!' gasped the other. 'Don't you know me – Bailie Nichol, of Levenford? Damn it all, Robertson—'

'I beg your pardon,' said Walter again. 'My name's Scott. Kindly let me pass.'

'But hang it all,' protested Nichol. 'Hang it all, Robertson, the whole town has been ringing with you. They've turned the place upside down looking for you. Every paper—'

'This young lady has to catch her boat,' remarked Walter, and, pushing past the dumbfounded Nichol, he drew Nancy to the pier and towards the boat.

'What was it, Walter?' she asked in astonishment.

'How should I know?' he answered. 'I never saw him in my life before.'

The bell on the boat clanged. She gave him a big, hurried hug.

'You've got my address,' she said. 'You won't forget me, dear? Please?'

When he returned to Cowal Cliff he had an idea that the manageress looked at him with a strange intentness, but he took no notice.

After tea he went out for a solitary walk along the promenade, and the stars came out and looked at his small figure strolling along with an air of vague triumph. It was impossible to tell what his thoughts might be, but that night he slept dreamlessly.

Next morning he lay late. It was about ten o'clock before he came down briskly, and found the manageress waiting for him in the hall.

'Somebody wants to see you,' she declared with an air of purpose and took him aside into a little room.

There he stared blankly at Bailie Nichol, accompanied by two women. One of the women was tall, large of bosom and hip, and flat of face. There were tears in her eyes, and her hands trembled. Beside her stood obviously her daughter.

'Now, Robertson,' said Nichol carefully, 'here we are. You're glad to see us, aren't you, old fellow?'

'What d'ye mean?' said Walter coldly. 'You are a damned nuisance, sir. And what are these women doing here?'

At this a groan broke from the elder female. She pushed forward and flung her arms round Walter's neck.

'Oh, dear! Oh, dear!' she moaned. 'Don't you remember me, dear? Don't you know me?'

Stonily, Walter withdrew from her embrace.

'Leave me be, woman. I can't understand such shameless behaviour.'

With a gesture of his arm, Nichol restrained the elder woman.

'Leave him in the meantime,' he whispered aside. 'We'll get him home. His memory's gone.'

The object of their sympathy and solicitude, Walter, was escorted with great care on the short journey to Levenford.

He preserved a cold and disgusted dignity when first one woman and then the other sobbed over him. But he made no demur about accompanying them, trotting with docility from boat to train and from train to cab.

'He's like a man bewitched,' sobbed the middle-aged woman, 'My poor Robert.'

When they reached the house at Barloan Toll, a young man was awaiting them.

'Oh, Dr Finlay, Dr Finlay!' wailed the woman, 'Look at him; it's just as you said. Oh, what'll I do? What'll I do?'

Finlay was very upset as he saw again the face of 'wee Robison' with its new, remote expression. He went up to him with quick kindness.

'Come away, man,' he said. 'Just sit down quietly, and we'll have a little talk. Don't you know me? You've had a breakdown man, and you just want to go very quietly.'

Walter seemed unmoved by this solicitude. He looked round in cold disapproval.

'What are those two women doing there?' he asked. 'Tell them to go away.'

Finlay signed to Mrs Robertson and Margaret to leave the room, and they went reluctantly, their sobs echoing down the passage.

Finlay and Robertson sat for some time in silence. It seemed to Finlay that Robertson's expression was changing. Just being in his own house, although he did not recognise it, was smoothing out that expression of tense remoteness. At last Finlay began to speak carefully.

'Now, listen,' he said. 'You've got to understand, my friend, that you have lost your memory. It's not serious, but you have completely lost your memory. You will have to wait until it comes back.'

The patient's face at last showed a look of frank interest.

'Is that a fact?' he said. 'And how long does it take?'

'Well,' said Finlay, trying to be reassuring, 'sometimes it comes back quite suddenly, the trouble passes over—'

A slow grin broke over wee Robison's face.

'Well, it's over now!' he said. 'So fetch them in!' He fingered an address slip in his waistcoat pocket, and his grin broadened. He dug Finlay slyly in the ribs.

'But, by God, man, it was grand while it lasted!'

The Man Who Came Back

One evening in early June as Finlay sat in his surgery there entered a man whom he had never seen before in Levenford. The stranger was perhaps between thirty-five and forty years old, but it was uncertain, for his features, lean, haggard, and jaundiced by tropic suns, wore that look of cheap experience which puts the stamp of age upon the face of youth.

The manner of this young-old man was easy, flashy, almost arrogant. He was dressed in a light suit of ultra sporting cut, carried worn-out yellow gloves and a chipped malacca cane, while his hat, which he had not troubled to remove, lay on the back of his head as if to mask the stains upon its threadbare nap by this extremely rakish tilt.

'Evening, doctor sahib,' remarked the unusual visitor with complete assurance; and without invitation flung himself into the chair beside Finlay's desk. 'Dropped in on you to get acquainted. I'm Hay, Bob Hay, Esq., of the North East India Company. Just back from Bombay to look the old town up again.'

Finlay stared at the queer individual in surprise. No one like this had ever been in his surgery before. Recovering himself he made to put a question, but before he could speak the ubiquitous Hay, tapping his pointed shoe – rather cracked about the uppers, but finely shined for all that – with his malacca cane, resumed his cocksure style.

'Pretty damn funny the old town looks after fifteen years. I can tell you, when a man's been out East and seen the world, he's fit to laugh his sides out at a chota spot like this. Ha! Ha! call it

205

the Royal and Ancient burgh. It's ancient all right. No life, doc, no bright lights, nothing! Damn my liver! I don't know how I'll stand it now I've come home.'

And with an easy, man of the world laugh, he pulled a cheroot from his waistcoat pocket, and stuck it nonchalently in his mouth.

With level eyes and a growing repugnance, Finlay studied the flashy Hay – Bob Hay, Esquire, as he styled himself – this son of Levenford, returned to his native town after many years abroad. At length he inquired brusquely—

'Seeing that you find it so unsatisfactory, may I ask why you came back?'

Bob Hay laughed, and airily waved his cheroot, which he had ignited by the simple process of borrowing a match from Finlay's desk and sparking it expertly upon his shoe.

'Reasons of health, doctor sahib! Climate plays the devil with a man's liver and lights out East. And the life y'know. Dinners, dances, regimental balls. God, doc, when a man's run after socially – oh, you understand how it is, old man! Had to give it up for a bit and come back. Couple of my pals in Bombay, big specialists out there, good fellows both, advised me to have a little rest and take a trip home.'

A pause while Finlay grappled with this specious information.

'You're returning to India, then?' he queried after a moment.

'Maybe, maybe,' evaded Hay. 'We'll see how we get on in the old home town. Might settle down altogether here. Buy a little estate up the country. Y'never know. Ha! ha! Company have been handsome, hang it all – confounded handsome! Settled a whacking pension on Bobbie Hay!'

'They've pensioned you?' echoed Finlay sharply.

For all his airy pretence, if Hay had been pensioned by his company, it was plain he would never go back to India. But why? Finlay stared with a new intentness at the other, whose pinch-beck outer husk revealed, on closer examination, the manifest seediness beneath. And, scrutinising even closer, Finlay became aware of a sickly pallor that underlay the sunburn complexion before him, of a shortened breathing, a quick and restless tremour of thin, yellow-nicotined fingers.

Decisively he pulled a sheet of paper towards him and picked up his pen.

'We seem to be wasting a fair amount of time,' he declared. 'Do you wish to consult me? Or what exactly can I do for you?'

'Oh, nothing much, doctor sahib, nothing much,' protested Hay with a gracious, deprecating gesture. 'I don't want to consult you. And don't bother about particulars or medicine. I've a prescription from my Bombay pals I take when I remember. As a matter of fact, I've only looked in because the company asked me to see my doctor sahib at home. I shall have to send them a medical chit from you every month.' He paused elegantly. 'Because of my pension, don't you see?'

'No,' returned Finlay, very precisely. 'I don't quite see. I cannot undertake to give you a certificate unless I know what's the matter with you. I'm sorry, Hay, but if you want a certificate out of me you'll have to let me examine you.'

There was a distinct and curious pause; then out came Hay's ready laugh.

'Right you are, then, old sport. I don't mind in the slightest. Not one chota peg. Ha! Ha! You go ahead. Put the old damn measuring tape across me. Bob Hay can say ninety-nine with the best of 'em.'

With the same conscious indifference Hay rose and slipped off his coat and vest, revealing the shabbiest of underclothing. Stripped, standing in his trousers and stocking soles, he showed a pitiable physique; his arms were skin and bone, his ribs standing out like spars, while in the centre of his narrow chest around his breast-bone there moved a curious pulsation.

Hay's whole bodily appearance indicated a wasted, ill-spent life. But Finlay was less concerned with the man's physique. His eyes remained riveted upon that pulsing movement in Hay's breast. It was laboured, that pulsing, and ominous – horribly ominous.

Finlay made his examination slowly and without asking a single question, using his stethoscope carefully, deliberately. Then, in a manner patently altered, he sat down at his desk again and remarked—

'You can dress up now; that's all for the moment. I'll give you a certificate.'

'Right you are, doctor sahib!' cheerfully exclaimed Hay. 'Knew there wouldn't be the slightest difficulty. Old warhorse is fit as a fiddle. Only a bit of nonsense on the part of these doctor wallahs in Bombay. Good friends of mine, mind you, but nervous, too damn nervous for words. I'll be all right once I dig up a little sport and gaiety in this one-anna town.'

Finlay did not answer immediately; he continued slowly writing out the certificate. But when Hay was dressed he looked up, and, in an unemotional, professional voice which masked the distaste he felt, he declared—

'Sport and gaiety are not for you, Hay. You're a sick man. You must have complete rest and freedom from all excitement.'

'Ah, a lot of tommy rot, doc,' laughed Hay. 'I'm right as rain.'

'You're not right,' Finlay repeated with emphasis. 'You surely appreciate why you've been sent back here.' A pause. 'Don't you realise that you're suffering from advanced aneurism of the acta?'

As the fatal name of that awful complaint echoed in the surgery, once again that curious silence fell. Then Hay smiled, though this time perhaps the smile on the pinched and sallow features turned somewhat ragged, merging insensibly into a grimace that almost was a sneer.

He stared at Finlay bitterly, defiantly, revealingly. But only for an instant. The ready laugh rang out again immediately, the easy, careless, blustering laugh.

'That's a good one, doctor sahib. But you can't scare me with those fancy tales. Ha! Ha! The lad's hard as nails and tough as leather, doc. The old pump's out of gear a bit, that's all. Nothing serious. You can't kill Bob Hay, doctor, no, by God, sir not for a hundred years.'

And picking up the certificate he folded it, tucked it deliberately in his waistcoat pocket, cocked his hat, pulled on the shoddy gloves, nodded to Finlay confidently, and swinging his malacca cane, strolled easily out of the surgery.

Finlay sat motionless at his desk frowning, surprised in a way by the odious effrontery of this strange patient, yet strangely arrested by Hay's indifference to the dreadful malady which possessed him.

Could Hay really understand the full significance of the terrible disease – aneurism – that swelling of the great artery leading from the heart, which was liable at any second to rupture and cause instantaneous death?

Was he ignorant of the fact that his life hung by a thread? That, at the outside, a few short months must see him cold in his grave? Finlay sighed, and, despite himself, a great curiosity possessed him as to who Hay was, and what his history might be.

Indeed, when the surgery was over and he came into the dining-room to eat his supper, he was moved to make a discreet inquiry.

Cameron was out upon a case, but Janet, never-failing source of information on matters relating to Levenford and its people, readily afforded him the information which he sought.

'Ay, indeed,' she responded, shaking her head, and drawing her lips together tightly – sure sign of condemnation and regret! 'Weel do I ken Bob Hay – and all about him. A sore heartbreak he's been to his folks, and a sorer heartbreak still to Chrissie Temple.' Janet paused, shook her head again, then severely continued—

'A fine young fella he was at a'e time, mind ye. He come o' decent stock, ay, his folks was highly respeckit in Levenford; they lived up Knoxhill way, an' had a braw big house. An' Bob was the only son. He went to the Academy like maist o' the other Knoxhill laddies, and then went into the yard to serve his time for the drawin'-office.

'Weel, he showed considerable promise in his wark, was likit by a' folks in the office, and took a pleasant part in the sociability o' the town. And to crown a', at the age of twenty-three he twined up wi' Chrissie Temple, and took to courtin' her serious and proper. Maybe ye'll ken Chrissie Temple, doctor?'

Finlay nodded in the affirmative, and reinforced by his interest Janet pithily went on—

'Ay, and a fine, sweet woman she is. Though, mind ye, in thae days she was bonnier by far. As ye maybe ken, she was the daughter of Temple, the writer in the town, oh, a sparky darke'ed lass, fu' o' innocence and speerits, an' fair desperate ta'en on with Bob. The two walked out for over a year. They were plighted, ye ken, and their devotion to each other was kenned and much thought o' throughout the hale toun.

'Weel, in the spring o' the next year it so fell out that Bob got the offer o' a post wi' one o' the big Indian companies out in Bombay. It's a chance that often happens in this toun, doctor, as maybe ye ken, what wi' the connections o' the yard and that like. Onyway, the post was offered to Bob.

'Oh, 'twas a grand opportunity, which baith Chrissie and Bob agreed he couldna afford to neglect, a chance for advancement which would bring him, at the end of five years, back to Levenford and the yard, in a braw superior possetion.

'So, after much haverin' and heart-burning, for ye maun understand that the Indian climate prevented Chrissie from going, and Bob was loth to gang by his lone and leave his Chrissie, 'twas a' agreed that he should go and serve his time in India. Chrissie would bide patiently until he came back, when they would be married at once, and settle down to a happy life in Levenford.

'So Bob took his leave 'midst tears and a' that show o' fondness, swearin' he would be true to Chrissie, as weel he might, and for some months a' went richt and proper.

'Then gradual-like Bob's letters home turned less regular. Soon they hardly came ava', and, finally, they stoppit a' thegither. Then, sure enough, to crown a', accounts o' Bob's wild doin's were brocht home from India by folks coming and going between the North-Eastern Company and the yard.

'At the start Chrissie flat refused to believe the stories, but a'e day, about a year after Bob had gone, she got a letter frae the bla'guard breakin' off the engagement. He wasna comin' hame at the end o' five years. The climate wasna suitable for her. He wasna good enough for her. These, and a hale pack o' excuses, were put forrit by Bob as the cause o' his decision, but Chrissie kenned, and everybody in the town o' Levenford kenned, that the real cause was the wicked life which Bob had ta'en till abroad.

'Weel, when she cam' at last to see Bob had failed her, Chrissie was fair struck down. She said nothing, answered nothing, took not a single step. But from that day a change cam' over the braw, douce lass. She turned quieter, more self-contained; she held herself awa' frae the life o' the toun.

'Douce and gentle as ever she was – ay, mair so – but somehow she come like to a solitary way o' leevin', takin' long walks by her lone, as though she couldna thole the company o' others o' her own age.

'Weel, time went on, and the long silence, the gap between Bob Hay and Levenford, widened. Nae mair was heard of him except at odd times, shamfu' stories o' his deevilries. He cam' to be a kind o' legend in the town for a' that was bad. Fair broken-hearted and unable to hold up her head i' the toun, Bob's mother just withered away. And, 'deed, his father was laid i' the graveyard not so long after.

'But Chrissie still kept up her heid. Off and on she had offers; some o' the best men i' the town spiered her, but she refused them a'. Faith, though she's bonny still and nae mair than thirty-twa, I'm thinkin' Chrissie has had enough o' men to last her for a lifetime.' A pause; then Janet concluded grimly – 'Now that he's back, if ever Bob Hay and Chrissie should meet again, as God's my Maker, I'd like to hear the way she'd speak to him!'

When Janet slipped out eventually and left him to his supper, Finlay reflected sombrely on what he had just heard. He knew Chrissie Temple, though up till the present, he had not known her story, and the combination of beauty and sadness which had always struck him about her now stood explained.

Aware of the tragedy that was Chrissie's life, Finlay felt an added loathing of this man who had come back; broken, debauched, and dying, but brazen to the last. Unlike Janet, he prayed with all his heart that Chrissie, for her own sake, might never see him.

Time went on, and Bob Hay continued to remain in Levenford.

The townspeople spurned him as they would have spurned a dog, meeting all his advances, all his attempts to recall himself to memory, with stony hostility. Yet Bob did not seem to care. Far from disheartening him, each rebuff seemed merely to encourage him the more.

He showed himself a great deal in public, stood at the Cross, paraded the High Street, forenoon and evening, dressed in his pinchbeck finery, swinging his cane, whistling carefree, shameless.

And every month, jaunty and disreputable, but irrepressible as ever, he appeared at the surgery for the certificate which entitled him to draw his pension.

Having explained that he preferred to pay his medical accounts annually, he always betook himself jauntily away without demeaning himself to offer a fee to Finlay.

Already it was rumoured that he was in debt all over the town. He seemed, indeed, to have no means of support but the allowance made him by the company, though this, he implied in a high-handed fashion, was a handsome, a magnificent sum.

On the first of September, however, Hay did not make his customary appearance at the surgery, and Finlay, who had somehow come to anticipate these visits with a mixture of aversion and interest, wondered what could have befallen the unfortunate reprobate.

He was not long in doubt. A message arrived the following day asking him to visit Hay at the Inverclyde Hotel. Moved by a queer curiosity, Finlay complied.

He found Hay occupied a small back room in the hotel, which, despite its grand-sounding name, was a mean, disreputable tavern lying behind Quayside. He was in bed in considerable distress, unshaven, pallid, and apparently in pain. Yet his demeanour was as careless and defiant as before.

'Sorry to trouble you, doctor sahib,' he croaked, 'Can't quite seem to get on the old pins today.' And then, reading the distaste in Finlay's eyes, he added – 'Not much of a place here. When I'm up and about I'll damn well give them notice. I'm going to stay with some friends, as a matter of fact, at the end of the next month.'

Finlay sat down quietly on the edge of the bed, drawing his own conclusions.

'You've been drinking, I suppose?' he asked.

For a moment it looked as though a hot denial were on Hay's lips; then his face changed, and instead he laughed lightly.

'Why not? A bit of a scatter does a fellow good once in a while. Shakes up the liver. Eh, doc?'

Finlay was silent, shocked, in spite of himself, by the sham, the pitiable travesty stretched upon the bed before him. He was not a man given to religious exhortations; he hated all display of sanctimony and righteousness, but now something, he knew not what, came over him, and he exclaimed –

'In the name of God, Hay, why do you go on this way? It would be bad enough at the best of times. But don't you realise – don't you understand—' he lowered his voice '—you've only got a few months to live?'

'Huh, humbug, doctor sahib,' wheezed Hay. 'You go and tell that to the horse marines.'

'I'm telling it to you,' persisted Finlay in that low, pleading voice. 'And I mean every word of it. Why don't you take yourself in hand, Hay?'

'Take myself in hand? Ha! Ha! That's a good one, doc! Why in the name of Allah should I?'

'For your own sake, Hay.'

Again a pause, while Hay, with unwavering defiance, met

Finlay's entreating gaze. It all seemed hopeless to Finlay, and, giving it up as a bad job, he was about to turn to open his bag and take out his stethoscope, when suddenly a strange and staggering phenomenon arrested him, held him as in a vice.

Through the shallow, callous expression on Hay's face there suddenly broke an unbelievable agitation; his cheek began to twitch, and, miracle of miracles, a tear fell from his eye and rolled slowly down his cheek.

Desperately he tried to hold his pose of indifference, but it was no use. The mask was off once and for all. He gave way completely, and turning to the wall, he sobbed as if his heart would break.

Unwilling pity welled up within Finlay.

'Don't take on, man,' he muttered, 'Pull yourself together.'

'Pull myself together!' sobbed Hay hysterically. 'That's good, that is! What do you think I've been doing ever since I came home but pull myself together? Do you think it's been nice for me, coming back like a beaten dog to die in the gutter?

'Haven't I tried to put a face on things and keep my end up? Oh, God in heaven, haven't I tried? You think I've been drinking? Do you know I haven't touched a drop since I came back? I don't care if you don't believe me. It's true. Do you know what my allowance is? Three pounds a month. A fine time a man can have on that! Oh, a hell of a fine time! Especially a man like me, whose heart's liable to burst at any minute.'

And, convulsed by an agony of pain and grief, Hay writhed upon the bed.

There was a long silence; then instinctively Finlay placed his hand on Hay's shoulders. He had a terrible feeling that he had misjudged this man, that what he had mistaken for cheap affrontery was merely the mask of courage.

'Cheer up!' he whispered. 'We'll do something about it.'

'No, it's no use. They won't own me here,' Hay retorted in a voice of anguish. 'Nobody speaks to me. I'm like a leper. Maybe I am a leper. They only want to spit at me, throw mud at me. Oh, don't think I'm complaining. I deserve it. I've earned it.

They're entitled to snarl and snap at me. The sooner I'm dead the better.'

As Hay spoke a curious expression appeared on Finlay's face – that look which usually betokened the taking of an important decision. He said no more; he did not even attempt to console Hay further; but, rising from the bed with a strange purpose in his eyes, he walked out of the room.

About an hour later, when Hay had sobbed his grief out, and lay staring at the ceiling in the blankness of his desolation the door opened softly, and someone came into the room. Apathetically, he did not at first turn his head, but at last he did so. Then a cry came from his lips.

'You!' he whispered as if in awe. 'You – Chrissie!'

Slowly she came forward – Chrissie Temple, quiet and unassuming, her dark hair braided from her smooth forehead above her kind and gentle eyes.

She sat down beside the bed and took his hand.

'Why not?' she said.

He could not speak; fresh sobs rising in his throat seemed to strangle him. At last he groaned—

'Go away and let me be. Haven't I harmed you enough? Go away and leave me be.'

'But I don't want to go, Bob,' she whispered. 'If ye'll let me, I'd rather stay. It's now that you need me.'

She smiled at him unflinchingly, and there was that in her smile which silenced him. He bowed his head against her breast, his pain forgotten in the knowledge of her love, of her forgiveness.

Later he tried to tell her, to explain haltingly his faithlessness – of how he had been swept off his feet by wild companions, led into wretchedness and debt, sent finally to a fever-ridden, up-country station, where he had surrendered to oblivion and fate.

She listened, compassionate and understanding, fondling his head, smoothing his ruffled hair.

The twilight found them thus, and drew a veil upon their reconciliation beyond which it was sacrilege to penetrate.

A week later Levenford was stirred by the news that Bob Hay and Chrissie Temple had got married.

The ceremony took place privately, and Finlay was there to witness it. Afterwards Bob was driven home to Chrissie's house, which stood right on the top of the Lea Brae, with a small garden from which there was a lovely view of the Firth of Clyde.

Healed in mind and spirit, if not in body, Bob knew the comfort and attention of a good woman.

Much of his time he spent in bed, but when winter passed and spring came again, Chrissie would take him into the garden, where, reclining in a long chair, he would rest his hands fondly in his wife's as she sat beside him, and his eyes on the view, watching the ships sail out to the great beyond.

A strange honeymoon, but a happy one! Finlay was a frequent visitor at the house, yet it was Chrissie's love and overflowing goodness rather than his skill which prolonged Bob's life.

He lived all through that lovely summer in great happiness and peace, his pretence and cheap flashiness gone, and in its place real strength and patience, with which he met all his pain and suffering.

When the first colours of autumn were creeping over the landscape, and the first leaves fluttering gently down from the trees, Bob Hay passed peacefully away, sailing away, like the ships, into the great beyond.

And Chrissie was there beside him when he died.

She still keeps much to herself, and still takes her solitary walks, but on the occasions when Finlay meets her and stops to have a word, it seems to him that, instead of sadness, happiness is written upon her face.

Miracle By Lestrange

The coming to Levenford of Lestrange, charlatan and quack healer, worked a strange miracle. But the miracle arose in a queer and devious way; took place in a woman's heart; and was far from the result Lestrange had intended.

Jessie Grant was a widow who kept the small tobacconist's shop at the corner of Wallace Street and Scroggie's Loan. She wasn't a tall body – rather to the contrary, in fact. Her hair was dark and clenched back tightly from her brow, and she dressed always plain as plain in a black serge gown. But she had a look on her pale, narrow face that struck and daunted you – a kind of tight-lipped, bitter look it was, and it burned out of her dark-browed eyes like fire.

Stubborn and hard was Jessie, known throughout Levenford as a dour and difficult woman who neither asked nor yielded favours.

The shop wasn't much – a dim, old-fashioned place, like an old apothecary's shop, with its counter and small brass scales, its rows of yellow canisters, and a stiff, weather-blistered door that went 'ping' when you opened it.

Ben from the shop was the kitchen of Jessie's house, with its big dresser, a wag-at-the-wa' clock, two texts, a table scrubbed to a driven whiteness, some straight chairs, and a long, low horsehair sofa – that made up the tale of the furnishings. And out of the room rose a flight of narrow steps to the two bedrooms above.

Jessie's husband, who in his life had been a graceless, idle ne'er-do-well, was dead and buried these twelve years. She had been left with one bairn, a boy called Duncan.

Soured and disillusioned, her subsequent struggle to secure a livelihood for herself and her son had been severe, and, although successful, had served further to embitter her.

As they say in Levenford, 'the wind aye blows ill wi' Jessie Grant'.

Strict wasn't the name for the way she brought up Duncan. Never a glint of human affection kindled her blank eye. To those that dared tax her on the matter she had the answer pat, and would throw Ecclesiastes xii., 8, right into their teeth.

Duncan, at this time, was turned fourteen years old, a thin and lanky lad who had fast outgrown his strength, a silent boy, very diffident and sensitive in his manner, but with the friendliest smile in the world.

At school, he had been a regular prize-winner, and had begged to be allowed to continue his studies and go in for teaching. But Jessie, implacable as ever, had said 'No', and so Duncan had left school a few months before to start work in the shipyard as a rivet-boy.

Folks murmured at such treatment of the boy, at such lack of motherly affection, but Jessie minded nothing. Bitter and harsh she was with Duncan in everything.

Naturally, such a woman had little to do with doctors – her Spartan principles and steadfast belief in castor oil and fresh air precluded that.

And so Finlay never met in with Jessie until one day in the spring he received a most surprising and wholly unexpected summons to her shop. It was not Jessie, of course, but Duncan – for once castor oil had not answered. And Finlay had not been ten minutes in the boy's dark little room before he saw the trouble to be really serious.

Duncan's right ankle showed a full swelling, a sinister swelling very white and boggy, yet without signs of inflammation. It looked bad: and it was bad.

Following a thorough investigation, Finlay had no doubt whatever in his mind; the condition was one of tuberculosis of the ankle bone.

Back in the kitchen, Finlay told Jessie, and he did not mince words, for already her critical attitude towards him and the coldness in her manner towards the boy had roused him to quick resentment.

'It means six months in a leg iron,' he concluded abruptly. 'And complete rest from his work.'

For a moment Jessie did not answer – she seemed taken aback by the seriousness of the complaint – then she exclaimed—

'A leg iron!'

Finlay looked her up and down.

'That's right,' he said bluntly. 'And some care and attention from you.'

Again Jessie was silent, but she glowered at Finlay from under her dark brows as though she could have killed him. From that moment she was his mortal enemy.

It showed itself in many ways during the weeks which followed. Whenever Finlay called to see the boy she was at his elbow, dour and critical, even contemptuous. She watched the fitting of the iron leg brace with a sour, forbidding frown.

She muttered openly at the instructions given her, and grumbled bitterly at the tedious progress of the case. Finlay was doing the boy no good at all; the whole thing was a pack of nonsense.

On more than one occasion hot words passed between them, and soon Finlay began to loathe Jessie every particle as much as Jessie hated him.

He began to study the relationship of mother and son, feeling Jessie's harshness to Duncan as wholly unnatural.

Here was a clever, sensitive, delicate boy, whose heart was bound up in books, forced to make his way through the rough hazards of the shipyard for which he was so clearly unfitted, when he might easily have made a career for himself in the scholastic profession, as he longed to do. But Jessie's thrawn will prevented it.

Every word she spoke was curt and brooking; never a single term of endearment passed her lips.

As time went on Finlay found the situation almost intolerable.

And then, with a flourish of trumpets and much bill-sticking on country gate-posts, Lestrange came to Levenford.

Now Lestrange, or, as he proudly styled himself, Dr Lestrange, was a mixture of the showman and the quack, hailing from America, who had toured the breadth and the length of the world, and now found himself at last in Levenford.

Armed with an impressive electrical equipment, he posed as a great healer, a man of miracles, who helped humanity, cured those hopeless cases where the methods of ordinary physicians had failed.

It was his custom, outside the hall where his performances took place, to display a breathtaking collection of splints, crutches, and steel leg irons, which, he claimed, had been cast away rejoicingly after their owners had been restored to health.

Humbug it was. But such a display did indeed appear outside the Burgh Hall on the occasion of the visit of Lestrange to Levenford, accompanied by photographs and testimonials galore.

Finlay himself observed the galaxy, which occasioned him no more than a mild, contemptuous amusement. He gave it no more than a passing thought.

But the fates decreed that Finlay would think and think about Lestrange.

Late that afternoon as he walked down Church Street towards his surgery he was waylaid by Jessie Grant. She had plainly enough been awaiting him, for there was a fiery gleam of determination in her eye. Straight outright she declared—

'Ye don't need to come any more to my Duncan. I've finished with you and your do-nothing treatment. I'm taking him to Dr Lestrange tonight.'

Caught completely unawares, Finlay could only stare at her, but at last he exclaimed – 'You wouldn't be so foolish!'

'Foolish, indeed!' she bit out. 'I'm sick of all your hummin' and hawin' and orderin' about, wi' not a thing to show for it.'

'But I explained it would be a long job,' protested Finlay.

'Duncan'll be well in another couple of months. For heaven's sake be patient!'

'Ye've kept on biddin' me be patient long enough,' she cried fiercely.

'But this Lestrange isn't a doctor at all,' protested Finlay indignantly.

'So you say!' flashed Jessie with a short, hard laugh. 'But the folk say different. I'm taking Duncan to him as sure as my name is Jessie Grant.'

And before he could say another word she darted a glance of final malevolence at him, and walked off down the street.

For a moment Finlay thought of hurrying after her, but he realised quickly the uselessness of further protest. With a shake of his head he resumed his way.

He knew Lestrange to be an impostor who could not possibly cure Duncan, and as such he left it, reflecting that nothing could result from the man's intervention but disillusionment and humiliation for Jessie Grant.

But here Finlay slightly miscalculated the methods and personality of the bold Lestrange. The so-called doctor had traded so long in human credulity he had become a past master in the art of roguery and deception. In his appearance, too, he was magnificently fitted for the part, tall and upright, with a patriarchal mane of hair, and a flashing eye which magnetised the beholder.

Matching his own arresting figure was his chief assistant, a beautiful young woman by the name of Marietta, silent, dark, and liquid-eyed, whom he claimed to be the daughter of an Indian chief. Small wonder, indeed, that the unwary were beguiled by such high-sounding effrontery.

That night, before a packed audience in the Burgh Hall, surrounded by Leyden jars, electric apparatus, and a weird instrument known as the Cage of Regeneration, Lestrange and Marietta worked their way steadily through their performance towards the climax of the evening, which was, of course, the demonstration of miraculous healing.

Then, with a spectacular flourish, Lestrange called for the halt and the lame to be brought to him.

The first case of all was that of Duncan Grant. Thrust relentlessly into the limelight of the stage by his mother, the little chap stood pale and trembling, while every eye in the crowded hall was turned upon him.

Lestrange advanced dramatically and laid a protective arm on Duncan's shoulders.

With assumed benevolence, he placed the boy upon an elaborate couch, and, in full view of the audience, made what was apparently the most profound examination.

Although his mask-like features revealed nothing as his hands slipped over Duncan's leg, Lestrange was inwardly delighted.

Although entirely without professional skill, long experience had acquainted him with those cases most adapted to his own ends. Duncan's was exactly such a case, for the leg, under Finlay's patient and persevering treatment, had responded finely. The swelling had subsided and the bone had healed; the ankle, in fact, was almost well.

Straightening himself theatrically from the couch, Lestrange raised his hand as though to compel the attention of a multitude.

'Ladies and gentlemen,' he began in his sharp-pitched nasal voice. 'I will now proceed to demonstrate my powers!'

Continuing, hypnotising the audience with high-sounding jargon, he condemned the old-fashioned bungling which had crippled the lad with a loathesome iron, then, in ranting terms he declared that he proposed to cure him.

Beckoning Marietta, who came forward with a winsome tenderness never seen on the face of any trained nurse, he raised Duncan from the couch, and, assisted by his beautiful partner, led the boy to the Cage of Regeneration.

Donning a long white garment, and drawing on rubber gloves, Lestrange took Duncan with him inside the cage. In a deathly silence various impressive rods and wires were adjusted; then in a stillness which was almost painful, the man's rasping command rang out.

Marietta threw over a lever, and the current passed in a quick crackle. Blue sparks ringed the cage with a screen of flame. Then the lever went back, the flame died, and the stillness was intense.

Spellbound, the audience watched Lestrange stoop to remove Duncan's leg-iron and cast it out of the cage across the stage with a gesture of triumphant insolence.

Then, as Duncan came shakily out of the cage, walked a little, and, at the man's hissed command, finally ran across the stage, a great sigh rose in the hall and swelled into a crescendo of sound.

Cheer after cheer rang out from the wildly-excited crowd as Duncan came down the steps and rejoined his mother, while Lestrange, with one hand outstretched and the other placed on his heart, bowed to the acknowledgement of his mastery.

It was a great moment – oh! a thrilling moment – for all within that tense, excited hall.

On the very next morning, when Lestrange and his associates, a tidy sum of takings to the good, had placed thirty miles between themselves and Levenford, Jessie Grant burst into Finlay's surgery with the light of baleful triumph in her eye.

So vindictive was she and so triumphant that the words broke from her lips with the rush of a burn in spate—

'You wanted me not to take the laddie to Dr Lestrange! You wanted to keep him crippled for life, nae doot! Well, in case you haven't heard, I'd have ye know I did take him. And he's cured – cured, do ye hear me? He started back in the yard this morning; he's fit to do it in spite of all your bungling. That's what a real doctor has done for him, and not a fushionless, know-nothing like yourself.'

Finlay stared at the enraged Jessie, unmoved by her vituperation, but strangely perturbed at the unexpected turn of events.

'Didn't I tell you?' he said slowly. 'This man's a rank impostor.'

'He made the laddie walk without irons,' she cried shrilly. 'That's a heap sight more nor you could do!'

'But don't you see,' answered Finlay quickly, holding his temper in rein, 'Duncan could have walked in any case. The trouble is that by putting away the irons too soon the good of all these weeks of treatment is undone.'

'Nonsense!' she shouted. 'A pack of lying nonsense! I know ye. Ye're only trying to save your face.'

Finlay's expression became a trifle strained.

'Mrs Grant,' he declared with firm gravity, 'say what you like about me. I'm not thinking about myself; I'm thinking about Duncan. I beg of you to let him wear the iron for another two months. Just let me go on that little bit longer then . . .'

'No, no,' she interrupted in a passion of violence. 'I'm done and finished with ye. The boy's cured in spite of ye. So don't ever dare to darken my door again.'

And with a laugh of triumph and contempt, she turned and banged out of the surgery.

Too late Finlay's anger flared. He was furious.

With a hot flush of indignation he cursed himself for having borne with Jessie for so long. She was beyond words. And he swore there and then to let her go her own intolerable way. He had warned her sufficiently; now she could run towards disaster and take the consequences.

But, as the days passed and turned into weeks, Finlay's resentment passed also, and instead he began to feel a deep concern for Duncan. It was his own strong professional sense allied to a profound instinct of humanity.

And then, one Saturday in June, almost a month later, as he walked along Church Street, past the Public Library, he came across Duncan, and all his suppressed feeling rose with sudden intensity.

The boy, emerging from the library, where he had been spending his few free hours amongst his beloved books, was limping abominably, hardly daring to place any weight on his right leg.

A pained frown formed on Finlay's brow. He remained in the middle of the pavement directly in Duncan's path, and despite the frown his voice was kind.

'How are you, Duncan, lad?' he asked quietly.

Startled, Duncan raised his eyes from the ground, where they had been fixed, and at the sight of the doctor his pale cheeks flooded with colour.

'I'm not so bad, thank you, doctor.' He paused awkwardly. 'At least . . .'

'At least what?'

'Well, I get about,' muttered Duncan miserably. 'I go to work. But, oh, I don't know . . .'

Finlay did know, however. As he watched Duncan go hirpling down the road he went home and raged to Cameron.

'It's iniquitous,' he threw out in conclusion, pacing furiously up and down the room. 'We've got to stop her. We can't stand by and let her do this thing. The situation is impossible.'

'Yes, it's impossible,' Cameron agreed slowly. 'Impossible for us to interfere.'

'But we must!' Finlay cried violently.

'We can't!' Cameron answered with a shake of his head. 'You know we can't. She's his mother. We can't enforce our treatment. I know that she's hard and bitter on him – that she doesn't care a hang for his welfare besides her own black pride. But makes no difference. You cannot get between mother and son.'

There was a long silence. Then Finlay ground out from between his teeth—

'She's a bonny mother. She doesn't care a pin for the boy. It's an insult to the name to call Jessie Grant a mother.' And, with a gesture of supreme contumely, Finlay walked out of the room and into the surgery, where he took a long drink of cold water, as though to cleanse a vileness from his mouth.

The days passed, and Finlay, although occasionally referring to the subject when Cameron and he were together in the evenings, began gradually to become absorbed by other cases. He saw nothing of Duncan, heard no news of him, and eventually – such was the press of work upon him – fell out of touch with the boy altogether.

And then one evening in the autumn Alex Rankin, a small and ragged urchin who often ran errands about the town, came to the surgery with an undreamed-of message for Finlay. It was a summons from Jessie Grant.

Finlay's first reaction was stupefaction. Then, flooded by the resentful remembrance of all Jessie's bitterness and injustice, he told himself hotly that he would not go. But finally came the thought of Duncan, softening him, making him resolve to bury his own sense of personal injury and answer the call at once.

It was a dark and squally night, without one single star showing through the heavy clouds which banked the sky.

As Finlay rounded the corner and came into Scroggie's Loan, the wind took him and almost bowled him from his feet. Jessie's shop was shut, but a faint light was visible through the small, square-paned window.

He pulled loudly at the bell, which jangled into the dim interior of the little shop, and was at once admitted.

Inside, he did not speak, but stared across at Jessie, who stood, a silent, beshawled figure, her hands folded in front of her, her eyes fixed impenetrably on his, her face harsh and formidable. She muttered at last:

'I want ye to look at Duncan.'

'So I thought.'

His tone was curt and hostile, and it seemed to him that in some vague fashion she winced. But her voice continued stern and indomitable.

'He keeps girnin' about the pain in his leg.' A pause, then, as though the words were dragged from her – 'And he doesna seem eager to walk, like.'

At this something broke loose inside Finlay. He could have slain her for her inhumanity.

'And what do you expect!' he cried furiously. 'Didn't I warn you weeks and months ago that this would happen? I knew it was madness, I told you it was madness the way you were behaving, but you wouldn't listen to me. You're a bitter woman and a bad mother. You haven't a spark of love or kindness in your whole body. You care nothing about your boy. It's a crying scandal the

226

way you've treated him all his life; you ought to think shame, once and for all, black, burning shame of yourself.'

Again that faint tremor passed over her rigid body. But she did not answer his outburst except to say coldly—

'Ye'll see him now ye're here.'

'Yes,' he shouted, stung beyond endurance by her icy indifference. 'But not for you. For his own sake, because I'm fond of him, because I want to try to get him out of your clutches.'

And without waiting for her reply, he turned away and walked into the back where Duncan lay.

Jessie remained quite motionless, as he had left her, her expression still drawn and curiously remote. He was a long time, a very long time, but still she did not move. Indeed, as the minutes passed, slowly recorded by the moving hands of the old wag-at-the-wa' clock behind her, she seemed to become more rigid, to contract, almost, into a statuesque immobility. Her features, pale against the dark shadows of the kitchen, were set and hard as granite.

At last Finlay returned. He came slowly, in a manner quite different to his tempestuous exit from the room. He busied himself for a moment quickly adjusting the contents of his bag, then straightening himself, not looking at her, he said gravely—

'We've finished with words now. It's time to act – or it may be too late. The leg is in a shocking state. There is only one thing to do, and mark my words, it must be done quickly.'

Silence. Her body, frozen and rigid, was convulsed by a violent inward spasm, yet her voice did not lose its stony note.

'What is't ye mean?'

Again silence; he looked at her at last. His tone was quiet, studiously even.

'I mean that your boy is seriously ill. The condition has entended. We must get him into hospital immediately, I think we'll have to operate. Amputation!' He paused, then spoke slowly, letting every word sink in. 'Your motherly behaviour may have cost the boy his leg.'

For a moment nothing was heard but the battering of the wind in the outer darkness; then, as though in the darkness of her soul there rose an echo of that fierce wind, she muttered harshly—

'Ye mean – he's like to lose his leg?'

He nodded in silence, and, picking up his bag, went out into the blackness of the night.

Duncan was taken to the Cottage Hospital in the ambulance which Finlay summoned, and within the hour made comfortable in bed. He was given a draught, and fell asleep at once. Then came the next morning, which broke fine and clear, and brought Finlay early to the hospital, torn by anxiety as to the fateful decision he must shortly make.

In the clean and polished ward, bending over Duncan's white bed, he made his re-examination, aided by the better light and the less fretful condition of the patient – testing, considering, balancing in his mind the case for operation and against.

Finally, he seemed to reach a positive conclusion, and with a tightening of his lips he turned to the matron who stood beside him. But before he could speak, a young nurse approached.

'His mother wants to see you, doctor. She's been waiting since six o'clock this morning. She says she must see you, and simply won't take No.'

Finlay made to brush the request away, then suddenly checked himself. On sudden impulse he went into the visitor's room where Duncan's mother awaited him.

And there, on the threshold, he paused. Jessie Grant was in the room sure enough – yes, it was she, though in the ordinary way never would Finlay have known her. She had a shrunken, shilpit look, as if she had fallen into herself, and in the space of that one short night her hair had turned to the colour of driven snow. Rocking herself back and forward, she was like a woman demented, wringing her hands like she was wrestling with something. And all the time moaning out Duncan's name. Then she lifted her head and saw Finlay. Instantly she came forward, her face revealing an emotion that was incredible.

'Doctor,' she grasped his arm, her speech broken and distraught. 'Tell me about him. Ye can't do it – ye won't take off his leg?'

He stared at her changed and ravaged features, bewildered, doubting the evidence of his senses. At last he said slowly—

'You're a bit late, surely, with your concern.'

But she only clutched his arm the more, her voice desperate.

'Don't ye understand, doctor?' Her whole body shuddered as with pain. 'I never kenned I loved the boy. But I do, doctor. I do. I've brought him up hard. I was feared he would turn out like his father, weak and soft, and a wastrel. I've used him sore and ill, but in my heart, doctor, I ken now that I love him.'

Finlay continued to gaze at her, profoundly troubled, half-doubting, half-believing this agonised revelation. She rushed on frantically—

'I've done wrong, doctor. I admit it freely. But I'll make up for it. Oh, I'll do anything you say. But for the love of the Almighty, spare my boy his leg.'

Now there was no mistaking the frenzied pleading in her tone. His eyes fell before the agony that lay open and naked in her face. There was a long silence. Then in a low voice he said—

'I've already made up my mind not to operate. I think, after all, we can save the leg. It'll mean months and months of treatment in plaster lying up here in the hospital.'

'Oh, doctor,' she breathed, as though it were a prayer, 'Never mind that if you'll just get him right.'

He did not answer. But, rooted to the ground at a strange and moving sound, he stood in pity and in wonder. It was the fearsome sound of Jessie's sobbing.

The tobacconist's shop in Scroggie's Loan has changed hands now, and Jessie Grant is seen in it no more. But there is a little white-haired woman, very gentle and quiet, who keeps house for

Duncan Grant, the young classical master at Levenford Academy, in a small, neat villa out by the Garslake Road.

When newcomers to the town remark how Mrs Grant spoils her clever son, Finlay holds his peace. Even when Cameron broaches the subject Finlay will take no credit, but with an inscrutable smile remarks that they owe the miracle to Lestrange.

The Wild Rasp Jam

Every year, when the fruit ripens, and the good earth yields its bounty, bringing douce housewives to their jam-making, Finlay receives unfailingly a fine big pot of raspberry jam from Tannochbrae, the snug little village on the lochside beyond Markles.

Many presents came to Finlay from the lochside folk, for they loved him, and he them; indeed, he always maintained this part of his practice to be by far the dearest to him. Yes, many a thing he had, from a goose, or a cheese maybe, or a salmon, or, in season, a brace of grouse. And in particular many a thing he had from Tannochbrae. But they were gifts solely of kindness and affection. They had not the spiritual significance, nor, for that matter, the strangely human story which lay behind that simple pot of jam.

And here, if you like, is the story itself.

Nessie Sutherland was the belle of Tannochbrae, a young spirited lass who, though poor, and often poorly dressed, was so bonny and blithe that her lovely hazel eyes played havoc amongst the young men of the lochside.

She was a sweet lass, right enough, maybe a trifle wilful in her ways, too sure of her power to fascinate, her head a little turned by the attention she received, but at heart unspoiled and inno- cent as the meadow queen that grew so freshly in the glens of Tannochbrae.

Nessie, though not yet turned twenty, had suitors galore, but amongst the crowd of them in the race for her favour and affec- tion, one seemed to stand far ahead of all the rest. He was Hugh

Riach, dashing, black-haired Hughie, six foot in his stocking soles, and broad in proportion, with a fine handsome head, a roving eye, and always the ready word, both glib and hearty, with which to greet the world.

Oh, he was a grand lad, everyone agreed, a man who could take his dram and hold it, fine company, a rogueish lad with many conquests, it was slyly rumoured, to his credit.

And there was more to Hughie than that! Beside the looks and his loud-voiced gallantry, he was heir to Tannochbrae Farm, which gave him a real advantage, especially in the eyes of Nessie's mother, who, shifty and needy, kept dinning in her daughter's ears the benefit of gear and siller to a tocherless lass.

That made little difference, however, though 'twas helpful in its way, for Nessie was swept off her feet by the dashing Hughie, and Hughie for once was equally swept away by her.

Out fishing in the loch that July day with his great friend Peter Donald, he boasted openly of his high intentions.

'I'm mad about her, Peter,' he declared in his ranting style. 'I'll no' be happy till I have her. She's fair bewitched me. Man, ye'd hardly credit it, but I've got to be that set on Nessie, even the thought of the show and winning the cup with Heather Pride means nothing at all beside it. I tell ye, Peter, I'll never rest till Nessie's mine.'

Peter Donald was silent, reflecting, maybe, how great Hughie's love must be to divert his attention from the tearing ambition which had consumed him for the last twelve months, namely to win the challenge cup at the County Show with his prize bull, Heather Pride. At length he muttered—

'Maybe I do understand, Hughie. I've always thought well of Nessie myself.'

Peter was like that, always moderate in his speech, a silent and rather uncommunicative chap who was studying for the ministry, with hopes ultimately of getting the manse at Tannochbrae. He had none of Hughie's good looks; his face was long and serious, and his brown eyes were not dashing, but sympathetic and kindly.

Yet, though he was shy and afraid of women and immersed in his books, he was far from being a bookworm.

Peter knew the woods and the birds and the beasts therein. He was the best fisher out of Tannochbrae, and for all his back was bowed by study his biceps were big, and he could toss a caber further than any man in the village.

At this moment Peter seemed to struggle with himself, as though he wanted to pursue the conversation further, but something, perhaps his shyness, restrained him. And then, all at once, he hooked a salmon, and the opportunity was lost in the stir of playing and gaffing the fish. But though the matter was dropped between Hughie and Peter, Hughie continued loudly to proclaim his passion that night in the Tannochbrae Arms.

Thumping the table with his fist, with a few drinks to give him pith, he roared—

'There's two things I'm going to do in the next few weeks. I'm going to win the cup with Heather Pride, and I'm going to have Nessie Sutherland for my bonnie bride.'

A silence of apprehension.

'That's poetry,' continued Hughie, leering round half drunk, 'the best lines of poetry that was ever wrote.'

Hughie's poetry, or at least the sentiment, was not long in going the round of the village, and reached the humble home where lived Mrs Sutherland and Nessie.

The old woman was in high good humour, and Nessie herself not displeased at such evident admiration on the part of her handsome suitor.

They sat outside the cottage in the warm dusk, discussing Hughie, enumerating his fine points, when Peter Donald strode along with the salmon he had caught that day.

'I thought maybe you'd care to have this, Mrs Sutherland,' he remarked unobtrusively. 'We have another at home, and we're not minding so much for it.'

His bashful way of presenting the gift made Nessie titter, and she thought how gallantly Hughie would have cried – 'Here's a braw salmon for ye, Nessie, lass, I caught it specially for yourself.'

Nessie was well aware of Peter's dumb admiration for her, which had existed since their schooldays together. It flattered her vanity, though, of course, there was small chance for Peter with such a dashing gallant as Hughie in the field.

Such was the general opinion of the village and the district, but there were those who, viewing both men, wished it were otherwise. And amongst them was our hero, Finlay.

Finlay knew more, perhaps, of Hughie Riach than most, and of his doings beyond the quiet confines of Tannochbrae – gay adventures in Levenford, for instance, of a Saturday night. And Finlay was far from sharing the general opinion of Hughie's worth.

Late one afternoon in the following week, driving out on his daily visit to Tannochbrae, Finlay took a short cut by the lane through Tannochbrae woods, and there, quite suddenly he came on Hughie and Nessie idling close together on the grassy pathway which lay between the lane and the woods.

In one hand Nessie carried a basket filled with wild raspberries which she had been gathering, and Hughie's arm was tight round her waist.

Something in the sight of those two wandering so close together in this unfrequented spot made Finlay frown, though it ought to have been an idyllic vision.

On a sudden impulse he drew up his horse and declared, with a pretence of jocularity—

'Why aren't you at your work, Hughie, man, instead of hanging about in the woods at this time of the day?'

Hughie's face clouded, and he said sullenly—

'That's my business.'

Unperturbed, Finlay went on, in the same light tone—

'And you, Nessie. You ought to be home at your jam-making. You know as well as I do that the berries ought to be sugared the minute they're picked or the jam isn't so good.'

Nessie looked up, her face flushed, her hair disarranged, too startled and confused to speak. It was Hughie who got ready another rude reply, but before it came Finlay made a gesture of invitation with the reins.

'Step up, Nessie,' he nodded. 'I'm driving past your mother's house. I'll drop you there. Come along now; you can't refuse a lift!'

Abashed and unable to refuse the invitation from such an august source, Nessie complied, and climbed up into the gig beside Finlay, who, with a curt nod to Hughie, drove off.

Finlay drove Nessie back to Tannochbrae slowly. At first he kept silent, surprised at his own action. But there was that in Nessie's eyes and in her shamed submission which told him how timely had been his interference.

Gradually the strain eased, and Finlay casually drew the conversation round to Peter Donald, remarking to Nessie what a fine fellow he was, how quiet and unassuming and kindly, and, above all, how fond of her. But Nessie, now a little angered at having been coerced into leaving Hughie, tossed her head petulantly.

'Peter's just a feared thing,' she said. 'If he's fond of me, why hasn't he got the courage to say so? I like a man that's got some spunk in him.'

Finlay sighed and dropped the conversation completely, thinking, as many a man had done before him, that no words of his could alter the case, that a wilful woman must have her way.

Time passed, and the day of the County Show drew near. The show, which took place at Levenford, was, of course, a great and eagerly awaited event, and this year more than ever the folks at Tannochbrae were keyed up to a high pitch of expectancy. They wanted Hughie's Heather Pride to win the Challenge Cup. Hughie himself seemed to have no question in his mind but that he would lift the prize. His boasting left no room for doubt.

Two days before the show, in a lordly fashion, he invited Nessie and his friend, Peter, to see his prize animal. It was sheer vanity on his part – the desire to impress Nessie with a sense of his possessions, for the humiliation he had received through Finlay still rankled; and bedsides, he had perhaps some inkling of Peter's feeling for Nessie, and, in his high-handed fashion, was determined to check such presumption once and for all.

It was a fine, warm afternoon when Nessie and Peter arrived at the farm, and Hughie led them straight away to the yard, where, in his arrogant fashion, he nodded to Dougal, the farm lad, to bring out the bull.

'There!' he remarked loudly to Peter, though his remarks were plainly for Nessie. 'Take a look at that, if you please, and tell me if it suits you.'

Peter and Nessie looked at the bull which Dougal had brought out from the darkness of the stall. It was a superb animal, jet black in colour, young, virile, indomitably alive. In the sunshine its black hide glistened, while the muscles of its neck bunched in a powerful hump, and its eye, shot with strange lights, rolled towards Hughie – sullen, unfathomable. Something latent in that eye seemed to fan the blustering bravado of Hughie's mood.

'Hup, man, hup!' he cried irritably. 'Don't look at me so dour. Ye'll never win the cup with that red eye. Hup, hup!'

And he twitched the steel chain attached to the beast's nose-ring until the beautiful animal arched its back angrily.

'Ye see,' Hughie remarked with a grin, 'it knows its master, the brute. And a noble brute it is. Hup, hup!'

Domineeringly he laid his big hand on the bull's pale pink nostrils, as though to show his power, his mastery. But at that moment the bull violently twitched its head and tore the chain out of Hughie's hands.

It broke loose into the yard and drew up, with its back arched and its forelegs together, stiff. Its hide, tense and living, glistened black against the whitewashed walls that enclosed the yard. The white glare of those walls hurt its eyes. This hot, yellow sand, strewn upon the square, was strangely irritating after the soothing darkness of its stall. Its eyes were fixed on Hughie with a kind of latent animosity.

Hughie started, nonplussed that the bull should have broken loose, forgetful of Nessie and Peter beside him, as they stood cornered in the angle between the byre and bull's stall. He took a step forward, surprised, cautious.

'Here,' he cried to the bull, 'here, man, here!'

But the bull made no response; it stood quite still, impassive, as if carved in ebony.

Hughie took another step forward, half-blustering, half-cajoling.

'What are ye doin', man? Here, man, here!'

By way of answer the bull made a run at Hughie, not a furious run, but a slow, rather considering run. Hughie jumped aside and swore as the beast barged heavily past him.

Springing forward, he tried to grip the bull's neck with both arms, bearing all its weight on his side, trying to steer it towards the open door of its stall. But the bull dragged him a few paces, shook him off easily, impatiently. Then, as he fell, it butted and nosed him about the back.

Hughie felt the horns rake the soft gravel beneath him as he rolled over on his side. He sprang to his feet again, bruised and shaken.

'Damn ye!' he cried. 'Damn ye!'

At which the bull, turning on its forefeet, very sharp and sudden, ripped its right horn through Hughie's shirt.

Swearing loudly, with his face suddenly alarmed, Hughie backed towards the shelter of the farm buildings, directly opposite the corner where Peter and Nessie stood. His torn shirt billowed off his shoulders like a cloak. He kept muttering, 'Ye would, would ye? Ye'd horn me, you brute! I'll learn ye – I'll learn ye something.'

But, alas! as the bull rushed towards him again Hughie's pretence of courage left him. He wavered, turned, and, seeing the kitchen door open behind him, he bolted as hard as his heels would carry him into the house.

At the sight of Hughie running away Nessie's heart constricted. Stunned, she could not credit it – Hughie showing such arrant cowardice! But she had little time to reflect, for at the same moment the bull swung, and, baulked in its rush at Hughie, lowered its head, then launched itself straight at the spot where she and Peter stood.

It was a savage, tearing rush, which, half-stupefied as she was, might well have proved the end of Nessie. But Peter acted quicker than a flash.

Pushing her violently to one side, while he leapt to the other, he saved them both. Nessie could feel the swish of the horn as it went past her side, and she saw Peter fall with the quickness of his own leap.

Peter jumped up again. His face was pale; not pale with terror, but pale with a hard, cold determination. He realised that Nessie and he, trapped by the angle of the walls, were in a desperate position.

Looking around swiftly, he caught hold of a rusty sickle which lay beside the water-butt. It was a feeble weapon, but he gripped the handle of the old hook till the white cords stood out on his hand. His jaw was set like a rock, his eyes were wide, staringly alert.

The bull, now thoroughly infuriated, came at him again, head down, back muscles humped. Peter held his ground to the last fraction of a second, knowing that the bull would strike to the right. Then, before he jumped, he smashed the back of the hook on the beast's neck.

It was a felling stroke, but it had little effect upon the bull, which turned short on its own momentum, and then, stopping, tore into Peter. Again and again Peter struck it with the heavy hook before he flung himself away to safety.

The bull paused at a distance of twenty feet, breathing heavily, eyeing the man sideways with one small, wicked eye.

Nessie, in an agony of terror, could see its nostrils widening. Then slowly, dangerously, it moved. No rush, but a slow sidle towards Peter, edging him back into the wall at the corner of the yard where Nessie stood penned in.

Peter backed a few yards, saw his mistake, saw that Nessie was in danger. At that instant the bull charged again. As the bull came in Peter did not move, but, crouching directly in front of Nessie, he took the full impact of the animal's rush. The bull's rush. The bull's horn buried itself in Peter's side.

Nessie screamed, as, clasping the beast's free horn with both hands, his face distorted, anguished, Peter wrenched himself away from the horn which impaled him, then slid down the bull's shoulders to his knees, while the blood came in quick spurts from his torn side.

Tossing its head in triumph, the bull again made to rush at Nessie, but Peter, swaying on his legs, his hands empty of any weapon, got up again to face the bull.

Full of fight and confidence, the bull bored in. Peter never moved. His head hung down, but his jaw was still grimly clenched.

As the bull charged he shut his fist and smashed it with all his force full in the brute's soft muzzle. The blow nearly broke his wrist, but the shock of it stopped the bull, which paused as though surprised. And in the same moment intervention came from the other end of the yard.

Dougal and Matt, the ploughman, attracted by Nessie's screams, raced into the yard, waving their arms to take the bull's attention, Matt was brandishing a heavy sledge, and as the bull came in on its next rush he planted his feet wide apart, whirled the sledge high in the air, and smashed it fair in the centre of the beast's brow.

The crack of the impact came clear and hard as a gunshot. The bull halted suddenly. All its venom seemed to wither into the air. Then, stunned, first one knee and then another buckled under it; it sloped over on its side, and finally collapsed.

Swaying on his feet, Peter looked stupidly at the fallen bull. Then he glanced at Nessie.

His face streaked with blood and dust, was filled with a great tenderness. He tried to lift his hand to wipe his lips, but he could not. Then he fell heavily across the body of the bull.

An hour later Finlay drove like a madman up to Tannochbrae. Ignoring the stir that his arrival caused, he made straight into the kitchen, where, on the horse-hair sofa, Peter lay stretched. Bending down amidst a dead silence, Finlay began to minister to the injured man. Beside him, holding some whisky in a tumbler, spilling half of it with a shaky hand, Hughie groaned—

'My God! He's all right, isn't he?'

Finlay rose slowly, his face dark and unfriendly.

'Yes, he's all right. It's only the muscle that's been torn. He'll be right again in three or four weeks.'

'Thank God!' cried Hughie again, and he tried to put his arm round Nessie, but Nessie broke away from him with a cold, pale look.

Hughie's lips began to quiver again. He glanced round the assembled company in a kind of desperate entreaty. But every eye avoided his. Then Hughie groaned again and stumbled into a seat, cowering and twitching like a man who has been in cold water too long.

A moment later he broke down completely. Blubbering, he whispered, 'Oh, God in heaven, I dinna ken what came over me.'

A week later, when Peter was well on the way to recovery, Nessie ventured round to see him.

'Is there anything I can do,' she said, her eyes steadily on his, 'to make it up to ye, Peter? I've always treated ye shameful. And now ye've saved my life. It was a brave, brave thing ye did, Peter.'

'Oh, I don't know,' he answered simply, colouring under her praise. 'It wasn't that much after all.'

This time Nessie did not smile at Peter's shyness, for she knew it as the mark of the man's great heart.

★   ★   ★

In the following year Peter and Nessie were married, and now they live in the square sandstone manse on the outskirts of Tannochbrae. But, though they are beloved and highly esteemed in the village, they are not so staid as Peter's learned profession might lead one to expect. They go boating on the loch in their little lugsail, and love to tramp on the moors above the village. There is nothing to mar their happiness.

Hughie, broken and disgraced, sold the farm and went off to Canada in a vain attempt to make a man of himself.

And now, when Nessie takes her children to the woods to gather raspberries, she does not think of him, such is her present happiness, except with pity. But she does not forget the doctor and his love of raspberry jam, nor the all-important fact that by driving her back to make it he saved her one August afternoon from herself and Hughie Riach.

And that is why every year, when the earth yields its bounty, Finlay receives from Tannochbrae the big sweet pot of wild rasp jam.

Who Laughs Last

'Don't go,' pithily remarked Cameron to Finlay that April morning when the call came in for Meg Mirless. 'Take my tip and give the guid lady a gey wide berth.'

Finlay looked up inquiringly from his finnan haddie which he had been discussing with a healthy appetite before his partner and patron spoke those sage words of admonition and advice.

'And why?' said he.

Cameron smiled.

'In the first place, you'll never sniff your fee, and in the second, there's nothing could ever be wrong wi' Meg Mirlees. She's the healthiest, hardiest, stingiest old faggot that ever drew breath by the grace o' God and the Provost in this Royal and ancient burgh.'

Finlay helped himself to more haddock, buttered another of Janet's famous home-baked bannocks, and listened interestedly while, with a wry and reminiscent smile, Cameron went on.

'Well do I mind the first time I ever waited on her. She had me in for a cough, making out that she had bronchitis, though hang the trouble I could ever discover in her tubes. I called all winter, for it was in my young days in Levenford when I was green and eager and easily led by the nose.

'Well, to cut a long story short, when I sent in my bill, I'm hanged if her ladyship didn't turn round and argue that she had only asked me to call the once, and the rest of the times had just been for my own pleasure, so to speak. She argued till all was blue, and at the end o't I lost my temper, tore up the bill, and flung it in her face.'

Cameron chuckled.

'Dod, 'twas just what she wanted. When I told her I wouldn't take a penny of her rotten money she laughed like an old cuddy and showed me to the door.'

'So that's her style!' exclaimed Finlay.

'Ay,' Cameron answered, 'It is her style. She's a miser, man; maybe not so much miserly as mean. Tcha! she's as mean with all her gear as a temperance hotel wi' matches. Mind you, it isn't as if she wasn't well off. She's worth any amount o' siller. She's got braw things in her house – antiques, ah, beautiful antiques.'

Cameron sighed with all the envy of a rival collector, for, besides his fiddles, the old doctor was desperately keen on curios and antique china.

'Why, she's got a plate there – a dish, to be exact, it's genuine Ming, brought back by her great-grandmother from Canton, and worth a mint of money. Land's sake! I'd give my eye-teeth to have the like o't.'

Finlay laughed outright at the sudden longing that had crept into Cameron's tone. He rolled up his napkin and thrust it in the ring. Somehow his interest had been awakened by the account of Miss Mirlees, and as he rose from the table he declared—

'I've a mind to have a look at your friend. She'll not get the better of me.'

'Ye say so.' Cameron cocked his head shrewdly. 'Why, man. I'll wager she'd get what she wants out o' you and never pay a penny piece.'

'Nonsense!' protested Finlay stoutly. 'You wouldn't catch me giving her advice for nothing.'

Cameron hid a smile, caressing his chin with a typical reflective gesture.

'On ye go and try, then. Try your hand at her, by all means. If you think you're a match for Meg Mirlees, Finlay, man, ye've no small conceit of yourself.'

Placed thoroughly on his mettle by this turn of the conversation, and, by the same token, curious to match his wits with the formidable old dame, Finlay, when he had visited his more serious cases that day, dropped in on Meg Mirlees about three in the afternoon.

Meg lived in Chapel Street, a narrow thoroughfare composed mainly of old-fashioned houses, very quiet and genteel, yet opening at the far end into High Street. The window of Meg's sitting-room did, in fact, afford a splendid view of High Street, and here, ensconced strategically, Meg would sit watching the passing life of the town, craning her neck, criticising, condemning, throwing out a tasty word of scandal to such of her cronies as had come to keep her company.

Meg had no friends, but only a tiny ring of toadies, who, by obsequious flattery, hoped to 'come in for something' in Meg's will.

Meg, however, was alone when Finlay entered, crouched in her customary chair – a gaunt, hard-bitten, shrunken old maid with high cheekbones, a healthy colour, and small, beady, bright eyes.

She was dressed entirely in rusty black, with an old, darned shawl happed about her, and a worn pair of elastic-sided boots upon her bunioned feet. A bag of small imperials – her one luxury – lay with the Bible on the fine needle-worked stool which stood beside her.

The plenishings of the room were really excellent; fine old furniture, crystal lustres on the mantelpiece, while, on a table by the window with its back to him, was the famous Ming plate. But the place, for all the value of its contents, had a frowsy smell and dank and chilly air.

'Well, well, doctor,' whined Meg by way of welcome, 'it's good of ye to look in to see a poor auld cratur like mysel'. It's no' a professional visit, of course. Ye wouldna think o' looking on it in that light. Ye see, it's just a wee bit private word I wanted with ye.'

Before Finlay could protest she went on quickly.

'Ay, ay, sit down there and rest ye. It's as cheap sittin' as standin'. I had a mind to light the fire, and then I just didna. I hope you don't find it cauld.'

Even as Finlay shivered in the frigid room he had to smile. He saw that it was more joy for Meg to sit without a fire to save coal than to be warmed with the cheerful blaze she could have well afforded. He took a chair, and gazed at the bleak and cunning old face before him.

'Well,' said he briskly, 'why did you send for me, Miss Mirlees?'

'Tit, tit, doctor!' cried Meg in a panic, 'dinna put it that down-richt way. A' I said was ye might look in if you happened to be passing. I was meaning to offer you a cup of tea, but 'deed I do declare, I've just discovered we're out o' sugar, and the kettle's this meenit gone off the boil forbye.'

She broke off, shook her head sadly at the strange coincidence which prevented her offering him hospitality, helped herself with relish to a small imperial, then, as an after-thought, half-offered the bag to Finlay.

'Ye'll no' be mindin' for one o' thae, doctor. Ye'll no' care for the peppermints.'

She had no idea he would accept, but before she could withdraw the bag Finlay, suppressing a smile, reached out his hand and helped himself liberally.

'Thanks, Miss Mirlees,' he cried. 'I've got an awfully sweet tooth. How did you know it?'

Meg's face froze at the inroads he had made on her precious imperials. She snatched back the bag and declared nippily—

'Ay, it wad seem ye do like them.'

Screwing the paper poke tightly, she gave him a glower and thrust the sweets safely in her pocket.

There was a short silence, broken only as they sucked their imperials at one another.

Finlay, warmed by the initial skirmish, was beginning to enjoy himself.

'And now, Miss Mirlees, that we're happy and comfortable, what is it all about?'

Meg darted a sharp glance at him, but, recovering her equanimity with an effort, she assumed a dreadful pretence of sprightliness.

'Weel, it's this way, doctor. Maybe I have something that might prove interesting for ye. Oh, I ken you doctors are aye lookin' for something extraordinary in the way o' complaints.'

She paused, considering him shrewdly.

'It's a bit lump on top o' my head. It doesna worry me ava', mind ye. I've had it these sax years, too, but, dod, it's been getting bigger lately, so, says I to myself, it might be real interestin' for young Dr Finlay to look in and maybe, in a quiet way, to try his hand at getting quit o' it for me. It'll be grand experience for the young man, thinks I, and, 'deed, I've no doubt at all, thinks I, he'd be glad enough to shift it without charge gin I gie him the chance.'

Her barefaced effrontery fairly took Finlay's breath away, but he restrained himself, and said—

'Let me look at it, then.'

'Weel, there's no harm in lookin',' responded Meg with a sharp little laugh.

Finlay rose and went over to the window.

Parting Meg's hair, still dark and thick, he examined her scalp, where, as she indicated, there was a round, pink swelling, as big as a pigeon's egg.

He recognised the condition at once. It was a simple sebaceous cyst; in plain language, an ordinary wen, a condition commonly met with, and easy to remove.

Resuming his seat, he explained to Meg in a few words what the condition was, and how, by a simple operation, he could put it right for her.

Her eye glistened. She rubbed her hands together.

'Ay, I thocht ye'd like the job, doctor. I knew from the start it would be grand experience for ye.'

Bubbling inside with merriment, Finlay surveyed her with assumed severity.

'I'm not needing that sort of experience, Miss Mirlees. I'll do

246

the operation for you, if you wish.' He paused significantly. 'But the fee will be a guinea and a half.'

Her face changed comically. She threw up her hands in horror.

'Doctor! Doctor!' she screeched. 'I'm surprised at ye. It's no' a thing to joke over.'

'I was never more serious in my life,' said Finlay coolly.

'Na, na,' entreated Meg. 'You're no' sae heartless, doctor. Havena I told ye . . .'

'Never mind what you've told me,' returned Finlay firmly. 'It's what I'm telling you that matters. One guinea and a half is the fee and not a penny less.'

Meg began to whine.

'I couldna afford it, I couldna, I couldna. Such a way to treat a puir auld woman. Oh, doctor, doctor . . .'

On she went, begging and praying. But Finlay was adamant. He had sworn to get the better of the stingy Meg. And he meant to keep his word.

In the end Meg must have seen this, for eventually she gave over, her face flushed with temper and vexation.

'Away with ye, then,' she cried. 'Ye're a bad black-hearted villain. I've wasted my time ower ye. Don't dare charge me for this visit, either. I'll not pay it, not a farthing. I've no money.'

Finlay rose to go, having enjoyed himself thoroughly, when all at once the great idea struck him.

It was indeed a grand idea, he thought, and his eyes sped towards the Ming Plate which Cameron had envied so greatly. He exclaimed—

'Never mind about the money then, Miss Mirlees, if you're rather hard put to it just now. We can't take the breeks off a hielandman. But I'll make a bargain with you. I'll do the operation if you'll give me that plate there by the window.'

The effect of his words could not have been more unexpected or disastrous. Meg exploded in a final burst of temper.

'My plate!' she shrieked. 'My bonny Ming plate that's worth

a heap of golden sovereigns! The idea! The very idea! To think ye wad try to take advantage o' me like that! As if I didna ken the value o't! Get out my house, you bold, bad villain, get out my house before I tak' my stick to ye!' And, brandishing the little black cane with which she hobbled about the house, she almost drove him out of the room.

Finlay retreated, laughing at his own defeat, meaning to relate the entire incident with gusto to Cameron that night after supper. But before evening there arrived a note from Meg, wholly unexpected and amazing, asking him to call without fail on the following day. Finlay marvelled, but, awaiting developments, he kept his own counsel, and next morning presented himself again at Meg's house.

She was strangely penitent, subdued, tearfully apologetic.

''Deed, I'm sorry at the way I behaved to ye yestreen, doctor. It was shameful, I ken, but ye maun excuse me. You see, I'm attached to the plate, and your demand fair took me by surprise. But I've been thinking since then, and I maun have my poor head seen to. It's an awfu' affliction. I canna rest it on the back of my chair at all, at all. I canna thole it, doctor.' And with her sharp little eyes darting gimlet glances at him, she added – 'And so I've decided to give ye the plate in payment for puttin' me right.'

A thrill of triumph shot through Finlay at having brought the old miser to heel, and also at having secured the plate for Cameron. He had always wanted to give Cameron something for his collection; and now here at last was the chance!

'Very well,' he said briskly. 'We'll consider it settled, Miss Mirlees.'

He went over to the window and took up the plate, and, while she watched him with avaricious eyes, examined it slowly.

Examined closely, it seemed an ordinary enough plate, plain blue and white in its colouring, rather like a dinner plate, but then Finlay knew nothing of antiques, and he was well aware of the store which Cameron, and, indeed, Meg herself, placed upon it. As he surrendered it back to her jealous hands he said firmly—

'Remember, now, Miss Mirlees, I'm to take this plate away whenever I've finished with you. It's to be this plate and no other.'

'Very well,' agreed Meg gravely. 'That plate and no other. It's a bargain!' Then quickly, 'But ye maun do the thing handsome, doctor. Ye're not to hurt me. Ye're to take the wen away so it will never come back again. Ye're to come in every day to see me.'

'All right,' said Finlay. 'It's agreed.'

'And forbye,' exclaimed Meg, 'ye'll throw in all the dressings and bandages complete. It's a' to be included.'

'Yes, yes,' said Finlay, trying to escape. But Meg, clutching at his arms, went on driving the hardest bargain that she could.

'And forbye, doctor, ye're to gi'e me a braw bottle of tonic for my bluid.'

'Good heavens!' thought Finlay. 'If I don't get out of here she'll be asking me to cut her corns.' However, he put the best face on it that he could, and promised to comply with even the most exacting of her requests.

He did, in fact, make a fine job of the operation, taking endless pains to make it satisfactory. He froze the round swelling thoroughly by spraying it with ethyl chloride, so that the incision should not hurt her. He dissected out the little cyst perfectly, stitched up the wound, and dressed it with iodoform gauze. It was a ticklish job, and took him, from start to finish, a full hour.

Meg, determined to get every ounce of satisfaction, made a great fuss, moaning and groaning and making awful grimaces. Such, indeed, was her attitude, as Finlay came every day to change her dressing. She was a perfect trial and tribulation, harassing him on every front. Only the thought of the beautiful plate he would get from her and be able to give to Cameron kept him from condemning her to everlasting torment. But he did endure it to the end, and at last, after a fortnight, the whole thing was finished, the wound healed, the wen gone, and Meg grudgingly satisfied. It was all over but the fee.

'Now for our bargain,' said Finlay determinedly. With an odd glint in his eye he went on – 'Here. This is the bottle of tonic I promised to give you at the end of the treatment. Take it and hand over the plate.'

She accepted the bottle of physic he held out to her. Then, with unexpected meekness, she hobbled over to the window, took the plate from its stand, and handed it to him without a word. He surveyed it proudly.

'Would you like a bit of paper to wrap it in?' she muttered.

Amazed at her liberality, he nodded – perhaps she wasn't such a bad old thing after all. He shook hands with her, then, with the plate wrapped in an old piece of brown paper and tucked under his arm, he left Meg's house and walked triumphantly home. Cameron was in the sitting-room, wandering about with his pipe in his mouth and his hands in his pockets. No moment could have been more propitious. With an assumption of indifference Finlay declared—

'I've a present for you.'

'Oh,' said Cameron. He looked surprised but pleased, and as, without further delay, Finlay launched into the story of his bargain with Meg Mirlees, the old doctor listened open-mouthed. When Finlay came to the climax Cameron fairly beamed.

'Well, it beats all, Finlay man, and to think you've got me the plate. Well, well, laddie, I can hardly believe it. I've had my eye on it for years.' And Cameron's hands, the hands of the connoisseur, fairly itched to get at the treasure.

With pretended modesty, Finlay unwrapped the plate. Cameron took it eagerly, stared at it with bulging eyes, then let out a shout.

'D'you like it?' said Finlay, fairly oozing satisfaction.

'Like it!' cried Cameron. The expression of eagerness vanished from his face. He looked at Finlay. He looked back at the plate. Then all at once something came over him and he began to laugh.

He laughed till the tears rolled down his cheeks. He laughed and laughed as he had not done for months, laughed till Janet came rushing to the door to see what it was all about.

'Oh, Lord save us! Finlay,' gasped Cameron. 'When I think of it. You, day after day – running after her – cutting out her wen – waitin' on her hand and foot . . .'

'Well,' said Finlay, faintly annoyed. 'Ye've got the Ming plate, haven't ye?'

'Ming!' choked Cameron with a fresh convulsion. 'My dear man it's no such thing. It's an ordinary dinner plate. You can buy this for three halfpenny in the Stores. I'll bet my hat that's where Meg got it. The window's full o' them.' And holding his sides he collapsed in a peal of fresh hysterics.

Finlay sat down on the sofa.

'Man, I can see it all,' went on Cameron. 'Right at the start Meg changed the plate. She's sold ye – lock, stock and barrel. At this very minute she'll be telling her cronies how she's worsted ye, tittering, and tee-heeing, rubbing her hands together. "This self-same plate", ye insisted, holding up the threepence-halfpenny article, driving your bargain by your way o't. And ye got the self-same plate. Ye've got no redress.'

There was a moment's silence while Finlay gazed across at the helpless, speechless Cameron. Then, slowly, reflectively, but with increasing enjoyment, Finlay began to laugh as well. And at that unexpected sound Cameron's mirth underwent a sudden change into sharp surprise.

'Wh—?' he exclaimed. 'What's this? What in all the world have you got to laugh at?'

'Oh, nothing,' answered Finlay nonchalently. 'Just nothing at all.'

'I should think not,' retorted Cameron with marked emphasis. 'I couldna find much to laugh at myself if I'd let Meg Mirless make a cuddy out of me so easy.'

'Maybe, maybe,' agreed Finlay with a sly nod. 'But to tell you the truth I had a feeling in my bones all along that Meg might make a cuddy out of me.'

'Well, I'll be hanged!' gasped Cameron, both astounded and perplexed that his young partner should take defeat at the redoubtable Meg's hands in so spiritless a fashion. A healthy fury he could have understood, but this easy laughter left him at a loss. He would have said more upon the subject, too, but Finlay, without further ado, walked out of the room to take the evening surgery.

At supper that night the matter was not mentioned again, but Cameron kept darting curious glances at Finlay, as though pondering what might be behind that complacent silence, wondering perhaps if, after all, in the classic phrase, Finlay had not something up his sleeve.

And, sure enough, on the following morning events took a sudden and more mysterious turn. It had barely gone nine o'clock when old Jeannie Glen, bosom friend and sycophant-in-chief to Miss Mirlees, came hirpling round as fast as her rheumaticky bones could carry her to bid Dr Finlay come post-haste to visit Meg.

Cameron, taking half an hour's ease before setting out upon his round, peered incredulously over the edge of his morning paper at old Jeannie.

'Another call for Meg?' he ejaculated. 'Has the dressing come undone?'

'Na, na,' panted Jeannie. 'It's no' her heid ava'. It's waur, far, far waur nor that.'

'What then?' queried Cameron.

'The Almighty alone kens,' answered Jeannie with palpitating emotion. 'But unless I'm far cheated, it's a summons. Ye maun come straight away, Dr Finlay, and I'll get back till her this meenit myself. Oh, dear; oh, dear, it's a sair fecht. I'm tellin' ye,' and muttering agitatedly old Jeannie hurriedly retraced her steps.

Cameron turned upon Finlay a look which held volumes of the most pressing inquiry. But Finlay took no heed. Whistling lightly, with an air both leisurely and aloof, he finished arran-ging

252

the contents of the famous black bag. Then picking it up, he donned his hat at an angle slightly unprofessional, nodded briskly to Cameron, and left the house.

His demeanour, however, as he mounted the steps of Meg Mirlees house was formality itself. He entered the back kitchen with real solemnity and marched up to the box bed where Meg lay, moaning and groaning, attended by the trembling Jeannie Glen.

'And what's the matter now?' asked Finlay briefly.

'I'm dyin',' articulated Meg, going straight to the point. With another hollow groan she writhed upon her couch and clasped her middle. 'My stomach's a mass of fire. I canna keep a thing down, not even a sip o' caul watter. Oh, doctor, dear, I'm near by wi't.'

And, as though to prove the truth of her assertion, she retched weakly into the basin which the trusty Jeannie proffered below her scraggy chin.

'What have you been eating?' inquired Finlay after a minute.

'Nothing, nothing,' protested the groaning Meg. 'I just had my breakfast, a sup parritch and a kipper, and a dose o' that braw tonic ye gi'en me. And I hadna been half an hour started to redd up the room when this awfu' burnin' and scaldin' took me just like a clap o' thunder. Oh, doctor, doctor, what in the name of heaven do ye think it is?'

A silence.

'Maybe,' said Finlay solemnly, 'maybe it's a judgement on you for swindling me out of the plate.'

A shiver passed over Meg's suffering form.

'Oh, doctor, doctor,' she whimpered, 'dinna bring up sic a thing at a time like this. I kept my bargain and you kept yours. Oh, give me something quick to ease my pain.'

Finlay fixed the old woman with an accusing eye. Then, without further speech, he bent over the bed, and, to the accompaniment of much audible tribulation on the part of Meg, examined her sombrely.

When it was over Meg retched again, then desperately groaned.

'Can ye cure me, doctor? Oh, dear, oh, dear, can ye cure me?'

Another silence, until with due deliberation Finlay answered—'Yes, I can cure you, but this time I'm standing no nonsense. I want the plate, the real Ming plate, or as sure as my name's Finlay I'll walk out of this room and leave you to your fate.'

Meg began to whine feebly.

'Oh, doctor, doctor, ye couldna be so cruel?'

'Very well, then . . .'

Finlay buttoned up his coat sternly, as though preparing to depart, but at that Meg cried out shrilly—

'All right, then, I'll gi'e ye the plate, only get quit o' this retchin',' and, raising a stricken hand, she indicated a cupboard in the corner.

Following a sharp instruction from the patient, Jeannie Glen waddled to the cupboard, produced the plate, and handed it to Finlay, who received it in dignified silence, and then, with all despatch, opened his black bag.

Taking out a packet of white powder, he mixed an effervescing draught for Meg. She drank it feverishly and relapsed upon the bed, declaring a moment later—

'Ye're richt. It's easin' me. Oh, thanks be to the Almighty and yersell, doctor. It's easin' me a treat.'

'Certainly it's easing you,' coolly retorted Finlay. 'By this afternoon you'll be right as rain. There's only one thing for you to remember.'

'And what's that, doctor?'

Finlay walked to the table by the bed, took up the bottle of physic he had given Meg on the previous day, then stalked over to the sink. Looking Meg straight in the eye, he declared deliberately—

'You mustn't take any more of this medicine.'

A pause while he uncorked the bottle and let the contents trickle down the waste.

'Ye see, Meg, this isn't a tonic after all. I felt in my bones you would try to swindle me, though I didn't know how. So, to be on the safe side, I gave ye a fine bottle of ipecacuanha. I knew ye'd need me after the first dose. It's an emetic, Meg – if you understand what that means – a grand strong emetic.'

'Ye young de'il,' cried Meg, struggling up in her night-gown from the bed. 'Let me get my claws on ye, and . . .'

But Finlay, roaring with laughter, the real Ming plate under his arm, was already halfway down the stairs.

Enter Nurse Angus

From that first moment when Finlay met Peggy Angus he knew that he detested her, and, naturally enough, he suspected the feeling to be mutual. But whether or not our young medico was right in such dour primary impressions the events of these chronicles may presently reveal.

Admittedly the meeting was unfortunate. Finlay was in a bad mood. Troubled over a case, bothered and overworked, he had got out of bed on the wrong side that morning, which, to add to the general gaiety, was teeming with rain.

He drove to the Cottage Hospital under the dripping heavens, jumped down from the gig, then, with his head lowered to escape the pelting raindrops, he dashed through the front door into the corridor beyond. Here he ran full-tilt into a nurse.

Angrily he raised his head and glowered at her. She was young and slender, and rather small, very neat and trim in her uniform, with a clear complexion, and lively, sparkling eyes. Her mouth was big and ready to smile, her teeth white and even, while her nose, small and decidedly upturned, gave her an air of vivacity and impudence.

Altogether she was, Finlay saw, uncommonly pretty; moreover, she was preparing to smile at him. But this, for some strange reason, added to his simmering annoyance.

He had realised, of course, right away that she was the new nurse they had been expecting at the hospital in place of Nurse Crockett, who had recently been appointed to Ardfillan. And he scowled.

'Can't you look where you're going? Or do you make a habit of running people down?'

Her smile, which had begun with much affected friendliness, immediately died out. Her eyebrows lifted, and her eyes sparkled more.

'It was you who ran into me,' she declared with emphasis. 'I tried to get out of your way, but you came through the door and down the passage like a bull at a gate.'

Finlay's temper flared. He was at his worst this morning, and he knew it, and the knowledge served to make him even more disagreeable.

'Do you know who you are talking too?' he barked.

Her expression altered to one of mockery.

'Oh, yes,' she returned, in a pretence of awe. 'You must be Dr Finlay. I've heard how nice you were. I couldn't possibly mistake you.'

His face flushed with discomfiture.

'Please remember your position. You're a nurse in this hospital, and I'm – I'm your superior.'

Again the sparks flashed from her pretty, dark eyes, but she was cleverer than he, and knew better than to display her anger. Lowering her lashes with mock demureness, she remarked—

'Yes, sir. I won't say a word the next time you run into me.'

'Why, hang it all!' Finlay exploded. 'How dare you talk to me like that?'

But at this point Matron Clark came out of her room and waddled along the corridor towards them, a short, rather stout, important figure, her round, fat face beaming with unusual amiability. Advancing, all unconscious of the scene which had occurred, she cooed to Finlay—

'So you've made friends with Nurse Angus already, Dr Finlay? I'm real glad. I was coming into the ward to introduce you. We're downright pleased to have Miss Angus with us. She's just finished her training at the Edinburgh Royal, you know, doctor, and now that she's come back home she's going to lend us a hand.'

Furious though he was, the open flattery towards the new nurse in matron's tone quite took Finlay aback. Junior nurses, he was fully aware, did not receive such signal recognition without due cause, and he was right, for while he stood speechless, matron's honeyed voice went on—

'You ought to know, of course, doctor, that nursing is a labour of love with Miss Angus. She doesn't – er – she doesn't have to do it for her living. You see, her father – oh, well doctor, you know all about the Anguses of Dunhill, don't you, now?'

Naturally enough, like everyone in the district, Finlay did know of the Anguses. Old John Angus, who owned enormous dye-works at Dunhill, employed close on fifteen hundred men, and was justly reputed to be worth a fortune.

His only daughter, Finlay remembered, had persuaded the old man into allowing her to take up nursing as a profession. All this occurred to Finlay as he stared fixedly at matron, who continued—

'So you see, doctor, under the circumstances, we're pleased and proud to have Nurse Angus here. Her father's such a large benefactor to the hospital. We must try and make things pleasant for her. Eh, Peggy?' And she beamed in motherly fashion at the young nurse.

A wave of repugnance swept over Finlay. He did not see – at least, he did not choose to see – the quick distaste which matron's too obvious flattery had aroused in the eyes of Nurse Angus. Instead, he declared, in a loud and surly voice—

'I don't care who Nurse Angus is, or what she is. She's come to nurse in this hospital, and not to be on the social register. I'll treat her exactly as she deserves.' And, pushing past the astounded and crestfallen matron, Finlay stalked his way into the ward.

An unfortunate beginning, you must agree, for the doctor and the nurse, in which each was represented to the other in a most indifferent light.

And, indeed, from that beginning, things went from bad to worse. Every time Finlay came into contact with Nurse Angus the air crackled with an electric hostility.

Quite frankly, Finlay was determined to put the young nurse down. He found fault with her on every pretext, real and imaginary, tried to catch her in mistakes, laid traps for her, and in general pursued her at every turn. Yet, for all his efforts, he found Peggy Angus more than a match for him.

When, in a bossy tone, he would make her fetch and carry for him in the ward, the derisive meekness with which she answered 'Yes, sir', drove him nearly frantic.

What annoyed him most of all was her extreme proficiency in her work and her extreme fondness for it. As he watched her deft and skilful movements with the patients, and saw her slight trim figure moving briskly down the ward, at times an almost unwilling admiration came upon him. But he checked it fiercely. He was resolved to subjugate her.

Another source of exasperation to Finlay was Nurse Angus's popularity. She had many friends in the town, was continually renewing old associations which had lapsed while she was absent at her training school.

Invited everywhere, Peggy went out a great deal in her spare time; she was on terms of familiarity with the very best families in the district.

Angrily, Finlay told himself that it was all due to her father's position and money. And he bristled at the very thought.

Once when she returned from spending a weekend on the family estate between Dunhill and the Loch shore he remarked with a sneer—

'Why don't you stay at home all the time? You're only playing at nursing here.'

For once the impudence left her eyes.

'Am I?' she asked.

'Of course,' he scoffed. 'And you know it. The lady bountiful stooping to suffering humanity! A fine pose. You're not genuine. It takes courage and real endurance to make a proper nurse.'

'Oh,' she answered in a quiet voice, 'then I suppose that rules me out?'

So much had Peggy Angus come to prey upon Finlay's mind it was a godsend when, at the beginning of the summer, she went upon night duty in the hospital. Thereafter he saw her seldom; indeed, for days on end he did not see her at all, and the relief, so he told himself, was tremendous. Though at moments he almost missed the stimulus of her disturbing presence, the sharp satisfaction of matching his wits and tongue against hers, he was once more, he told himself, infinitely better off now that she had vanished from the sphere of his activities. And he hoped that it would be long enough before she reappeared to worry him again.

But here Finlay little reckoned with the fates, which held more in store for him than ever he visioned in his wildest dreams.

It was, by this time, the summer season – a hot summer which made fishing indifferent sport, and caused Finlay to spend most of his leisure on the Levenford lawn tennis courts. He was a keen player, and, though he played little in his student days, now, with regular play and practice, his game had rapidly improved, and he had become quite adept at the game.

It was, then, in a spirit of considerable enthusiasm not unmixed with optimism that he put his name down for the Nimmo Trophy, the big annual tournament. This competition was for mixed doubles, partners to be drawn by ballot, and it was looked upon as the main event in the tennis season of the town, and, indeed, of the entire county.

On the Monday evening following that on which he had made his entry, Finlay strolled up to the club after surgery hours to see what his luck had been in the draw.

A pleasurable excitement stirred him, for he was aware that on this particular turn of fortune much of his chance depended. It was late, the dusk falling, and most of the Club members had gone home.

He entered the pavilion, sauntered up to the notice board, and let his eye run down the list of names on the white sheet. Suddenly his expression altered to incredulous dismay. Bracketed with his own name was the name of Peggy Angus.

Finlay stared at the offensive name, with muttered exclamation he was turning away from the notice board when Doggy Lindsay and some others came in from the changing-room.

'Congratulations, Finlay, old man!' cried Doggy in his usual offensive style. 'You're the lucky man right enough.'

'Lucky?'

'Certainly! To draw Miss Angus!'

Finlay frowned at Doggy.

'I didn't know she played. I didn't know she was even a member of the club.'

'Of course she is,' cried the irrepressible Doggy. 'And a jolly fine little player, too. When she was at school she won the junior championship here. See?'

'I see,' retorted Finlay again. 'So she does know something about the game.'

'Why, of course.' Here Doggy laughed and slapped Finlay on the back. 'Not that it really matters, Finlay, old man. I've drawn Anne Brown. We'll wipe the floor with the rest of you. We're the winners, Finlay, and don't you forget it.'

Unheeding of Doggy's banter, Finlay nodded blankly, and as soon as he could get away he slipped out of the club, his face brooding, still marred by that unpleasant frown.

Impelled by some secret, inner force, his steps took him not in the direction of home but towards the Cottage Hospital. It was after nine when he got there, and, as he expected, Nurse Angus was on duty, writing up her charts in the small side room which opened off the ward kitchen.

He entered without a word, and, standing with his hands in his pockets, surveyed her with Napoleonic gloom. At last he spoke.

'I thought I'd come in and tell you the glad news. We're drawn together for the Nimmo Trophy.'

If he had expected to dismay her he was disappointed. Swinging round in her chair, she surveyed him calmly.

'That's grand,' she said with satirical emphasis. 'Couldn't have been better.'

He gave a grunt.

'I wasn't aware that you knew one end of a tennis racket from the other.'

'Oh, yes,' she answered sweetly. 'I believe I can just tell the difference.'

'The junior champion, weren't you?' he derided. 'A kind of infant prodigy, I suppose?'

'That's right,' she answered with a humorous smile. 'I began to play before I'd finished teething.'

He had to bite his lip to keep back an answering smile. Really her good nature was infectious. And she was as pretty as a picture.

All at once Finlay felt a warm tide pulse within his breast. Did he really dislike Peggy Angus after all? With dramatic suddenness her loveliness and charm took him by storm. He grew confused, and muttered—

'Well you'd better begin to play in good earnest this time. You've got to put your back into it and show some real spirit. I expect you to practice and practice hard. Do you hear me? It's pluck that counts in any game, and if you've got any I want you to show it just for once.'

Without giving her time to reply he nodded awkwardly, turned on his heel and left the hospital.

He did not see Peggy Angus again until the date appointed for his first round tie. So far from indulging in any practice, she seemed never to have been near the courts, a defiance of his instructions which served to increase his growing admiration for her spirit.

With a queer sense of anticipation he made his way to the club and arrived there punctually at half-past five in the evening.

Six o'clock, being suitable to all parties, had been fixed as the time of the match. Despite Doggy's assurance, he did not expect Nurse Angus would prove herself expert at the game. But if she were any good at all they ought to win this tie, for they were drawn against Tom Douglas and May Scott, neither of whom were any class as players.

Douglas and Miss Scott were already on the court, and at five minutes to six, sharp, Miss Angus arrived, already changed, looking prettier than ever, and very efficient and neat in her smart white dress and white shoes. She carried two rackets under her arm.

The sight of her sent a thrill through Finlay. He knew now how much he had looked forward to playing with her, and the knowledge for some reason made him angry with himself. He met her with a pretence of brusqueness.

'Late as usual!' That was his polite greeting.

She gave him a quick glance, in which there was neither mockery nor impudence.

'Surely it isn't six o'clock,' she answered quietly, then looked away.

It was as though this final rudeness had subdued her at last, for there was no raillery in her manner and no roguishness in her face.

He ought, of course, to have exulted, having sworn to put Peggy in her place. But instead he cursed himself for a boorish prig. He wanted more than ever to take back all he had said against her.

The game began. And here again Peggy proved her mettle. Although obviously out of practice, from the moment when, with a clear note, her racket met the first ball, it was evident that Peggy Angus was a skilled player. Indeed, Finlay saw that without a doubt she knew more about the game than he.

She served crisply, volleyed neatly, and drove with remarkable vigour. Her placing was accurate and subtle, and after a few errors, made before finding her touch, she played a really brilliant game. Douglas and Miss Scott were completely swamped.

The first set went to Finlay and Miss Angus at six-one, while the second they won to love, and with it the match.

Douglas and Miss Scott took their beating in excellent part, and smilingly shook hands across the net.

'Nobody could stand up to that stuff,' grinned Douglas as he struggled into his sweater. 'It's a perfect education!'

Finlay nodded in agreement. He accompanied his partner off the court with a sense of genuine pride. He was delighted to have won, and thrilled at the brilliance of Nurse Angus's game.

All his natural generosity acknowledged her superiority as a player, and exalted in the wonderful game which she played. He felt that once and for all it was time to make amends. And, as they reached the pavilion, he turned to her abruptly—

'Nurse Angus you played marvellously, far better than I did. You'll have to take me in hand and give me a lesson before our next tie.'

But, alas, though Finlay's intention was good, the result was unhappy, for, in the light of his previous behaviour to her, Peggy mistook his appreciation for the cruellest satire.

She flushed to the roots of her hair, and looked up at him, her lips straight, her eyes strangely hurt. Then she said—

'I've got to play through those ties with you. And, come what may, I'll do it. But don't you think it would make things a little easier if you left me alone!'

He saw in a flash that she had misunderstood him. Quite taken aback, he tried to set things right, but even before he could answer she had left him.

He did not see her until the day of the next tie, and then her attitude, reserved and cold, precluded all explanation.

In a strained silence they played through the tie, which they won by an even wider margin.

By this time public interest, all unconscious of the internal tension, began to centre on Finlay and Nurse Angus, because of their fine play, and a fair number of people turned out to witness their fourth-round tie. This Finlay and Nurse Angus also won, and, amidst a buzz of congratulation, it was agreed that their chance of going to the final was excellent.

Actually, they made an admirable combination, for Finlay's natural impetuosity was countered by the accuracy of Nurse Angus's play.

While her own game shone with a level brilliance, she seemed, at the same time, to steady Finlay, and somehow to excite him to bring off scintillating winners. A pity, everyone went about remarking, that this nice young couple could not win the trophy.

Naturally, in Doggy Lindsay, the club champion, and Miss Brown, who had been ladies' champion of the county these last three successive years, they would meet an invincible combination.

The fifth round came, and the sixth, then the quarter-finals, and eventually the semi-finals. Finlay and his partner went. through them all formally, distantly, and with scarcely a word spoken between them. Indeed, Finlay determined to postpone all speech until the final tie was over, and the trophy won.

Not for his own sake, but for Peggy's, he became increasingly set on winning. He told himself that when he had steered Nurse Angus through the contest, and defeated Doggy and Miss Brown, he could adjust the painful situation which had arisen between them.

It came at last, the day of the final, a fine, bright, sunny August day. Quite a stir was about, for the event always aroused interest and excitement in the town.

Even Cameron, at breakfast that morning, facetiously remarked—

'You seem to be going strong with Nurse Angus. Well, well, she's a fine lass. I'm not surprised she's taken a notion of you.'

Finlay jabbed at the marmalade savagely.

'That's where you're wrong,' he said. 'I'm pretty sure she hates the very sight of me.'

'Aha!' said Cameron dryly. 'Then, in that case, the pair of ye deserve to get beat.'

But Finlay had no intention of getting beaten. Following a light luncheon, he arrived early at the club, and changed in good time for the great match, which was to begin at three o'clock.

A crowd of several hundred people was in the ground, members and their friends, and a section of the public perched on the temporary stand, which, following the usual custom, had been erected for the final match.

Doggy and Miss Brown, full of confidence and spirits, were already in evidence, and, in company with some of the club officials, were exchanging good-natured banter on the verandah.

'Where's your partner, Finlay?' cried Doggy boisterously. 'She hasn't turned up yet.'

'She'll turn up all right,' said Finlay quickly.

'Perhaps she's going to let you down at last?' persisted the grinning Doggy.

'She's not the kind to let anyone down,' retorted Finlay with sudden indignation.

But, indeed, when three o'clock came, and there was no sign of Peggy, a whisper ran through the crowd, a rumour went round that Nurse Angus would not play. And at this a sensation of dismay, mingled with compunction, swept over Finlay.

Perhaps she was not coming. Perhaps she disliked him so much she had refused to appear for the final match.

A sudden despondency took him, but at that same moment a shout went up from the crowd collected at the gate, and Nurse Angus made her appearance.

She did not quite look herself, somehow, for her face was extremely pale and almost drawn. It seemed as if she had been hurrying; at least, her distress was attributed by Finlay to this cause, but he had no time to dwell upon it, for immediately she led the way towards the court.

Together, with Doggy and Miss Brown, they went out into the bright sunshine of the centre court, and their appearance was greeted by a cheer. Then began a warming-up in preparation for the match. But, as he tossed a ball towards her, Finlay observed that she wore a wash-leather glove on her right hand. He eyed the glove oddly.

'You'll never play with that thing,' he declared. 'Why don't you take it off?'

She shook her head, moistening her lips slightly.

'I've blistered my hand,' she answered rather uncertainly. 'Oh, it's nothing at all. Probably from playing so much. I hope it won't put me off my game.'

Her answer left him rather at a loss, but before he could pursue the matter, Doggy sang out to him, and the game commenced.

It was going to be fast and furious, Finlay saw. Their opponents having won the toss, took the service, which Doggy smashed in relentlessly. His service was his strong suit, and it won him the first game easily.

Finlay set his teeth and pulled himself together. He saw that Peggy was not playing nearly so well as usual, and he felt that she was wilting under the excitement of the event.

When he had won his own service, and Miss Brown had won hers, Peggy served badly, and lost her service, making the score three–one in favour of Doggy and Miss Brown.

In the next game Doggy again served and won a smashing service, making the score four–one. And when Finlay, too eager, served a double fault, and went on to lose his own service, making the score five-one, a groan ran through the onlookers which deepened as Miss Brown easily served her way, to win the first set for her side at six–one.

It was to be exactly as anticipated, then, an easy victory for Doggy and Miss Brown.

The crowd, sympathetically disposed towards Finlay and Peggy, resigned themselves to the slaughter of the innocents and settled down to watch the massacre of the second set.

Before that set began Finlay remarked in a determined undertone—

'We've got to buck up, partner. Come on, now! We've got to win.'

Though he meant to be encouraging, for some reason Peggy grew even paler under those words.

But it seemed as if they took effect, for, setting her teeth and playing feverishly, she flung herself into the match. With complete abandon she smashed, and volleyed, and drove, and served, and every one of her desperately-executed shots came off miraculously.

Cheer after cheer rang out from the crowd.

Inspired by this turn of events, Finlay also played well. He reeled off the last game with four cannon-ball services, and he and his partner took the second set at six–three.

One set all, and the final set to go. Excitement amongst the spectators knew no bounds. It was to be a match after all, and a grand one too!

Gripped by the drama of this gallant recovery, the crowd held its breath and focused its attention upon the last deciding set.

Wiping the perspiration off his face, Finlay backed to the base line to await Doggy's serve. In the short interval he had exchanged no words with Peggy.

Subconsciously he felt something unusual about her game. Although she had played so brilliantly in the second set, when she struck the ball it seemed as if she did so with a conscious effort of will, and he could have sworn that after she had hit an extra power-ful shot an expression of acute distress flashed across her face.

But now Finlay did not pause to reason. Straddling his feet, he balanced his racket and took Doggy's first ball.

A beautiful serve and a beautiful return; but in spite of it Doggy won the service. Undismayed, Finlay followed by winning his. Then quickly Miss Brown won hers, and Peggy the next. Two games all.

A gasp from the crowd. And a succession of such gasps at the end of every game as, in turn, each player won the service until the score stood at five all. It was plain as a pikestaff that whoever broke through the service would win the match.

Excitement mounted higher and higher. Every shot evoked a cheer, every rally a burst of prolonged applause. Finlay felt the quick drumming of his pulse. He wanted, with all his heart, to win, to win with Peggy Angus. It would symbolise his whole feeling for her if they could win this match and share the triumph together.

Another shout from the crowd. The score was now seven all, and it was Peggy's turn to serve.

The gruelling match had taken toll of her, and as she took up her position she appeared nearly worn out. Little beads of perspiration stood on her upper lip, and when she gripped her racket it struck Finlay that a little shiver of distress went through her whole body.

He glanced at her doubtfully as she served – a fault, and, again, a double fault. Her next service lacked its usual sting and the next also. Quicker than it takes to tell, Peggy had lost her service.

This time a groan rose from the spectators. The score now stood eight–seven, and it was Doggy's service, which he was almost certain to win. It was the end at last.

'Are you all right?' inquired Finlay of his partner with sudden anxiety. But she did not answer.

Deep silence as Doggy served. Finlay, feeling the position hopeless, returned out. Fifteen love.

Doggy served to Peggy, who, setting her teeth and hitting fiercely, scored a winner right in the far corner of the court. Fifteen all.

Doggy served to Finlay, who returned badly into the net. Thirty–fifteen.

Doggy served to Peggy, who again made a brilliant winner right down the side line, and once more evened the points, earning a loud and prolonged cheer from the crowd.

Plainly unsettled, Doggy served to Finlay, who, encouraged by his partner's daring, returned hard to Doggy, who, making a weak, backhand shot to Peggy, allowed her to run in to volley the ball away safely and win the point.

The score was now thirty–forty.

With an expression of anxiety on his face for the first time, Doggy served to Peggy. It was a fault. He served again. It was right and Peggy, playing with the utmost determination, steered the ball short over the net, and Miss Brown was unable to return it.

An almost hysterical burst of applause from the crowd. Thanks to Peggy's brilliant play the scores had been levelled and now stood at eight games all.

The excitement was intense as Finlay served and won his service. Nine–eight in favour of Finlay and Miss Angus.

Miss Brown now served. She served to Finlay, who returned the ball and made the point. Love–fifteen. She served to Peggy, who made a brilliant winner, and won the point.

Miss Brown, looking very worried, served to Finlay, and in the rally Peggy again made the point. The score was love–forty. It was set and match point.

A deadly stillness settled upon the court as Miss Brown served to Peggy. The first service was a fault. The second was right, and Peggy met the ball firmly, and, with tremendous force, sent it right to the base line between Doggy and Miss Brown.

It was a marvellous shot, and it won the game, set and match.

Cheer after cheer rang out. It had been a thrilling match, a magnificent recovery and a marvellous finish.

The din was tremendous as Doggy and Miss Brown ran round to congratulate the winners. But all at once the general jubilation changed to a gasp of consternation. As Finlay turned exultantly to take her hand, quite quietly Peggy crumpled up and collapsed upon the court. Finlay rushed forward.

'Good Lord!' cried Doggy. 'She's fainted.'

'Drink some water,' said Finlay, bending down and supporting Peggy's head.

They brought a glass of water, and he held it to her lips. In a few seconds she opened her eyes.

'I'm all right,' she said faintly; then, as though realising that he held her, she added, 'Please let me get up.'

'The excitement was too much for you,' he muttered. 'You shouldn't have played if you didn't feel up to it.'

She gave him a pale, cold glance, then in a voice only audible to him she said—

'A nice opinion you'd have had of me if I hadn't played! Even better than you have already!'

Then she insisted on getting to her feet, and assisted by Miss Brown and some others she went into the pavillion.

Finlay stood for a moment, alone, cut to the quick by her bitter words. Then he changed quickly and left the ground. He ought to have been delighted that he had won, thrilled with the joy of victory. But instead he burned with a queer shame. He tried, to no purpose, to banish the whole thing from his mind. The memory of her white, drawn face haunted him.

In this desolate fashion he turned across the common towards Arden House. And then as he entered Park Street he saw an agitated figure hurrying down the road, apparently making for the tennis club. It was Matron Clark, and when she reached him she did not stand on ceremony.

'Have you seen Nurse Angus?' she demanded straight away. 'I left her in bed at the hospital, and she's gone, she's gone.'

He considered her flushed, concerned face in real amazement.

'But why not?' he asked. 'She had to play the tennis match with me this afternoon. She's up there now.'

'Oh, Dr Finlay,' wept the matron, 'how could she, how could she? After me begging and praying her not to go.'

'What do you mean?' he cried.

'Don't you know? Didn't she tell you? Last night when she was on duty the patient in bed fifteen knocked a bottle of pure carbolic acid over. It went right over Nurse Angus's hand and gave her a shocking burn, an acid burn. Don't you understand? Why, this morning she could hardly hold a teacup. And to think she's gone and played . . .' And in a perfect frenzy of concern matron rushed off towards the tennis court.

Turning, Finlay surveyed her retreating form with a horrified expression on his face. So that was it. That was why Peggy had fainted. He saw now the reason of the glove, remembered how she had winced each time her racket had met the ball in that last thrilling match! 'It's nothing,' she had said, 'only a blister.'

Because of his behaviour to her at the beginning, because he had questioned her pluck, she had stubbornly refused to tell him. She had played the game with a badly burned hand, a hand that could hardly clasp the racket.

No doubt she despised him, had set herself thus to humiliate him. He groaned aloud at the very thought. And, all at once, a great tide seemed unlocked within his heart.

He wanted to turn, to run after the matron towards the tennis club, to apligise to Peggy Angus, to get down on his knees, to say how sorry he was, to ask pardon humbly. But he did not. How could he? She would not even listen to him now. So he turned instead, and walked slowly towards Arden House, trying to take comfort from the thought that he would see her again, that perhaps, if the chance came he could make amends.

And through it all there pressed upon him an understanding unfathomable and bitter sweet.

He knew at last what his feeling was, had been from the first, and always would be, for Peggy Angus.

Known as Inflammation

After the final of the Nimmo Cup, as related previously in these chronicles, life went hard for Finlay. He moved in a queer preoccupation, ate poorly, slept worse, and in general offered every evidence of a man suffering from deep and compelling emotion.

Peggy Angus, following a short spell at her home at Dunhill to allow her injured hand to heel, was back in hospital, quietly efficient, once again on day duty.

Nothing passed between Finlay and the young nurse but a few brief words exchanged in the ordinary routine of the ward.

Yet Finlay would have given everything he possessed to break down this barrier of coldness and misunderstanding which had arisen and stood, it seemed, permanently separating them. He knew at last, in his secret heart, that he loved Peggy Angus. And it cast a mortal sadness upon him to feel that now she could never care for him.

As if to escape his melancholy, he threw himself desperately into his work, and more particularly into study.

Mark you, the conscientious strain in Finlay, though often overlaid by the natural impetuosity of the man, was strong, and this at all times caused him to try to keep up-to-date in his work. It was not easy, since usually the practice occupied him so fully he had little time to read.

Nevertheless, he did make an effort to keep in touch with modern research in medicine and surgery. And now more than ever he sought a weary consolation by burning the midnight oil

273

over the recent advances of his profession. Not without result, as shall presently be seen.

To be dramatic fiction, the drama which ensued ought to have been staged on the grand scale. But it was simply bare reality, and concerned a poor family of foreigners named Pulaski, and in particular the little boy named Paul.

The Pulaskis were Lithuanians who had come, like many others of their countrymen, to work in the mines of Lanarkshire. But, when the industrial situation became depressed, they drifted to Levenford. The father was fortunate in getting work in a humble capacity as labourer in a shipyard.

They lived in impoverished conditions in the Vennel, and there was a brood of children, amongst them Paul, aged eight, who spent most of his spare time playing on the pavement of the squalid slum.

When Paul fell ill with vomiting and a bad pain in his stomach no one paid much attention to the fact.

Certainly Mrs Pulaski had no thought of the doctor, for this was an expensive luxury far beyond the means of her humble establishment. But when Paul, dosed with some dark concoction and put to bed, showed no signs of improvement, she held an uneasy colloquy with her husband, the result of which was that Finlay arrived next morning to see the patient.

He found the little boy in bed with a furred, dry tongue, a flushed face, a high temperature, and severe pain and tenderness low down on the right side of his body. The vomiting had stopped, but, instead of bringing relief, this seemed merely to have aggravated the condition.

'I don't know what he takes to upset him!' exclaimed Mrs Pulaski brokenly, with her dark foreign eyes fixed intently on Finlay. 'Or maybe it's a chill on the stomach he would have – the inflammation, eh, doctor?'

As the familiar word fell on Finlay's ear he remained silent. Inflammation! – the convenient receptacle into which all manner of doubtful and unknown conditions were cast.

He continued his examination, not satisfied that this case before him was a simple chill or disturbance. Something in the signs and symptoms, in the boy's attitude, struck him vividly and reminded him of a certain condition which his recent reading had brought before him.

He said nothing, however. Turning from the bedside, he prescribed a simple remedy and a fluid diet, and indicated to the mother that he would return with Dr Cameron.

At midday he went over the points of the case with Cameron, making no bones about the fact that he considered the condition serious, and about two o'clock the two doctors walked down the road and arrived at the mean home in the Vennel.

Cameron made his examination of Paul, who seemed worse, in greater pain than ever, and unable, as his mother related, to retain even the sips of water she had given him.

Later, in consultation together in the little kitchen, Cameron passed up and down dubiously.

'He's bad, right enough, the little chap,' he threw out. 'It looks to me like inflammation of the bowels. What do you think yourself?'

There was a silence. Inflammation again, thought Finlay, and he answered slowly—

'I think it's appendicitis.'

At the mention of the strange new word which at the beginning of this century was causing open war amongst the pundits, Cameron threw up his head like a startled horse.

'That!' he said abruptly.

Finlay nodded slowly, and before the old doctor could intervene he launched into a rapid explanation.

'I've been reading Englemann's treatise and Mitchell's account of his cases. This boy here has got all the typical symptoms. It's not just inflammation, I'll swear it's this new thing they're talking about in London, and Paris and Vienna. Appendicitis! Oh, I know it sounds trashy and newfangled to you, but I'm convinced in my very bones it's a genuine case.'

275

Cameron inspected Finlay quietly.

'I don't think it's trashy,' he said slowly. 'And just because I'm not acquainted with the condition, because maybe I'm a little old-fashioned and behind the times, I don't propose to deny its existence.'

There was a silence. Moved by Cameron's generous attitude Finlay did not speak, and eventually the older man resumed—

'But talking doesn't help us much. Granted you're right, what do you propose to do?'

Finlay started forward eagerly.

'Well, believe me, castor oil and linseed poultices won't help us here. There's only one thing to do. Operation!

Another silence. Cameron stroked his chin reflectively.

'Well,' he said at length, 'maybe you're right But it's a serious step, man, a gey serious step. I wouldn't like you to take it on your own responsibility. No, no! Suppose anything happened to the boy? Bless my soul, they'd swear the operation had killed him. You'll need to have another opinion. I can't help you here, though I'm with you heart and soul.'

He paused. 'Suppose you call in Reid and see what he says?'

Finlay's eyes fell. Though he knew Cameron's suggestion to be a wise one, it was not, to him, a happy one. He was fairly friendly with Dr Reid, a young man like himself, with a fair-sized practice in the Newtown, and a bustling go-ahead manner, which was hearty enough, though perhaps a little jeering at times. Yet Finlay was loth to submit to outside interference. He was an individualist. Nevertheless, he saw the wisdom of Cameron's advice, and at last he raised his head.

'Right!' he said. 'I'll have Reid in at once.'

Without delay he called Reid, and while Cameron set out alone on the afternoon round the two younger doctors went into consultation at the Pulaski's house.

Reid, deeply gratified by Finlay's invitation, professed full knowledge of Mitchell's recent work, and he made it plain in no uncertain fashion that this new condition known as appendicitis was to him an open book.

'I went through the reports of the John Hopkins Hospital only last month,' he added. 'You've seen them I suppose?'

'No,' replied Finlay dourly. 'But I've seen this case.'

Reid said no more for the moment but went on with his thorough examination of the boy. When he had finished he followed Finlay into the other room, lit a cigarette, and, planting his legs apart, blew a long cloud of smoke towards the ceiling. He seemed absorbed in thought, but at last, with a certain diffidence, he spoke.

'Frankly, Finlay,' said he, 'I can't agree with your diagnosis. As I've told you, I'm up to this thing. Absolutely, man. But this isn't it. I don't look on this as any more than a simple inflammation. The boy's vomiting has stopped, his temperature has fallen, his mother says he is complaining of less pain.'

Reid waved his cigarette. 'I'm sorry, Finlay, to disagree with you, but I'm confident you're wrong. There's no appendicitis here. I couldn't, under the circumstances, become a party to advising operative treatment. Wait and see, my boy, that's the idea here – a masterly inactivity.'

And with a friendly little nod, Reid took himself away.

But Finlay did not leave the house. Somehow he could not. Far from reassured by Reid's words, he wandered back into the little bedroom where Paul lay, and stared at the passive figure of the boy.

It was perfectly true, as Reid had said, the vomiting had ceased and the pain was less, but this, in Finlay's eyes, marked not an improvement but a rapid deterioration in the patient's condition.

He took Paul's hand.

'Does it still hurt you?' he asked.

'It doesn't hurt me so much. But I feel awful queer. It's kind of black in the room.'

Finlay bit his lip. The pulse, racing under his fingers, coupled with a falling temperature, bore down upon him ominously.

Here, in this poor and squalid home, he felt himself faced with that awful figure – the dark angel of death. He must do something

– he must. Cameron could not help him, Reid had failed him; the decision rested entirely with him.

For a full five minutes Finlay stood motionless, staring down at the narrow disordered bed. Then across his set face a light spread suddenly.

He had it! Why hadn't he thought of it before? He would ring up a certain professor in Glasgow. The professor knew him, remembered him as his house surgeon, would undoubtedly with his unfailing charity, run down and see this humble case. The professor on occasion could demand a hundred guinea fee and a special train to transport him to his lordly patients; but on other occasions he would come obscurely, and for nothing, in the cause of mercy. This was such an occasion, and Finlay was sure of his man.

Turning, he went into the other room, where Mrs Pulaski stood with a clutter of frightened youngsters clutching at her skirts, and in as few words as possible he explained that Paul would have to go to hospital immediately.

'Hospital!' echoed the frightened woman. 'Holy mother! Is he that sick, doctor?'

'Yes,' said Finlay, 'and he'll be worse unless we do something quickly.'

Sitting down at the table, he took his prescription pad and dashed off a hurried note to Matron Clark at the hospital instructing her to send the ambulance for Paul and prepare for the operation by the professor that evening.

Then, comforting the weeping mother as best he could, he hurried back to Arden House, where, without delay, he put through a call to Glasgow, and was connected to the professor's house.

But here he received a rude shock. The professor had left two days before to spend a fortnight's vacation in the south of England.

Completely dismayed, Finlay replaced the receiver, and rested his head in both hands. He knew no other surgeon well enough to ask him to undertake the journey to Levenford and to perform the operation without fee. Caught in a dilemma of his own making, he felt trapped and helpless.

But time was not standing still, and he could not afford to waste one precious moment. Though he did not know what he was going to do, he was still conscious that he must act – act immediately.

Rousing himself, he went out of the house and walked rapidly across the Common towards the Cottage Hospital.

He entered the hospital, and went straight to the matron's room, but she was not there, and so he turned and made his way into the ward.

Nurse Angus was in the ward, standing beside the clean white bed in which Paul now lay, and as Finlay entered she looked up and met his eyes, not in her usual impersonal manner, but with a strange intentness.

'He's very bad,' she said in a low voice. 'Temperature subnormal, and the pulse almost imperceptible. He seems to be slipping into coma.'

With his gaze upon the bed Finlay saw that she was right. He muttered—

'It's a bad lookout, I'm afraid,' he paused, then blurted out – 'The professor can't come. I can't get anyone to tackle it. We'll have to do the best we can without an operation.'

He did not look at her, but waited instinctively for some cold reply. He knew that now she must despise him more than ever. His heart sank. But to his amazement she did not speak. He lifted his head and found her warm eyes fixed steadily upon him.

'Do you mean that there's no one to do this operation? And you know that it must be done!'

He nodded his head dumbly, conscious of her presence, of her disturbing scrutiny. There was a long pause, then she said slowly and distinctively—

'Why don't you do it yourself?'

279

He stared at her, staggered at the suggestion, yet strangely thrilled by it. And, all at once, inspiration flowed to him from the composure in her face. He had never dreamed of tackling the operation himself, for although he knew its technique from reading, he had felt it far beyond him.

He had operated, of course, in a small way, but a major abdominal operation had stood always as difficult, dangerous, and obscure, something quite outside his power. But now, with this sudden suggestion offered so unexpectedly, his purpose deepened.

He realised that it was the only thing to do, that he must make the attempt.

At that moment the matron came waddling up.

'The theatre's ready,' she announced officiously. 'Whenever the professor arrives we are ready to begin.'

Finlay faced her with real determination.

'He's not coming,' he declared. 'But for all that, we'll begin at once. I'm going to do the operation myself.'

'You!' gasped the matron.

'Exactly,' said Finlay abruptly.

'But, Dr Finlay—' protested the matron.

Finlay did not wait. Before the astounded woman could say more he walked out of the ward and into the little office, where, picking up the telephone again, he rang through to Reid's house.

It would have been easier by far for him to have asked Cameron to give the anaesthetic, but now he did not want the easy way. He wanted Reid to be there, since he had disagreed with his diagnosis, to see everything, to witness the best or the worst that he could do.

Three-quarters of an hour later Finlay stood in the operating theatre ready to begin. The theatre was hot. The sun had been shining through the ground glass windows, and it was full of a hot bubbling and hissing from the small steam steriliser.

Exactly in the centre of the theatre was the operating table, breathing unevenly under the anaesthetic was Paul.

At the head of the table, very disturbed and unwilling, sat Dr

Reid. He had made it perfectly clear that he came merely to give the anaesthetic and would take no responsibility for the issue.

Beside her tray of instruments was Nurse Angus – still calm, and impenetrable in her demeanour – while beside the metal cylinder of oxygen, as though she felt that she would soon be obliged to use it, was Matron Clark.

It was the moment at last. With a quick prayer, Finlay bent over the table and reached out his hand for a lancet.

He concentrated on the one neat square of Paul's body surrounded by white towels and coloured a fine bright yellow with iodine. It was inside the square that everything would take place.

He tried, in the hot room through the daze of his conflicting emotions, to remember everything that he must do.

Aware above everything of the presence of Nurse Angus, he drew a deep breath.

First there came the incision. Yes, the incision came first. The warm, shining lancet drew a slow, firm line across the bright yellow skin, and the skin parted in a red gash.

Little voices whispered inside Finlay's brain, mocking him, telling him he would never be able to accomplish the impossible task he had undertaken.

On and on he went. He used more instruments, and the rings of forceps lay deeply one upon another.

The confusion of the instruments seemed inextricable, and, all at once, through the steaming heat of the theatre, the broken breathing of the patient, the latent uneasiness in Reid's eyes, there came upon Finlay the sudden paralysing thought that he could not continue.

He was a fool, a hopeless, incompetent fool, muddling about in the darkness looking for this thing they called the appendix, which did not, could not exist. Beads of sweat started upon his brow. He thought for a moment he was going to faint.

And then, through the anguish of this horrible uncertainty, he felt the eyes of Nurse Angus upon him. There was something open and revealing in those eyes; suffering because he suffered, enduring every pang which he endured, yet strangely courageous and pleasing. But there was something more which glistened there, and entered into Finlay's soul with a stab of ecstasy.

In a flash the mist passed, he took command of himself, and, bending, went on courageously with the operation.

All this happened quicker than can be told. It was the turning-point, the crisis of the operation. A second later Finlay's searching hand discovered the appendix and withdrew it to open view.

A kind of gasp broke from Matron Clark's lips, and Reid's face expressed unwilling admiration, for there, exposed for them all to see, was a round swelling, an abscess in the appendix, almost gangrenous.

Filled with a rising exultation, Finlay hurried his movements. He was vindicated, completely vindicated. Out came the appendix, and in went the sutures.

Quickly the operation drew to a close. Confident now, Finlay put in the stitches with a beautiful precision. It was nearly over now, sealed up beautifully and finished.

The matron coughed diffidently, and ended the long silence. Nurse Angus had begun to count the swabs. At last it was over, and the door swung open, and the wheel-stretcher went out, bearing Paul to the ward.

Finlay watched the swing-doors close upon the wheel-stretcher as Matron Clark ushered it officiously into the ward. He knew that Paul would recover now.

He turned and saw Reid coming towards him. He no longer looked cold and remote and uneasy. He said with real cordiality—

'I want you to know, Finlay, that you were right and I was wrong. Man, I admire you for what you've done.'

He held out his hand, and Finlay took it. He was grateful to Reid, but when the other doctor left the theatre the strain of what he had gone through struck him again, and he sat down quite weakly on a stool.

Then he was conscious that Nurse Angus was still in the

theatre. She stood looking at him, then went to the tap, ran the water hard, filled the tumbler, then gave it to him. Finlay drank it, then gazed at her with a surging gratitude.

'I want to thank you,' he muttered, 'for helping me, advising me. Oh, I'd never have done it but for you.'

Then he broke off.

There was a silence. Her face was turned from him now, but tears were in her eyes. At length she said—

'I knew you could do it. And you did. It was splendid.'

Her voice, low yet thrilling, set his heart thudding.

He sensed the pulse of some secret feeling in her which suddenly intoxicated him. A light of understanding broke over him. Had he been wrong in thinking she disliked him?

Her name rose instinctively to his lips. But before he could speak she turned quickly and was gone.

The Fête at Dunhill

Finlay was in love – deeply and hopelessly. He knew that without Peggy Angus beside him to share his life he would not be happy.

And yet he could not put his fortune to the crucial test. For, on the day following his dramatic operation on the little boy, Paul, the most unexpected and banal occurrence took place. Peggy's summer holiday fell due, and she left quite quietly and unostentatiously to spend the fortnight with her folks at Dunhill.

When she had gone Finlay had full opportunity to examine his own position. He had begun by distrusting Peggy because of her family, good position, and obvious command of wealth. He had been suspicious, feeling that it was wrong for her to be a nurse, and that she was posing, insincere. And, behaving contrary to his own generous nature, he had at the outset created a painful misunderstanding between them, a gulf which later on he had despairingly felt he would never bridge.

But now a ray of comfort shone for him.

Peggy's interest in his work, as shown so sincerely and spontaneously at the recent operation, gave him fresh hope. Perhaps, after all, she did care for him a little. His heart bounded at the very thought, and he longed for the chance to ask her that question humbly and openly. The chance came, too, sooner than he anticipated.

A few days after Peggy had gone on holiday, Matron Clark greeted Finlay at the hospital in great good spirits.

'They're having a fête at Dunhill next Saturday,' she declared. 'Mr Angus has lent his grounds. A lovely place they have up there. And the funds are to go to the hospital. Isn't it splendid? Nurse Angus has arranged the whole thing.'

At the very mention of Peggy's name and the thought that he might see her at the fête, Finlay's pulse quickened.

'That's fine,' he said to the matron, trying to keep his tone unconcerned. 'You'll be going up?'

'I am indeed,' agreed the matron with a brisk nod. 'And I'm counting on you to drive me up, doctor.'

Finlay shook his head diffidently.

'They'll not want me up there,' he answered, hoping to be contradicted. 'I'm not exactly a favourite in that quarter.'

'Nonsense!' replied the matron. 'And besides, it's your duty to be there, seeing it's a charity for the hospital.'

A slow smile came to Finlay's face.

'Oh, well,' said he, 'if that's the case, I'll not deny I'd like to go.'

From that moment Finlay began to look forward to the proposed function with his whole heart.

On the following afternoon when he got home he found a letter from old John Angus cordially inviting him to the fête. Finlay studied it in silence. Had Peggy mentioned him to her father? Perhaps she had spoken for him kindly.

Overcome by a feeling of mingled ecstacy and suspense. Finlay sat down and quickly wrote his acceptance.

It was, he told himself, an almost providential opportunity, and as the day of the fête drew near his beating sense of antici-pation increased. On that day he would ask Peggy to be his wife.

Saturday came, bright and clear, and Finlay himself made arrangements to drive matron up to Dunhill. But at eleven o'clock on that forenoon an accident happened at the shipyard. Bob Paxton, son of old John Paxton, the foundry foreman, fell from the upper deck of the Argentine cattle boat then in No. 5

Graving Dock, and was brought to the Cottage Hospital suffering from serious internal injuries and concealed haemorrhage.

Finlay, long since a friend of the Paxton family, was called to Bob, and his view of the lad's condition was grave. So grave, in fact, that he hesitated about leaving the case for long, and with a dubious frown, he indicated to matron the inadvisability of his going to Dunhill.

'It's the haemorrhage I'm afraid of,' he added. 'I think we might have to do a transfusion.'

Matron raised her hands instantly.

'That's not a thing to rush into, doctor. And, besides, you wouldn't think of doing it till this evening, anyhow.'

She was all ready for the expedition, and provoked to think of any interference with her pleasure.

Finlay's look grew still more doubtful. He, too, wanted to go to Dunhill with all his soul, but the strong sense of duty in him revolted at the idea of putting himself out of touch with this critical case.

He refused to commit himself until he had seen his patient again, and at two o'clock he returned to the hospital and again made his examination of the lad.

This time he had to agree that the symptoms were more encouraging. Bob had recovered consciousness, and, though very pallid from the effect of the internal bleeding, stoutly protested that he was 'fine'.

Added to matron's pleadings, this persuaded Finlay. He instructed Nurse Cotter, who remained on duty, to keep a constant eye on the case. He himself would be back without fail at six o'clock sharp.

So matron and Finlay set out together just after two. Thanks to the splendour of the day and the enjoyment of the drive, the grim reality of the hospital ward which they had left behind them soon faded.

After all, Finlay could not tie himself to the bedside the whole day long. Such exacting service could surely be demanded of no man.

Long before they reached their destination his thoughts had flown ahead, and he was longing eagerly for his first glimpse of Peggy.

Towards three o'clock they arrived at Dunhill. The Angus estate was a beautiful place, approached by a long, winding drive, guarded by a lodge, and flanked by rhododendron bushes.

The house itself was of fine white sandstone, built in the baronial style, with imposing turrets and a high crenellated coping.

The grounds were at their best, bright with flowers and steeped in sunshine.

On the close-cropped lawns stalls, tents and marquees had been erected, around which there thronged crowds of people enjoying the gay display always found at such local charitable fêtes. There were, for instance, various booths devoted to the sale of needlework and home-made cakes, candies and jellies.

Side shows offered their attractions and competitions, and their prizes, notably a fine cheese to be won by the lucky individual who would correctly guess its weight.

In the midst of all stood a large marquee, at which ices and teas were served.

At the head of the drive Finlay surrendered the horse and gig to a waiting groom, and, accompanied by the stout, thoroughly excited matron, made his way on to the front lawn.

They had not gone very far before they encountered Peggy, and at the sight of her Finlay felt his heart stand still. He had never seen her in other than her hospital uniform or in her plain tennis dress, but now she wore a lovely frock of flowered muslin and a shady hat, which showed the coils of her beautiful hair clustered above her white neck.

She was surrounded by her family and friends, and her face, a little flushed by the sun, wore an expression of gaiety.

At that moment she turned her head and saw Finlay and matron. Immediately she came forward to welcome them, and, having shaken them by the hand, introduced them to her father and mother and her small brother, Ian.

Finally, with an air which might have been that of mild embarrassment, she turned and made them known to a young man who stood close beside her.

A very personable fellow he was indeed, upright and handsome, with brown eyes and a close cropped moustache, perhaps about twenty-seven, and his name was Dick Foster.

Finlay stared at the unknown and unexpected Foster with a sudden cold premonition, quite taken aback, hardly responding to the other's easy greeting. His awkwardness passed apparently unnoticed, however, for Foster was socially expert.

There was the usual exchange of conversation and laughter in the group, and eventually Finlay found himself beside old John Angus, a grand old man, stocky and bespectacled, with broad shoulders and a fine open face, known in the district as a model employer and philanthropist.

Old John said a few pleasant words to Finlay. He explained that his daughter had really wanted to be a nurse, and he added with a sly laugh that he was willing enough for her to carry on with this profession until she followed the more satisfactory one of marriage.

As the old man spoke this word which had for days been graved upon his heart, Finlay's eyes remained stonily fixed upon the figure of Dick Foster, who, with an air of proprietorship, had now taken Peggy's arm and was gallantly leading her towards one of the stalls.

A terrible sensation shot through him, a shudder of bitterness, mingled with sudden despair. Vainly he tried to fight it down. He turned to old Angus.

'You think your daughter will be getting married soon, then, sir?' he asked, though hardly able to speak.

'Oh, ay, we hope so,' said old John with a fond paternal laugh. 'Don't ye think she's ower bonny to be a nurse?' And laughing at his own witticism, he patted Finlay's shoulder and moved away.

To Finlay the allusion seemed clear, bracketing Peggy and the handsome Foster in happy alliance. He bit his lip fiercely. And, as though his cup of wretchedness were not already brimming, at that moment matron sidled over, her eyes following Finlay's after the retreating couple.

'Don't they make a handsome pair?' she gushed. 'I've just been hearing about it from the minister's wife. Why, they're practically engaged! Imagine, doctor, and we never suspected a thing. Why, by all accounts, everyone at Dunhill is hoping they'll be married next spring. Oh, it's quite romantic. Isn't he good-looking, doctor? Comes from a fine family, too, they tell me. Went to college at Edinburgh, and now he's going in for the law.'

As the matron rattled on, singing the praises of Peggy and this young Foster, in all ignorance of the havoc she was creating, Finlay's heart turned to ice within him. Was it for this he had built all his high hopes? All the life went out of him, the scene lost its brightness, the words and laughter round about fell dully on his ear.

He broke away at last from the garrulous woman, and tried to lose himself in the slowly circulating crowd.

With his hands plunged in his pockets, he wandered about desolately, thinking that he might perhaps catch another glimpse of Peggy. He might see her from a distance; even that would be some consolation to his aching heart.

But he had bargained without young Ian. At first sight the boy, aged twelve, had taken a fancy to Finlay, and dogging the young doctor's footsteps with all the intensity of an Indian sleuth, he collared him at last and dragged him towards the various stalls. Finlay was in no mood to resist.

They tried their luck at the coconut shy, the dip in the tub, guessing the cheese and sundry other games of skill. Then, in increasing friendliness, Ian forced Finlay into the house, lugged him upstairs to his den to exhibit all his precious trophies – his air-gun, his fishing-rod, his collection of butterflies.

He was a great little chap right enough, and drawn towards him, despite his misery, Finlay was moved to question him.

'Is it true,' he asked in a low voice. 'That your sister is engaged to Mr Foster?'

'Oh, yes,' answered the boy carelessly. 'I suppose so. They're going to be married soon. I think he's terribly sloppy on her. I don't like him.'

'Come now, Ian,' said Finlay, striving painfully to be fair. 'He seems a fine chap.'

'Oh, not bad, I suppose,' said Ian grudgingly. 'But I just can't stand him. Don't let's talk about that, though. Here, I want to show you my catapult.'

The afternoon passed, and with it, despite the cheerful chatter of the boy, Finlay's spirits sank steadily to lower than zero. He felt humiliated in spirit, wounded, utterly wretched.

At half-past four they went downstairs, Finlay hoping with all his might that he would make his escape unnoticed. But in the hall they encounted Mrs Angus, who immediately declared—

'Good gracious! Dr Finlay, where have you been? We've been looking for you everywhere. Has my wicked young man,' she tugged Ian by the ear, 'monopolised you all this time? Come along and have some tea. We're going in just now.'

There was nothing to do but accept, and, mustering all his resources, Finlay put the best face on it possible and followed the gracious white-haired lady into the drawing-room.

There were a number of people there – old Angus and a number of friends, most of them notables of the district. And when Mrs Angus entered tea was served. She herself presided in the good old-fashioned style behind the big silver teapot and dispensed the fragrant beverage in thin china cups, while cakes were handed round by two maids.

Finlay felt the gracious atmosphere of the place, the silver, the flowers, the deft service, the atmosphere of refinement and charm. This was Peggy's by birth and breeding. She was part of this, charming and gracious and sweet, and at the outset of their acquaintance he, the upstart, had dared to humiliate her.

Well, it was now his turn to feel abasement utter and complete! He groaned inwardly, and raised his cup with nervous fingers. Dumbly he wondered where Peggy was, and yet he had no need to wonder.

He knew instinctively that she was with Foster, that they were alone together, had probably stolen away from the crowd. Obsessed by the thought, he became more agitated still when suddenly Mrs. Angus casually remarked to her husband—

'Where's Peggy? She ought to be coming in for tea.'

Before John Angus could reply the irrepressible Ian burst out—

'Don't worry about them. They'll be out spooning together!'

'Ian, dear!' said Mrs Angus reprovingly. But her rebuke was lost in a general laugh, and Peter Scott, one of Angus's friends, remarked pawkily—

'It's the right sort of day to pop the question.'

No sooner had he spoken than Peggy and young Foster entered the room. Naturally they were immediately the subject of general chaffing.

Though it hurt Finlay to the quick to do so, he raised his eyes and gazed at them.

Peggy's face was turned away, he could not see it. But Foster's, slightly flushed and very self-conscious, wore a look which Finlay construed instantly as that of an accepted lover.

All that Finlay wished now was to get away, to vanish instantly and completely from this happy scene.

Finlay remained for a moment immovable in his chair, battling with his thoughts. Thank God he had work to do. He remembered almost with gratitude Bob Paxton, whom he must see at the Cottage Hospital at six.

And, when the general conversation was again flowing, he rose, unobserved, and slipped over to Mrs Angus.

'I must go now,' he said. 'I've got to get back to a case.'

'But can't you wait?' she murmured, raising her brows in

disappointment. 'We're going to have a bonfire this evening, and fireworks.'

He shook his head stiffly.

'I am sorry, but I must go. Someone else will give matron a lift back. As for me, I've got work to do.'

He knew that he was uncouth and graceless, but he could not help himself. His tongue was dry in his mouth.

He thought for a second she was about to speak, to reveal in all nakedness his painful secret. But apparently she changed her mind.

'Very well, then,' she said, 'If you must, you must.' Smiling slightly, she shook hands with him kindly, indeed for quite a while she retained his hand in her own warm clasp, then, turning to her daughter, she declared, 'Peggy, you'll see Dr Finlay to the door.'

Thus bidden, Peggy accompanied him into the hall. He felt rather than saw her beside him, for once again he dared not look at her.

The sense of her nearness, coupled with the knowledge that she could never love him, filled his breast with a suffocating pain. But at the door he faced her, thrusting down all the insupportable feelings which surged in him. He said simply—

'Thank you for having me up here. You have a lovely place. And altogether it's been a wonderful day.'

She did not answer immediately. Indeed, he thought her cheeks pale and her voice slightly strained as at length she said—

'I am glad you have enjoyed yourself.'

Silence. Then she remarked in that same tone—

'It's all gone very quickly. I hardly seem to have seen you.'

He did not answer. Indeed, he could not answer. Blindly he held out his hand, touched hers for a moment, then ran down the steps.

The drive home was misery. He felt alone in the world.

His work – that was what the future held for him – and he must work alone.

Arrived in Levenford, he made straight for Arden House. Cameron gave a whistle of surprise at seeing him home so soon.

'You're back early!' he exclaimed. 'Did you hate the fête all that much?'

'No,' said Finlay gruffly; 'the fête was all right.' He paused. 'I wanted to see Paxton at the hospital.'

Cameron inspected his young partner shrewdly, discerning something of the bitterness which these simple words concealed. He said presently—

'As a matter of fact, Nurse Cotter was on the phone for you from the hospital half an hour ago.'

Finlay nodded. He had half expected such a message; troubles, in his experience, never came singly.

Pausing only to snatch a bite of food – he had eaten nothing at Dunhill – he hastened down to the hospital and entered the ward where Bob Paxton lay. Here his brow clouded.

Bending over the supine figure on the bed, Finlay made a rapid investigation, collapse due to haemorrhage, he thought, and there and then he decided upon immediate transfusion.

His face lit up at the coming battle.

Ordering Nurse Cotter to send for Halliday, the porter, who from previous experience could be counted on as a safe and generous blood donor, Finlay passed hurriedly into the side room to prepare for his delicate and difficult task.

The trouble would, he realised, be Nurse Cotter. She was a bungler, the last person he would have chosen to assist him. But the need was urgent, and he must make shift with her the best way he could.

In a sense, too, the blame was his. It was while he had been playing the lovesick swain at Dunhill that Paxton's condition had deteriorated.

All this was in Finlay's mind, forcing a look of pain and bitterness upon his features as he crossed to the theatre to see about his instruments.

He pushed open the swing doors with nervous vehemence,

then suddenly drew up, petrified to absolute rigidity. There, in the theatre, dressed in her neat uniform, methodically arranging his instruments, was Nurse Angus.

He gazed at her, unable to believe his eyes, while the colour ebbed slowly from his face. Then, with a rush of bewilderment, he gasped—

'Why are you here?'

Without looking at him, she answered—

'My holiday is over tomorrow. I thought I might just as well come back for duty tonight.'

He could only stand and stare at her, as though still dazed at her return. And she seemed to sense his incredulity, for in that matter-of-fact voice, she went on—

'Matron told me about your case, of course, and after you'd gone I thought you might need me. So I came on.' And bearing the tray of instruments with impassive precision, she went past him into the ward.

He followed a moment later like a man walking in a dream.

Halliday was already at the bedside with Nurse Cotter, who manifested every sign of satisfaction that Nurse Angus should be back to relieve her of responsibility. And, without delay, Finlay set himself to carry out the transfusion, swabbing Halliday's muscular arm with iodine, puncturing the vessel accurately, transmitting the precious life fluid from the healthy porter to the collapsed and languid figure on the bed.

It was done at last. Kneeling, Finlay watched the change in Paxton, who now, as by a miracle stroke, was filled with new life, breathing quietly and vigorously, saved.

Finlay remained there a long time, in profound meditation, long after Halliday had returned to the lodge, and Nurse Cotter began to fuss with her charts in a far corner of the ward.

Then, with a deep sigh, he rose and went into the side room where Peggy stood, cleansing the last of his instruments.

Mechanically he stumbled into speech.

'I want to thank you for coming down. I couldn't have

managed nearly so well without you.' He raised his hand to his brow dumbly. 'It always seems to be that way somehow – you seem to help me out!'

A long pause. She did not speak. And so, his shoulders sagging a little, he went blindly on—

'I want to congratulate you, too – on your engagement. He seems a fine fellow, Foster – I hope you'll be happy.'

Now, indeed, she raised her head and gazed at him steadily. And her voice was also steady as she answered—

'You're making a mistake, I think. Dick Foster is nothing but a friend. People have drawn all sorts of stupid conclusions. If you don't believe me . . .'

The colour rose to her brow, and her eyes fell.

'Today he proposed to me, and I refused him.'

A start ran through his entire body. He dared not breathe. Then, his heart leaping into his throat, he came towards her.

Though he did not, could not speak, his love for her was written openly in his face, and at that sight she cried, with a little, choking sob—

'Oh, my dear, don't you know that it is you – that it always has been and always will be you?'

The next instant she was in his arms.

A melting tenderness filled his soul, his whole heart sang with a wild and matchless joy. He knew that the crowning glory of his life had been achieved.